For Jimmy,

with best wishes,

Jauliko P. H.

Avil 1986

The City Beneath the Skin

The City
Beneath the Skin

An adventure by
JONATHAN GATHORNE-HARDY

HAMISH HAMILTON
London

First published in Great Britain 1986
by Hamish Hamilton Ltd
Garden House 57–59 Long Acre London WC2E 9JZ

Copyright © 1986 by Jonathan Gathorne-Hardy

British Library Cataloguing in Publication Data

Gathorne-Hardy, Jonathan
  The city beneath the skin.
  I. Title
  823'.914[F]   PR6057.A84
  ISBN 0–241–11868–9

Typeset by Input Typesetting Ltd, London
Printed in Great Britain by
St Edmundsbury Press, Bury St Edmunds, Suffolk

For Tim Behrens

Acknowledgements

The reader may be assured that the facts upon which this book is based are true.

For that my thanks are largely due to Amanda Claridge, Assistant Director of the British School at Rome. One of those principally responsible for the remarkable Pompeian Exhibition in London in 1976–77, she was unstinting in her help and as ingenious in her suggestions as to what was feasible as she was rigorous in her rejection of what was not.

I should also like to thank Geoffrey House of the British Museum; Carmine Zuccaro; Fan Behrens; Failings Supply Ltd, Portable Drilling Equipment; Capitano Benedicte of the Rome *Carabinieri;* Dr Sara Bisel; Dott. Maria Cerulli Irelli, Soprintendente Archeologico di Pompeii; and Dott. Umberto Pappalardo, Soprintendente Archeologico di Herculaneum. (No one, incidentally, who has met this brilliant and dynamic young archaeologist would need my assurances that he bears not the faintest resemblance to the doddering figure who holds his position in this book.)

There are hundreds of books on Pompeii and Herculaneum. For those interested in pursuing the subject, I would recommend the following: *Pompeii AD 79 – The Treasures of Rediscovery*, Richard Brilliant (New York, 1979); *Pompeii and Herculaneum*, Marcel Brion (London, 1960); *The Destruction and Resurrection of Pompeii and Herculaneum*, Caesar Conte Corti (London, 1951); *Cities of Vesuvius – Pompeii and Herculaneum*, Michael Grant (London, 1971); *The Gardens of Pompeii*, Wilhelmina F. Jashenski (New York, 1979); *Pompeii and Herculaneum – The Living Cities of the Dead*, Theodor Kraus, photographs by Leonard von Matt (New York, 1975); *The Shadow of Vesuvius*, Raleigh Trevelyan (London, 1976).

For those interested in volcanoes, *Volcanoes* by Frederick M.

Bullard (Edinburgh, 1962) and *Volcanoes* by Kent Wilcoxson (London, 1967) are both informative. For the latest theories on the eruption of Vesuvius in AD 79 see the articles by Haraldur Sigurdsson in *The American Journal of Archaeology* (1980/81) Vol. 84, nos. 2 and 3.

As to whether or not anything like this has taken place at Herculaneum, the answer is that it has not. But then, only a small proportion of Herculaneum has been recovered. Most of that strange city is still buried.

It hasn't happened yet. That does not mean it can't or that it won't. On the contrary, that *something* like this will happen is virtually certain. And no doubt – just as it did on that sunlit day 1906 years ago – it will happen when we least expect it.

Chapter One

The morning of 24 August AD 79 round the bay in front of
Neapolis began as those hot midsummer mornings always
began – as they still do today.

At about ten o'clock it had been just possible to discern a
black bar across the horizon. It had drawn swiftly nearer,
gradually resolving itself into a line of rippling waves. The
molten flatness of the great bay darkened, and at the same
time increasingly sparkled, a bowl filling with smashed sapph-
ires, filling to the brim as the waves reached shore. Now the
leaves began to rustle, the flowers to sway. In a few minutes
a sea breeze was sweeping in over the farms and villas and
little cities that surrounded the beautiful bay – Neapolis itself,
Herculaneum, Oplontis, Pompeii, Stabiae. . . .

This cooling zephyr would blow all day: some beneficent
giant was slowly, steadily, filling his lungs in the mountains
of the interior. It would cease just before sunset. For a few
hours the air would be still, the houses, the pavements giving
off the heat they had absorbed during the day. But after a
while, far up in the mountains, the giant would start to exhale,
his breath rolling down across the snows. Soon the leaves
would again rustle, the tree-tops murmur, and from then on
and all night long a refreshing stream of air would flow
through the gardens, the terraces and the now silent streets
with an effect indescribably refreshing.

This perfection was set in yet further perfection, ringed by
it. About five miles away splendid Mount Vesuvius rose like
a backdrop 6000 feet high. It had until recently been thickly
covered in groves and woods, but now vines and olives and
rich grazing plots fell from the very top of its almost flat peak
in an organised cascade down the fertile slopes.

And throughout these hazy vistas of cultivated scenery,

1

marked intermittently with the blue-green, black-green brush strokes of tall cypresses, stood the great villas of the rich, with their parks and pools and statues and lovers.

As a civilisation, it has had no rival for brutality. For standards of comfort, it bares comparison with late 20th century California; perhaps only 18th century Versailles saw furnishing and decoration of such sophistication, elaboration and expense.

The great houses – filled with bronze and marble busts and statues – were like art galleries: pillars, walls and ceilings elaborately painted, sparkling with greens, golds, crimson, aquamarine. Innumerable murals, mosaics and tapestries of landscapes and seascapes gave a feeling of spaciousness. *Trompe l'oeil* fish and fruit decorated dining rooms, painted flowers and creepers twined round the walls of bedrooms – *trompe l'oeil* so skilful it deceived birds and butterflies.

These elegant, luxurious and lovely houses – teeming with slaves – had flushing lavatories and hot and cold running water. Ice and snow from the mountains provided refrigeration in summer; central heating warmth in winter. A good cook cost as much as three well-bred horses.

Only two things threatened this Eden of the wealthy.

The first was the poor, in the form of thieves. Made reckless and desperate by hunger, enraged by cruelty, numerous as an invading army – the situation resembled that of a guerrilla war. Outside walls were windowless, the few doors massive and iron-studded. Some houses had huge shutters, barred and iron-studded also, made of oak or chestnut, to protect upper floors. At Herculaneum, where space was restricted, the rich had begun to build upwards. Light was often dispensed from light-wells where pointed sides might descend to a little chamber.

The second threat was invisible, invincible, unsuspected – and inescapable.

The giant forces which order the surface of the earth, melting or freezing ice-caps, splitting continents or letting them collide, raising and lowering seas and mountains, move with such ponderous slowness that between one step and the next the whole history of mankind can start and come to an end.

The Tyrrhenian sea is that part of the Mediterranean lying

2

between Italy and the islands of Sicily, Corsica and Sardinia. Once land, a million or so years ago it began to sink and the Appennines began to rise. The crustal rock dragged down in the process – a process still continuing – melted under the intense heat and pressure. From time to time the molten rock forced, and forces, its way up through the fracture down the west coast of Italy which also results from their combined rising and sinking.

But the moves the giants made here were not all so far apart. Vesuvius first erupted about 10,000 BC, as the ice rolled back at the end of the last Ice Age. It may have erupted again about 1200 BC. In 72 BC there was still a relatively shallow, vegetation-choked crater where Spartacus hid his slave army before launching a successful attack on a Roman camp below. One or two Roman scientists (Strabo, Vitruvius Pollio) knew that Vesuvius was not the massive, placid mountain that she seemed – but a volcano.

In AD 79 the giants were about to take another step – and one, now that human life was there, of unprecedented destructive power.

Here, too, the event was not completely unpresaged. On 5 February, AD 62, the region had been struck by a savage earthquake. The epicentre had been close to Pompeii, which was badly damaged. So too, though less so, was Herculaneum. Near that little city, a great chasm suddenly opened in the earth and 600 sheep vanished. People went mad with fear.

Even Naples was shaken – and not just by the trembling earth. That very night Nero appeared in the theatre there, having chosen that moment and that place to test out his belief that he was a gifted singer. Guards were posted to drive anyone trying to leave back into his seat. There they sat, the court, the richest people of the coast, shaking with fear, the ground quivering, statues swaying, chunks of plaster falling off the pillars, pinned to their seats by spears while the Emperor shrieked and warbled on the stage.

It is not known whether there was any warning in AD 79, on that morning of 24 August. It is likely there was. Certainly there had been lesser quakes after AD 62. The bodies discovered at Herculaneum recently (1983/84) were all

3

comparatively young. The older ones, the majority, recognising the signs, had fled.

But even if there was nothing as dramatic as a minor earthquake, these events are invariably preceded by clear signs that something is going to happen – and that it is imminent. Animals are restless and frightened: horses break loose, even kicking down their stable doors, and gallop away; pigs and sheep stampede. Birds fall silent. Fountains cease to play and springs dry up.

An air of waiting for something to happen would have hung over the little city – over the whole silent, sunlit region. The remaining people – disturbed by the warnings of those who had fled even though they had chosen to ignore them – would have been nervous of staying indoors and would have kept coming outside to look apprehensively around.

This expectancy was rewarded in the middle of the day. At one o'clock the whole region was shaken by a gigantic explosion – so loud its thunder was distantly heard in villages over seventy miles away. Nor was this a single event. The explosion continued on without pause into a sustained and deafening roar. The source of this cataclysm seemed to be somewhere directly behind Herculaneum, in the direction of Mount Vesuvius.

[2]

The force of that first colossal explosion blew two thousand feet off the top of the mountain. A writhing pillar of pumice and fire mounted swiftly to a height of about 64,000 feet and held there for eleven hours. Here the top was caught by the powerful stratospheric winds and blown flat. It looked from a distance as though some monstrous mushroom, or one of the Mediterranean umbrella pines, had sprouted from the top of the volcano.

Almost as swiftly, a great darkness swept from Vesuvius out over that sunlit countryside like an ink cloud from an octopus. It was a darkness that was to last for three days of terrifying destruction.

Through the whole of this period the volcano threw out an endless stream of missiles with indiscriminate ferocity. Lumps weighing thirty tons were hurled over two miles; those of ten tons and more landed five miles away in the sea, to sink in columns of bubbling, boiling water to its bed.

This terrifying night – through which swept swirling clouds of hot, sulphur-smelling gas – was lit by intermittent gashes of fire and lofty fountains of sparks from the mountain. Sheet and forked lightning flashed continually.

Nor was it silent. Vesuvius roared and sometimes screamed in the darkness. The electrical charges sent great thunder-claps rolling through the night. Every now and then there was the colossal detonation of a fresh explosion in its depths and these alone shook the cities to their foundations.

The Romans had an explanation for such events. There had been a great battle in heaven between gods and giants. The giants had lost and been forced down and imprisoned beneath the regions of this coast. Earthquakes, the smoking of the ground, were their periodic and frantic efforts to break free.

That night it seemed that they had done so. Several people afterwards swore they had glimpsed their towering forms rampaging past.

'You might hear the shrieks of women, the screams of children and shouts of men,' wrote an eye witness; 'some calling for their children, others for their parents, others for their husbands, and seeking to recognise each other by the voices that replied; one lamenting his own fate, another that of his family; some wishing to die from the very fear of dying; some lifting their hands to the gods; but the greater part convinced that there were no gods at all, and that the final endless night of which we had heard had come upon the world.'

After eleven hours – in the middle of the first night – the column of fire and pumice sustained by Vesuvius at 64,000 feet collapsed for the first time. This sent a huge wave of super-heated steam and other gases – the *nuave ardente* – surging down the mountainside at several hundred miles an hour. It was this that killed most of the people in Herculaneum – destroying their lungs through heat.

The volcano now entered a new phase, hurling its column into the heavens and then periodically letting it collapse to send another surge of superheated steam and gas racing down

5

its sides. Not until the fourth collapse, on the morning of the second day, did one of these deadly surges reach Pompeii, now buried under about nine feet of pumice particles.

Each steam and gas wave was followed by a very fast-moving pyroclastic flow – an avalanche of ground-hugging pumice at high temperature. These did not overwhelm Herculaneum, but where they struck they did so with very destructive violence. Roof timbers from the rear of the town have been found flung right across it to the beach at the front.

The continuously striking lightning, the crashing descent of hot fragments and boulders of lava, had already started numerous fires. So did these raging, pyroclastic flows of extremely hot volcanic material. The cities of the plain, the stately villas, would have all been totally destroyed by fire – had it not been for the rain.

Rain! It is clear from the surviving evidence that it was not so much rain as an endless fall of solid water.

It has been estimated that during the eruption of AD 79 Vesuvius ejected seven cubic miles of matter with a weight of 33 billion tons. But this matter was only a fairly small proportion of what was actually thrown out. Aside from relatively minor quantities of miscellaneous gases – carbon dioxide, nitrogen, sulphur, hydrogen, chlorine – by far the greater part was water.

At first this staggering quantity of water is held in the magma – the liquid rock – deep in the earth's surface. And these depths can be very great. That of the magma chamber of Vesuvius is known – its top lies 16,500 feet below the ground. At depths of this sort the temperature, 870° centigrade, is far above that at which water turns to steam. But the enormous pressure forces it to remain in liquid form.

Slowly, sometimes over many centuries, the magma works its way to the surface. At a certain point, where the pressure has finally fallen sufficiently, the water trapped as a liquid can suddenly start to expand into steam – at which point, in that instant, its volume increases a thousand times.

This is the force which fuels a volcano of the Vesuvian type. It creates a series of tremendous explosions in the chimney causing local earthquakes. Finally there comes the vast one which blasts the way to the surface and starts the eruption.

6

These are the most violent natural phenomena known on earth. There was no conventional lava in AD 79. The force of the expanding water and steam racing up with the magma was far too great. It 'frothed' the lava into the tiny particles we call pumice – particles for the most part the size of walnuts and peas.

For a day or two this frothed pumice is flung out, along with lumps of matter, often weighing many tons, from the magma chamber roof, from the chimney and the top of the volcano. Finally the throat and funnel of the volcano are clean and much expanded. Now the gas blow-off follows – a mighty discharge of those huge quantities of exploding steam which can last several days, and which rapidly condenses into water as it roars into the sky.

It was this wall of water that fell upon the regions surrounding Vesuvius and completed their devastation. It fell from the start, preventing any fires catching hold; but the real solid fall took place over the last two days.

The slopes of the volcano were now covered with forty feet or more of freshly fallen frothed pumice. Combined with the thousands of millions of tons of water and the slopes of the mountain itself, this created a vast flow of lava-mud. It swirled down a mountainside increasingly disintegrating, and swept into Herculaneum, completely engulfing it to a depth of seventy feet or more.

So enormous was the quantity of mud and pumice and water, so high as it flowed in successive waves did it eventually reach, that it swept on, seventy feet deep, out into the sea in front, pushing the shore half a mile further out than it had been before. This mud and pumice then swiftly hardened, entombing the city in a substance, on the surface, as hard as rock.

On the fourth day the volcano at last fell silent. Light slowly returned, shining luridly through clouds of drifting vapours. As these cleared it was revealed that all had changed. The sun now shone on a scene of vast and terrible desolation.

Everywhere was white with ash as in a thick winter snow. Many thousands had been killed, dozens of villas had been destroyed, as had the towns of Oplontis, Taurania, Tora, Sora, Cossa and Leucopetra.

The largest of them, Pompeii, was buried under twenty to thirty foot of pumice, above which the gaunt roofless outlines of the taller houses still rose. As the years passed, these collapsed in ruins, soil formed, the city vanished.

Soon the name of Pompeii itself was forgotten. But the legend survived that there had once been some ancient city in the region – and the area became vaguely known as Civita.

Pompeii's sister town did not survive even as a memory. Totally sealed and preserved in the rock-hard mud, no sign remaining, another town called Resina grew up on the site during the Middle Ages. Sixteen hundred years later Herculaneum had been forgotten entirely.

Chapter Two

Alexander Mayne took his road map of the Campania and tried to smooth it on the café table.

Both it and the adjacent *Calabria* – from Edizioni Iter – were marked with inked notes, and as creased, stained and torn as if it had actually been on their thread-like lines that he'd driven for ten days instead of letting them guide him clumsily and inexpertly – many villages were unmarked – along the tiny, often still unmetalled roads – many of them also unmarked.

It was, apparently, very dry for April, and already hot. Three days before, leaning against a pine tree, lunching off two long, crisp rolls, salami, olives and swigs of the harsh red wine that had done considerable damage the night before, Alex had noted how the dust plumed behind a battered pick-up rattling across the bare valley below, like spray behind a destroyer or the clouds that accompany galloping cowboys.

'Suitable for Westerns and similar,' he wrote in slapdash hungover scrawl on the margin and ringed the area in blue.

In fact the film whose possible location and local co-operation he was supposed to set up was about kidnapping, but he knew that information of this sort, though probably useless, would give David McKeown the feeling he was getting his money's worth.

He'd chosen three possible villages without difficulty and invariably found in those remote spots someone – an ex-waiter thirty years in Chicago, a hairdresser returned from Manchester – whose atrocious English and his own even worse Italian allowed him to negotiate with the small, nut-brown, villainous-looking man produced as a figure of authority.

As nearly always, the mention of possible film work produced reactions of the utmost amiability. But Alex knew, as he wrote down names and took the number of the only village telephone in the bar, that even more than usual with film projects he was almost certainly raising false hopes.

A 'decision in principle' had been taken to set the film in southern Italy. Nevertheless he'd rung McKeown Productions before he left to make sure a visit to Sicily wasn't necessary. David's 'Don't bother' was far too quick.

'Is *Kidnap* still on?'

'Very much on. Slightly off the boil.'

'How much off the boil?'

David McKeown hated his ex-brother-in-law's financial precariousness. He thought it was catching. 'Look – EMI and Telco together paid £25,000 for the option. They're prepared to spend £150,000 on the project.'

'But you know that means nothing. Are they going to take up the option?'

Pause. 'Yes.'

The pause was far too long. Alex had estimated he now owed £20,000. This ghastly figure had accompanied him like the knowledge of a fatal disease all the way up from Reggio. If the film *didn't* come off . . . despite a lifetime of such juggling, he felt a wave of panic.

He leant over the crumpled, note-studded, drink-stained map and followed the road with his forefinger. It went up over the mountains behind Ravello and down to join the Salerno-Naples road. Ercolano was on this road.

David had also asked him to look out some romantic or unusual localities, for love scenes, for the snatch – or for both. 'You know – temples, cathedrals, ruins.'

Alex had consulted his *Blue Guide* and, starting with Paestum that morning, had dutifully chosen all three in that order on the route back.

He stood up, folded the map, paid for his Campari soda, and set off towards the *cattedrale di San Pantaleone*. The guide had strongly recommended the twelfth century bronze panels in the doors.

Alex bent and looked at them in the late afternoon sun. It caught the extraordinary yellow of his hair. He still looked oddly boyish despite his thirty-six years. Or perhaps not oddly. A close observer might have gained more than a hint that he was on the way to being beaten; would have noticed something slightly wild, or slightly desperate, in his expression. But to a casual glance, taking in the expensive camera, the notebook, the hooked nose and sharp blue eyes intently peering, he might have seemed an eager young transatlantic academic in pursuit of a thesis.

In fact he was wondering whether, suppose he slipped out of his hotel that night, he would be able to saw out one of the twelve-inch bronze panels, and if he did where he'd sell it and for how much. And realising at the same time that like all the odd but petty criminal fantasies that quite often assailed him, he would never dare attempt it.

[2]

'Six radiators have exploded in recent months,' said Thomas. 'In one case a thirty-foot fountain of scalding water was sent into a room containing early Egyptian pottery. Fortunately the exhibits there are in tough glass cases.'

He paused and glanced at his notes to give the journalists time to get it down. Twelve of them. Average. As usual he noticed how, the smarter the paper, the scruffier the journalist. That impeccable solicitor came from the *Sun*. The man from the *Observer* might have been a tramp.

'Actually, floods burst up through manholes in the basement every time there is really heavy rain. This has been going on for ten years. Quite often keepers, porters, guides, anyone around has to rush down and see what they can rescue from everything sloshing about.'

Thomas paused again. It was raining and dark outside and he inadvertently caught a glimpse of himself, bent, massive, in the long, rain-streaked windows. Hastily he looked back.

'The Property Services Agency is responsible for all National Museums. Last year they gave us £6 million for repairs. It will cost £25 million to put all these things right. But I would, finally, not like you to go away blaming the PSA. They are doing what they can. The fault lies with the Treasury and the Government.'

There were a few simple questions.

'What is bronze disease, Mr Henderson?' asked the tramp from the *Observer*.

11

'Without going into technicalities, it's something bronzes can catch,' said Thomas. 'A form of spotting and encrusting.'

The last questions came from Tony Liddell, the *Times* correspondent. 'You are saying this isn't a proper way to run a museum?'

'It is an appalling way to run a museum,' said Thomas.

It hadn't gone badly, he thought, as he walked back through the museum, empty now of the public, lights dimming, doors being secured. It was Tinling's idea that Keepers of departments should address these conferences, although they had a more than competent press officer. It was an integral part of his orchestrated campaign to get money. The people in the museum – that is the museum *itself* – must be seen to need help, to be seeking it.

He turned right through the Egyptian galleries. He could feel himself limping. The wound he'd received in the last year of the war didn't impede him. He played squash at least twice a week, sometimes three times. But it was always more pronounced when he was tired.

The huge statues loomed up in the semi-darkness. Thomas had always thought Angus Wilson's transposition peculiarly apt. Museums *were* zoos. At night he would hear from the windows of his large flat the sounds of Africa across the tame sward of Regent's Park – the sudden trumpeting of elephants longing for the open savannah, the echoing roar of the lions. Museums, too, came alive at night. He could feel now the great bulk of Sobkemsaf I and Amenphis III aching for Egypt, hear from all over the acres of building the silent cries of statues for their ancient villas, urns and swords for their burial mounds.

He unlocked the first door of the Greek and Roman antiquities department, closed it, crossed the small anteroom, unlocked the further door and limped past the tables and shelves where the assistant keepers worked, to his office.

'Mrs Henderson called.' Only Miss Brough's hands and forearms were visible arranging something on his desk under the circle of light.

Thomas felt himself contract. Still, he thought, after twenty-three years you can affect the pit of my stomach. 'If she rings again, say I'm out.' It only happened every six months now, once or twice a year. This time he would not respond.

'It's after 6.30, Mr Henderson. I'm off home.'

'Of course. I'm sorry, Miss Brough. Good night.'

He lowered himself wearily into his chair and stared, unfocussing, at the two piles of papers she had left for him. He could have retired three years before at sixty; but when they, or rather Sir Edward Tinling, asked him to stay on he'd agreed. He'd insisted only that he should have seven weeks' holiday a year. He also intimated that he would expect to travel away from London more than usual – or normal.

As his desk gradually sharpened below him he saw the latest fulfilment of this condition in one of Miss Brough's tidy piles – the tickets, itinerary and programme for his trip to Naples next morning. Next to this she had put the letters and memo to be signed before he left.

The most interesting of these concerned the purchase of the bronze head. He was ninety percent sure the trustees would agree at their meeting tomorrow. They liked nothing better than spending money, provided they were convinced it would be well spent. And if they got the first-century AD bronze head in perfect condition for what he hoped, it would – as his memo convincingly argued – be well spent. There remained only the choice of dealer to bid for the Museum. Thomas thought Lesters, but he could decide that on his return.

He stood a moment before leaving. Should he call Cynthia? It had been over a week – but at his age sleep frequently seemed more important than sex.

Thomas was woken by the telephone at 11.30, fifty minutes after he'd turned out the light. He was wide awake instantly and reached out his hand.

'Hello.'

He thought there was no sound at first but, listening intently, could detect the faint sound of heavy breathing, as if a large overweight man was holding the telephone some way from his face.

Thomas replaced his receiver and lay on his back, his heart thudding. After a few minutes he picked it up again. Still the sound of breathing, slightly louder.

It occurred to him that thriller writers were wrong to cut

13

telephone wires. You could paralyse a telephone by ringing in from outside. Each time the terrified victim tried to ring the police they would hear the hoarse, menacing breathing.

Thomas put back the receiver, turned on the light and heaved himself out of bed. This would have to be faced after all. He pulled on shoes; a sweater and trousers over his pyjamas.

Outside the air was cold. There was no sound across the park from the animals cringing in the alien rain. Thomas drove out past the mosque and turned in the direction of Paddington.

The lights were on in the basement flat and its area door unlocked. There were three pints of milk and another had been kicked over and broken – quite recently, because the pale dissipating pool of milk was still diluting in the rain. Thomas bent automatically and picked up the full bottles as he went in.

The flat stank of stale drink, unemptied ash trays, urine and something going bad – fish or meat. The central heating was on and the windows closed. The tall gilt-stemmed standard lamp had been knocked over, books pulled out of shelves. He could see the uncleared remains of a meal on the table at the back of the living room by the kitchen door.

His wife – his ex-wife – Sheila, lay sprawled along the sofa wearing only a pink slip. The telephone receiver was on her shoulder. He was thankful she'd passed out. At a certain late stage of drunkenness she felt compelled to abuse him.

But it was not ancient hate that had prompted this call. As he bent to replace the receiver, he saw that her lap and the floor around the sofa were strewn with childhood letters, photographs, school reports, even the birth certificate of their son Philip. Beside the green leather case from which these had been pulled lay an empty bottle of South African sherry.

Thomas carried the milk bottles through to the kitchen and put them in the fridge. Here there was chaos. The table and sink were piled with dirty dishes. The pedal bin was full of rotting food and empty bottles. He opened the window over the sink, turned off the central heating, and recrossed the dining room to the corridor which led to the bathroom and bedroom.

There was an empty whisky bottle and two empty wine

14

bottles in a waste basket by the bed and a half-full one on the dressing table. The bottom sheet had a large damp stain where she'd pissed after passing out. Unable to find a clean one, he turned the mattress, put the top sheet to the bottom and roughly made the bed.

In the past, he would have searched the flat and removed any drink he found before leaving. But in recent years he'd learnt that his call meant the bender was over. He wondered how long it had lasted – three days? Four?

Back in the living room he stood staring at the heavy-breathing figure on the sofa. He could just discern, larded about with chins and cheeks, like a tiny pink kidney in its great coarse case of fat, the raw anxious little face that still sometimes came to him in his dreams. There was a gash of lipstick on her chin. It was for him. She'd tried to make up. She'd known he'd come. Indeed it was probably impossible now, at any rate very difficult, for him to refuse any violent cry for help.

It had not always been so. Before . . . before what had happened he'd quite often ignored her. But since then, knowing he'd come, she'd called far less often.

Thomas squatted by the sofa. He forced one arm under her shoulders, the other under her knees. He pulled her almost to the edge, tilted her towards him and slowly straightened his legs till he was standing up. The muscle laid down so many years ago as army middleweight champion and a bit later boxing for Cambridge had never entirely gone away. As well as the squash, he could still surprise the porters at the Museum. But she must have weighed eleven or twelve stone by now and hung very heavily over his arms.

He lowered her gently onto the bed and turned her over, face on one cheek, before pulling up a blanket. His fear – a fear remembered with such horror he would not admit its source – was that he'd arrive on one of these half-yearly visits and find she'd breathed in her vomit and choked to death.

Thomas turned off the light and walked back to the dining room. Hate was the lust of divorce. He remembered those rages which had suddenly flared up and consumed him, consumed them both, for years after they had parted. Was it this – stronger, or at least more long-lasting than love – that still bound them?

He went on his knees at the sofa. He couldn't tackle the whole mess. He'd call that woman in the morning. But this he had to clear.

He'd felt no hate carrying her to bed. Weariness mostly, indifference, a fleeting pride in his strength, pity. Not hate.

And as he gathered the photographs, letters from prep school, school reports, the first passport, everything she'd preserved of their son Philip's childhood and youth, there was nothing at all, not a flicker; that total blankness which betokens its extreme opposite; emotions – guilt, anguish, pain, love – entombed somewhere far too deep, thank God, to be any longer felt.

[3]

Alex stopped just after the little pass between Ravello and Corbora and got out to take the view. McKeown Productions liked plenty of photographs of any conceivable location.

The whole of the Campania was spread below him, a vast roughly circular plain, twenty or thirty kilometres across, rimmed by jagged peaks. Geologists believed, said the guide, that the region had been created by a gigantic volcanic explosion 36,000 years ago. The distant mountains were extinct volcanoes.

The only one left active was Vesuvius which, high as he was, rose from the plain opposite still higher – to over 4000 feet. But even that, to whose base he was about to descend, had not erupted for many years. It seemed quite dead, no plume of smoke, as in the old prints, flowing from its flat top.

Alex drove down the steep road, with its *serie di curve* and *caduta massi*, extremely slowly. Fantasies engendered by the dust clouds of the Calabrian roads had resulted in rather reckless driving. Ominous clunking came from the body of the brand-new hired Fiat.

The modern town of Ercolano, which had replaced Resina, was really just another Naples slum – joined to it by urban sprawl. The quickest way, by the map, would have been by the Salerno-Napoli *autostrada*.

Alex chose a smaller road, also signposted Napoli. Quickest

16

in was quickest out – and also the most obvious and most easily blocked. Not a route for kidnappers.

The smaller road, further off, was less obvious, and a great deal less easy. Part cobbled, heavily pitted and holed, it was deafening with horns and bicycle bells, stinking with exhaust, lined with little workshop garages, shops, slum houses, occasional vegetable patches under plastic.

It took him an hour and a half to reach Torre del Greco. After this, suddenly emptier, the road became the Corso Resina and led into Ercolano. Alex steered with the map on the wheel. The *scavi* – the excavations of ancient Herculaneum – were halfway along this road.

There was a small semi-circular space for cars, inexplicably barred off with metal fencing, in which a gang of youths kicked a football.

Alex parked on the pavement before this space. There was an imposing entrance with 'HERCULANEUM' written above it. He passed below this, paid 2000 lira for a ticket at a window marked '*Biglietteria*', and went over to a rickety balustrade guarding the drop into the ruins.

The street level of Herculaneum was about sixty foot below that of modern Ercolano. A sloping road lined with tall, dark green cypresses ran down the left hand side of the excavations, round the front and to the entrance into the Roman town.

Looking at the plan in the *Blue Guide* from his vantage point at the top of this road, Alex was surprised how little had been excavated. Built like most Roman towns on a system of *insulae*, or rectangular blocks of houses, divided by a grid of straight streets, a square of only four blocks – about 200 square yards – had been completely revealed.

Trees and shrubs grew haphazardly, weed-like in the ruins, which looked curiously drab in the light April sunshine. Some of the houses were square shells, but most still stood quite high – a few to two storeys, some complete. The sound of a pneumatic drill came thumping over these ancient roofs from somewhere at the front of the town. April was not a tourist month and he could see no one moving in the narrow streets.

Indeed, he thought he might have Herculaneum to himself, until he turned and saw a girl coming in past the '*Biglietteria*' window.

Alex stared, desire like a sudden sharp pain. He thought

17

he'd never seen a face so openly and frankly sensual. She had an abundant mass of bouncing dark black curls above a narrow forehead, slanting black eyes, a short nose with marked nostrils, a wide, upward-curving mouth with dark lips, the lower one bulging slightly fuller above a small round chin, and skin that was a pale olive brown. As she passed, Alex – his senses fired by hangover and what now seemed like months of abstinence – thought he could smell warm skin. He set off in pursuit.

Thomas, feeling slightly self-conscious, realising he should have seen Cynthia after all, had followed the same billowing sea-blue skirt and white shirt all the way down the main street, the Via IV Novembre, from the station. He came past the *Biglietteria* in time to witness this little pantomime. At once he stopped, baulked, deflated, feeling suddenly foolish.

Yet it was not just this that pulled him up. Never normally allowing such observation, the events of the previous night no doubt still stirred in him and he could not help noting the quite striking resemblance of the young man to his son. It was not just the colour of his hair – Sheila used to say it was the colour of gorse blooms – but the way he moved. Something precipitate.

He stood and watched them walking away, a couple now, joined by that thread as old almost as life itself – a couple if only for a few moments, for as long as it joined them, even though the girl was as yet unaware of it. Or was she? Thomas saw her stop and with a quick sideways glance move to look out over the excavations. The young man slowed, appearing engrossed in his guide. He would have been the same age as Philip, near enough.

The girl set off again. The young man looked up from his guide. Resuming detachment with an effort, Thomas started to descend very slowly himself.

His morning at the Museo Nationale had been fruitful. He had been able to promise Dottore Giuseppe Montesano, whom he'd met a number of times before, that the Museum was quite prepared to lend its collection of first-century Roman glass, even the beautiful blue glass from Pozzuoli. More important, from Thomas's point of view, he'd arranged to read a paper on his speciality – antique marble – at Giuseppe's conference at the end of September.

Yet the most important reason for coming to Naples was not official at all.

Thomas had now reached the end of the entrance road. The noise of the pneumatic drill, where two men were digging down to the last four yards of beach, was deafening. To the left were the new Antiquarium and the offices of the Soprintendente. To his right, the excavated fragment of the ancient town of Herculaneum. Looking across he saw the gorse-bloom yellow head passing the House of Argus, the *casa d'Argo*. Alone. Thomas was ashamed to feel relief. He watched the young man draw level with the House of the Skeleton.

He turned off the road and took a long, steeply sloping ramp, still barred to the public, down to what had once been the beach in front of and below the town. Now, facing outwards, the immensity of the catastrophe that had overwhelmed Herculaneum rose starkly above him – the smooth 100–foot high, 200–yard long vertical cliff of mud-rock.

It looked like the rampart of some colossal ancient fortress. And this towering cliff of destruction had swept over the city and then flowed inexorably on – a mile wide – another half a mile, thrusting the sea back to where it was now.

The old Roman shore had been cleared almost to the limit of the present excavations. The pneumatic drill, its thudding racket less now he was below it, came from where the last five yards were being laboriously gouged out. It was near there that the marble had been found. Some time he would have to see that.

Water which had drained down from the excavated city had filled the narrow stretch where the sea had once been and sparkled now in the sun. The beach beneath his feet was composed of the same moist dirty grey-black sand he would have found on the real beach half a mile away at that moment, except that it was scattered with millions of the pea-sized pebbles of feather-light pumice.

Thomas turned and scrunched up the beach of Herculaneum and through the tall, hoop-shaped entrance to one of the fisherman's boat chambers built into the sea wall. The remains of so few people had been found in the town itself that it had once been thought all the inhabitants had fled in time. But a few years back 150 skeletons had been discovered along the beach and in these boat chambers.

Thomas stood and looked at the twelve skeletons huddled in the mud in front of him. It was obvious enough, and yet always strangely evocative and moving. To his left was the skeleton of a twelve-year-old girl. She was crouched protectively over the skeleton of a much younger child – one three or four years old. All the skeletons were face down, many with an arm or hand covering the face. And all without exception had their teeth clenched in agony against the fiery rush of hot gases that must have caused their clothes and hair to blaze and burnt up their lungs.

Thomas stood, his eyes fixed. For an instant he could hear the lapping of the sea behind him, as it must have lapped when it curled onto the beach that hot afternoon of 24 August nearly two thousand years before.

It was for this, this precise moment, that he had come to Naples and then to Herculaneum.

The current lot of Keepers and Assistant Keepers at the Museum were scholars. Their drive was a scholar's drive: exactitude, detail, to master painstakingly and totally a small area, to cite sources, as many as possible. Not that Thomas's scholarship was negligible. His work on ancient marble was pioneering and well thought of.

But he came from an older and perhaps more romantic generation. His compulsion came from his sense of the past, of history. And by his sense of history he did not mean anything very complicated or even very sophisticated. It derived ultimately from just such images as that of the beach behind him, from these little constructed pictures in his head.

There were a number of places scattered round what had been the classical world to which he had to return from time to time to recharge. Herculaneum was one of them. Pompeii was more successful. Far more had been recovered, far more people went there; as a result its ghosts had fled. Herculaneum – this tiny, empty, nearly complete fragment of Herculaneum – was still haunted.

Thomas turned and stepped out of the shade into the sun and the present day. He started to climb slowly up the ramp. He'd wondered whether he should present himself to the new Soprintendente, the aged but apparently flamboyant Dr Gandolfino. However, Montesano had earlier advised against it. The Assistant Soprintendente Dr Dorothy Schultz, whom

20

Thomas had met once or twice, was taking being passed over very badly. 'Shocking' was how Montesano had described it. '*Scandaloso*.' Thomas didn't want to exacerbate things.

Desire makes cowards of us all. In order to let the girl get a little further ahead, Alex had paused too long on entering Herculaneum, to study his plan again. When he looked up, she had vanished.

He walked rapidly to the first intersection, that of the Decomanus Inferior. This too was empty. As he ran down it the thud of his feet echoed off the high windowless wall of the house on his left which stretched its entire length.

At the next intersection he stopped, panting. It was extremely silent. The pneumatic drill, muffled now by the intervening houses, seemed to come from another world. Where had everyone gone? Why?

To calm himself, he opened his camera and took some random shots for McKeown Productions. He was standing at the junction of Cardo IV and the Decomanus Inferior. The guide pointed out that the streets were narrow and the houses tall for the same reason they still were in Naples and other towns of the Campania – for shade in summer, warmth in winter.

Alex turned right into Cardo IV. Two of the houses further down had their second storeys jutting out, as in a medieval town. He saw that these were resting on steel beams and had concrete in-filling. How much had they reconstructed?

The first house was out of bounds. A flimsy wood trellis door had a sign, '*Divieto di Accesso*', hung on it. However, the padlock had broken and it swung half-open. Glancing up and down the deserted street, Alex stepped through.

The ground floor, said the guide, had been a shop. He could see through to a patch of sunlit space at the back, either a little garden or where the roof had fallen in on a room. It was choked with brambles and nettles.

Alex stood listening. It was completely silent, but a peaceful silence now. He could imagine that everyone – or perhaps not quite everyone; was there someone upstairs, asleep and waiting? – had gone to the beach or the games or wherever it was Romans spent their late April afternoons.

On the left was a wooden staircase, the bottom two steps missing. It was modern, but halfway up glass protected the

21

black carbonised remains of the original steps. Here were several little rooms with thin, partition-like walls. Most had no windows. It was warm, still, almost dark.

His rope-soled shoes made no sound. Coming up the stairs his sense of someone waiting grew stronger. It grew more and more powerful as he moved slowly and silently from room to room. At the last one, he stood beside the door listening intently.

At last, with an effort, he stepped inside. At once there was a loud scream and a figure rushed from him to the far end of the room.

'Christ alive!' cried Alex, jumping back. 'Who's that?' His mouth dry, he peered into the gloom.

At last the figure came away from the wall. It was the girl he'd been following. Alex let out his breath. 'I'm sorry, but you gave me a fright.'

Still she stood looking at him.

'Do you speak English?' said Alex. '*Parliamo inglese?*'

At last. '*Me* frighten *you*,' she said indignantly. 'I've never been so scared in my life, creeping about like that. I thought you were a ghost. You still look like a ghost – a huge ghostly dandelion.'

She stopped, suddenly embarrassed. They stood in silence.

'Actually I have to go soon. I have to be at Naples airport,' she said after a moment.

Alex led the way down. At the bottom of the stairs he took her left hand to help her over the gap. He felt a ring on the finger next to her little finger. The confirmation that it was a wedding ring sent another pulse of attraction through him.

The girl caught his glance and was aware of his reaction. Not for the first time she reflected that Black Jake – whom she'd married at eighteen, left at nineteen, and whose face she could scarcely now remember – had been more use to her as a ring – protecting or attracting – than he'd ever been as a husband.

'I'm Alex Mayne,' said Alex. 'What's your name?'

'Catrina. Catrina Webb.'

After another silence, Alex said, 'It's so peaceful here. I thought it was as though they'd all just left for the beach.'

'It's always like this. I remember when I came when I was sixteen. I thought it was like the *Marie Celeste*.' After a pause

22

she added, 'I suppose everyone thinks the same things really. And the other obvious thought about the peaceful summer afternoon, blue sky and suddenly – *bang!* The eruption and the destruction. It must be very, very difficult to have an original thought about Herculaneum.'

'Very, very difficult,' said Alex.

They stood in the sun outside the swinging door. 'The House of the Wooden Partition,' said Alex, looking at his plan. They walked slowly up Cardo IV, Alex leading them into the House of the Carbonised Furniture and the House of the Neptune Mosaic.

Catrina seemed to know nothing. 'House of this, House of that,' she said. 'Is that what they were really called? How do they know?'

'It doesn't say,' said Alex. 'Do you often come here?'

'No. In fact, not since that time. But my mother's family live here. About an hour away. I've been staying with them. We left our luggage at the airport and then my grandmother wanted to do some shopping in Naples. But Naples traffic is complete hell and anyway the shops aren't particularly good, so I made her put me off at the Circumvesuviana at Garibaldi. I thought I'd come here to kill time and see if it was as I remembered.'

'Was it? Is it?'

'Exactly the same.'

They turned along the Decomanus Maximus and into a house unmarked by the guide. 'It should be called the House of the Huge Beam,' said Catrina, pointing to the roof.

Her mouth, her dark red slice of mouth. When she opened it to speak it was a more delicate pink, like the wet inside of a watermelon. He swallowed. 'When's your plane?'

'I have to be there at six.'

Alex looked at his watch. 'I could drive you if you like.'

'That would be nice.' After a slight pause, Catrina said, 'What about you? What are you doing here?'

'We may be going to shoot a film here.' He paused. He always enjoyed this moment. He could see her ravishingly end-tilted eyebrows already arched in interest. 'I work in films,' he said.

Catrina was thinking: I bet not all that high up. She suddenly felt drawn to the slightly battered figure beside her.

'A film? What about?'

'Kidnapping. What do you think of Herculaneum as the location for the snatch?'

'Not bad. It's nice and near the *autostrada*.'

'Too easily blocked.'

'Nonsense. You don't know anything about it. You'd have to take it – anything else would be far too slow. There are dozens of exits. You could get off long before they could do anything. I could show you.'

The Decomanus Maximus was the highest point of the excavated town. Alex took more photographs; several of Catrina against the high cliff of tufa with the houses of Ercolano at its top.

'Let me take one of you.'

Alex unslung his camera, and it was their two heads – one gold as pollen, the other black – that Thomas saw bent close together over it as he came slowly round the corner at the top of Cardo V, the street parallel to the one Alex and Catrina had taken.

It had been some years since he had been there last, but the streets were familiar. He too had been looking up at the outline of Ercolano seventy foot above them. And he remembered that, at the sight of that little crust of slum houses straggling along the drab grey cliff, he'd thought then as he thought now. It was like looking at some great potential work of art. There was an enormous sculpture – a whole city of streets, temples, taverns, houses, rooms, statues, furniture, perhaps even clothes and food – latent deep in the rock below Ercolano and still waiting after 1900 years to be carved out.

But at the sight of the two heads bent together, to his eyes as intimate as if they'd been on a pillow, he turned abruptly round and strode back down towards the bottom of the town. It was not true that all the world loved a lover.

As he turned up the first stretch of the entrance road, he saw two figures burst precipitately from the new Antiquarium to his right. One he recognised, though Dorothy Schultz was an acquaintance more than a friend. He'd met her twice. He turned his head quickly to avoid being seen; but a second glance showed that she was far too occupied with the tall elderly man to whom she was speaking while following, or rather – there was something about the way he did not look

24

back – chasing him. Nevertheless, Thomas quickened his pace.

Shortly afterwards Alex and Catrina followed him in the same direction. They also saw the same two figures, now stopped facing each other about forty yards from the road, both gesticulating, and, struck by the vehemence of the scene, they stood and watched.

The woman was tall, nearly six foot, fifty-five or sixty, with black-grey hair coiled massively into something almost the size of a table top and pinned tight to the side of her head. Although she was large, her bulk was hidden by a long green garment, tent-shaped from neck to below the ankles.

Her companion, or antagonist, was even taller, exceptionally tall, and extremely thin. A man of seventy perhaps, with a brown, bony, bald head fringed by a froth of grey hair. He had long thin moustaches, and long, shaking, bony fingers.

Both were clearly very angry. But as they watched the woman was seized by an extra paroxysm of rage. Her green garment billowed and shook like a marquee hit by a gale. Shouting hoarsely, she raised both arms above her head. The man too flung up his arms, either to strike back or to protect himself, then he turned and retreated again, arms pumping at his sides. The woman, still shouting, at once surged in pursuit.

Alex and Catrina watched till the man disappeared back into the Antiquarium, closely pursued by the woman who, her feet hidden by her tent, appeared to glide across the ground like a hovercraft.

'Did you hear what she was shouting?'

'It was difficult to understand. She had a very strong American accent. Something about over my dead body, or it might have been your dead body.'

At the car she told him to put the map away.

'I'll guide you.'

Alex's bare arm brushed along her slender brown calf as he bent to shove the map into the compartment opposite the passenger seat. He shivered.

'It's amazing how they don't mend the roads,' he said, clearing his throat. The crack over which the clanking Fiat bumped was a good inch and half wide and stretched six feet across the bottom of the Via IV Novembre.

'I like that,' said Catrina. 'You can still *use* the roads. The Italians have the right priorities.' She pointed to a long crack running up the front of the building they were passing. 'In fact the whole region hasn't really recovered from the earthquake in 1980. There's still scaffolding up, even in parts of Naples.' Whatever he'd done to cause the clanking was getting worse. He couldn't get the Fiat into fourth gear. Catrina began to worry she'd miss her plane.

'We'll make it,' said Alex.

When they reached the airport he ran beside her through the automatic glass doors, and carried her two cases from the left-luggage to the check-in point.

At the gate to the departure lounge he said, 'Let's meet in London. How can I get hold of you?'

Catrina looked at him, her face serious. 'All right. I don't know where I'll be. I'll give you my grandmother's number in Wiltshire.'

Alex wrote the number on the back of his cheque book and then stood and watched her walk through and put her hand luggage through the X-ray machine. She did not look back, not there, not after walking through the X-ray arch, not when she turned left and walked out of sight towards the departure lounge. Thinking of her as he walked back to the Fiat, of her dark red mouth, of the smell of her next to him in the car – the smell of warm skin, no doubt at all this time, of clean cotton, of recent and very faint, fresh sweat – he shivered again. 'All right.'

That night, by chance, Thomas and Alex took the same *rapido* to Rome. They both had dinner in the restaurant car. But Thomas took the first sitting, Alex the second, and they did not see each other.

Chapter Three

A return to London is a return to bills. Even Catrina was driven from Alex's mind by the pile of brown envelopes and forms about recorded delivery letters which had gone undelivered. He so dreaded what he knew he'd find that he didn't dare touch it for three days.

Yet beneath these two major preoccupations, as though connecting them, he was surprised to find a third. He could not stop thinking about Herculaneum. This was nothing to do with the obvious fact that he had met Catrina there.

He had rung Wiltshire the afternoon he had returned, and twice again that evening. Not until the following morning did someone reply.

'Hello.'

'Is that Mrs Webb?'

'Yes.'

'It's Alexander Mayne here. Could I speak to Catrina?'

'Catherine? I'm afraid she's not here. She doesn't usually give much advance warning. I haven't heard from her recently.'

'Oh well,' said Alex, 'I'll ring again in a few days, if that's all right?' He paused, listening. 'Well, goodbye,' he said with a feeling of mistiming. But the receiver had already been quietly replaced.

Yet Catrina no longer had any connection with Herculaneum. She was in England, and he did not think about her when he thought about the excavated city. The little streets, the two-storeyed houses, returned to his mind with an odd persistence on their own. Again and again, walking to the Tube, standing at the window in his bedroom, waking at night, he found he was trying to remember something that had happened without having the faintest idea what it was.

27

It was as if he had lost something there, or been told, and forgotten, some vital information about the Roman town.

Mrs Webb's responses grew increasingly, then totally monosyllabic. Yet what a lot even those clipped yesses and nos revealed. Each time she spoke he saw greenhouses and gravel sweeps. I'll bet there's a Trust Fund, he thought.

Not that Alex went after girls because they had money. Nevertheless, his girls often seemed to have money as a sort of chance adjunct. And his need for money, always pressing, had now become desperate.

When at last he faced the brown envelopes and collected the recorded delivery letters, he found his estimate of £20,000 was too low. It was £20,000 before even considering the life support systems which, starting with Access and Barclaycard, were all about to be cut off. He owed £10,000 to the bank. They had held off on his promise to send the Deeds of the flat – already held by the building society, who now not only refused a second mortgage but were threatening repossession unless he paid the arrears on the first mortgage. The restaurant crew were threatening to sue. The garage was threatening to sue; it would in any case sell his car in part payment of his bill. The other travel agent was suing.

Once again, he felt panic. The balls, so long kept in the air, were all about to crash to the ground.

[2]

David McKeown, short, plump, pink and warily welcoming, was no help at all.

'This is fine, just what we wanted, Alex,' he said, flipping swiftly through notes and photographs. But the cheque, when he handed it over, was for £2000.

'But you said £1500 *a week*,' cried Alex.

'Alex.' David had on his 'spare me' expression. 'I said £1000 a week now, £1500 a week when they started shooting and if you went on location.'

'Oh *shit*,' said Alex. He flicked the cheque with his finger. 'This will hardly cover my travel expenses.'

He stared at the ground. He'd suddenly remembered the rates were due in soon – £450. If he could somehow raise a further £2000, open a new bank account, keep some of them at bay with small cheques. God, life was awful.

'What's whatshisname – that scriptwriter chap – getting?' he asked at a tangent. Were any of them still employed?

'Two thousand quid. But I'm dropping him as a matter of fact.'

It was dead. He could tell from the tone of David's voice it was dead. He had been quite mad to rely on it.

At first, when he'd started to do work for McKeown's six years before, the volatile life of the film world had suited him. So ten projects vanished into the air; ten equally promising rose to take their place. Alex was at home in a world of hope. He slept with girls who thought he'd get them parts. One month, when he was short of cash, he worked as an extra for £50 a day. Also it allowed him ample time to follow other ventures: plans to bulk-buy secondhand books; handling the publicity for a pop group; a scheme to smuggle marijuana which in the end he was too scared to join; a share in a restaurant ('No cash, Alex you fool. Just guarantee ten per cent of the bank loan and rake in ten per cent of the profits').

Then about eighteen months ago McKeown's hit a rough patch. David lost a lot of money on cable. He had less and less work for Alex. Indeed, the *Kidnap* project was the only thing that had come up in the last year. Alex had had to rely, or rather gamble on, his other schemes, which in turn had become more and more desperate.

It was in fact the author of one of these – one that at the time he had rejected – whom he rang after leaving Wardour Street.

'Certainly,' said Eddie Segal. 'It so happens I might have something, my dear fellow. I'm going to a sale at Christie's tomorrow. Ten-thirty. Why don't you join me? Ask for the Antiquities sale. We could have some lunch afterwards.'

When Sotheby's had been taken over in 1983, the brilliant, still relatively young Lebanese had left, taking with him four other disaffected directors and a lot of influential and wealthy clients. They had recruited similar figures from Christie's and Phillips and set up – though Eddie's had been the dominant hand – their own auction house: Dexter's.

Dexter's had made its way by flair, by reducing the buyer's premium to five per cent and in some cases to nothing, and

29

by sailing rather close to the wind. Alex had not taken the decision to ring easily. He still remembered with a qualm the time Eddie had telephoned out of the blue two years before.

They had not met since they had briefly shared a room at Cambridge sixteen years before. After some resuming-contact generalities, Eddie had said, 'Forgive me asking, Alex – I wouldn't dream of asking if I didn't need help – but would you like to make some money?'

It had been at the start of the McKeown vacuum. 'Well, yes I would,' Alex had said. 'As a matter of fact I need money rather badly.'

'I should perhaps warn you it could be dangerous.'

'*Dangerous?*' said Alex. 'How dangerous? What makes you think I could do something dangerous?'

'I heard you were being a stunt man in a film.'

'No, no,' said Alex hastily. 'Film *extra*. And that was some time ago. I couldn't possibly have been a stunt man. I'm a physical and moral coward. Surely you remember that?'

Eddie Segal didn't seem to be listening. 'Extra – stunt man – what's the difference? Anyway, if you're interested come to Duke Street tomorrow about twelve. You'll see the sign.'

It wasn't so much interest as being short of money. Not desperate, but short. Alex had turned up.

It seemed that a number of Russians, despite ferocious laws, liked to sell things in the West – gold objects particularly, also icons. These had to be picked up, sometimes deep in Russia via a series of contacts, and smuggled out, mostly across the Black Sea.

'Do you speak Russian?'

'No.'

'Well, doesn't matter. Our contacts usually speak a little English.'

'What happens if I'm caught?'

'You won't be caught, unless you're incredibly foolish. We've only had one carrier who was rumbled. He's doing five years in Yakutsk.'

'Where's that?'

'Central Siberia.'

'I see. Pretty hairy.'

'You'll make a lot of money,' said Eddie. 'But yes – hairy.'

'It sounds just up my street,' said Alex, terrified out of his

30

wits. He'd waited a day or two and then made one of his other schemes suddenly become urgent.

The difference between that episode and this, he reflected as he followed the doorman's directions to the Antiquities sale, was that this time he was well and truly desperate.

Eddie Segal was standing reading and marking his catalogue at a large entrance door. About fifty people, added to all the time, were jostling, waving, talking, sitting in the small but lofty East Room just beyond him.

Eddie's soft, dry, olive-coloured little hand was framed in a dove-grey, very clean cuff. He looked just the same as two years ago, only even richer.

'This should be quite fun. There are some nice things.' He led Alex to two seats at the side in the fourth row upon which was laid a grey coat with a velvet collar. 'We can see nicely from here.'

'Is this a lot of people?' asked Alex.

'There'll be more. Especially later on. Most of the dealers are here already. There's Ogden, Robin Symes. That's Raffi-Soleimani. Ingrid McAlpine. You see that woman sitting in the front in the black suit?'

Alex saw an upright figure with high-piled grey hair. One boney, age-spotted hand, the fingers covered in large rings, was removing her spectacles.

'She's from Wolheim's. They sometimes do the bidding for the Getty Foundation.' He turned his sleek head. He missed nothing. 'You see that man sitting down at the back of the room? That's Thomas Henderson from the British Museum. Their Antiquities people are brilliant.'

Alex looked over his shoulder, and saw a big man with thick grey hair, fleshy nose and a deeply lined, rather melancholy face. Even sitting down he rose above the people around him; but the buyers of antiquities – Greek, French, German, several Japanese – seemed on the whole rather small.

'Are you bidding for anything?'

'No. We're holding a sale of antiquities in the middle of October. I just wanted to see what was going on. But I'm quite interested in that – lot 265.' He pointed. Alex noticed that he polished his nails.

'You mean the head?'

'Yes.'

31

A rampart had been formed facing the audience of low display cases full of what looked like the detritus of archaeological sites; slightly to the left was a high pulpit with 'CHRISTIE'S' emblazoned on it; and further left again, completing the rampart, was a higher display case full of vases. Prominent on one of the lower cases was a bronze head a foot or so high. It was the head of a man about forty, with short curls frozen by the dark green bronze – a fine face, strong, sardonic.

'How much will it fetch?'

'What do you think?'

'I haven't the faintest idea,' said Alex. 'I don't know what any of these things cost. Twenty thousand? Fifteen thousand? You can see the eyes are missing – ten thousand?'

Eddie smiled faintly. 'Wait and see.'

Alex wanted to reach for Eddie's catalogue and see the estimate, but at that moment a plump, pink-faced man slipped through the half-dozen people behind the rampart, had a word with one of them, mounted the pulpit, opened a ledger, looked up, smiled, and began at once.

'Good morning ladies and gentlemen. There are a few withdrawals this morning – lots 48, 49, and 66. There are three additions for which most of you will have received slips. These, and various other corrections, I'll deal with when we come to them.'

'Now, for lot number one, I have – ' he looked up and seemed to catch some figure from the air – 'a bid of three hundred. Four hundred. Five hundred. Six hundred. Six hundred pounds. At the back. Going for six hundred pounds. For six hundred pounds then. Going. Going. . . .' Pause. *Tap*, went his small ivory hammer on the pulpit. 'To Gibbs at the back. Six hundred pounds.'

The only auction Alex had been to before had been country sales of furniture, old cookers, piles of books. He was amazed at the speed, the skill, the intimacy. The auctioneer's eyes were everywhere, swift flickers of communication passing between him and the bidder, to the new bidder, back to the old. 'Five thousand pounds at the back. Against you, sir. Six thousand pounds. Six and a half. Still against you. To the Hadji Gallery. At six thousand five hundred pounds. Going. Going.' Tap.

But above all he was amazed at the money: at the amounts poured out, it seemed unthinkingly; at the ruthless, battering power of the larger over the smaller.

The sums were far, far higher than he'd imagined. Even trivial objects – rings, glass bowls, clasps, bits of things – went for £600, £2000, £3500. A marble bust – 'AD 120 – very good condition' – went for £150,000. A marble head of Asclepius, first century AD, for £72,000. Is bronze, thought Alex, more or less valuable than marble? Three marble to one bronze, so perhaps bronze. There were few battles. The winner usually seemed to emerge quite swiftly.

It was not until just before one o'clock that anything like a battle did develop – and it was in fact over the bronze head. Two young men in green aprons, like servants at a Cambridge college, held up each item as it was auctioned. As one of these lifted lot 265 and stood facing the now crowded room, the murmuring and coughing and rustling died away for the first and only time in the entire sale.

Something about the bronze head caught Alex's attention as it was held up, staring out unseeing over the audience. The face was dominated by the holes of eyes, black, blank – blank with horror at what he'd seen, his people, his family dying in agony, his city destroyed. To be buying and selling was suddenly tasteless, shameful.

Yet it was the bidding that gripped. It began with a jump to £50,000, and then leapt upward in bounds of £10,000 – Lesters against the old woman from Wolheim's – to £150,000. Here there was a long pause. Lester's seemed to have won, when all at once a new figure entered.

'£155,000? I have £155,000. Against you sir. The Hadji Gallery – £155,000.' Alex saw the mottled hand holding the spectacles, whose minute tap on the chin had sent the bidding back across the room each time, fall to her lap. Wolheim's was finished.

And now, as if the players had come up to the net, the bids got closer, faster, 'Sixty thousand; £165,000. One-seventy. Seventy-five. £180,000.'

The auctioneer, very alert, very polite, pink face pinker, looked now to one side, now to the other, an umpire. The odd thing was that the bronze head, having scorned it, seemed to be following the sale too. As the young Cambridge porter, holding it in both hands at his waist, turned left and right after the bidding, so did the head move – not completely, but slightly, listening as sightless people do.

'£185,000. Ninety. Ninety thousand. Ninety-five. Two hundred. Two hundred thousand pounds.' There was a long pause. Against Lester's. But Lester's too was finished. The Hadji Gallery had won.

But suddenly, amazingly, as if partially revived by the rest, Wolheim came back. Very slowly, shaking, the spectacles were raised to the chin again.

'Two hundred and five thousand. 210,000. 213,000 pounds.'

It wasn't like a game. They were mountaineers climbing step by step to impossible altitudes, oxygenless, exhausted. As the air got more and more rarified, the steps got smaller and slower.

'Two hundred and sixteen thousand, 218,000, 220,000 pounds.' Higher and higher, slower and slower. At 225,000 pounds they began to mount in thousands. '226,000, 227,000, 228. . . .' They were only just moving. 'Two hundred and twenty-eight thousand. And five hundred.' Pause. 'Two hundred and twenty-nine thousand.' Pause. '229,500.' Pause. '230,000 pounds.' Pause. No one moved. It was clear that Wolheim's was, at last, really finished. The spotted skeletal hand could not move. 'Two hundred and thirty thousand pounds. Do I have any advance on two hundred and thirty thousand pounds? Very well then, going at 230,000 pounds. To the Hadji Gallery. Going. Going!' *Tap!* With a combined sighing, coughing, rustling, talking, scraping, and standing up the auction room relaxed.

It was time for lunch. Alex stood up. 'Who gets the head?'

'I don't know,' said Eddie. If Wolheim's had been bidding for Getty they would have got it. But I don't think the Getty Foundation need any more of that sort of thing now. And the Hadji Gallery could have been bidding for them. They often switch dealers to stop people bidding them up. It might have been one of the pension funds. But the Hadji have a lot of clients. It could have been a private collector.'

'Not the British Museum?'

'I don't think so. Henderson didn't bid. Lester's often do

their bidding and Lester's dropped out at 200,000. It was a high price for something like that, nice as it was.'

Alex looked back to see if he could see the man Eddie had called Henderson but there was no sign of him.

'I'm afraid I can't offer you a great deal, Alex,' Eddie said after they had ordered.

'As long as it's not as terrifying as last time.'

'What was that? I forget.'

'Smuggling stuff out of Russia and highly likely to end up in Siberia.'

'Oh yes – and you had to rush off and do something or other; what was it – stunt man or something?'

'No Eddie. I've never been a stunt man. I don't know – probably my restaurant,' said Alex, remembering with a stab of panic.

'That's it. How did that go?'

'It went bust. It's rather a mess. I had to get out. That is, I'm in the process of getting out.'

'I see.' Eddie did see. He looked at Alex's still handsome if now rather haggard face and felt a warm glow. Partly at his own success and wealth. Partly sentimental. Like many foreigners educated in England, the experience had had an exaggerated effect on him. This was what it was all about, as they said, being an English gentleman, helping old varsity friends who were on their uppers.

'It's bound to be a bit like last time, Alex,' he said, filling his glass. 'A lot of our work is helping private individuals sell their possessions abroad, that is here – which in my view they have a perfect right to do, but which the law of their own country forbids. But no law *here* forbids it. Italy, for instance, is the same.'

In fact it turned out to be exactly the same proposition as before, only in this case getting goods out of Nigeria.

'But isn't that pretty dangerous? What happens if I'm caught?'

'There is not the remotest chance of your getting caught. The laws are completely bogus. The government is frantic for foreign currency. In fact, the individual in this case is a highly placed member of the government. They would normally use diplomatic baggage, but there are reasons here – I haven't quite fixed it up, I'll explain later – but I promise you categorically you will have no difficulty getting out of Nigeria. The journey afterwards might be a trifle tricky. But only in a geographical sense.'

'How much would I get?'

'Two and a half thousand pounds fee. All expenses. A commission on the sale. Primitive African sculptures are making very good prices at the moment. You'll clear at least £6000 for two or three weeks' work. Perhaps a bit more.'

Alex had no choice. He agreed at once. Eddie would ring him in a day or two.

Walking slowly back to Green Park Underground, he found himself thinking of the auction, of the fine, proud, bronze head held up – worth nearly a quarter of a million pounds. And had those staring empty eyes looked on the volcano's fire?

[3]

The following day he was about to set off for a business lunch when David McKeown rang.

'Your notes don't really say where we might set the snatch. Were none of the places any good?'

The call and the questions surprised Alex. Perhaps *Kidnap* wasn't so dead after all. 'Herculaneum,' he said without thinking.

'Why?'

'It's a strange place. You could set the love scenes there, too. Also, it's near the *autostrada*.'

'Is that the place with ruined houses? You didn't mark them.'

'Yes.'

'Who's sexy face?'

'Sexy face?' said Alex. 'What do you mean?'

'There's a girl in one of them. Taken against a cliff.'

'Oh, that's just a girl I met there. I thought I'd taken all of those out.'

'Is that why you suggested it for the snatch?' asked David suspiciously.

'Of course not,' said Alex irritably. 'Could you send that picture back to me? Like I said, it's a very strange place.

36

Haunted. And ideally suited for the getaway. Look David, I've got an urgent business lunch. I've got to go.'

The business of the lunch was to borrow money. It required a good deal of drink to raise the question and still more to get over the polite, regretful but quite definite refusal. On the way back in the Underground Alex fell asleep and went beyond Stockwell to Clapham Common. He decided to clear his head by walking back to the flat.

He'd gone fifty yards or so past the bookshop when he stopped. He'd seen something interesting in the window, but not taken it in, not acknowledged it. Was it a book by someone he knew? It was a curious sensation, as if one half of his brain was trying to force a message through to the other half.

He walked back and saw the book at once, at one side, not very prominent. *Pompeii and Herculaneum: The Living Cities of The Dead,* by Theodore Kraus, Leonard von Matt: half-price.

The connection was finally made next morning. It was one of those sudden explosions among the synopses caused by hangover.

The lunch-time drinking had sent him out to supper wanting a great deal more to drink. The couple he went out with hardly touched the stuff. He had, effectively, two bottles of wine. There was half a bottle of Sainsbury's sherry in the fridge when he got back.

He was woken, it seemed at dawn, by the most appalling thumping and crumping actually going on in the bedroom. He realised after a while, unable to blot it out, that it was in the street. Still half-drunk, shuddering, he got out of bed and went to shut the window.

It was a pneumatic drill. They were smashing up the road. Alex leant his forehead on the cool glass and watched the drill bounce maniacally and deafeningly up and down – *woof*-bang, *woof*-bang, *woof*-bang.

He felt his stomach rumbling. He needed a drink. Suddenly a scene flashed into his head. Alex stood stock still, gripped by it, holding his breath. *Christ!* he thought. *That's it. That's what it was.*

He pushed himself off the window, trembling now, partly with hangover, partly excitement. He pulled on his dressing gown. He wanted to tell someone. But he could tell no one. If he told *anyone,* they'd steal it. It was so obvious perhaps they already had. He stumbled downstairs. What he needed was two really stiff drinks, two snorters.

He stood in the kitchen. The empty bottle of sherry was on the table with the glass beside it. All at once he picked up the telephone and dialled.

'Hello?'

'Mrs Webb? It's Alex Mayne here. I just wondered if by any chance Catrina had turned up or rung up or anything? I'm terribly sorry to disturb you so early in the morning.'

'It's eleven o'clock,' said Mrs Webb coldly. 'No, she hasn't.'

There was a pause. Alex hoped the volcanic rumbling of his stomach couldn't be detected.

'Look, Mr Mayne, I don't think there's much point in your continuing to ring up like this. Why don't you give me your number and your message and if Catherine appears, I'll tell her.'

'Yes,' said Alex. '01–627 1176.'

' . . . 627 1176. Go on.'

'How do you mean, go on?'

'Have you no message?'

Message? Trembling, rumbling, sick, Alex thought. Then at last, with relief, he said, 'I know. I've got it. Tell her this.'

'Yes?'

'Tell her I've had an original idea about Herculaneum.'

Chapter Four

Alex spent the next three days reading in the Brixton Reference Library. He also bought the half price-copy of Kraus's *Pompeii and Herculaneum* he'd seen in the Clapham bookshop.

Herculaneum had been discovered in 1709. A peasant on the outskirts of what was then still called Resina – now Ercolano – found that his sixty-foot well was no longer filling with water.

While deepening it, he was astonished to find that at about eighty feet or so he was digging up slabs of polished marble. The local dealer to whom he sold them was even more astonished. He recognised the marble. It was antique – a type hitherto only found in the ruins of the ancient world.

A high-ranking officer in the Austrian army, Prince d'Elboeuf, had recently bought a villa at nearby Portici which he was busy decorating. When he learnt that the marble he was buying from the local dealer came from the bottom of a peasant's well on the outskirts of Resina, he immediately bought the entire holding.

Prince d'Elboeuf's servants now enlarged the well, sank it deeper and dug out little tunnels from the bottom, bringing up columns, statues and more marble. But eventually digging became too difficult and in 1715 it was abandoned. D'Elboeuf still had no idea what the peasant had discovered.

In 1738, King Charles of Naples and Sicily bought the villa at Portici. His wife Maria was very excited at the idea of digging. Work was resumed, and with the vastly increased resources of a reigning monarch results were swifter – statues, marbles, and then, on 11 December, 1738, an inscription: '*Theatrum Herculaniensum*'. It was onto the stage of this theatre – lined with marble, set with statues – that the peasant had accidentally dug his well. After 1700 years, Herculaneum had returned to the light of human knowledge.

The realisation that eighty or ninety feet down there was a buried city perfectly preserved – albeit in solid rock – produced a frenzy of treasure seeking. Tunnels were forced out in all directions, narrow passages, some a mile long, winding in pitch darkness through the streets, the squares and the houses. A new and much wider shaft was sunk to let them haul up the larger finds.

Digging continued spasmodically, with long gaps, throughout the eighteenth century, becoming less and less intense. The work was difficult and it was continually compared to that at Pompeii, which was now being excavated. Pompeii had been buried under dense showers of the pea-sized pumice *lapilli* – the 'frothed' lava. These, except at the surface where they had been compacted into a crust by rain, could be shovelled into wheelbarrows and carted off. Besides, no one had built on top of Pompeii as they had at Herculaneum, and it was the existence of Resina which made proper excavation impossible. By the mid-nineteenth century the digging at Herculaneum had got no further than at the end of the eighteenth century. The partially hollowed-out stage and the tunnels were reached by a stair descending twenty-seven metres into the dank depths. They were now just a sight shown by flaring resin torches to distinguished visitors. Dickens went down and was terrified.

The last significant work was done by the great Soprinten-dente Amedeo Maiuri from 1927 on, and again after the Second World War. He organised the purchase of seventeen acres from the outskirts of Ercolano and it was from these that the present small patch of Herculaneum had been labori-ously dug.

From Alex's point of view, his reading was both exciting and also, in some respects, maddeningly vague. Throughout its recent history there were references to the hardness of the mud-rock in which the Roman city was entombed. That was why tunnels were abandoned. A letter from Johann Winkel-mann of Dresden, which appeared in 1762, described how difficult d'Elboeuf's excavations had been. In 1738 pickaxes and gunpowder had been used. One account described the rock as hard enough for a pickaxe to strike sparks and set off an explosion of mine gas.

But precisely how hard was hard? There was evidence the other way. If a lone peasant could dig down sixty feet – using what? Pick? Shovel? Bucket on a rope? – and then down a further twenty feet, it couldn't be all that hard. In 1738, shafts were filled with earth and stones to prevent subsidence. In the 1750s, when the props were removed from galleries dug in and out of the theatre, the galleries collapsed. Clearly, therefore, not *rock* hard.

Nor could he find out if the flow had filled the town solid right the way through. Was every crevice, every cupboard, every jug and bowl filled to the brim and then itself entombed? Had all those myriads objects already found – from tooth-picks, helmets, mirrors, knives up to over-life-size busts and torsos – had to be chipped piecemeal from mud-rock? Just as, thought Alex (and thereby showed it was indeed difficult to have an original idea about Herculaneum), just as if the whole town, its entire contents, were like some giant conception in a sculptor's mind waiting in the solid rock to be carved out?

Vesuvius had erupted over seventy times since AD 79. On many occasions the region had been riven by tremendous earthquakes, the last major one on 23 November 1980. Several of these eruptions and earthquakes had been of colossal violence. Surely great cracks must have opened over the centuries. And there must have been, too, some rooms that had escaped the flow, particularly as it slowed up and grew sluggish – cellars, rooms sealed to protect valuables.

And Alex was irritated by the continual reference to sixty or seventy feet of mud. In fact, as he remembered it, the great rampart at the front of the town was higher than this. It had seemed, as he pursued Catrina down it, and then again when they walked up together, a cliff of at least 100 feet. But if it had built up here, by the same token the mud, as it flowed down, congealing, would be shallower at the back.

Even where there was talk of sixty or seventy feet, this meant to the street. Alex tried to envisage the houses he'd seen at Herculaneum. Some were at least two storeys high. These then would be under, say, thirty or forty feet of mud. One book said that houses at Herculaneum, in AD 79, were being built to three storeys, with sometimes a fourth storey left open to the sky. Yet how could they know this for certain? Another book said that the layout and construction of houses in Herculaneum were remarkable for their variety and for the degree they departed from normal patterns of Roman building. And only a tiny bit of the town had been excavated. He discovered that at the same period, mid-first century AD, there were houses of eight and nine storeys being built at next-door Neapolis; at Rome, at Ostia, twelve storeys were quite common. A house of five storeys, provided it had not been toppled, could actually have stuck up above the deepest mud, and in fact some writers suggested this had happened.

But about one thing all the books agreed. Herculaneum had been a resort for the wealthiest Romans. Charles Waldenstein had argued in 1904 – and was later proved right – that far more important works of art were buried at Herculaneum than had been, or would be, found at Pompeii. And for Alex 'works of art' meant one thing – money.

Nearly £230,000 for a single eyeless bronze head, no bigger than – well, than an ordinary head. Alex couldn't get over the sum. From the Villa of the Papyri alone, not inside Herculaneum, admittedly, but only just outside, had come some ninety-odd sculptures – bronzes, marbles, busts, animals, satyrs, boys, men, women.

If he were to stumble on just one such object of this sort his fortune would be made. But suppose he struck a terrace or some crowded vestibule, or even a craftsman's studio. . . .

And it was money made, the quantities involved, as he'd somehow always known he'd have to make it – or not make it at all. A killing in the manner of the film world. With no particular application of effort or skill; just the courage to take, when it mattered, the big, the really big, decisive gamble.

It was all this he planned to tell Catrina when they finally met up five days after his revelation.

[2]

'I can't think why I gave you Granny's number,' said Catrina, who'd done so for it to provide precisely the test it had. 'I hardly go there now.'

42

'"Granny" doesn't suit her at *all*. Is she as pinched and disapproving as she sounds?'

'Not really. Very English, I suppose. Rather lonely now. Most of her close friends are plants.'

'Why does she call you Catherine?'

'I was christened Catherine. My mother wanted there to be something Italian in my names. So she started to call me Caterina, and that turned into Catrina. I think Granny's about the only one left who calls me Catherine.'

He had to lean across the table to hear her rather low voice, with its sudden trill of laughter. *Al Ben Accolto* was one of those Italian restaurants which ensured the privacy of each table by enveloping it in noise so deafening that no one further than a foot away could hear what was being said.

Alex looked across at her, her wide mouth as dark as the wine she was drinking. He wanted to ask her what had happened to the husband who now no longer circled the finger of her left hand. Was it a signal of encouragement? The evening hadn't quite reached that point.

'Tell me about your original idea,' said Catrina.

Alex refilled his glass for the second time with Chianti. Nervously finishing half a bottle of wine waiting for her arrival at the flat, he'd decided not to talk about it after all. It was so obvious that he felt, superstitiously, just to mention it would put it into someone else's head. He would do the whole thing on his own.

But now, faced with her, the desire to show off to her, to appeal to this beautiful attentive girl for help and support and admiration were all suddenly irresistible.

'Do you know the history of Herculaneum at all?'

'Not really.'

Thus Alex embarked on a rough condensation of his three days' reading. He described the overwhelming of the city, its rediscovery, the protracted excavations, the uncertainty – in Alex's view – as to the depth or shallowness of the mud-rock, as to its hardness or softness, of whether it had penetrated everywhere, solid right through. But above all he talked about the one thing that was certain, the possibility of really big money.

Catrina listened carefully but, towards the end, with growing perplexity.

'So,' finished Alex, totally convinced. 'What do you think?'

'I think it's very interesting. But,' she paused, frowning, 'what exactly is your original idea?'

'Original idea?' said Alex, very surprised. 'I've just told you.'

'What you described was fascinating. I don't see how it was an idea exactly.'

'But don't you see – if we rented a basement flat or a house in Ercolano above the buried Herculaneum we could dig down and get some of the stuff out.'

There was a long pause. At the next table two animated middle-aged men could have been spies exchanging details of the latest missile for all anyone could hear.

'You mean smash down through the kitchen tiles and then dig down through sixty feet of rock?'

'If necessary,' said Alex. 'If the kitchen was in the basement. But I explained – it may not be all that solid.'

'Yes, but it might be sixty feet,' said Catrina. 'Suppose you miss the houses, you'd have to dig right down to the street.'

'You might,' agreed Alex, 'but the streets were narrow to keep out the sun. The chances are you'd strike a house. If not, you'd have to sink another shaft.'

'Move into the dining room and smash that up too?' said Catrina, giggling. But the practicalities didn't really convince her either way. 'Of course,' she said suddenly after a short pause, 'I know why it isn't possible.'

'Why?' said Alex.

'Because you don't know the Italians,' said Catrina. 'Look, last summer my Aunt Isabella, who lives a little way outside Rome, dug a big new swimming pool at the bottom of her garden. They soon found a mosaic, bits of pillar, etc. Obviously an old villa. Now the Italian government says these things belong to them, to the state. You can keep a few unimportant things, and buy back the rest, or most of it, cheap. But you have to hand it all over to be registered and catalogued – which takes weeks, months. And if you happened to find something really marvellous then the government would pay you – but about a tenth of the value.

'Well, of course no one dreams of bothering with all this nonsense. In fact, Aunt Isabella kept a nice, very battered marble head and sold some coins. Everyone does it. All Italy is like Rome. You know – there's the Colosseum, and all those statues, and the door of your hotel is a Roman Column. They all *know* the place is *made* of Etruscan stuff and Greek stuff and Roman stuff. You said that man who dug the well was surprised when he found marble. I don't suppose he was surprised at all. He probably expected it.

'What I mean is, if it were possible to dig down, someone would have done it. If one person could and did, lots would have done and it would have leaked out. If it hasn't, then it isn't possible.'

Their intimacy advanced, in the din of *Al Ben Accolto,* by the measure of her first long speech to him. Alex wanted to take her small hands, as active as a pair of tumbling doves, and kiss them.

'You may be right,' he said. 'But the fact is, it hasn't leaked out. It has been done, done once by a peasant on his own in the eighteenth century, and it hasn't been done since. I want to try.'

Catrina looked at him, not speaking. Drink made him look like a wild schoolboy.

'The fact is,' said Alex, 'I've got to try. I'm desperate for money.'

'But I thought you said you worked for a film company. Don't they pay enough?'

'That wasn't strictly true,' said Alex. 'Anyway, it's far far worse than that. I owe thousands and thousands of pounds. They're about to take back my flat. I'm in the most ghastly terrifying mess at the moment, in fact.'

Enjoying the drama, he looked at her face, concerned, flushed, and filled their glasses again.

'Anyway, don't you even think this is worth finding out about? The obvious place to go to find out is Ercolano. I thought I'd go next week. Would you like to come with me?'

This was two questions, in their essentials unrelated. Catrina answered the most important.

'Yes, I'd love to come with you,' she said.

Alex allowed the drink, which the strain of exposition and seduction had to a certain extent kept at bay, to sweep forward through the cortex. 'I know one isn't meant to notice, or at least comment, but what happened to the ring you had on your left hand? Have you just split up?'

All sexual love seems inevitable to the two caught in its powder train, who forget the far more numerous times the leaping sparks die out half-way or fail to catch at all. So, much later, lying in bed, Alex's head heavy on her shoulder, Catrina thought how she knew this would happen from the first instant she'd become aware of his eyes on her as she'd walked down into Herculaneum.

And this was the best moment, as yet unalloyed by reality, by past or future, when even the thick cloying fumes of stale wine smelt good, his snores sounded sweet, and the tousled gold of his head seemed to echo the half-full moon rising above the acres of grey corrugated roofs of the Clapham warehouses and workshops outside his bedroom window.

[3]

The next morning, while Alex still lay dazed by hangover and love making, Catrina prepared breakfast. Half-way through she had to answer the front door two floors down from his flat, which occupied the top two floors of the late Victorian house. It was a recorded letter, delivered along with three bill-like envelopes.

'Your kitchen could do with the delicate hand of a woman.'

Alex struggled up, then reached down for one of the pillows. 'Is it an awful mess?'

'Actually, I detected the hands of at least five women.'

'Nonsense,' said Alex, feeling a vague male glow. 'As I told you, there's no one in my life except you. You look delicious. Is that my shirt?'

They sat side by side domestically in bed, the tray over both their knees. After a while Alex opened the recorded delivery and groaned.

'What is it? Shouldn't I have accepted it?'

'They would have got me in the end. It's a bit complicated. I guaranteed part of an overdraft for a new restaurant. It went bust. They said I owed £10,000 and they'd sue. Now they are suing. I've been ignoring their letters. Really I would have to flee the country anyway, even if it wasn't for my brilliant idea.'

'Oh yes, your idea,' said Catrina. She remembered her

determination the night before to protect the wild-eyed drunken school-boy from plunging too deep into his crack-pot plan. 'What do you propose to do when you get to Erco-lano? Go to the head of excavations or whoever it is, say you want to dig a hole through a basement flat and is it feasible?'

'No. I shall pretend I'm making a film, or finding out about one. You can get anywhere like that. Could you pass me the phone?'

'But do you know anyone out there who could help?' said Catrina, remembering guiltily that her Barracco grandmother knew one of the archaeologists at Pompeii.

'I know someone who may,' said Alex, dialling.

But he couldn't get hold of Eddie Segal. A cool, incredibly upper class girl made an appointment for him at three o'clock.

'Eddie picks his telephone girls from *Debrett*,' he said.

'Cheaper,' said Catrina.

David McKeown sounded guarded. He had a meeting at twelve o'clock. Another at two. There was no news on *Kidnap*. Would tomorrow do?

'Look David,' said Alex, exasperated. 'I don't want work. I want money. There's an idea come up and if necessary I just want to be able to say I'm working for McKeown Productions. Do you have any of those cards left with my name on them? And could you write one of those all-purpose introductory letters?'

'Ah – some freelance work,' said David, with evident relief. 'Yes, I should think so. I'll leave it with my secretary. Of course, you'll. . . . You won't forget. . . .'

'I'll see McKeown's is brought in if it starts to look promising.'

Before Alex left, Catrina said she'd tidy the flat. 'And I'd better get some things,' she said. 'Don't think I'm moving in on you, but I'll need a certain amount if we really are going to Italy.'

'We really are going and move in all you want,' said Alex lightly.

David was very much not at a meeting though Alex arrived in Wardour Street by chance at exactly twelve o'clock.

'Here are some cards and a letter,' he said. 'I've left it vague. What is it you're on to – telly, is it? A film? Is there anything else I can do?'

He meant: Can you tell me more? 'You know these things, Dave,' said Alex, enjoying the reversal. 'This could come to nothing. On the other hand, it could be very big. Like I said, if it looks like coming off, I'll try and involve you. It's a film. African money.'

African money, thought David McKeown when Alex had gone. Did he mean *South* African money? Or Arab money? Extraordinary man, Alex. For months – years even – nothing. And then suddenly – *bingo!* Up he came with something, like with that man from Germany.

By the time he saw Eddie Segal Alex had worked out a more coherent story.

'Could I postpone Nigeria, Eddie? There's something come up I've got to see to first. A documentary about the excavations at Pompeii and Herculaneum. The BBC are interested.'

'Oh,' said Eddie. He looked disgruntled. He'd got Alex securely placed – on his uppers. To have him get off them or out of them devalued his charity, as well as being inconvenient.

'It won't take long, and it almost certainly won't come off,' said Alex quickly, anxious not to close any possible source of money until quite sure it wasn't needed.

'Ah – a long shot,' said Eddie, partially restoring Alex to his uppers. 'When will you know definitely?'

'Within a week. Anyway, when I said postpone I meant postpone. I'll need to do your Nigerian thing as well. But I ought to check this out. Do you happen to know anyone in Italy who could help? Anyone with contacts or influence in Herculaneum? Or Pompeii?'

Eddie looked at him. 'Well, it so happens I did Dr Montesano of the Museo Nationale in Naples a service. Actually, I was going to write suggesting he might like to send someone to our sale – or come himself.' He paused. Old varsity friend or not, the essence of the Levantine way was the bargain, favour given for favour received. 'Alex,' said Eddie, laying a single slender olive finger with its polished nail on Alex's forearm. 'Can I absolutely *rely* on you for Nigeria?'

The connection was not lost on Alex. 'Absolutely,' he said.

'OK. I'll write today,' said Eddie decisively. 'When do you go?'

'As soon as I can get a seat on a plane. Tomorrow. The next day.'

'Then I'd better ring up.' Eddie looked at his watch. 'He may not be back yet. I'll try later. A film on the excavations at Herculaneum and Pompeii, you say? For the BBC?'

'I do work for a group called McKeown Productions. But the BBC is very interested. We often get films together for them.'

'I'll concentrate on the BBC side of things,' said Eddie.

[4]

The post next morning brought Barclays Bank's final solution. Alex passed it to Catrina sitting beside him having coffee.

'Oh dear,' she said, 'what are you going to do if they won't cash any more cheques?'

'I used the miserable little McKeown cheque to open a new account at the NatWest down the road.'

'Well, I can pay for my ticket to Naples,' said Catrina.

'When I'm rich, I'll give you a huge allowance,' said Alex, running his fingers up through her thick curly hair. He paused, then said, 'What is your money situation?'

'I've still got about £400 from working in that Italian paper shop I told you about. But when Daddy died I was left some money. It's in a small trust fund.'

Sunrise Travel had return tickets on a charter flight to Naples in two days. Alex paid, receiving her cheque – Coutts – with feelings much the same as a general, long beleaguered, receiving written news of reinforcements.

The following morning Eddie rang up and said he'd spoken to Dr Montesano, who'd be pleased to help Alex. He should make an appointment on arrival.

'I stressed the BBC side,' said Eddie. 'The BBC has great prestige in Italy. Great prestige.'

'Thanks, Eddie.'

'Oh, and there's a lead you might follow.'

'What?'

'Ask him in passing about the stealing and smuggling of

antiquities. I have a feeling something odd may be going on down there. And Alex. . . .'

'Yes, Eddie?'

'You won't let me down over Nigeria?'

'No.'

Next afternoon – Tuesday, 9 May – Alex and Catrina caught the 1515 Alitalia charter flight to Naples Capodichino – AL 528.

[5]

Later that same day, indeed the last thing he did before leaving the Museum, Thomas also contacted Dr Montesano of the Museo Nationale. In his case, however, it was a letter written after reflecting on his contribution to the symposium.

Naples – its changing role in the ancient world – was the very wide subject of the various papers. It had recently been discovered how much more extensive the connexion had been with Roman North Africa than had been realised before – particularly in the first century AD. This could be well demonstrated by a study of ancient marbles. But Thomas felt he would have to make one further visit to various sites in the region – as well as doing some work in the Museo itself – before completing his paper. He suggested the end of July.

Finally, before leaving the letter for Miss Brough to type in the morning, he confirmed the despatch of the Museum's Pozzuoli glass.

He still enjoyed his work at the Museum, even after all these years. In fact, he thought later as he set out for his regular Tuesday dinner with Cynthia, the ability to invest matters of habit with enthusiasm and conviction was one of the secrets of a satisfactory life, and this was as true of sex as of anything else.

Often more true of sex. But his affair with Cynthia Freeling had started two years before and no particular ingenuity was as yet required. Indeed, driving to her, feeling desire kept at bay, latent, he noticed, as often, how effectively that impersonal force created a temporary simulation of love – charging his arrival, her appearance, their first drinks together.

And how swiftly, once satisfied, the current vanished.

50

Waking at four in the stifling dark of the bedroom he felt almost nothing for her. Could he feel love? Had he ever felt love? The disgust he felt at the sense of having performed – and had done to him – a service, forced him from the bed. Yet as he rose from placing his unfeeling and automatic kiss, he felt an anguished stab of pity, behind which lay, as so often, a deeper stab of self-pity.

After their supper, Cynthia had become unusually silent. Eventually she'd said, 'I know you don't like to talk about it, Thomas, but I'm terribly worried about Barnaby. Look – does this mean anything? I found it under his bed.'

Barnaby was her teenage son. At the sight of the heat-stained strip of aluminium foil, Thomas had felt a familiar dread. With difficulty he'd kept his voice even. 'Seventeen or eighteen years ago it was called "chasing the dragon".'

'What does that mean?'

'You put heroin in a line down the foil and apply heat underneath it. As the heroin fires you follow it with your nose. For a while,' finished Thomas, his voice flat, 'you can still smell the heroin.' He sniffed the foil. 'Not on this one.'

'Oh Christ Christ *Christ*. I *knew* something like this was going on.' Left elbow on the sofa, forehead in palm, Cynthia stared down. 'What should I do?'

'Confront him. Explain that you know – that you don't blame him – that you'll help. And get a good doctor. I'll give you a name. I should think he's still practising.'

Driving back to his flat through lightening but still lamplit grey streets, Thomas knew that this was one night he should have stayed with her. That was why he'd left. He reminded himself to look up Dr Ifford's number.

He'd tried to comfort Cynthia after that – but what comfort was there? They'd soon gone to bed. She'd lost herself in their love-making and then – somehow it had seemed the reaction of a wounded animal – fallen into a deep sleep.

When his wife Sheila had told him that their son Philip, golden-haired Philip, was taking drugs, his feelings had been different: terror, guilt – and fury.

The break-up of their marriage had been due, in part at least, to completely opposing views on how to bring up Philip. Thomas, while not a violent disciplinarian, insisted on some elementary boundaries. Sheila believed in a system he christened 'Piss in the soup' (based on an actual incident). So little Philip wanted to stay up till twelve? Miss school? Tear up *The Times*? Piss in the soup? So what? Let him piss in the soup.

Their separation, Philip thirteen, at least brought an end to their rows – or rather relegated them to the telephone. But it introduced new complications. Seeing his son less, Thomas realised how much he loved him. And this love had to compete at the brief weekends with the need to instil discipline. Love often won.

As Philip moved deeper into adolescence, Thomas began to find him maddening. This did not lessen his love. On the contrary, guilt at his uncontrollable exasperation increased his love in the periods separating their meetings – periods which themselves increased as a result of that same exasperation. Sometimes Thomas didn't see his seventeen-year-old son for six or seven weeks.

And then – 'I've found out that Philip is taking drugs.' The first wave of anguish was swamped by an even greater anger. *She'd* brought him up. It was *her* fault. He'd always known, he'd always said that piss in the soup would lead to something like this.

But guilt and anger in turn were swept away in horror at what heroin was doing – and how rapidly – to Philip. His wife had always drunk a good deal. It was during the year and a half that they fought to save Philip – tried to force him to save himself – that she started to drink heavily. It was now she would ring him at three in the morning and ramble on in slurred tones till he'd put the receiver down in exhaustion. Finally, he took to leaving it off.

Philip dead – his terrible death – brought them briefly together in a way their son had never managed when alive. It was from this point on that Thomas forced himself to respond to the drunken breathing on the telephone.

Philip's death. He could review the past. He would not engage with it. He ran the car into the garage, swung down the door, locked it. Looking across into Regent's Park he allowed himself to think only of the glistening mist-dampened trees, the black canal. How seldom could one see the dawn in London. He'd long discovered that an even more important secret of a satisfactory life – more important by far than the revitalising of old habit – was learning how to forget.

Chapter Five

Despite the double windows, the noise in the room in the Hotel Arena had been deafening since seven o'clock.

'All Italians use the horn as sort of one of the major instruments of driving,' said Catrina, pausing naked, arms full of tubes and pots and bottles, on her way to the shower. 'The Neapolitans *only* use the horn.'

Alex opened the windows and looked out. Gauzy swirls and drifts of exhaust stung his nostrils even four floors up. Shutting the windows was like muting the treble on a loud-speaker.

'How long does it take to get to the Museo Nationale?'

'Twenty minutes,' shouted Catrina above the swishing water behind her green plastic curtain.

He still had time for a shower. They'd telephoned Dr Montesano on their arrival. In halting Italian, Alex had introduced his BBC self. In equally rudimentary English, Dr Montesano had recognised his name and made an appointment for eleven o'clock.

The water was tepid, the shiny bright blue tiles as slippery as soapy skin. Alex trod gingerly, gripping the towel rail. People were badly damaged by the showers in Italian hotels – smashing femurs and skulls, getting electrocuted.

They set off at ten-thirty. As the concertina door of the lift rushed shut with a clunk, and the lift began to descend, Catrina said, 'Did you take those vitamin pills?'

'I forgot.'

'They're vital,' said Catrina.

The man behind the desk took their key and smiled.

'*Buon giorno,*' said Alex.

Immediately – there was the traffic: bang outside the door, locked motionless, roaring, the exhaust now choking.

'How do we get there? No bus or taxi's going to crack this.'

54

'The Metropolitana's quickest. But we've time. I know short cuts. We'll walk.'

The cobbled streets down which she led him were as narrow, the houses as tall, as in Roman times. Washing was slung between them. Every now and then Alex felt drops of water from the drying clothes. Even these streets were cloudy with exhaust fumes, filled with honking cars, mopeds, bicycles, people. The road-wide empty sky above was blue.

One or two new buildings were being squeezed up where gaps had been cleared in the crumbling cliffs. Concrete-block floors rose storey after storey balanced on clusters of rickety ten-foot toothpicks. But he noticed that quite a number of old houses were draped in dense trellis works of rusty iron scaffolding.

All at once he stopped. 'Is that the scaffolding put up after the 1980 earthquake that you were talking about?'

'Yes.'

'But that was years ago.'

'I suppose they're too poor to do the repairs.'

'No, no you don't understand. I didn't mean that. There was an earthquake some years before the eruption in AD 79. I wonder if this is the same. We must check what Vesuvius is doing.'

Catrina looked at him quizzically. 'You mean, if you were deep in one of these crevices or cracks you talk about, chipping out some million-pound bronze head with eyes, how awful to be buried in lava again?'

'Exactly,' said Alex, deaf to all irony. 'We'll have to check up.'

His brief foray, on the telephone, into Italian had convinced him it was far better to leave such things to Catrina. He watched her while she talked to one of the eight doorkeepers inside the main door of the Museo. Not having to engage in the struggle to understand or be understood gave him a curious feeling of detachment, almost of absence – as though he were in a dream or only half-visible.

Dottore Montesano was expecting them. Would they come this way? They followed the wizened little doorkeeper past the pillars and over-life-size classical statues of the lofty entrance hall.

All the employees of the Museo Nationale seemed minute.

Dr Montesano himself was scarcely over five foot, thin, with a large bald head and thin secretive face with piercing black eyes. While he spoke one thin-boned, long-fingered, faintly nicotine-stained hand gestured with a cigarette, the other spun a globe.

After much polite introduction and extravagant praise of the BBC, Dr Montesano said that he understood the *documentario* was to cover the excavations at Pompeii and Herculaneum. He pulled two large sheets of paper in front of him. He had done a little preliminary work to help the BBC and Signor Mayne and perhaps. . . .

Perhaps, Alex rather hastily made Catrina interrupt, suddenly sensing a real lava-flow of Italian loquaciousness, perhaps he should just explain that the BBC had now decided that Pompeii was so well known in Britain that it would be more interesting to concentrate on Herculaneum.

'*Soltanto* Herculaneum?' said Dr Montesano.

'*Soltanto,*' said Alex.

With evident disappointment Dr Montesano pushed the most densely covered sheet of paper to one side. He turned to Alex.

'*Che cosa ha letto il Signor Mayne?*' What had Signor Mayne read? How well did he know the subject?

Alex told Catrina he had read six or seven books. There was one by Kraus, another by a man called Caesar Corti.

Well, said Dr Montesano, for accounts of the very first diggings he should look at *Symbolae Littorariae Opusculum Varia*; for the nineteenth century and the great Giuseppe Fiorelli, he should see the *Giornale degli scavi di Pompeii*, which contained also accounts of Herculaneum. For the work of the great Amedeo Maiuri he would find accounts and photographs in Herculaneum itself, in the Antiquarium. He believed there was even some early film.

Dr Montesano handed Alex a large amount of homework, some located at the Museo, some at the Biblioteca Nationale. He would speak to the librarian.

'*Oggi parliamo degli scavi,*' Dr Montesano stopped and gave the world a lightning agitated twirl with his fingers. He lit a fourth cigarette, the third, forgotten, lying half-smoked and still smoking on a volcano mound of ends and ash.

'*Oggi parliamo degli scavi,*' repeated Dr Montesano gloomily.

Two months ago it would have been simple. A call to his old friend Dottoressa Dorothy Schultz, an appointment, she would have explained everything. Today. . . .

It appeared that Dr Schultz was an American archaeologist who had devoted the last thirty years of her life to Herculaneum, the last fifteen as Deputy Soprintendente. Everyone expected that on the death of the great Alberto Barba she would become the next Soprintendente. Instead, at the last moment, Dottore Arturo Gandolfino from Milano had been appointed.

Certainly, said Dr Montesano, it was nothing to do with her being a woman, as Dottoressa Schultz felt. After all, the present Soprintendente at Pompeii was a woman and one of the most distinguished archaeologists in Italy. It did, however, have everything to do with her being an American.

Dottoressa Schultz had taken her reverse badly. It had unfortunately coincided with trouble of a private nature. There had been scenes at Herculaneum of considerable embarrassment. '*Orribile*,' said Dr Montesano, giving the globe a rapid twist.

It had also meant a radical change of excavation policy. This the BBC would have to deal with. As Signor Mayne obviously realised, the ultimate aim of any Soprintendente was to excavate the entire city. To this end it would be necessary to purchase considerable areas of present-day Ercolano and indeed there were vacant buildings on the fringes of the *scavi* which could be bought.

But what to do meanwhile? Dottoressa Schultz's plan had been to re-open and extend the eighteenth century tunnels; and also to dig new tunnels, but this time with all the care and skill of modern archaeology, out into the buried town. In this way fresh finds could be expected. Exciting and valuable finds which would stimulate publicity, tourist trade and thus revenue. It would also be possible to improve the eighteenth century maps of Herculaneum and so determine which parts of Ercolano needed to be bought. Her plan had the enthusiastic support of Signor Carlo Vincenzi, the Chief Civil Engineer on the site, in charge of the actual physical digging, who had come to the *scavi* as a young workman in the same year as Dottoressa Schultz.

Dottore Gandolfino had reversed all this overnight. He

planned to re-open the vast Villa of the Papyri, just outside Herculaneum. This had been abandoned in the eighteenth century because of poisonous fumes in the tunnellings. Its site had been lost under the metres of mud-rock. Recently it had been rediscovered.

Who was right? Dr Montesano shrugged his shoulders. It was not for him to say. But for an account of the last thirty years they would have to speak to Dottoressa Schultz. But perhaps . . . well, would they allow Dr Montesano to see how she was at the moment? As for Dottore Gandolfino – why, said Dr Montesano, looking at his watch, he would ring him at once.

There followed a long and voluble exchange in which the words '*Bee-Bee-Chee*' were at first prominent. Dr Montesano finished it triumphant – what luck! Dottore Gandolfino would of course help all he could; and the very next afternoon, at 4.30, he was leading a party down into the buried theatre. They were invited. What was more, Dottore Gandolfino spoke English.

This appeared to be the end of their meeting. They had shaken hands, thanked Dr Montesano, and were about to depart, when Alex remembered what Eddie Segal had said.

'Ask him about the stealing and smuggling of antiquities,' he said to Catrina. 'Is there, has there been much of that?'

At her question, Dr Montesano sat down abruptly. Once again he set the world in rapid motion. Why was Signor Mayne interested in *that*? Surely the film was on the excavations?

Alex explained all aspects were important. He had to know the background. Besides which, as he had said, a series of films were contemplated.

Dr Montesano lit what must have been his seventeenth cigarette. It so happened that some alarming developments had taken place over the last nine months. Police contacts in the Italian underworld had reported that an unusual supply of first-century BC and first-century AD antiquities had been surfacing. Some astonishing source must have been discovered – almost certainly in Sicily. So valuable were one or two items that the police were seriously worried. It seemed that the Mafia had plans to move into this area which was by tradition local, entrepreneurial, and free of gang violence

58

or rivalry. He was in fact about to write to various museums to warn them. To the British Museum. No doubt they knew, or knew of, Signor Thomas Henderson. . . .

As Catrina translated and paraphrased this increasingly rambling discourse, Alex became gradually gripped by a terrifying suspicion. Before it finished, he suddenly interrupted.

'*Scusi, Dottore Montesano, ma da dove venire tutta questa roba? Queste teste e cose? Da questa zona?*'

This question pleased Dr Montesano. That of course could be possible. The Campania, as Signor Mayne knew, was particularly rich – the Villa of the Papyri had been filled with things. But dozens of such villas had been overwhelmed in AD 79, and not yet found. At any point a farmer, an amateur with a metal detector, might stumble on one. As well as Herculaneum and Pompeii, six other cities – Oplontis, Taurania, Tora . . . Tora. . . .

Unable to stand the gropings of Dr Montesano's memory, Alex burst out, 'But do they *know* where the stuff is coming from? Is it coming from Herculaneum?'

On this, apparently, there could be no doubt. The antiquity robbers never went into known sites like Pompeii or Herculaneum. Here, everything was catalogued and registered, and to some extent guarded. Besides which, as he'd said, it had been established that the source was in Sicily.

'But are they *certain?*' insisted Alex.

Certain, Dr Montesano said. Capitano Barbatelli of Napoli I, the *carabinieri* of the Special Operations Group, was completely sure of this. If Signor Mayne wished to pursue this aspect further, he would arrange a meeting. And with many handshakes and repetitions of '*Prego – prego; non e niente*', the miniscule Dr Montesano ushered them out.

The Naples traffic surged and roared and crashed eternal as the sea. It was not until they'd struggled back to the Hotel Arena and were standing on its roof, reached by a narrow staircase next to the lift, that Alex spoke about the meeting.

'I wish I hadn't gone on so much about if they were getting that stuff out of Herculaneum.'

'Well, at some time you're going to have to ask someone who knows, point-blank, if it's possible to dig down and find anything – otherwise how will you ever know?'

'Yes.' Alex looked across to the tangled vista of roofs. 'I wonder whether it is possible. I'm not getting anywhere.' he had a feeling familiar to him from many such expeditions, the same feeling of waste that he had when researching a film he knew would never be made.

'But you're doing *wonderfully*, Alex. You only thought of it a week or so ago, and already you've seen the head of the Naples Museum; tomorrow you see the head of Herculaneum! And anyway, it may not be possible – I don't really think it is – but it's great fun.'

She put her arm tight round his chest, and the fragile vulnerable curve of his rib cage made her all at once long for it to be easy; for Ercolano to be built, not on rock, but on something as soft as snow or as full of huge cracks as a melting glacier down which he could effortlessly slide to piles of treasure.

They stood pressed close, looking out between tower blocks and TV aerials and factory chimneys to where Vesuvius rose, massive, placid in the distance.

'Neither of us was born when it last erupted,' said Alex.

'It looks as though it never has and never could,' said Catrina.

'Yes – and how much more then, when it was covered in woods and vines and wild boar.'

[2]

The Piazza Garibaldi and the Stazione Centrale were only three minutes walk from the hotel. At 3.30 they were on the Circumvesuviana, and thirty-five minutes later had taken a humble double room in Ercolano's only *Pensione*, the Pensione Eden.

'How long do we want it for?' Catrina had asked.

'Until we've proved my idea is possible.'

'*Non più di una settimana*,' said Catrina to the plump *Custode* who was booking them in.

As they walked in the warm mid-May sun down the Via IV Novembre towards the *scavi*, Alex felt they might as well leave that evening. It seemed quite ludicrous to think of trying to dig down through the solid streets and buildings of the crowded noisy little town. The cobbled road was packed with cars and bicycles, trams trundled past powered by the taut cat's cradle of cables.

Catrina increased his gloom while they waited, as instructed at the *Biglietteria*, in a small grove of cypresses at the bottom of Herculaneum. She suddenly pointed over the edge of the eighty-foot cliff edge beside them.

'Do you remember the terrible noise of the drill last time? Doesn't that show how hard the stuff is?'

'Not entirely,' said Alex. 'I think I read somewhere that lava and tufa are much harder where they are exposed to the sun.'

At the sight of his face, she wished she hadn't spoken.

'Have a cherry,' she said, offering him the bag she'd bought on the way down.

One of the people waiting with them was a German archae-ologist with her daughter. The three others came from Naples University. Dr Gandolfino was in no hurry. At 5.15 the cher-ries were finished and Alex was wandering irritably round the edge of their cypress grove.

'You couldn't really set the kidnapping here,' said Catrina, joining him where he was staring morosely down at the drab little streets and remants of houses. 'Think of the struggle as she tried to escape. It'd have to be outside the entrance.'

Alex didn't answer. After a pause, he said, 'When is that damned man coming?'

Dr Gandolfino finally arrived at 6.15, accompanied by a stocky assistant carrying two powerful-looking torches. As he strode towards them, Alex said, 'Surely that's the man we saw having a row when we were leaving last time?'

'Yes it is,' said Catrina; 'and the woman must have been Dr Schultz.'

Dr Gandolfino apologised for being late, introduced himself, paying special attention to the BBC, and then intro-duced his Chief Engineer Signor Vincenzi, a stocky man with toothbrush-short grey hair and a deep scar down the left cheek, due no doubt to some excavatory hazard. This completed, Dr Gandolfino raised his bony fingers – '*Andiamo!*'

He led the way down to the excavations and across to two tall gates which opened in the Via Mare, a narrow, slightly sunken road running up beside the low stone wall bounding the left of the *scavi*. Here he paused a moment and gripped Alex by the shoulder, gesturing up to the opposite side of the road.

'For the *documentario*, Signor Mayne, over there lies the Villa di Papyri. I show you later, later.'

At its top the Via Mare was crossed by a bridge carrying the Corso Resina. Steps led up to this on either side. On the left was a small red-walled building flanked on one side by tall slum houses. Dr Gandolfino unlocked the door, stooped and strode in.

Inside, a small summer-house-like room was strewn with fragments of statue, cornices, tiles; four eight-foot lengths of marble column leant against the wall beside the door. To the right-hand side, half a dozen steps led down into a similar room. At the side of this a steep stair led down into the rock. Dr Gandolfino stopped here dramatically.

'*Stiamo per scendere nel teatro Herculaniensis. . . . Bisogna annunciare questo. . . .*' Then, translating himself for the benefit of the BBC, 'We are about to descend the *teatro Herculaniensis*. I have to announce this: the Comune di Ercolano, the Society Archeologico, I myself, can take no responsibility for what 'appens.'

About sixty steps led at an acute angle deep into the rock, lit feebly from the bottom by a single bulb. The walls, gleaming wetly in Chief Engineer Vincenzi's torchlight, were thinly covered in some mineral deposit. The stair turned at the bottom, and a short tunnel branched off. At its end a balcony hung out over a wide well.

Looking up, Alex saw the top forty feet or so above covered by a glass-paned skylight; forty feet below were the seats of the old auditorium. Beside him, Dr Gandolfino boomed loudly and at length. Here the King and Queen of Naples once had sat watching great statues spin as they were winched to the surface.

Another twenty steep, slippery steps and they were standing in semi-darkness at the top of the theatre.

Only the top row had been cleared completely – a six-foot wide passageway sweeping a whole semi-circle at the back of the auditorium, lit by infrequent light bulbs. Elsewhere, groups of six or seven rows had been cut out leaving the mass of the rock intact.

Only when they reached the stage itself was there a sense of space, of being in a theatre. It had been cut clear to a height of 30 foot, except for two massive squared blocks left in the middle to support the roof. The area in front of the stage had also been cleared, a ten-foot space across to a blank wall of rock. There were three gaps in this leading to three ramp-ways up between the sparsely cleared rows of seats. It was cool, dimly lit, and totally silent except for the sound of water dripping. Even Dr Gandolfino did not speak.

In the roof above the stage was a small, round, black hole about two feet across. It was the bottom of the peasant's old well.

Signor Vincenzi now turned and led the way through a large square opening in the back of the stage. It was the entrance to the eighteenth-century tunnels, and as he bent and followed them into the darkness, bending now even lower, Alex suddenly remembered a film about a mining disaster he'd seen as a boy – *Kameradschaft*. A hot panic wave of fear left him shivering. He felt the huge weight above them, crushing them. They were trapped, crouching, under ninety feet of solid rock.

Yet not exactly solid rock. The tunnel followed a street. At his feet, to the left, he saw the raised edge of a pavement by the light of Dr Gandolfino's torch shining from the back. The tunnels went up and down, turned at right angles, branched at junctions, as the old roads had. It was a warren. He could feel the city all round them, only a foot or two away on either side: doors, windows, houses, courtyards, shops, inns – all frozen into the mass of rock.

And rock which crumbled under the fingers. Every twenty feet or so the walls were actually soft with infill. The eighteenth-century tunnellers had dug out ten feet or so blindly on either side, taken anything they'd found, and then moved on and dug out again, filling up the two side tunnels behind with the fresh debris.

At one point the tunnel rose over a mound and, detecting some change, Alex stopped and stamped his feet. To his surprise, it rang hollow. He asked Dr Gandolfino what this was.

'*Niente-è solo un bernoccolo,*' he said. 'Nothing. It is a bump.'

Indeed Dr Gandolfino, so voluble before, seemed to have

been silenced by the claustrophobic depths. Signor Vincenzi, who clearly knew the tunnels backwards, had, in robbing him of physical leadership, robbed him of his voice as well. Ungainly bent, he brought up the rear; several times Alex heard sharp cries as the Soprintendente's bald head struck the roof.

They explored – that is to say followed to their ends – three tunnels, returning each time to the theatre. Then Dr Gandolfino and Signor Vincenzi had some slight altercation. Dr Gandolfino, as far as Alex could gather, wished to go down a particular tunnel, his Chief Engineer didn't. Dr Gandolfino was adamant.

This time Alex counted each step. They stopped, after passing several side turnings, at 264 paces. It was wider there and slightly higher. Dr Gandolfino gathered his party to Signor Vincenzi's evident irritation, and directed his torch at the end.

'They fill up in the eighteenth century,' he said. 'It go on a hundred metres north.'

'It looks completely fresh,' said Alex, and indeed the tumbled infill – what they could see of it past a Signor Vincenzi now almost demented with impatience – might have been piled up yesterday.

'That is Herculaneum for you,' said Dr Gandolfino, regaining his *amour propre* with each word. 'Two thousand years ago is just today.' Alex noticed flecks of blood on the top of his brown scalp.

'Where are we?' he asked.

Dr Gandolfino laughed. 'How do I know? If we dig up, perhaps we find the mayor in his bath.'

'But what if the Mayor dug down?' said Alex, his heart beating. 'Isn't that the way? Why don't you dig down from the top?'

'Tunnels?' said Dr Gandolfino.

'Tunnels, shafts – yes,' said Alex.

'*È impossible – completamente impossible*,' said Dr Gandolfino with emphasis. 'Impossible.'

'Why?' said Alex.

'Why?' cried Dr Gandolfino. 'Why you say? I tell you why. You know how they dig this out in the eighteenth century? They 'ava to use miners and convicted *criminali*. Often they

64

usa convicted murderers. Only these can do it, it is so hard. And whata you find if you dig your tunnels? Eh?' demanded Dr Gandolfino. 'You finda chaos, nothing. Thees town is flattened. You know the mud, just the *blacklash* throw a 'eavy marble bath right across a room. A 'uge rock of a hundred thousand kilograms is carried one kilometre by a river of mud just *one metre* deep! Big houses were moved, flattened. Look!'

Dr Gandolfino passed his torch over the roof and walls and Alex saw now that they were in fact a jumble of tiles, bricks and debris caught in the rock. Dr Gandolfino fastened his torch on a strip of blackened charcoal.

'And thees mud isa very hot,' he said. '*Molto caldo*. Silver melt. There ees no wood in Herculaneum. All ees carbonised. Burn without oxygen. No, no my friend,' said Dr Gandolfino, growing calmer, 'take ita from me, digging tunnels is quite impossible, isa biga waste of time. That is why no Superintendente – not the great Maiure heself – try it. I tell you later what we do.'

Alex felt despair closing over him like the mud that had buried the city. He was aware that Catrina had slipped her hand, wet with sweat, into his. The German archaeologist was asking something. Alex took his hand from Catrina and pretended to examine the wall.

It was dark when they at last re-emerged from the theatre. Alex realised by strength of his relief how oppressed he had been. Catrina's hands were still wet with sweat.

'I was absolutely terrified. I get claustrophobia quite badly.'

'You should have said something.'

'I knew if I opened my mouth I'd've collapsed or been sick.'

They walked in silence, Catrina behind him. Alex was stunned by his misery. Now what – Nigeria? Even more than Gandolfino's categorical statements, the cool night, the streets, completed the destruction of his dream. In particular the streets, the harsh, ordinary, still crowded streets exposed by their noise, their reality, the fantasy he'd created – the fantasy quality of their twins seventy feet below, down which he and Catrina had been groping not ten minutes before.

They went into the first restaurant they came to, the *Caffè Ristorante Fauno*, at the bottom of the Via IV Novembre next to the Banco di Napoli. Alex drank three tumblers of wine fast, looking down the long, narrow room to the three people scattered about the off-season emptiness.

With his head up and averted face he looked like a little boy hiding some bitter disappointment. Catrina felt a spurt of the protective anger with which, despite being almost fully occupied fighting her panic, she'd reacted to Dr Gandolfino's lecture in the tunnel.

'At least that conceited unpleasant man proved one thing.'

'What – apart from the obvious?'

'That your idea really could work.'

Alex turned slowly from his unseeing survey and stared at her. 'He seemed to me to prove the exact opposite.'

'No,' said Catrina. 'When experts like that say something exciting and original isn't possible then you know jolly well it *is* possible.'

'He seemed convincing enough. The hardness for example.'

'It was *because* he was so convincing I knew he was wrong. And you could *see* he was wrong. What about the peasant's well? He couldn't have dug that tiny hole if it was really hard.'

'Perhaps. But what about the whole city being flattened?'

'*Parmigiano, signore?*' said the water.

'*Si,*' said Alex. 'Ask him for another bottle of wine.'

'*Un'altra bottiglia di vino,*' said Catrina. '*Exactly.* How can he say it was all flattened when we'd been waiting two hours looking at the whole excavated bit that *wasn't* flattened? And the theatre wasn't *flattened*. They got all those statues out of it.'

They spent the rest of the meal each arguing the case the other had put in earlier discussions. Her hands became Italian in their excited emphasis – acrobats in front of him, swallows, flags. Just as reason had played no part in her opposition, nor did it in her conversion. She had changed purely to raise Alex from despair and protect him from Dr Gandolfino's coarse certainties. And it was to this – the femininity, the sexuality of it – to which he responded and which he allowed to comfort him.

They were smoking and drinking coffee, when Catrina suddenly said, 'Isn't that the woman we saw that time with Dr Gandolfino?'

Alex looked over his shoulder. In the corner by the pizza oven there was a large slumped figure with her back to them. She had a big loosely looped plate of hair on one side of her head. 'I think it is,' he said.

Catrina stood up and went out to the *gabinetti*. On the way back she talked for some time to the barman.

'It is Dr Schultz,' she said; 'he says she's been coming here alone a lot recently and drinking a lot. It's much worse than just her job. She's had an Italian lover – a woman, a research chemist in Naples – for fifteen years. Suddenly – the woman left and got married. He feels very sorry for her. I think we ought to talk to her.'

'What, try and cheer her up?'

'Well, yes I suppose so. But Dr Montesano said you should talk to her. She must know Herculaneum better than anyone. I think we should take the chance.'

'All right. You do it. She'll probably fancy you,' said Alex, emptying the rest of the bottle of fizzy local wine into his glass. 'But don't say anything about what we want to know. I've had enough expert opinion for one day.'

Her skirt swirled as she turned away. Two men at a table paused to watch her pass. She could *only* walk provocatively, even traversing a restaurant. Dr Schultz seemed to have dozed off because Catrina had lightly to shake her bowed shoulder.

But a few minutes later, sitting at the table, she was beckoning Alex across. He walked over.

'This *is* Dr Schultz, Alex. She said she'd be glad to help. This is my friend, Alex Mayne.'

'Sure, sure I'll help.' Dr Schultz held up a strong masculine hand. 'Glad to meet you, Mr Mayne.'

Her face was pale, square and determined. It was somewhat blurred by drink, but not particularly unhappy. Belligerent, rather. She looked like the old Churchill in a particularly eccentric wig.

'So you're the BBC guy,' she said. 'I heard there was some guy from the BBC expected. So what d'ya want to know?'

Alex paused, and then with a sudden decisiveness pulled out one of his McKeown cards. 'It's true, I'm doing some research for the BBC,' he said, pushing it across, 'but actually I work for these people, too. They're planning a major film here. I was wondering if I could talk to you about that?'

Dr Schultz had closed her eyes as soon as he'd started to speak. Now she whispered, 'Say "ectually".'

'What?' said Alex.

'Say "ectually",' said Dr Schultz, slightly louder.

'Actually,' said Alex.

'Marvellous,' breathed Dr Schultz. 'Can you *talk* to me? You *gotta* talk to me. Both of you. D'ya know, I've been here thirty years speaking their lousy language. If I don't speak English I'll crack up. I *need* to speak English. Have some grappa with me. Hey Attillo,' she yelled across the room. '*Una bottiglia di grappa per i miei amici.*'

The young man hurried across from the bar with a plain bottle half-full of white spirit and three small glasses.

'*Ho ordinato i bicchieri, da questi non si beve un bel niente,*' said Dr Schultz impatiently. '*Mi porti tre bicchiere veri.*'

Attillo placed the bottle beside her empty litre carafe of wine, and fetched three tumblers. Dr Schultz sloshed in the grappa, and Alex's nostrils caught the fumes – faint, acrid – of distilled steel.

'So, what's this film?'

'Well I won't go into the plot,' said Alex. 'It's about stealing and smuggling antiquities. The Mafia get involved.'

'Yeah?' said Dr Schultz, beginning to glaze. She took a huge swig of grappa.

'The basic idea is they sink a shaft down from Ercolano into the buried city, and cut tunnels. That's how they get the stuff. But it's important that this is possible, or at least plausible. Dr Gandolfino raised a lot of objections.'

At once Dr Schultz's grey blurry eyes snapped into focus. 'He did? Like what?'

'Well – like it wasn't possible because it hadn't been done before.'

'Not been done before!' cried Dr Schultz scornfully. 'Of *course* it's been done before. Where does he think this is – Pennsylvania? This is Italy. They've been down there. Sure. That town's as full of holes as a Gruyère cheese. What else?'

'That the rock was too hard, that the mud had swept everything away, that it was too hot – everything had melted or been carbonised.'

Dr Schultz filled up her tumbler and banged the bottle onto the table. 'That mountebank' she said viciously. 'D'ya know why that old man got this job? Because he's a *man* – if he *is* a man. You can't talk about Herculaneum till you've been here ten, twenty years. This is a complicated place.

'Hard? Of course it's hard. But it's not *all* hard. You get soft patches, where water is. You should talk to my Chief Engineer, Carlo Vincenzi. He saws it out, lets it dry in the sun, then sells it as building blocks. I remember when we excavated the beach in 1984, at the bottom it was *exactly* the same as it had been two thousand years ago – the consistency of wet mud.

'Same with the force. Okay, okay – we know now that it came in with one hell of a kick. I've found roof tiles and timbers on the beach that probably came from the back of the town. But in one place the mud came in so slowly and gently it didn't even move a cradle. In what we call the Trellis House you get your *opus graticum* – that's a really delicate frame of wood and reeds *still* dividing the rooms. Maiuri found unbroken *glass* wrapped in straw; he found whole *eggs* preserved, their shells unbroken.

'So they were carbonised. The wood is carbonised. Sure. The mud was hot. There were hot gases. But not everywhere – there's lots of lead and gold and silver not melted. You get wood *not* carbonised – specially fresh wood. D'ya see what I'm getting at? This was like the effects of blast. You get all sorts of freak effects.'

Flushed with the energy of her counter-attack, Dr Schultz's huge earphone of hair had now become completely unravelled. 'Anything else ya wanta know?' she said.

'Where should we dig?' said Catrina. Alex took such a huge mouthful of grappa that it was actually painful to swallow.

'That's a very interesting question,' said Dr Schultz, suddenly seeming to wake up to Catrina's presence again. She emptied her tumbler of grappa, filled it, all the while staring at Catrina without speaking. Then she laid her large hand over Catrina's small bunched fist.

'Nobody knows how *big* this goddam town was,' she said.

'Okay – they say five thousand inhabitants. But it's a guess. That theatre *alone* holds five thousand. What *was* this? Some kinda Bayreuth? This could have been a big place. So where d'ya dig? Ya dig at the back. The *elevation* must have bin the same as today. The mud could only build on what was there. So there was high ground at the back and the mud would have been shallower. That's one place. Where else?' Blearily, she looked into the past. 'The Romans probably had ribbon development, same as we do. The town could've straggled out north on the road to Neapolis.'

Dr Schultz stopped, her eyes returning to Catrina. Then slowly she drew her hand back to her big breast with Catrina's reluctantly captive inside it. 'Those stones *speak* to me,' she said. 'D'ya know what they say? They cry out – come down here and let us out. *Rescue* us.'

She stared at Catrina as though mesmerised by her beauty. But it was evident that, with a sudden onset of grappa, private griefs had begun to surface. Two huge tears had formed above her cheek-bones. 'They won't let me do it,' she said. 'Carlo and I are banned.'

She raised her glass and seemed to study the tough, oily meniscus of the fiery spirit. The tears wobbled but, equally tough, held on.

After a long pause, 'Lousy country,' muttered Dr Schultz. There was another long pause, then she whispered, 'Lousy double-crossing bitch.'

Alex stood up and coughed. 'I think we really ought to be going, Dr Schultz,' he said gently. 'You've been marvellous. You really make the film seem possible. I can't thank you enough.'

Catrina too stood up and with some difficulty freed her hand. 'Yes, you were marvellous,' she said.

Dr Schultz, tilted in her chair, her hair like a Valkyrie, one eye now closed, sighted up at them with the other.

'Any time,' she said. 'Any time you want help you come to me. And they tell you something's impossible? *Bullshit*. Nothing's impossible. You could find a living man down inside there. I've told them – those frogs in the theatre – they're *Roman* frogs.'

70

'You can never tell which clothes are going to be really useful,' Catrina sat on the right of the little beds they'd pushed together. 'I bought this little white sweater in Selfridges and I often put it on and feel really pleased.'

Her chat amused and soothed Alex. Sometimes he learnt things about her.

An Arab couple had come to sit at the table behind him in a restaurant in Naples. Catrina's wide mouth had parted slightly and her eyes glowed with interest.

After a considerable time observing she said, 'I like Arabs in their context. I don't like the ones who get out. They're threatening and vulgar.' There was a long pause. 'The way they eat their food is threatening. She spits out the bits she doesn't like.' Long pause. 'The way she spits is really *disgusting.*'

When he finally turned to look, Alex saw that the most noticable thing about the Arab girl was that she was strikingly beautiful.

Catrina never screwed tops back on. Bottles, toothpaste, shampoo – if he picked them up after she'd used them, they fell apart.

At first he'd slightly resisted the flow of pills. 'It looks as if a couple of geriatrics were staying here. What's Efamol for?'

'PMT.'

'I don't suffer from PMT,' said Alex.

'It also preserves your brain cells from drink. I suppose you're going to say you don't need *that.*'

Quite quickly he acquiesced: Vitamin B and B6 for drink; A for cancer and skin; calcium for nails, teeth and hair; E for sex; C for everything. Soon he wondered how he'd survived without them. 'You can't be with a pill maniac and not take them. You feel you might be missing out.'

Catrina observed with detachment – preparing for the terrain ahead – that he was fairly selfish in small matters. She did not mind because she'd noticed that middle-class Englishmen often used good manners and consideration as a substitute for feelings. Some of them really thought good manners were a form of love.

For Catrina, the evening with Dr Schultz and what had preceded it meant the automatic assumption of Herculaneum into her crystallising goal to be with him.

For Alex it was not so straightforward. That sense of destiny he'd felt so powerfully had promised neither success nor failure. It had simply been a sense of something inevitable. He too now linked their affair to Herculaneum, but he could regard this either as marking a stage towards something more permanent or as setting a term to it.

They spent the morning after meeting Dr Schultz searching Ercolano for a basement flat.

The barman at the Ristorante Fauno, where they'd had their breakfast of *cappuccino* and a cake called a cornetto, was astounded they wanted a flat in that area.

'*Perchè qui? Nessuno abita qui.*'

His uncle had a nice place on the fourth floor of one of the apartment blocks near the station.

Catrina explained that they were working for people making a film and had to be there. The barman Attillo shrugged. He'd ask around.

The Tourist Office in the Via IV Novembre said no one took apartments *anywhere* in Ercolano. Torre del Greco, yes. Not Ercolano. There weren't any estate agents.

'We'll have to look ourselves anyway,' said Alex. 'We must look where the back of Herculaneum might have been.'

Dr Gandolfino had given them a note in his flourishing script which allowed them into the *scavi* without paying. The distance from the top of the excavation to the bottom was about 200 yards. Alex paced the same distance up the gentle incline of the Via IV Novembre and then stopped.

'*Here* we shall dig!' he cried, pointing.

It was a bewildering sight. To their left was a long, single-storeyed building surrounded by iron railings and with pillars set in its faded, pink, plaster walls – the *Scuola Media Statale*. A lattice-work of unstable new scaffolding was in the process of being put up. The two roads which ran either side were filled with people, jostling, shouting, pram-pushing, all bargaining, poking, buying at the stalls and barrows which crammed them from end to end.

A market. Alex and Catrina pushed past cut-price jeans, piles of cheap crockery, a stall of biscuits, a stall of cheeses –

ricotta, yoghurt – a stall of soap powders, plastic basins of glistening black olives, a stall of dun-coloured corsets, trays of second-hand tapes, one being loudly played, and endless piles of vegetables and fruit already, in May, pouring from the fertile earth of Vesuvius.

'At least they wouldn't hear a drill,' said Alex.

Behind the *scuola* was a ramshackle block of shops – a *macelleria,* an *alimentari,* a *farmacia.* The market flowed all round this too, ending in the fish stalls. Here, under awnings, or vast, fading, patched umbrellas were tubs of slimy water crawling with snails, trays of polypi, mounds of squid and octopus, piles of vongole, a seventy centimentre red mullet, its mouth gaping. One old woman was trying to sell eels writhing in a bucket. There were barrows heaped with mussels.

'You mustn't eat those,' said Catrina. 'The shit goes straight into the rivers and then out to sea where the mussels and clams eat it up. After a rainstorm the rivers *pour* out a great pale stain, a fan-shaped stain into the sea. From above it looks like the land has diarrhoea.'

'It's not going to rain today,' said Alex. It was English July heat.

'My grandmother said it would be a hot summer.'

It was here they saw their first '*Vende*' sign. It was on a tall building at the end of a narrow cul-de-sac opposite the fish stalls. Alex took the number – Napoli 432 886.

For two hours they wandered the little streets, trying not to stray further north than the buried theatre or west than the Corso Resina.

It was a maze, a spaghetti tangle of crumbling, cracked courtyards and small, squalid squares with outside stone staircases or steps leading to crowded flats and even what looked like one-roomed dwellings. The huge tilted broken flags had gaping holes for drainage. Washing hung so thickly on windows or across the narrow streets that it seemed to be raining from the cloudless sky.

'Friday's traditional wash day,' said Catrina. 'They wash every day, but more then, like we eat fish.'

Some of the courtyards were ruined and empty. In one of these Alex saw a neat yellow coil of child's shit. The air smelt of sewers. One 'door' was the springs of a bed secured by wire. A rusty pipe carrying water through a wall had its holes bound with old stockings. There were no '*Vende*' or '*Vendita*' signs here. There were often no names to the courtyards or numbers on the doors at all.

And everywhere there were *bambini* – tiny children yelling on broken bicycles or carts made of pram wheels, babies with filthy dummies, children on the balconies and at the broken glass of windows – so many it was as though they were spawned by the filth and debris. They were fascinated by Alex and Catrina, staring, whispering, following them.

Everyone was fascinated by them. The groups of women chatting and laughing on the steps or balconies stopped at once and watched them pass in absorbed silence. Some younger girls – fifteen or sixteen, with wide faces and strong, squat bodies – burst out laughing: 'What ees the tima?' they trilled, helpless with giggles. 'I speeka Eengleesh.'

Quite often Catrina asked several women if they knew of any houses or basement rooms to let.

The women looked astounded. *Here*? Why? *Basement* rooms? Basement rooms were for storing, for animals. How much? They said would ask. The braver of the swarming *bambini* had come up with hands outstretched for money. This made Alex increasingly agitated.

'Don't worry,' said Catrina. 'They're used to being refused.'

But his concern was not primarily philanthropic. 'How do they live? The crime rate must be appalling.'

'It is. It's a way of life. I'd say eighty percent of the men in these families are unemployed. In 1975, fifty thousand families around Naples supported themselves by smuggling.'

'You're very well informed. How do you know?'

'My grandfather was a judge in Naples,' said Catrina. 'I suppose all told I've spent about a quarter of my life here. We used to come out for the whole of the summer holidays; after my father died, far more. I'll take you to meet them, all my Barracco relations. It's not far. About half an hour away. You'll like them.'

'No, no,' said Alex hastily. 'The fewer people who know we're here the better.' He was thinking, We must get padlocks, chains, locks for windows.

After two hours, Catrina said, 'This is hopeless. You look too English. We both look too rich. I'll manage far better on

74

my own. I can pass as Italian. I'll dress differently. I know I can find something because they're so poor.'

As they walked back to the Pensione Eden, Alex said, 'Do you think we're mad to have decided so quickly?'

'No. You always meant to do it no matter what anyone said. I think that's the only way anything gets done.'

'I suppose so,' said Alex. He didn't see how they'd ever get a house or a room in the slums of Ercolano, and if they did, how they'd escape such avid curiosity. How could they drill if twenty neighbours were listening to see if they had another row or broke another bottle? And as the scheme moved terrifyingly into the open out of the warm, indistinct realms of fantasy, this, all the practicalities, started to look overwhelming.

'I think the drilling may be the hardest problem,' said Alex, as they passed under the tram cables of the Via IV Novembre.

[5]

Amongst the little pile of brown envelopes, three showed the life support systems on red alert. A fourth suggested a solution to the drilling.

Alex introduced himself as a ratepayer on the telephone to the Lambeth Council. He had plans to break up a concrete yard at the back of his house and make a garden. He might excavate a shallow pond. Could the council suggest someone in their employ who might help with advice about pneumatic drills and so on?

After a preliminary skirmish to establish he didn't require planning permission for this major restructuring of the Stockwell landscape, the council suggested Mr Ballan.

'I can help you, lad,' Mr Ballan strode across a wide marshalling area, a waste dotted with lorries, mobile diggers, drums of cable. He stopped at a portakabin set down on a surface of cinders. A number of drills lay on the ground.

'What's the problem again?' said Mr Ballan, frowning thick grey brows at the envelope in his hand. Alex explained.

'You need a simple compressor like these 'ere,' said Mr Ballan. 'These compressors will do *anything*, lad.' Mr Ballan was as confident as a rock. Alex bent and raised one. It was extremely heavy. Mr Ballan cupped a hand and bellowed, 'Here, lad,' then he picked up a chunky, six-inch spike which lay on a pile of bits. 'Fix 'er up and turn 'er on, lad,' he said to a boy of about eighteen who'd come running from a second portakabin.

Alex watched while the lad expertly slotted in the bit and then picked up the long tube of the compressor's umbilical cord and walked uncoiling it towards a squat green diesel engine about the size of a chest of drawers. It was a grey cold May day – winter to an Ercolano dweller. The diesel coughed, then burst into the familiar racket of street repair.

Mr Ballan kicked a two-inch-thick plank towards Alex. ''ave a go on that,' he said. 'Just squeeze the 'andle.'

Alex raised the drill and was just able to lift it on to the plank. He squeezed. There was a deafening *woof*-bang, *woof*-bang, a violent leaping and juddering and the drill had gone straight through the plank and was ploughing up the cinders. He released his hand and laid the drill down.

'Powerful,' he said.

'Yer arms would aike after 'arf an 'our,' said Mr Ballan. 'Likely they'd swell up. But my men can do a twelve-hour day, 'alf an 'our off fer lunch.'

'I might have to dig a hole,' said Alex. 'How long would it take to dig a hole one foot deep, five foot long and five foot wide?'

'Well, you'd need a jack 'ammer,' said Mr Ballan. 'I ain't got one 'ere. That's a compressor with a rotary percussion action. Take yer a couple of hours, near enough.'

'And the expense?' asked Alex, scribbling 'jack hammer' in his notebook. Mr Ballan reckoned fifteen quid a week for the tool, five quid a week for the bits, sixty quid a week diesel engine. Drilling Equipment Supplies Ltd, were the best people to hire from.

Alex could see that Mr Ballan was proud of his equipment. He therefore approached with tact the central difficulty – noise. Mr Ballan said Alex would be surprised what a lot of noise the public could take. However, it transpired that it was possible to get a compressor that worked off domestic electricity. The only drawback was that it was half as powerful. It also required a transformer to bring the power to 110 volts. No, he didn't know the voltage of the Italian domestic electricity supply. Mr Ballan looked slightly surprised at the question, which had sprung from Alex before he could stop it.

But as for the compressor itself, well, you could fit an acoustic hood. Actually, Alex's deafening tool already had an acoustic hood.

'That canvas bag there,' said Mr Ballan, pointing. 'Don't make a blind bit of different, frankly. But the public think that something's bin done, and they think it's quieter. You'll just 'ave to wear earphones, lad.'

Catrina was still out when he got back. She'd asked him what she could do and he'd told her to find out what the chances were of Vesuvius erupting in the near future.

'How?' said Catrina.

'I don't know,' said Alex irritably. 'Try ringing the *Daily Telegraph* information service.'

He made some tea and then set out his notes from Mr Ballan. He'd decided that initially they should dig no further than twenty-five-feet. If they hadn't struck anything significant by then, it would mean they were either digging into a street, or that the houses beneath had been flattened.

A hole, one foot by five foot by five foot, would take two hours by compressor with diesel. A hole of twenty-five foot would therefore take fifty hours. The debris would have to be hauled up and disposed of – needing a block and tackle, rope, bucket. Say a further fifty hours. If they worked seven hours a day that was about twenty-five days. Add a week for travelling. Add a week for contingencies. Say six weeks. On Ballan's figures that was £420 for hire of equipment. Okay – say the first shaft was a dud and they had to dig another – £840.

But the diesel was out of the question. Alex envisaged the astonishment in the super-curious slums of Ercolano as the BBC television researcher installed his equipment. It would have to be the compressor run off domestic supply. That would take twice as long to dig, the same time to clear the debris. Estimate £45 a week for the transformer. No – £20; plus £25 for current: £780 for one shaft; £1560 for two.

Woof-bang, *woof*-bang, *woof*-bang thought Alex. Wrap an eiderdown round it, an acoustic eiderdown. Woof-bang. It was hopeless. As he explained to Catrina, *any* compressor was impossible. She must remember the noise in the *scavi*.

She herself looked cheerful. Ashamed of his earlier sarcasm, he asked her how she'd got on. She'd taken his remark about the *Daily Telegraph* perfectly seriously. They'd suggested she ring London University. She was to see a vulcanologist, Professor Williams, on Wednesday afternoon. The rest of the afternoon she'd spent in the Brixton Library reading about volcanoes.

And it was sweet Catrina's simple approach that, indirectly, solved the drilling problem. She said, 'Why not look in the Yellow Pages?'

'The Marjeeling Drill Company Ltd: Atlanta, USA and Sutton,' said simply, *'For all drilling problems.'* Alex rang them and eventually spoke to Mr James. Mr James had the total confidence that seemed to pertain to anyone connected with drills. 'No details over the phone, Mr Mayne,' he said. 'If you've a drilling problem, Marjeeling can solve it. I've a slot of half an hour at 9.30 tomorrow. Can you make it?'

Mr James was about fifty-six, tall, square, with square-ended, perfectly manicured nails, and as pale as if he spent most of the time underground with his drills. He was delighted to hear he was to advise on a film. 'We were advisers on *The Army Game* and *Oil*. I'd tell them something, they'd do the opposite. *Oil* gave us a mench in the credits,' said Mr James a little wistfully, the faintest twang of Atlanta in his voice. Alex promised him a 'mench' too. After much shuffling through files and looking at leaflets, Mr James 'came up' with a solution.

What Alex needed was the Acker Packsack portable core drill kit. This was unique to the Marjeeling Drill Company. It was a smallish portable drill running off a 10h.p. petrol/oil engine with a six-gallon pressurised fuel tank. It made less noise than a small motor mower – the equivalent, say, to a washing machine. You could drown it with a transistor. It would drive a 1½-inch coring bit with a soft diamond formation at 150 revolutions a minute. You could sink a bore down seventy feet in under a day. Each tube core was three feet long, to be coupled on as the core got deeper. When you'd drilled to the required depth, you wound up the drill rod and core pipe, tapping out the core of each three-foot length.

Alex studied 'Acker Bulletin Sheet 14' which showed two hefty tin-hatted prospectors drilling in Canada. 'How can I drill a hole five foot square if the pipe is only one and a half inches in diameter?' he asked.

'That's the beauty of tufa,' said Mr James.

'But it's solid rock.'

'It's solid,' said Mr James. 'It's not rock. This bit *will* do solid rock, though you wouldn't do seventy to eighty feet in a day or anything like. But I've drilled tufa in north-west America. A soft diamond formation will take you through easy. And you won't need so much water to cool the bit. A bucket every quarter of an hour. Or fix up a drip feed. But here's how you drill your hole.'

Mr James beckoned him round his desk and drew a square on a piece of paper. He then drew a line of little circles along the top of the square.

'Okay? You drill a series of holes along the top. Leave two to three inches between each hole. Then you drill another line, and another and so on right down the area of your hole.' Deftly Mr James drew little circles. 'When you've drilled it out, you take a pick and you'll find you can hack it out, joining the holes together.'

'*Hack* it?' said Alex. 'Will it work?'

'Oh yes,' said Mr James. 'I've seen this done more than once. That's the beauty of tufa. You've already drilled out about half your hole. You'll find it splits up. Then you shovel it out. It'll work all right – though you may occasionally find yourself wishing you had a compressor.'

By chance, Mr James had two Acker Packsack kits awaiting shipment in the basement. He broke one out for Mr Mayne. The drill itself, with its engine on the top, seemed almost unliftably heavy, designed for lumberjacks.

'Whole kit weighs four hundred pounds,' said Mr James, whose polished hands revealed unexpected strength. 'Comes in four cases of a hundred pounds each. Enough drill rods and tube cores for fifty feet.'

He showed Alex how to couple the rods together. He showed him how to attach a Jo-bar to exert extra downward pressure. He showed him how to pump up the fuel tank. 'And fix your hosepipe here. Steady trickle. I'll take out the pump and leave the hose.'

'What can go wrong?' asked Alex, his arms already aching. 'Will that drill thing wear out?'

'The bit's meant to do several thousand feet. One will be plenty. You can get your drill pipe breaking – but that's at three thousand, eight thousand feet. Not in your case. Don't do the holes too close together – let's say three or four or five inches – or your pipe will bend in.'

He agreed that Drilling Equipment Supplies (South London) was the best place to hire and he knew they could supply. 'In fact, that's our supply depot. I wear two hats here.'

'About how much?' said Alex.

'To hire? The kit'll cost you about £15 a day. Plus your bit, you'll have to buy that, obviously. Say £300.'

'Three hundred pounds?' repeated Alex, aghast.

Mr James shuffled his leaflets and catalogues. 'No, even better,' he said. 'Three hundred and twenty-nine *dollars*.'

'Oh good,' said Alex.

Catrina returned exhilarated by research and the attentions of Professor Williams.

'I *like* crusty old professors. You feel their passions have been frozen for years. Think of the explosion when you release them.'

'For years?' said Alex. 'That's not the impression one gets from campus novels.'

Since 1631, it seemed, Vesuvius had erupted in moderately predictable cycles. These consisted of small eruptions every two, three, five, even ten years, culminating in a colossal one. The latest gaps between large eruptions had been thirty-four and thirty-eight years. These had been in 1872, 1906 and again in 1944. Since then, Vesuvius had reposed in total silence. Although the cycle could be as much as ten years out, there was a feeling now that it had returned to earlier, pre–1631 patterns.

'Professor Williams – or Bill, as I now call him – thought it might be about every hundred years,' said Catrina, consulting the notes written in her extravagant hand. 'That was what happened after AD 79. After 1139 it was quiet for five hundred years, till 1631. So there you are. Impressed?'

'Very,' said Alex. 'What did you say you were doing?'

'Writing a travel article for *Vogue*.'

'And how old was this crusty unerupted volcano?'

Catrina giggled. 'About thirty-five. How did you get on?'

'As usual, the whole thing boils down to money.' Alex too had several pages of notes and calculations. The great advantage of the core drill method was that it didn't need two shafts. Testing what was underneath was just a matter of one swiftly drilled hole. Mr James had said seventy foot a day. What was a day? Say eight hours. That was seven minutes a foot. Make it eight. Alex had reduced the shaft to four feet by four. Ten holes by ten holes left three inches between them and gave a hundred holes to be drilled, each of twenty-five feet. Time had to be allowed to get out there, to test-drill the whole basement, to dispose of the core debris.

'It seems to me we'll need the equipment for two months – that's twelve hundred pounds. We'll need to buy rope, block and tackle, pick, tools. We'll have to get chains and padlocks – obviously the place is crawling with burglars. We'll need to hire a van to take the stuff out, getting around, carting debris. We'll need to live and pay rent a great deal longer while I dig the shaft. I think we'll need about six thousand pounds. I've got about twelve hundred pounds left in my new account.' He smiled at her. Catrina smiled back, the great generous boat of her smile.

'And what can I provide? Well, I *know* we'll get it back. I'm sure I can help. I've got a few hundred in the bank. Granny has an old Ford van she let me take to Scotland once. If I say I want it for a holiday in Italy, I'm sure she'd lend it. I get seventy pounds a month from the trust.' Catrina paused and thought. 'If only we could get at my trust.'

'Your trust – what are the conditions, do you know?'

'The trustees are Robert Jarvis, an old friend of daddy's, and our solicitor. They decide. But it's for big things – a house or a flat. Robin did say they would consider a car.'

'A car,' said Alex thoughtfully. 'A car. I've got a sort of friend who deals in second-hand cars. I'm sure if we gave him twenty-five quid, he would give us the cash and say he'd sold you a car.'

The arrangements took two weeks. Alex insisted they bought or hired everything they possibly could in England to allay suspicion. 'Two English people trying to hire an Acker Packsack in Naples? They'd call the *carabinieri* at once.'

81

Drilling Equipment Supplies had the kit, but insisted on a month's rent in advance and three hundred pounds deposit, for which they accepted post-dated cheques. Alex bought fifteen hessian sacks, a pick, a spade, a small sledgehammer, a tool chest, a London Pattern Pulley Block (£18.97), and a hundred feet of nylon rope. He bought four heavy padlocks and some lengths of chain. It was exhilarating, but easier to do if he thought it quite unreal. He had a fantasy about being Robinson Crusoe allowed to prepare.

Catrina's grandmother lent the van. Her trustees could 'see no objection to a small car'. Alex's acquaintance thought twenty-five quid would fit the bill. The money came through at the end of ten days. It turned out that a constellation of trusts surrounded the Webb family – A Trust, B Trust, Grandfather Davidson's 1934 Will Trust. One of these supplied cash while shares were sold in Catrina's sweet little private-to-her trust. Alex arranged with his delightfully polite new bank manager for travellers' cheques and also that funds would be sent to open an account in Italy when he sent the name and address of a bank. After all the purchases and tickets, they had just over three thousand pounds left. It would be tight.

Letters arrived from the solicitors of the restaurant consortium and the legal department of Barclays. The Lambeth Council rate department joined gas, electricity and telephone on red alert.

On Thursday, 1 June, Alex set off in the van. He was booked on the Paris-Milan car train and hoped to reach the south in about three days. Catrina had flown to Naples the day before to find an apartment in Ercolano.

Chapter Six

Alex arrived at the Pensione Eden in Ercolano late in the evening on Saturday. Catrina was in the dark, high-ceilinged small square room they'd had before – twin beds shoved together, one dim light bulb, the smell of the noisy communal *gabinetti* outside echoed in the pale urine walls.

He held her tight, desire rising instantly through exhaustion, her mouth tasting of the red wine from the bottle on one of the flimsy bedside tables.

'Let's get into bed now.'

'I can't, Alex. I must tell you what I've done.'

It had been almost impossible to get a room, an apartment, anything, in the area near Herculaneum. Apartments in the big blocks near the *stazione* were possible. But the Comune di Ereolano had vague, heady plans to sell the fringe slums for vast sums to the *scavi*.

'They're only lived in by really poor people still without homes because of the earthquake. Do you know there are still people living outside Naples in those containers that go on the backs of lorries?'

The slum dwellers themselves were not just amazed at her, they were suspicious. 'I couldn't have bribed them. They would have suspected something completely criminal.' In the end Attillo the barman at the Fauno introduced her to Francesco Iannucci. For some reason she couldn't fathom, he had got permission to renovate one small house, and was building a completely new one on the very outermost edges of their area.

'I haven't actually said we'll take it, but I practically have. We won't find anything else. It may be too far out.'

Terrified that someone would look inside and at once suspect what they were doing, Alex had buried the drill containers, ropes, pulleys and picks under the sacks inside the van. He insisted on driving it down to the Fauno to keep his eye on it.

'I've said you're writing a book,' said Catrina. 'There's too much money in films. You're a poor author writing a travel book about the *scavi* and this coast. A *scrittore* is always admired in Italy.' She paused. 'I've also said we're married. Otherwise I'd get no respect.'

'Have you?' said Alex, his tone flat.

He was too drunk to drive the van back. But not too drunk to make love to her. It always amazed Catrina how drunk he could get and still make love.

The Via Ascione was some way past the buried Teatro Herculaneum, left off the Corso Resina as you headed north up slightly rising ground to Portici and Naples. The street itself, paved in massive old flags with chisel marks for winter walking, was quite short. At its end, after thirty-five slum terrace houses on either side, was a six-foot-high iron railing with a new gate, heavily padlocked.

Alex put his head to the cold metal of the gates. To his left were the last three terraced houses. Two were in semi-ruin, but the third showed signs of rough rehabilitation. A short stone stair led to the front door. To the right, a cleared space, bags of concrete, a mixer, a diesel motor, a pile of concrete air bricks showed where Signor Iannucci was about to build. Ahead, the ground fell away. The Via Ascione was on a short bluff or promontory, stretching out into the large area of cultivation next to the *scavi*. Somewhere buried out there was the Villa di Papyri.

'It may just do,' said Alex. 'Obviously, the ground must have been higher here then too. And being to the side may be an advantage. The mud flow wouldn't have been so violent. And it could have been shallower. As long as we're not too far to the side. Wait here and guard the van.'

Catrina watched him stride up the flagged street. How vulnerable he looked. And oblivious. He was completely unaware he was running a gauntlet. From every house, between the looped necklaces of washing, at doors, on crumbling balconies, the women were not peeping or peering as in England – but staring. Each woman took a prolonged,

84

unashamed, intense, enjoyable *look* at the tall yellow-headed *scrittore inglese*.

'It's about 240 paces to the Teatro,' said Alex on his return ten minutes later. 'That's about twenty less than the long tunnel which I counted.'

'Which tunnel?' said Catrina. 'They all seemed miles long to me.'

'The last one. The one that engineer – Dr Schultz's friend, Vincenzi was he called? – tried to stop us from going down.'

'I don't remember.'

'Yes you do. He tried to stop us going down it. Then when we got to the end he became more or less demented. He tried to stop us looking at it, jumping about. Anyway, when we were there, when I asked what would happen if you dug down, we *could* have been standing twenty paces further out than the *Via Ascione*. Also, I've thought of something else. Dr Schultz said Herculaneum was probably partly ribbon development. Well, I bet the Corso Resina lies on top of the old Roman Naples-Salerno road. I remember how straight it looks on the map. The mud would just have driven a two-mile or so wedge across it. When it hardened, they'd have joined the ends in a straight line – like the original road. I think we'll take it.'

'I don't dare describe the inside,' said Catrina. 'But I'll make it nice.'

They stopped halfway back down the Corso Resina and Alex paced out the distance between the Teatro and the entrance to the *scavi*. This was two hundred and eighty-two paces, forty more than to the Via Ascione.

As they turned up the Via IV Novembre on the way to Signor Iannucci's apartment near the *stazione*, the van bumped badly over the split in the road. 'This place is cracking up,' said Alex, his hangover jarred. 'That bit's got worse in the last three weeks.'

Signor Iannucci was a stocky dark man of about forty-two, with an abundant mat of chest hairs that would have curled over his collar had it been buttoned. He spoke volubly to Alex, holding him intimately by the arm, until Alex indicated that Catrina would translate.

The renovation and decoration of Via Ascione 46 was little short of farcical. Three small rooms had been roughly decorated – that is, whitewashed – and furnished à la Pensione Eden.

The front door opened into the kitchen, a five-foot wide corridor into which, rather high up, a window had been knocked. It contained a gas fridge the size of a picnic basket and two gas rings. Signor Iannucci showed Alex how, if you stood on the single chair, you could just see the sea.

From this, to the left, three steps descended to the tiny living room (*anticamera*) – a square white box with a table and two chairs.

'He says,' said Catrina, 'that the table's perfect for a *scrittore's* typewriter.'

'I suppose so,' said Alex, 'in that a typewriter is all it could hold.'

The bedroom was another whitewashed box. It contained only two iron beds. The *bagno* was in fact the windowless side of the bedroom partitioned off with a lavatory at one end and a shower at the other.

Sensing a growing lack of enthusiasm, Signor Iannucci said of course he'd be bringing bedclothes, bedside tables, a cupboard, a chest of drawers, chairs, a cabinet for the *anticamera*, etc. that afternoon. If you put your head to the left-hand side of the window which, like the *anticamera*, looked across the vegetable fields to the *scavi*, it was possible – Signor Iannucci rammed his cheek hard against the side and squinted at an acute angle – to get a magnificent view of the *mare*. And of course the window this side meant less noise.

'*Noise?*' said Alex. 'What does he mean? Why should there be any noise at all?'

Catrina asked, but Iannucci just smiled non-committally.

After a short silence, Alex said, 'Well, we haven't any choice. How much did you say it was?'

Catrina spoke to Iannucci. 'A hundred and twenty thousand lira a week.'

'What's that? About £50. It seems rather a lot.' Alex looked at the bare room.

Iannucci now became extremely voluble. Eventually Catrina said, 'We can have it for sixty thousand lira a week if we take it till September and also sign something saying we've paid a hundred and fifty thousand lira a week. It's something to do with a government tourist grant.'

'All right,' said Alex, 'as long as he gives us curtains and some smaller lamps with shades.'

Signor Iannucci was delighted. There was no hurry about payment – a week, two weeks. He pressed keys on to them: a key to the gate padlock, to the front door, to the *autorimessa* – the garage.

Signor Iannucci showed them this before he left. It was reached by a second door and a rough wooden stair from the living room. Although Iannucci called it the *autorimessa,* it still smelt strongly of horse. The partitions dividing the loose boxes had been pulled down but there were still mangers and straw racks in the twenty-foot side wall with its single boarded-up window facing the large double doors. These were new, as Iannucci showed by pointing to the old ones leaning against the far wall.

'Always you keep locked,' he said to Catrina. 'Much thieving here. In Ercolano they know here is Francesco Iannucci. No one come. But many wicked men in Torre del Greco. You tell your husband.'

When he'd gone, Catrina passed on a much milder version of this message. Then she said, 'But haven't you noticed the huge advantage of this place?'

'Where?' said Alex, looking round the dark stable, lit by a single feeble bulb from its central beam. He looked at the boarded-up window. 'You mean if I hung out of that by my toes I'd see the sea?'

'No you fool,' said Catrina. 'The floor. The ground. Don't you see? It's *earth.*'

Signor Iannucci returned that afternoon with bedding, curtains and more spindly *pensione* furniture. Catrina found an open *alimentari* and bought food and wine, but they decided to eat at the Fauno again.

So close under the thin-tiled roof was their little room that it was, already in June after the long sun of the day, too hot for anything more than a single sheet.

[2]

They learnt the meaning of Iannucci's enigmatic reference to noise the following morning at seven o'clock. There were two sleep-shattering explosions, the sound of a diesel engine coming on to full throttle, and then what so far seemed to have been the *leitmotif* of Herculaneum – the familiar *woof*-bang, *woof*-bang, *woof*-bang percussion of a pneumatic drill.

Glaring dazedly out of the front door in his dressing gown, Alex had the terrifying impression that the two workmen opposite were engaged on the same task as himself.

Catching sight of Alex, the man with the drill waved, then resumed his deafening pounding. It was a trench, not a hole. However, he noticed that the cleared earth seemed about three feet thick above the mud-rock.

After breakfast, they went down through the living room to the stable. The noise of the pneumatic drill was very slightly less here than in the kitchen, but still very considerable. They had almost to shout to make themselves heard.

'I'm going to start right away,' he said above the racket. 'But you can go shopping if you like.'

'I might be able to help,' said Catrina.

'What?'

'I said I might be able to *help*,' said Catrina loudly.

He piled the ropes, pulley, sledgehammer and tool chest under the sacks, and leant one of the old wooden doors to further hide everything. Then he pulled out the four cases containing the Acker Packsack.

It was when he'd opened the fourth that he realised Mr James had inadvertently left out the length of feeder hose.

'*Hell!*' shouted Alex. 'We'll have to go to Naples.'

'Why?'

'We can't possibly buy thirty or forty or however many metres it is to the kitchen of garden hose here. They'll smell a rat.'

'Nonsense,' said Catrina. 'They all have flowers and plants in tubs or pots or boxes. The poorest slummiest houses try and have something. I'll go. I've masses to get anyway. You put that thing together. I'll measure to the kitchen.'

She paced her way to the stair and was gone.

With the aid of the manual and what he remembered of Mr James's demonstration, Alex started to assemble the core drill. He coupled the first three-foot drill rod and tube core barrel together and fitted the soft diamond core bit. This assembly, once fixed to the 10 h.p. drill motor, would drill a one and a half-inch hole down fifty feet. The recoverable core was seven-eighths of an inch diameter.

To assemble all this, with frequent reference to the manual, took nearly an hour. Once all together, it was heavier than he remembered. But there was an item James hadn't mentioned, a chain anchor with a two-foot spike. Alex had to use the sledgehammer to drive this into the compacted earth. About two inches before it was completely embedded it struck rock.

He attached the fuel pipe, pumped up the pressure tank, attached the Jo-bar so that Catrina could help steady the drill and then leant it against the wall.

He'd decided to modify and extend the plan he'd made in London. He'd drill a series of twenty-one-foot-deep holes two feet apart in a square grid covering the whole stable floor. He'd start at the near right-hand side at the living room end, work up beside the long wall opposite the double doors to the far right-hand corner, move in two feet and drill down again to the near wall. Not until a core revealed some sign of habitation or remains underneath would he embark on the main shaft. And if nothing were found . . .

'I've got the hose,' shouted Catrina from the top of the stair. 'No one noticed. People buy hose every day. What shall I do with it?'

They fixed one end of the hose to the kitchen cold water tap, the other to the nozzle on the drill assembly. Alex turned the tap to just above a drip in the kitchen. The reliable little Biggs and Statton engine started second pull of the rope – and such was the din from the pneumatic drill it was scarcely audible, even in the stable. Alex turned the water tap to 'on' at the drill head. At 9.45 on the morning of Monday, 5 June, they began to drill down into the buried city of Herculaneum.

Alex had used a sledgehammer to knock the anchor stake through the earth. The core drill sliced down in about thirty seconds. There was a slight jar, and then he felt a satisfying quiver – a feeling that was to become familiar and eventually almost maddening in its monotony – the quiver of the soft diamond core bit cutting down into the mud-rock.

With Catrina holding the Jo-bar, it took a little over ten minutes to drill a foot. After sixteen minutes, counting the eighteen inches of earth floor, it was necessary to fit another drill rod and core barrel. This took five minutes. By the end of the next half hour Alex's arms ached from gripping the drill and there was an acute pain across his shoulders.

'It's getting impossible to breathe in here,' he said, straightening and swinging his arms. He turned off the engine. 'We'll have to unblock that window.'

He levered off the planks that had been roughly nailed across it, and at once became aware of a faint through-draught coming from the double doors. Wisps of blue-grey exhaust trickled out under the top of the window.

Alex leant on the sill for a moment. The colour-flattening sun beat on the rich black earth and the rough plastic-covered greenhouses where the *pomodori* and other vegetables ripened so swiftly. The ground sloped away fifteen feet below. He tried to see into the distant *scavi*, but they were just too low.

He added another drill rod and tube core and pulled the string start.

By the time of the next change, Alex was stopping every five minutes to rub his forearms and stretch his shoulders. As they coupled on the new drill rod and core barrel, Catrina said diffidently, 'Do you think you need to *grip* it so hard? I would have thought if you just somehow rested on it it wouldn't be such an effort.'

'Oh for Chrissake,' said Alex. 'Who's doing this, you or me? If I don't hold it the rod will bend and snap and the whole thing will have ended before it's begun. Anyway, I don't need you. Why don't you go and get the lunch ready or something?'

He knew she was right. It was not anxiety about the drill rod, but tension. Somehow it was impossible to release his grip.

Ten minutes later he felt her hand press cool on his neck, and then her fingers ran up into his hair making him shiver. She bent and kissed him. Without stopping the drill, Alex smiled at her. Catrina took the Jo-bar. It was eleven-thirty.

At one-fifteen they had drilled to a depth of seven drill rods, or twenty-one feet.

'This is the moment of truth,' said Alex, winding up the top core barrel and drill rod.

As the Acker core drill bit down into the lava, it forced the core gradually up into each newly attached core barrel. Thus the last core barrel fitted contained the first core drilled – in this case the compact earth of the stable floor and first foot of mud-rock. Alex tapped this out on to the ground. The next three cores were of the same uniform dark grey, hard, granulated consistency. The fifth was different. It was lighter in colour and slightly less dense.

'Obviously the flows would be different,' said Alex. 'Some with more mud; some more pumice, like this.'

The sixth was similar. With sinking heart, Alex wound up the last core barrel and tapped it out. The same.

The disappointment was immediate and surprising in its strength. They stared at the grey fragments of slender core. At last Alex said, 'Well, I don't know what we expected.'

'I know exactly what *I* expected,' said Catrina vehemently. 'I expected about ten foot of that mud stuff, then a few inches of roof tiles and timber, then more mud stuff, and then a foot of bronze or marble where we'd landed bang on top of some marvellous statue.'

Although Iannucci's workmen were still pounding at the foundations of his new house, Alex said his arms were too painful to continue. Catrina made him soak them in hot water, and then rubbed one of her creams into them. 'I'll get something from the *farmacia* this evening,' she said. 'And you must take extra vitamin pills.'

At two-fifteen, as they were finishing lunch, the pneumatic drill at last fell silent. It was as though someone had stopped shouting at them.

'Let's go to bed,' said Alex.

If they propped the door wide and had the window open they could feel, naked, flickers of coolness – eddies from that breeze that was flowing in from the sea. His arms were so painful it hurt even to hold her. After they'd made love they both fell immediately asleep in spite of the discomfort of the shoved-together beds.

They were woken promptly and violently at four-fifteen by the pneumatic drill exploding almost, it seemed, beside their bed.

Alex turned the water on in the kitchen and they went down to the old stable. He shovelled the core fragments into one of the sacks where they filled barely a quarter, and moved the drill three paces further on beside the wall.

'It's no good having them too close together,' he said, surveying the expanse of floor still to be drilled.

With frequent stops and helped by Catrina on the Jo-bar, he could manage no more than two hours drilling. Then, soaked in sweat, shaking with exhaustion, he said his arms had to have a rest. It was all he could do to hammer two of the short planks back across the window.

While he had a shower and then soaked his arms, Catrina went to the *farmacia* and came back with something called Aspercreme.

'Did you say I did it typing?' asked Alex, as she rubbed it gently into his forearms.

'I said it was fibrositis,' said Catrina. 'It's the same idea.'

Iannucci's two men stopped at eight o'clock. Alex said they should now test to see how noisy their own drilling was. He ran the little Biggs and Statton engine while Catrina walked about outside the stable doors.

'It's not loud. You can hear it. You can hardly hear it at the gates. It's rather as though something were wrong with the car and you were running it to see what.'

'I still think we ought only to do it under cover of other noise. I hope to God they take more than two days to complete their trench.'

'What we have to face,' said Alex as they lay in bed on their inadequate mattresses that night, 'is that I haven't really taken any exercise for eighteen years.'

'Making love?' said Catrina, sliding her agile hand over his bare stomach.

'Drilling down into that lava or whatever it is isn't like making love,' said Alex, 'not even remotely.'

The next morning his forearms were noticably swollen and extremely tender. With Catrina providing all the pressure on the Jo-bar, forcing himself to relax his grip, and stopping every five or six minutes for massage and rest, they managed the second hole. The cores revealed the same pattern as the first lot.

'Let's leave it,' said Catrina. 'You'll only make them worse. Let's do the money and the shopping we were going to do this afternoon.'

Alex fastened the double doors with chain and padlock both inside and out. He re-boarded the window and concealed bit, drill rods and core barrels under the sacks behind the old doors.

He insisted they drive the kilometre or so to Torre del Greco. 'No one would expect an impoverished writer to open an account with three thousand pounds. It would soon leak out. Anyway, it's a far bigger place with far more shops.'

They found a Banco di Napoli, paid in the travellers' cheques, and arranged for the rest of the money to be sent from England. They bought more cutlery, a cast-iron frying pan, candles, and a double bed mattress to augment the two pain-filled wafers Iannucci had provided.

'We must remember we'll soon be rich,' said Alex, momentarily exhilarated by the merging architectural motifs of their crisp 50,000 lira notes which they'd got to pay the rent.

'In that case, I think we should buy a typewriter,' said Catrina.

The euphoria was short-lived. During the late afternoon Alex was able to manage another two hours before having to rest his arms, by which time, also, the pneumatic drill had stopped.

'Look at it,' he said, leaning wearily on the drill head. 'Two and a half holes in two days. And found nothing. At this rate it will take two months just to test the area. Imagine when it comes to digging! It's far too difficult. No wonder no one's tried it. What's the point?'

'But you've done marvellously,' said Catrina. 'Look at what you've achieved – getting all this together, the ropes, and drills. Getting it all out here. Made your plan. Started on it. You can't expect immediate results. You'll get stronger. I think you've *already* achieved a great deal.'

'Do you really think so?' said Alex. 'Perhaps you're right. Let's go and have several large drinks.'

Then, and many times later during the following weeks and months, she was to marvel at the swiftness with which he responded to her encouragement; as though his despair was not really over the reality of the situation – and goodness knows it was real and despairing enough – but due to some inner and quite different crisis of confidence which she could reach and assuage.

Later, as he lay asleep, her arm under his neck, she embarked on one of those meandering, fruitless and enjoyable speculations which centred on how much he loved her, or whether it was love at all. She ended by wondering whether it was not exactly that – a cry – but a cry less deep than she supposed, simply the ordinary male/child cry for support and reassurance in endeavour? If so, was what she felt love either? Perhaps it was just an eager but equally automatic female response to that male need?

She was also aware of some latent violence in him which she half-wanted to provoke and half-feared. Why, for instance, did he drink so much? It worried her and several times she'd decided to speak. So far she hadn't dared.

[3]

Next morning, Wednesday, Alex's arms were a good deal better. There also came a faint encouragement from the cores.

He finished the third hole mid-morning and began the fourth. The pneumatic drill stopped an hour before lunch and Catrina reported that the trench was finished. But to Alex's great relief Iannucci's men started up the cement mixer.

He had just attached the second drill rod of the fifth hole at 7.20 when Catrina, who was emptying the cores of the fourth hole, gave a cry. 'Alex! Look at this!'

She was pointing to the middle of a slender grey core cylinder. There, at what would have been about twelve feet underground, marking the boundary between the different coloured mud-rocks, was a piece of unmistakable red roof tile, very faded, and below that two inches of black material. Alex broke the core and rubbed this between his fingers, smelling it.

'Earth,' he said. 'I thought it might be carbonised beam.' He crumbled the compressed grains and let them fall. 'Herculaneum was very crowded, the gardens small. We may be in a garden going towards the house that tile came from.'

Small though this was, it was the first sign of life in the uniform grey – someone was down there.

During the week Alex's arms recovered and he became more and more efficient. By Saturday it was taking about six and a half minutes to drill a foot. Alex could add a drill rod and core barrel in three minutes. Tapping out all the cores took about fifteen minutes. This was left to Catrina, while Alex continued with the spare drill and core barrels. Twenty feet could now be done in two and three quarter hours, slightly less if they used the Jo-bar.

By Saturday evening they'd drilled twelve holes and Alex got drunk. They went to the Fauno and ended up on grappa. Attillo said he hadn't seen Dr Schultz for four days. There was a rumour she'd gone to Rome to get Dr Gandolfino's appointment rescinded. '*Quella donna è forte. Uno vera combattrice,*' said Attillo admiringly.

This time, her heart beating, Catrina said Alex drank too much. Don't have another one. To her surprise, his smile charmingly weak, he agreed. He'd been trying to cut down for years. However, he immediately waved to Attillo for his tumbler to be refilled, and there was something more than happy amiability – a momentary flash of that latent violence – in his silent smiling toast to her.

She woke into familiar wine-skin fumes, the sound of the cement mixer emerging out of Alex's snores. She thought of letting him sleep, but finally shook him awake. He was like a teenage boy going early to school, clogged, automatic. He hardly noticed the extra Efamol.

The weather had been growing steadily hotter since they'd arrived. Catrina said one of the wives she was making friends with in the Via Ascione had told her it was officially *un'ondata di calore* – a heatwave. By one-thirty Alex was covered in sweat, uncooled by the occasional inadequate wisps of breeze.

'Christ,' he said, straightening from the drill as the seventh rod reached its end. 'No wonder there are strikes. Now for another twenty-one feet of that fucking grey stuff.'

But where they were now – at the living room end of the stable, finishing the last hole of the second line – this was to be expected. The great disappointment had come as they emptied the cores at the opposite end – where the 'house' should have been. The thin layer of earth remained, but that was all. Since Wednesday, the inhabitants of Herculaneum had given no further sign of their existence.

'Oh let's leave it,' said Catrina. 'We don't have to work on Sunday just because Iannucci makes his men do it. You've

95

done enough. Let's go and see that place Attillo told me about – La Pinetta.'

This was a municipal swimming pool attached to a filling station midway between Torre del Greco and Ercolano. They had *spaghetti con vongole* first – Catrina's shit-fed clams – at the *ristorante* beside the filling station. Taped music thumped. A large television flickered unwatched in the corner.

They bought two 2000–lira tickets and pushed through a door – '*Piscina*' – at the back. At once the music became loud; louder as they descended the steep internal stair, and then, as they stepped out into the brightness, deafening – a great soft heave of sound, and they were lifted, wafted, several feet off the ground, engulfed in the huge swelling operatic sobs of Italian pop.

At the sight of the glittering kidney, the municipal punctuation mark lying in the sun, Catrina gasped, 'Oh my God – this is what I've been missing.'

Alex followed more slowly as she ran ahead towards the *spogliatoii*. The '*Uomini*' side of these was a square concrete box with '*Vietato orinare*' on the wall. Urine crystals glistened on a depression in the floor and Alex had to breathe through his mouth.

As he came out, clothes rolled in his trousers, he looked across the pool and saw that Catrina had laid out her towel in one of the empty areas between the twenty or so Italians spread over the considerable expanse of blue tile. She waved, walked towards the edge, dived in.

Alex did the breast stroke and couldn't put his head under water. Catrina only emerged to breathe, like a dolphin or a seal. Women had evolved from sea animals: Catrina's mouth tasted salt in the morning, you could see her gills when she was drunk. She pulled herself onto the side and immediately dived back into the water as though she could not bear to tear herself from its arms. The tape thumped Julio Iglesias.

Except to look at the progress of Iannucci's building, he hadn't been outdoors since the visit to the bank. The woman on the towel ten yards from them had breasts like white cheeses slung from her shoulders; a third breast was clamped between her teeth, a large powdery bap.

'Aren't you going to swim?' Catrina lay beside him panting, her ice-cold seal-thigh pressed against his hot shank.

'I wonder why swimming is always compulsory?' said Alex.

He walked reluctantly towards the clear chemical-blue water, receptive, menacing, a feminine symbol trapped and distorted in its oddly masculine container, a plump spermatozoa concreted in the act of swimming. It was freezing, practically castrating him.

'Did you know chlorine alone doesn't make your eyes sting? It's the reaction with urine that does it – though I'm surprised they've any left after changing.'

'I don't care. I'd like to come every afternoon.'

Returning to Via Ascione 46 was like returning to prison, a prison that was already underground. During the following five days Alex only went out once.

Iannucci's men often left the cement mixer churning during their long lunches and their siesta. Alex forced himself to start drilling before they returned. On Monday he worked for nine hours. On Tuesday he had to stop at seven-thirty – eight and a half hours. That night he got drunk again and was exhausted by two o'clock on Wednesday. The single trip outside took place that afternoon.

Although the cores had so far only filled four sacks, they decided they should find somewhere to empty them.

'I'm sure there were several places on the road down from Ravello,' said Alex. 'But that road through Pompeii to Torre del Greco is a nightmare. It took me hours.'

'Why on earth didn't you use the *autostrada*?' said Catrina.

To his astonishment, they reached Corbora in twenty-five minutes. Shortly after it, as the *serie di curve* and *caduta massi* began in earnest, they found a long-disused quarry, overgrown with brambles and saplings.

'It would be even quicker at night,' said Alex.

He drilled a further nine hours on Thursday. He would have done so on Friday, had it not been for a somewhat alarming incident.

Catrina had gone shopping. Alex was in the trance-like condition drilling rapidly induced ('simple manual labour is a form of meditation' he'd said to Catrina) when he became aware that he had heard and had ignored prolonged knocking at the kitchen door. It had now stopped and Alex had a sudden terrified intuition that someone was breaking in.

He turned off the drill, sprang up the stairs and, sweating, shirtless and filthy, arrived in the living room just as Signor Iannucci came in from the kitchen.

Much mutually incomprehensible explanation took place. Iannucci had heard a faint noise from the *autorimessa* – *una macchina da scrivere elettrica*? – he looked curiously at the dishevelled figure of the *scrittore inglese* – *scusate l'interruzione,* but naturally he had a spare key.

Alex waved aside the one word – *scusate* – he vaguely recognised. '*N'importa, n'importa.*' The van was only running on two cylinders. 'See-lee-dar?' asked Iannucci. '*Cylinder,*' said Alex. 'Boom-boom-boom-boom?' He moved his right hand vigorously up and down as though demonstrating how to masturbate.

'See-leen-dar?' said Iannucci again, puzzled; '*cos'è quello?*'

Alex went into elaborate pantomime of faulty car engine, *macchina* limping – finally he demonstrated masturbation again.

'Ah *cilindro,*' cried Iannucci, revealing himself, Alex thought, to be a good deal thicker than he looked. At once the fixer took over. He had a brother-in-law, a marvellous *meccanico* in the little Via Giardini down the road. Mention Francesco Iannucci.

Alex thanked him. He went and stood by the cheap portable typewriter, which Catrina had arranged on the table by the window to re-establish his *scrittore* credentials. '*Si multo tempore perdita,*' he said. '*Terribile, terribile.*'

Iannucci had come with the rent declaration to be signed. Alex said how comfortable his beautiful house was. Iannucci said that he would be honoured if Alex would come to a meal, bringing of course his wife. Alex, wincing at the word, said that he and his, er, *moglie* would love to have a meal. And perhaps Signor Iannucci and *his moglie* would do the same?

'We'll have to get bolts to put on the front door and the door down to the stable,' he said to Catrina when she returned. 'I think I ought to fix up a bell. And he wants us to go and have a meal with him.'

'I think we should. You remember those louts? I'm sure he's powerful round here. We must keep in with him.'

She referred to an incident that had taken place the week before. Returning with shopping by a circuitous, idly exploring route, she had been suddenly confronted by two youths who'd clearly been following her. The street was empty except for a young boy some distance away. One of the youths had asked her what a nice girl like her was doing there. The second said her handbag looked heavy, could he help carry it?

She was wondering whether to scream, to run, or simply to hand everything over, when the boy in the distance came running up. She recognised one of the urchins from the Via Ascione. He muttered something to the two youths. She had caught clearly only the name Iannucci. They had looked sullenly at her. One had spat. Then they had slouched off.

Saturday, Alex managed nine hours, and again on Sunday. But during Monday he became steadily more depressed. Catrina, at his insistence, had gone to Torre del Greco for bolts, plus, if possible, a bell. He guessed she'd stop off at La Pinetta. Somehow when it was her emptying the cores it was less dispiriting.

At eight o'clock the cement mixer fell silent. Moments before, Alex had completed drilling the twenty-ninth hole, the last hole of the fifth row. He began to wind up the drill rods and tap out the core barrels. The single bulb, the largest Ercolano could provide, cast the muted light of a partial eclipse. It was difficult to make out details.

Not that it mattered. At the living-room end of the stable there was not even the earth layer; only the slight discontinuity at twelve foot where the lava-mud changed colour. Alex tapped out the last grey core of matter and stood wearily upright.

He looked across the pocked floor; in the dim light the neat rows of little rimmed craters made it a fairy battlefield. Craters – or were they graves? Alex had a sudden sharp clear certainty. He was wasting his time. What he was doing was absolutely futile. As usual, he'd failed.

He heard the van outside. Catrina had returned. He unpadlocked the double doors and stepped outside. She was coming round the back of the van, carrying two full plastic bags.

'Sorry I'm late.'

'Come in here.' Alex took the bags and put them against the wall inside the stable.

'Look at it.'

Catrina looked at the pockmarked no-man's land. 'Goodness, you've finished the row – that's marvellous Alex.'

'Catrina – I can't go on. It's pointless.'

'What on earth do you *mean*, Alex? You're doing *marvellously*. Another few days and you'll have finished the testing. You don't realise how strong you are now.'

'I don't mean that. I know I'm *able* to – with your help. But look Catrina – what's your nearest town in Wiltshire with six thousand inhabitants?'

'I don't know. Warminster? No, that's much bigger. But say Warminster.'

'Now imagine you're moving a platform the size of this stable, about twenty-four foot by fifteen foot, sixty foot above the town. And then for no reason you just stop. How likely are you to be above a house or anything special?'

'I don't know. You might be,' said Catrina, not envisaging the scene.

'OK,' said Alex. 'But now we've tested five-sevenths of the platform. We've found nothing at all. We've just got that four-foot by fifteen-foot plank to test. That little strip above a whole town. It's obviously ridiculous.'

'What shall we do?' Catrina had her familiar vision – no longer funny – of garages, stables, basement rooms all over Ercolano studded with little holes.

'Do? We pack it in. Go home. Give up.'

This was no time for argument. 'Alex, you can't stop now. At least finish this bit we've started. I've so admired you, the way you've set it all up, the way you've stuck to it. Please, just finish it, if only for me. Then we'll go home. Will you?'

He looked at her. How much easier it was to say yes, no matter that you felt no. 'All right.'

She was quite surprised and very relieved he didn't get drunk that night. Or not really drunk – a bottle and a half. He talked about his father, who had died when he was three. He told her about the co-educational school he'd been to. 'I learnt nothing. I'm really totally uneducated. I learnt some Greek at my smart little prep school and that's all. I had to go to a tutorial for a year to get to Cambridge. In the fifth form all I learnt was driving. I can do skid turns. I'll show you.'

'Was that really all?'

'Skid turns, and fucking.'

'Yes – you're marvellous at that.'

But later in bed while Alex slept she wondered if their affair would survive Herculaneum. As he had drilled towards it, as they both worked, she'd had a sense of them being drawn down together deeper and deeper into a primitive subconscious of love and sex. Now that base, that world, that magnet, seemed to have been removed from under them.

[4]

Nothing disturbed the monotony of drilling, except that each day, notch by notch, the temperature seemed to rise another fraction of a degree. The few eddies that managed to twist in from the cool breeze that blew off the sea did something, but not much, to stir the stagnant, stifling, exhaust-smelling air of the stable.

Catrina suggested again that they might go and call on her Barracco grandparents who lived about twenty kilometres away. But Alex, his paranoia notching up steadily as if in tune with the heat, again turned the idea down vehemently. 'We don't want *anything* about us to leak out to *anyone* – least of all our presence.'

On Monday 21 June, at eleven-thirty, Catrina had gone on a lightning visit to La Pinetta and Alex was drilling as usual. He had just fitted the sixth drill rod and core barrel and resumed drilling when there was a momentary shudder of the drill head and then the drill began to race.

His heart beating, Alex switched off the engine and wound up the drill rods, tossing the core barrels one by one into a heap.

As he pulled the last one out of the ground he saw at once what had happened. The drill was headless. The diamond core bit had sheered off and must now be lying eighteen foot below the ground.

'So that's it,' thought Alex. 'Fucked up. Finished.' It was almost a relief.

He was sitting in the kitchen with a glass of wine and a cigarette when Catrina got back.

'We've had it,' he said. 'It's over.'

'Why – what on earth's happened?'

'The drill's had it.' He got up, throwing his cigarette into

101

the sink, and walked down into the stable. 'The end's broken off.'

Catrina stood holding the drill rod helplessly in her hands. 'Isn't there anything we can do? Can't we get a new one?'

'What the hell's the point? I told you we were wasting our time – and money. I want to get out of this awful place now.'

There was a pause. Suddenly Catrina threw the drill rod on the ground. 'How *can* you give up now?' she said furiously. 'You really *are* a failure. You promised me you'd finish this bit. Is this all it takes?'

Alex stepped towards her and for a moment she thought he was going to hit her. '*This* all it takes, you say? It's easy enough for you – fucking off to the Pinetta whenever you feel tired or bored. It's me does the fucking drilling. I've done it nearly a month now. How long do I go on? Six months? A year?'

He was trembling. The sweat had made marks like tears on the grime of his face.

'I'm sorry, Alex. I'm sorry. You're quite right, it's far harder for you. It's only because I love and admire you. Somehow you've so nearly finished. Please Alex – just one more go.'

They stared at each other. The cement mixer had stopped. It was very hot and still in the stable.

'All right. I suppose so. I'll do it. But if we find nothing – that's *it*. I'm fucked if I'm going to move about Ercolano drilling holes. Okay?'

'What can we do?' Catrina went and put her hand on his bare arm, but he shook it off.

'It'll set us back at least four days. I'll have to fly to England and get a new one. I'd better get two in case it happens again. They cost about £300 each. God knows how much money we've got left.'

Catrina knew. Just over two thousand pounds. 'Why can't we get one in Naples?'

'That man, Mr James, said they were unique. You can only get them in London.'

'But there must be something. A hook or something. It must always be happening. Why don't you ring him up?'

'For Christ's sake, Catrina, why don't you do the whole thing yourself? You madden me sometimes.'

Nevertheless he took the van down to the Fauno and borrowed the phone behind the bar. It took nine tries before he got through to London.

'Hello there.' Mr James's American accent was more noticable across a thousand miles. 'So what can I do for you this time?'

'I'm in Italy,' said Alex, wishing to alert him to the speeding digits on the cost-indicator behind the bar.

'So how's the film going?' said Mr James.

'Film?' asked Alex blankly.

'You started shooting yet?'

'Oh yes – yes – yes, we've been shooting for some time. Look, we've run into some trouble. The bit has broken off quite deep down.'

'You've lost your bit. That often happens.'

'What shall we do?'

'You could get a new bit.'

'Out here? Where?'

'Masarenti in Naples. They handle the Packsack for us. But that'll set you back. What you need,' said Mr James, getting into the saddle, 'is a fishing tool.'

'Fishing tool?' Had Catrina been right? A rod and line?

'It's pointed, with an acme thread. You put it into the drill pipe and rotate it *very slowly* into the bit underground. Then you pull it out. You need – hang on, I'll just look it up.'

Alex reached over the bar and with a *prego* took Attillo's biro.

'You *can* do it with magnets,' said Mr James, 'but that's damned expensive. Get a fishing tool. You'll need an "N" Acme thread, and the part number is C–205–A. Masarenti will know what you want.'

Alex scribbled onto the back of his cheque book. 'Anything else?'

'Your thread's broken, that's why it ripped off. You'll have to get the thread mended. There's usually enough meat to get a new thread cut. Masarenti should be able to do that too.'

'Right. Thank you very much, Mr James.'

'No bother,' said Mr James. 'You won't forget the mench?'

'No,' said Alex. 'I won't forget the mench.'

As they drove into Naples that afternoon, Catrina said, 'Suppose he asks what we're doing?'

'Say we're drilling to see if there's water for a well.'

Masarenti were at Via Cuma 30. The sallow elderly man who dealt with them had grown weary in the service of drilling. Yes, he had that particular fishing tool. Yes, he could cut a new thread, provided enough metal remained. More exactly, he would arrange to have it cut.

The old man was wearied, too, by the occasional dishonesty of drillers. Alex had to deposit a cheque for the full value of the fishing tool – exactly twice what he was charged to hire it out.

It was clear at once how the tool worked. About fourteen inches long, the threaded diameter at the top was two and a half inches, to fit onto the bottom of the drill rod; at the tapered end the threaded diameter was seven-eighths of an inch, to screw into the centre of the separated core bit.

Although it was past seven o'clock, Alex insisted they try and retrieve the bit as soon as they got back to Ercolano.

He screwed the heavy 7lb fishing tool into the drill rod, and then painstakingly assembled the pipes and fed them down the hole. At seventeen foot, Catrina holding the Jo-bar, they gently lowered the drill rods until the fishing tool came to rest. Alex now started to rotate, so slowly that the rods barely turned.

It took twenty minutes, the transistor blaring to drown the noise of the Biggs and Statton engine. Again and again Alex stopped the drill, wound up the drill rods and then, finding he'd caught nothing, lowered them and the fishing tool back down the hole.

But at last, the threads caught. His arms quivered to the vibration he'd become so bored with. Held fast by the fishing tool, the bit had begun to drill again.

They wound it up – nervous all the time that it might drop off the end – until finally Alex was holding the core bit to the light, inspecting the bright new shear marks slanting up the threads where the bit had torn out.

There was another day in Naples while Masarenti had a new thread cut (40,000 lira), and then Alex was able to resume drilling.

He resumed drilling, but his attitude had changed. He was no longer in pursuit of something. It was a job. He'd finish it. They'd go.

Or split. Sensing that he too, though quite differently, associated their being together in some way with Herculaneum, the fact that they were soon to leave filled Catrina with apprehension.

By Sunday 27 June, Alex was starting the final line of exploratory holes. Catrina was in the kitchen, depressed. She'd grated her finger painfully doing the parmesan. The mayonnaise had separated twice and she had no eggs left.

At 11.30 she heard a shout from the stable. Then the door into the living room banged open. 'Catrina – for Christ's sake. . . .'

As she ran she thought, Oh God, make it not the drill again, make it good news.

Alex was standing at the far left-hand corner of the stable. The drill was buried to the hilt, the drill head and motor actually resting on the earth floor.

'I've broken through into something. I was half way down the last rod when the drill began to race and the whole thing just collapsed down like that. It could just be a crack or an air pocket, but there's *something* there. You'll have to help me lift it.'

They fixed the Jo-bar and managed to heave the drill and twenty-one feet of rod and core sufficiently high to support it on two of the empty Packsack cases. Alex wound up the core barrels and tossed them in a heap without bothering to empty them.

When the hole was exposed, he knelt and sniffed, half expecting some faint remnant of that ancient air – sulphuric, volcanic – to rise to his nostrils. But he smelt only earth and horse.

He stood up. 'There *are* hollow places. Do you remember how it rang hollow when I stamped in that tunnel?'

'Not really,' said Catrina. 'I was far too busy fighting my claustrophobia. How deep is this bubble or crack of yours?'

Alex measured out forty feet of string and tied a nut to the end. It was difficult to be accurate but the crack seemed to extend about four feet below where the drill would have stopped.

'Right – this is the place.'

Paced out, a four-foot square was clearly inadequate. He paced one of five foot, and then stood back pointing. 'That's where we dig the shaft.'

From that moment the drilling routine became relentless. Alex began immediately. He planned to cover the five-foot shaft area with holes six inches or so apart, but first he wanted to discover the extent and if possible some evidence as to what they'd broken into.

This took four days and involved drilling twelve holes.

The crack extended three foot from the left-hand corner of the stable down the left-hand wall towards the double doors. It occurred each time at the twenty-one-foot limit of the drill. It was no wider than six inches since it wasn't struck by the next row of holes, seven inches in from the first. Alex didn't dare drill them closer because he'd become fairly neurotic since the core bit had sheared off. Mr James had warned the pipe might bend in if too close. The depth of the crack continued to be about four feet.

The cores offered somewhat limited evidence as to what was going on below. It didn't look as though they'd broken into some Roman artefact, like a sealed lead water tank for instance, because the cores showed no signs of Roman-made material. They were all of the uniform grey lava-like matter.

At the same time, the six cores nearest the wall, which led to the crack, did show a further variation. At the twelve-foot level where the earth line usually occurred the drill entered a third type of lava. It was more variegated and at the same time denser. This occurred along the same six-inch strip as the break. They took samples of each type of core and put them in plastic bags so that Catrina could show them to her professor.

Alex said he thought the most likely explanation was that they had struck some deep fissure or crack opened up, at a point where three lava-mud flows met, by some ancient post-AD 79 earthquake.

Yet the meagreness of this discovery, and of the evidence, didn't seem to discourage him. Each morning he struggled into a day which, although it had only a few hours before grown cool, was already starting to heat up again. The cement mixer was only used intermittently now. When it wasn't running, Alex played the transistor full volume – like the rest of the Via Ascione. He'd rigged up the bell to ring in the stable from the front door if Catrina was out, when he also bolted all other doors on the inside.

In order to wake up without the mixer they bought an alarm clock (20,000 lira). 'It's the first time I've got up regularly at seven o'clock since . . . since I was . . . Actually,' said Alex, 'I suppose it's the first time I've got up regularly at seven o'clock in my life.'

He also began to feel better than he ever had before. It had virtually nothing to do with Catrina's re-iterated anxieties, simply that drilling with a hangover was so frightful he was forced to drink less.

His diet was as near perfect as she could make it. Each meal was accompanied by a supplementary pile of vitamin pills nearly as large as the meal itself.

Catrina herself could not bear to remain in their hot little house all day, and always found a reason for escaping. She'd made friends with the young wife she'd first met in the Via Ascione, Carmela Pastore. Her husband Mario was a *carte-maro*, a man who collected old cardboard boxes and sold them, for almost nothing, to be reconditioned. Carmela was twenty-five and had seven children. Six of them slept in one bed; Carmela and Mario had the baby with them.

Catrina returned with tales of drama and gossip. Mario had been knocked off his bicycle and had a whole day's collection stolen. Sophia Zuccaro had accused Maria Auletta of trying to sleep with her husband.

'She pulled three whole handfuls of hair out. You can see the bare patches.'

'Really?' said Alex.

It sounded quite unreal. He sometimes didn't go out for four days at a time. When he did, he noticed things with the random inconsequentiality and sharpness of convalescence – the insect antennae of the TV aerials all cocked, quivering, in the same direction; the growing smell of drains in the tremendous heat.

The buried streets and houses of Herculaneum were far more real to him; at least, far more important. He could feel them beneath him as the bit drilled slowly down. He pretended he stayed in because it was taking longer than he'd anticipated and their money would run out. Or Iannucci might call when they were both out and discover the holes and the equipment.

In fact he stayed in because he had recovered his sense of inevitability. His destiny lay down there. If it was simply a crack opened up by an earthquake – so be it.

By Tuesday 27 July, the five-foot square was covered with ninety-seven holes and the temperature was regularly reaching 34.5 Centigrade, or 94 Fahrenheit, by midday. It was time to start on the main shaft.

Chapter Seven

[1]

Alex had often had fantasies while the Acker Packsack vibrated under his hands that he was a Klondike prospector or a miner at the coal face.

He realised, immediately and painfully, that what he'd been doing bore as much relationship to hard manual labour as icing a cake did to surfacing a road.

Even loosening the compacted earth of the stable floor with the pick and then shovelling it into the sacks was back-breaking. He dug out an extra foot-wide strip beyond the five-foot square so that the earth shouldn't slide down the shaft – if it were ever dug. This took two and a half hours and by the end he was exhausted, covered in sweat and developing blisters on both hands.

Not only that, he'd filled ten of their fifteen sacks. The weeks of drilling had only filled six more than that. A trip or so a week to the quarry was all very well. But every other day, or even every day . . .

'You'll have to take the stuff out at night,' he said to Catrina.

'Why?'

'Endless van trips would look extremely odd.'

'Honestly Alex – no one would notice. You're totally para-noid. You may not realise it, but they actually think you're an ordinary *scrittore*. They don't seem to notice you play your radio full blast in the stable for days on end and only lurch out into the sun every five days blinking and covered in sweat and dust. As for me, they see me go in and out all the time. We're certainly not accepted exactly; but they're not violently curious about us any more.'

However, this particular fear vanished the moment Alex started on the mud-rock, that very afternoon.

The first blow with the pick did, it was true, dislodge a six-inch sliver. But it also pulled the reddening skin off a half-formed blister and sent a jar up his arm that made him gasp. He clenched his teeth and swung the pick again.

After ten minutes he stopped and leant on the pick handle, panting.

'This is going to take bloody years. The stuff's like concrete.'

'It'll get easier. Especially when you've got down a bit and can see the progress. And don't you fill the sacks. Just throw it on the edge. I'll buy a shovel and I'll fill them.'

By the end of the day he'd managed to break up the surface to a depth of about three inches. Catrina bathed his hands and rubbed cream into them. She put elastoplast strips on the raw skin.

'Some Gruyère,' said Alex, watching her. 'Dr Schultz was talking through her bun. I simply do not believe that anyone in Ercolano has ever tried to do this before.'

The following morning, as the alarm pulled him awake, he remembered something he'd read as a boy. The sailors on the old windjammers had urinated on their hands to toughen the skin against the rasp of the ropes. After breakfast he did the same. His urine was opalescent under the naked bulb and stung slightly. Alex shook his hands dry before joining Catrina in the stable.

He was astonished to find how unfit he was still, even after nearly two months drilling. He had to pause after half an hour, then after fifteen minutes and soon every ten minutes to rest his arms and get his breath. By the time they ate, he thought he'd have to give up altogether. He realised why Mr James had said he'd wish he had a compressor.

Yet almost imperceptibly the shaft began to appear. On Friday he cleared five inches: on Saturday a little more. By the end of Monday he'd added a further nine inches. He'd also managed to dig for eight hours, though with regular rests and three hours off for lunch.

Catrina looked down at him. Wearing a bra and jean shorts, she too was streaked with dirt and sweat. Even though most of it was earth, the depth of the shaft was well up his thigh.

'See what I mean? It's a proper hole. And I think you look marvellous in it.'

She jumped down beside him. Alex put his arm round her and pulled her head back by the hair. 'I'd do almost anything for your mouth.'

His hands grew harder and finally ceased to blister. It was impossible to say if the urine had helped. As the obsession to dig increased, he found it more and more difficult to go out.

In fact, it wasn't for seven days – in the middle of the second week of the shaft – that he managed a brief trip into Ercolano.

It was towards the end of the morning's digging. The reason was a violent new anxiety. The van was now well overdue its 3000–mile service. Alex had become beset by fantasies of a breakdown on the way to the quarry. The *carabinieri* pulled up. They found the chippings of mud-rock in the back, at once put two and two together, and . . .

'Two and two together indeed,' said Catrina scornfully, who had in fact been on a trip to the quarry that morning with the first full load. 'How could they put two and two together? They'd have to put two and twenty million together to guess what you're doing. But if you're going near the market, get some cheese and some fruit for lunch.'

[2]

Thomas Henderson had spent a useful two hours in the Antiquarium at Herculaneum. A year before, while excavating near the end of the beach, Dr Schultz had found a load of marble where the ship carrying it had foundered while trying to escape. Thomas had read about it but never seen it. He was slightly relieved that neither Dr Schultz nor the new Soprintendente were able to be there to assist him – though Dr Gandolfino had left a flowery and regretful note.

Now, returning slowly through the hot sun towards the station, he turned off for a moment to look at the market.

The people of Ercolano, like the slum dwellers of Naples and for the same reason, were, although strongly built, seldom over five and a half feet high. Thomas caught sight of Alex's yellow head and sharp haggard face immediately – even though fifty yards and a hundred jostling heads and faces separated them. Just as he'd seen him immediately, and with the same sense of shock, from the back of the Christie's saleroom.

For a moment a chill ran down his spine. The boy was haunting him. Then he pulled himself together. What was so odd about it? The uncanny resemblance to his dead son was neither here nor there. The lesson was to learn how to forget – and Thomas had long since learnt it.

Clearly this was a person here studying some aspect of the classical past of Italy, as also at Christie's. Thomas himself had studied like this – what, thirty-four, thirty-five years before. It was in fact a reason for making the young man's acquaintance.

As Thomas started to push through the crowd, Alex, his purchases complete, hurried through the strong smelling fish stalls at the end of the market and headed for the Via Giardini and Iannucci's brother-in-law, the mechanic.

Thomas was just in time to see him turn down into it. He quickened his pace and limped hurriedly after him.

It was a narrow, short street, hung with washing. Forty limped paces and he was at the right-angled bend halfway down it and could see to the end. But there was nothing, nobody. Just washing. It was empty.

Thomas ran to the end and looked left and right up the Corso Resina. This time there was a fair distance in either direction before anyone could have turned off – and he couldn't have been more than a minute behind the young man. But there was no sign of him.

He turned in some perplexity and looked up the Via Giardini again. A student of archaeology, or post-graduate working on a thesis, would visit Herculaneum. But he wouldn't live there. And certainly not in this revolting little slum street.

Thomas shrugged the incident aside. He was due back in Naples at 2.30. But as he limped sweating back to the station the reason, or lack of reason, for his impulsive pursuit lay uncomfortably close to the surface of his mind. It had nothing to do with the desire to make the acquaintance and perhaps help a young fellow academic. The real reason had been to satisfy himself that he had in fact not seen, was not continually seeing, a ghost.

[3]

They carried the typing table out into the tiny patch of shade thrown by the house and ate lunch overlooking the temporarily silent building site.

'The van won't be ready till tomorrow,' said Alex.

'Why not?'

'I don't know. Really you should have come with me. I thought he said he'd have to make something-or-other.'

'I hope it isn't too expensive.'

Alex poured out more wine. It frothed pink-topped in the little glass.

'Something rather odd happened in the market.'

'What?'

'I think I saw a chap called Henderson.'

'Who's he?'

'He works in the British Museum. I saw him with Eddie at the sale I told you about.'

There was a pause. 'I hope he didn't see me,' said Alex.

'Why? I don't see that it matters.'

'Don't you? Suppose he also noticed me at Christie's?'

'Oh, I see. You mean two and two together again?'

'It's all very well to laugh, but that's exactly how murders and bank robbers are discovered. If it was him, I think it's highly suspicious he was here at all.'

Towards the end of the second week it was becoming difficult to throw the waste up to Catrina. Alex really needed a ladder to get out of the shaft easily. On Wednesday afternoon they drove into Torre del Greco to buy a ladder and a bucket.

They were getting out of the van on their return to have a *cappuccino* at the Caffè Fauno when Alex saw a familiar figure windmilling at them from the far side of the Via IV Novembre.

It was Dr Gandolfino. He crossed over to them, bony fingers outstretched. 'So the BBC hava return! You hava come to make *documentario*?'

113

'Not quite yet,' said Alex. 'but we make soon. We are here now to finish the research.'

'*Molto bene*,' said Dr Gandolfino. 'Tomorrow you come to my office and I tell *tutti i miei piani per Herculaneum* – all my plan for Herculaneum. You come haff four o'clock?'

They watched Dr Gandolfino stride away into the heat.

'Do you suppose there's any chance he'd hear I was a travel writer from someone or other? Iannucci?'

'Not the slightest,' said Catrina. 'Extraordinary the way he walks. As though he were trying to take off. I thought he looked a bit shifty when he saw us. Caught out.'

Alex worked furiously the following morning to make up for the time he'd have to waste with Dr Gandolfino.

He shaved and changed and before they set off bolted on the inside both the front door and the door from the living room to the stable. They left by the main stable doors, padlocking these behind them.

As they walked down the Corso Resina, keeping to the shade in the fierce heat of the afternoon, Alex said, 'Don't bother to come to Gandolfino. See if you can find Dr Schultz. Ask her about the level of the water-table in Herculaneum. I've suddenly started to have nightmares about needing to pump out water.'

'There wasn't much water in the Theatre. They weren't pumping there.'

'I know. But it might be different.'

Dr Gandolfino's office was below the bottom eastern end of the *scavi* in the one-storey administrative block. One of the patrolling guides told them he thought Dottoressa Schultz was working in the Antiquarium a hundred yards up from there. Catrina stopped and watched Alex slouch gloomily on in the glare of the sun, then she turned back to the Antiquarium.

She eventually located Dr Schultz in one of the basement storage rooms. It was long and cool, lit by neon. Dr Schultz was at the far end sitting beside a large table covered in bones.

Catrina walked up to it. 'Excuse me, Dr Schultz. I'm sorry to barge in without an appointment, but could I have a word with you?'

114

Dr Schultz looked up and then stood up. 'Why Catrina – hi. Good to see you again. How's the film?'

Catrina held the strong, dry hand, toughened by years of archaeological scraping. 'Fine thanks – and the film too. In fact,' she said, trying to remember what role they'd assigned him, 'Alex has been working on the script for a few weeks.'

'Well, it's lucky you got back now. I'm getting out.'

'Leaving? Why?'

'I've had enough of this lousy country. But that ain't the only reason.' Dr Schultz looked up the room, put down the bone she was holding, and came massively round the table. 'I purrhaps shouldn't tell you this, but purrhaps you shouldn't stick round here that long.'

'Why ever not?'

'Because something weird is going on inside that mountain.'

'Inside Vesuvius? But I thought it was quiescent.'

'That's what a lotta people thought. But I was talking to Salvatore Pasquilino, a friend of mine who works at the Observatory up there. In the past two months they've detected swelling in the side of Vesuvius. This side.'

'But if it's dangerous, shouldn't they warn people?'

'You're damned right they should. But d'ya know what scares the shit out of them? Apart from chaos in these little towns? Tourists. If they start warnings, who'll go to Pompeii? Pompeii brings in a lotta money. They'll wait till after August.

'But it's not Pompeii where weird things are happening. Have you seen the new scaffolding going up here? In the town? There's some in the *scavi* right now.'

'I'm not sure,' said Catrina. 'But there's always scaffolding. It's the result of the earthquake.'

'*Earthquake?*' said Dr Schultz. 'That earthquake was in November *1980*, for Chrissake. Did you know that in the last six months, Salvatore was telling me, the whole area three or four square miles round Ercolano and Torre del Greco has risen one foot?'

'Risen a foot? The ground?' said Catrina. 'But that isn't possible.'

'It most certainly is possible,' said Dr Schultz. 'A few years ago – 1970 – Pozzuoli rose five and a half feet in under three years. But the authorities are so shit-scared here they . . .

they. . . .' Dr Schultz suddenly seized a bone and pointed it savagely and dramatically in the direction of the mountain. 'You can't monkey with Vesuvius. You know that bulge, that bloody great crack in the road at the bottom of November the Fourth Street? D'ya know what the Comune say that bulge is? *Roots.* The roots of a tree. What tree? There's no damn tree in a hundred metres of that bulge, for Chrissake.'

Breathing heavily, Dr Schultz put down her bone and relinquished Catrina's arm which she'd gripped in her fervour.

'I get carried away by what these people do. I say too much. What was it you wanted to ask me?'

'Well, it may not be relevant now,' said Catrina, considerably shaken. 'But Alex wanted to know about the water-table in Herculaneum. Will he – would the character in the film find a lot of water?'

'The water-table seems to have changed over the centuries. Right now, if you dig thirty foot under the present street level of Herculaneum you'll hit water. But I'm kinda vague as to the details of your film. As I recall it was really opening the old tunnels. You won't find much water there.'

'Do you think the Corso Resina lies above the old Roman-Salerno road?' said Catrina, eager to get as much out of Dr Schultz as possible.

'I doubt it. Medieval towns hardly ever followed the Roman pattern. And certainly not here where Resina grew up on bare rock.'

'But mightn't it be the Salerno-Naples Road? I thought you said there'd been ribbon development.'

'Well, like I say – we don't know where the Naples-Salerno road ran, as far as Herculaneum goes. As for ribbon development – yeah, there's a thing about it. But there's absolutely no evidence.'

Catrina stared at Dr Schultz aghast as she casually overturned in a few sentences the work of months. But then, she thought, was there any point if the whole place was about to blow up?

'But are you getting out because it's dangerous?'

'Dangerous? Who said it was dangerous? Well, yeah of course it could be dangerous. Like I said, you can't monkey with Vesuvius. But Pozzuoli's been going up and down like a yo-yo for two thousand years. Two thousand years ago it was twenty foot higher than it is today. You can see the foundations of Nero's palace on the bottom of the bay. It's never happened here before as far as I know. But this whole area's unstable. I'd like to stay and see what's going on.

'But I've got to lecture in the good old USA on some of this.' Dr Schultz turned and waved her arm vaguely over the bones. Then she swung back and glared at Catrina. 'Or so *they* think. In fact, I'm also going to apply a little light leverage to the *Società Archeologico di Pompei e Ercolano*. I'd organised some US funding to open up and extend the eighteenth-century tunnels. Well, now they've put that decrepit old sham in charge there's going to be some *unfunding* done, I can tell you that. Do you know what that windbag plans to do. . . . ?'

It was ten minutes before Catrina could extricate herself. At the administrative block she was told the Soprintendente was still engaged with Signor Mayne, so she wandered over to the little grove of cypress trees where they'd waited before going down into the theatre.

Not since then had she looked at the little Roman town. It lay silent and peaceful, the drab greys and pale browns bleached to nothing by the fierce sun. A lizard flickered through the dust at her feet. On just such a hot still afternoon. . . .

She wouldn't repeat what Dr Schultz had told her. Alex's moments of despair had returned. And she noticed how his anxiety that the whole thing would fail expressed itself in anxiety about peripheral details. They'd be burgled. Iannucci would come in. They'd run out of money (this a certainty, in fact, even if they stayed only till the end of August). A man from the British Museum had seen him shopping. He'd strike water. There was no point in adding to them.

It had earlier just been possible, at least for her, to imagine and joke about a series of test drillings in different garages and stables or basements. It was not possible to imagine a series of twenty-foot shafts. Besides, Alex couldn't manage another.

Or might he? He was much tougher than he seemed. The anxieties were actually irrelevant. The holes got drilled. The shaft got deeper.

She wondered whether her surprise at the swiftness with

which she could restore his confidence wasn't misplaced. In fact his confidence – at least his resolve – was far greater than hers. His response was really nothing to do with that. It was a playing out of roles – hers to encourage, his to do. It was once again, therefore, part of their love-play. It made her glow, gave her a feeling of power to see him pull himself together at her words and swing his pick into the rock again. Just as she felt power, power and pleasure mixed, when she whispered in bed, 'You're so strong, you're marvellous,' and felt the surge of his strength.

Catrina suddenly saw that the little house where they'd met, where he'd picked her up – the House of the Wooden Partition – had scaffolding up it. So did several of the houses, particularly the tallest.

They must hurry. It would be too cruel if an earthquake or some volcanic event stopped them. Yet she wanted to hurry in any case.

Her speculation about their love evolved and became more elaborate over the months. She had always realised it had a function – to penetrate into Herculaneum. This was both its strength and perhaps its weakness. It bound them together. Nothing else was necessary. But she now felt the buried city somehow contained the heart of their love. Her fear was that she'd been deceived. That to Alex the love and its function were the same. Sometimes as she emptied the sacks laboriously out of the back of the van in the deserted quarry she too imagined the shaft coming to a stop, a blank, when they reached its bottom. Then Alex would leave. Only if she could get inside would she find if the heart was real, find what it was like, would at last possess it, control it, change it.

She saw Alex emerge from the administrative buildings and stand blinking in the sun as though he'd emerged from underground. After a moment he started towards the Antiquarium.

She called and joined him. 'You look a bit shattered.'

'He's a nightmare. A sort of word volcano in continuous eruption. I shall try never to see him again.'

'There's no need to.'

'Apparently in December it's the 250th anniversary of the discovery that this was Herculaneum. He's planning a big party in the *scavi* before that to celebrate. We're asked.'

As they walked slowly back under the blasting sun, the shadows of the cypresses no more than black pools at the base of each trunk, Alex said, 'Apparently Henderson was here. I was right.'

'Oh.'

'He's giving some lecture here. Gandolfino asked if I knew him. I said I did vaguely.'

[4]

As the shaft grew deeper it grew darker. Alex added thirty foot of flex to the light, wound it round the beam and hung it down to illuminate the digging. He also fixed the pulley and the nylon rope and every so often Catrina would lower the bucket for him to fill with the mud-rock loosened by the pick.

The second bucket she pulled to the surface, she said, 'Look, it's pointless my emptying it into a sack, putting the sack in the van, driving out and then emptying the sack. If I park the van here, I can empty the bucket straight into the back and then just shovel the stuff out at the quarry.'

'I suppose so.'

'And it would hide the hole from a casual viewer standing on the stairs, the unexpected visitor.'

Alex no longer seemed to notice such ironies. To him they weren't ironies. At night he undid the heavy pulley and locked it in the van. He laid the old double doors of the stable across the top of the shaft. This left the Acker Packsack containers exposed, so Alex carried them up to the bedroom and put them under the bed.

'If Iannucci breaks in and wanders up we'll say it's spare electric typewriters.' Catrina giggled.

Alex didn't smile. At night he pulled up the light bulb on the end of its flex, and also the bell. He'd added forty feet of flex to this so that he could have it ring beside him when Catrina went out.

Five days after seeing Dr Gandolfino, they had lunch with Signor Iannucci and his wife. It was a vast, disgusting and rather embarrassing meal but Catrina said it had cemented their relationship. Apart from anything else, she now seized every opportunity to save money.

On 12 August Alex reached twelve foot and the change of stratum. The flakes and chips were denser, harder to dig; the colour paler.

On 17 August, hacking at the shaft floor below the stable wall, he reached the third strata of lava – a vertical five inch irregular seam of grey mud-rock closer in colour to the second stratum.

'It looks as though something got embedded.' He pointed to the uneven margin where the two materials met. 'You can see where it has broken up this denser, paler stuff.'

Two days later came the *scirocco*. They'd both overslept the alarm and woke an hour later bathed in sweat. Normally at that hour – eight o'clock – the air was still, the sun steadily heating the town before the insweep of cooler air off the sea at around ten o'clock. Today, irritably and hurriedly dressing, Alex was aware of an unpleasant mugginess. All at once the bedroom door was slammed shut by a gust of warm air.

'I think it may be the *scirocco*.' Catrina was standing naked by the window, pencil strokes of whiteness from her bikini straps across the brown skin of her back and bottom.

'What's that?'

'It's a hot wind that blows from Africa.'

The digging, to Alex's mind, began to resemble something from some crass overdone film melodrama about Devil's Island. It had been very hot before – no wind, not the slightest eddy of breeze reached him down the shaft. But the *scirocco*, as it swept in burning waves off the Sahara and across the Mediterranean, sucked up water. In the saturated air, Alex hadn't swung the pick for five minutes before sweat was pouring off him, drenching his shorts, running into his eyes. He kept a jug of water and a towel down with him and every hour or so he went up and stood in the shower.

'How long does this fucking *scirocco* of yours last?' he called up to Catrina as, herself wet with sweat, wearing as usual only her jean shorts and bra, she pulled up the bucket.

'Not long. Two or three days.'

'I'm going to make the hole smaller. I think I can manage four foot square. It's all we'll need.'

She knew that the *scirocco* could in fact last as long as

two or even three weeks. It had once been an extenuating circumstance in cases of murder. Alex's bursts of anger, his continual irritability, the claustrophobia of the stable soon drove her out, even though it meant he had to empty the shaft of debris. She delayed returning from the quarry; out shopping, she lingered and chatted – the price of *parmigiano* had gone up again, someone had cornered the market in Milan; the heat had killed another baby of a family still living in a lorry container outside Naples.

Alerted by Dr Schultz, she noticed new cracks in the crumbling plaster of the slums, paving stones tilting and rising as the earth bulged. Scaffolding was going up. Carmela passed on the rumours. Some great inter-faction war was brewing in the Camorra. Another earthquake had been predicted. Smuggling was finally going to be stamped out. Cholera had broken out in Salerno/Naples/Torre del Greco/Torre Annunciata.

As in all disaster areas – beseiged cities, war zones, refugee camps, prisons – imprecise rumours were always sweeping the slums of Ercolano. But there was an increase in August, a new sense of unease.

[5]

As Alex cursed and sweated, the shaft grew deeper. Each day he tried to get up at six in a vain attempt to escape the heat. Each day or day and a half, the twenty-two-foot aluminium extending ladder had to be opened a further rung. At nineteen foot it curved alarmingly as Alex climbed exhausted to the surface. At twenty foot he hung a rope from the beam so that he could more easily pull himself up.

On the evening of Thursday 26 August he didn't stop digging until eight-thirty. 'Tomorrow we'll know. There can't be more than a few inches to go.'

For the second time that week they overslept the alarm.

'It's this sodding *scirocco*,' said Alex, pulling on his shorts. 'I thought you said it only lasted three days.'

He worked furiously all morning but by lunch time at two-thirty still hadn't reached any crack. There was no means of telling how much further since the drill holes were now blocked with fragments of mud-rock. Perhaps they would find the crevice itself was now full of chippings.

Catrina slipped out and, although she was getting desperate about their money, bought two 7000–lira bottles of sparkling Blanc de Castellblanch. If they found anything, they'd celebrate. If they found nothing, they'd need it even more.

Alex resumed at four o'clock. At five-thirty, washing her face and neck in the kitchen, she heard him shout from the bottom of the shaft.

He was crawling on his knees, head to the ground. As she leant over, he turned to call again.

'What can you see?'

'It's not a crack. It's something far deeper. I think it must be a well. Come down.'

Together they knelt before the eight-inch hole in the rock. Alex picked up a two-inch sliver of mud-rock and dropped it down. Two seconds later they heard a faint sound as it struck the bottom.

'It must be at least forty feet,' said Alex.

Catrina put her eye to the hole, but the blackness was impenetrable. She sniffed but could smell nothing. Yet it was Roman air. 'I suppose air is eternal,' she said.

'If only that bloody flex was longer, I could hang the bulb down. Go and get that torch from beside the bed. It's practically run out but we may see something. I should've thought of this.'

'We didn't dare expect it would be necessary.'

Even before she'd left the stable she heard him hacking fiercely at the rock face.

Excitement caught her in the bedroom. As she stood beside the bed, she found she was trembling, her teeth chattering. *We've done it,* she thought.

She stood and watched by the light of the bulb as Alex swung the pick in a frenzy against the sides and bottom of the shaft. She could hear the lumps of lava resound as they hit the bottom of the well.

When he paused for breath, she said, 'Alex – you've done it!'

'Bring the torch down,' he said, panting. 'We'll see if we can see what I've done.'

He had hacked out a rough hole approximately eighteen

inches across, though the actual opening into the well was little more than a foot wide.

They crouched down again and Alex directed the torch through the gap. 'Look,' he said.

Below them, at an angle of about sixty degrees and about nine feet away they could just see in the dim light a curve of metal rail and a patch of pale ground. The jagged top and sides of the opening, as well as the fading torch, made it impossible to see any more.

Alex forced himself forward, put his head into the hole with the torch at his cheek.

'I can't see any further across,' he said when he eventually pulled back. 'The rock hangs too low. And the torch is too faint to see very far down the well. But I think the sides are painted. Do you think the Romans painted their wells?'

'Probably. Let me look.'

It was true. On the smooth plaster just below her face she could see something green on a pale green ground. Then it merged and vanished down into the terrifying blackness.

Alex stood up. 'I'm going in.'

'Now?'

'I'll widen the hole, then stick the bottom half of the extending ladder across. I think it will just reach that railing.'

'For Christ's sake be careful, Alex. The whole thing may collapse.'

'Get me the bucket down. I'll tie the nylon rope round my waist. You should be able to hold me on the large pulley if anything happens.' He blessed his foresight in buying a sufficiently large and powerful one.

Catrina climbed to the top of the shaft and waited once again while he hacked furiously at the bottom of the shaft. Then she lowered the bucket and climbed down herself with the rest of the nylon rope. Alex began to untie it from the bucket handle. 'Get the towing rope from the van. It's under the spare tyre in the back.'

When she'd joined him again he'd tied the nylon rope round his chest. He knelt, so the loop caught under his armpits. 'Take my weight. See if you can hold me.'

Catrina took the rope in both hands and braced herself as he reached above his head.

'I can hold you. I couldn't possibly pull you up.'

'There's no need to. Put it twice round your waist and pay it out as I go down. If anything happens, you just hold and lean back. I'll climb back up.'

He pulled the collapsing aluminium ladder down and detached the halves. He tied the tow rope to the bottom rung of the lower half and, while Catrina held it taut, knelt and pushed the ladder out over the well. It came to rest at the bottom of the railing with six inches to spare sticking through the hole.

Alex kicked the top rung. 'Seems firm enough.'

'If you do it safely, I'm coming afterwards.'

'No you're not.'

'Why not?'

'Someone may come. You've got to stay and answer the door.'

'How on earth can I answer the door stuck down here with only half a ladder? No one's going to come. The outside gates are locked by now. No one ever comes. We've done this together. I'm coming too.'

'All right.' He smiled at her, secretly relieved.

She wound the nylon rope twice round her waist and then, as he manoeuvred himself onto the ladder and began to lower himself down it, played it out. 'It's a tight fit,' said Alex, and was gone.

A few moments later, far far too few, she heard him call. 'Okay – it's firm. I'll hold the ladder.' His voice was muffled, faintly reverberant. 'Bring the other end of the rope with you,' he called.

She undid the rope and re-tied the end round her waist. Then, too frightened to look, she went and knelt with her back to the hole, lifted one leg onto the ladder, then the other, flattened herself onto it and, with her eyes shut, heart pounding, slowly let herself down. She felt the lava-rock scrape her back as she disappeared.

Chapter Eight

[1]

Thomas read the letter from Dr Montesano with sympathy, and also a certain wry amusement. This was not just because the translator at the Museo Nationale wrote a form of menu English.

Dr Montesano apologised for writing so late when the affair Sicilian had already been in progress nearly a year. But as Signor Henderson knew, the British Museum was very unlikely to be involved. Swiss dealers were the main culprits. Also, he had mentioned the subject on Signor Henderson's two recent visits.

However, it was now necessary for something more formal. The press had got hold of, and much exaggerated, the Sicilian finds. Priceless treasures were streaming across borders. The heritage of the nation being stolen, squandered. There was an election in six months. The government. . . .

It was a long letter. Thomas dictated a polite reply. Yes, the Museum would certainly keep an eye open for stolen antiquities. As always. Dr Montesano of course knew well the Museum's policy in these matters. They would purchase nothing they had any reason at all to believe stolen.

Yet Thomas knew that Dr Montesano and the Italian government were in a dilemma here. Antiquities that had been registered and catalogued and which were then smuggled abroad and sold all foreign governments had agreed to return. But where they had not been registered . . . that was more difficult. How after all could you be sure they'd been stolen? It was often impossible for the Italians to ask for things back. If they did, other governments would frequently not comply.

Nor was the dilemma confined to governments. Museums were staffed, essentially, by scholars. They depended for their

125

papers, their expertise and knowledge, the depth of learning displayed in their catalogues, to a very large extent on the number and variety of artefacts that they were able to see and study. For much of this they relied, in turn, on what people brought them – to have identified and explained, or to try and sell. If they got the reputation for refusing to look at anything that might be stolen, or even for calling the police, the flow of objects would considerably decrease. Something *known* to be stolen would, of course, be reported. Once, six years before, faced with a famous object only recently stolen from a well-known private collector, Thomas had actually called the police. But this was exceedingly rare. In the vast grey area in which what was brought might not have been obtained strictly honestly, the whole weight of a museum's self-interest was to say nothing. They – at least the British Museum – would not purchase. But they wouldn't do anything else.

Thomas could do little or nothing about all this. However, his somewhat paradoxical feelings about museums were well-known in that little world. That, though necessary and in many respects beneficent, they were also in fact zoos; that ideally the relics of antiquity should remain in the country whose past they represented and if possible in the actual spot where they had been found or where they belonged – he made no secret of his ideas about all this.

Dr Montesano, knowing this, under pressure from his government, wondered whether some demonstration of public solidarity could perhaps be engineered. Perhaps a statement to the British press?

Here Thomas could oblige. Miss Brough had told him that the *Sunday Times* – no doubt having picked it up from the Italian papers – wanted to question him about the supposed discovery of something startling in Sicily. He could certainly use this occasion to say something in aid of his colleague in Naples.

He had hardly finished dictating his letter to Dr Montesano along these lines when the telephone rang. Miss Brough, still at his side, picked up the receiver, asked who it was and handed it to him.

'Mrs Freeling.'

'Cynthia?'

'Hello Thomas. I'm sorry to ring you at work – but it was such a relief that I thought you'd like to know too. Barnaby has finally agreed to attend Dr Ifford's clinic.'

'Yes, that is a relief.'

He listened to the details of her son Barnaby's capitulation, then agreed dinner the next day and ended the conversation.

He had a sudden longing to go. He rang Miss Brough on the internal phone.

'Have you booked my tickets to Montesano's conference?'

'Not yet, Mr Henderson. It isn't until' – minute pause – '19 September. There will be no difficulty.'

'Nevertheless I should book them now. Get me the same hotel as before.'

'Very well.'

[2]

Alex caught Catrina's shoulders as she reached the bottom and helped her backwards off the ladder. Only then did she dare open her eyes.

They were standing in front of a low railing which curved one third of the way round what must have been a light-well. Over this, in front and two feet or so higher than their heads, there projected downwards the jagged underside of the great rock which had blocked off the top of the light-well and so saved it from the mud flow.

'Do you think it crashed down in the eruption?' whispered Catrina at last, pointing. 'You said some really huge lumps were thrown four or five miles.'

Alex paused so long before replying it was almost as though he were waiting for someone else to do so. At last, his voice almost as soft as hers, he said, 'I doubt it. It would have done more damage. I think it must have rolled in. You can see there are only a few cracks in the side.'

The torch was scarcely bright enough to see across. It was impossible to distinguish any of the painting.

Nevertheless they stood looking across at it, unable to move or speak, for some reason reluctant to break the deep silence, to stir the dead, curiously inert air.

'We must hurry,' said Alex, with an effort speaking in a

127

normal voice and untying the nylon rope from his waist. 'This torch is about to give up.'

She took his hand as they turned. 'I feel frightened. Dr Schultz was right. You expect at any moment to see a Roman.'

Her eyes now accustomed to the gloom, Catrina saw that they were in a short but wide corridor. Immediately to their right a portion of the wall had collapsed in rubble. She was about to step forward when he held her back. 'Watch out.'

He put out a foot as though testing ice, took a step and tested again. The floor was strewn with lumps of plaster and very dusty, but it was completely firm, not even quivering when Alex jumped. Clearing the dust, they saw the floor was made of small alternate black and white marble squares.

At the end they had their second indication as to the events nearly two thousand years before. Incongruously flanked by two slender painted pillars, they were faced with a wall of the familiar mud-rock. Two-thirds was blank; but against the other third were stuck a good number of bronze plates, crossed by iron bars. There were other plates and bars on the floor.

Alex stood close, examining these in the small dim orange circle cast by the dying torch. 'There's wood here. See – fragments of wood, quite a lot. And it's not carbonised. Dr Schultz was quite right. It's rotted away over the years. This must have been a big wooden door strengthened with bronze panels and iron bars.' He bent and peered at the ground. 'You can see the groove in the floor where it fitted. And the imprint of it against the mud.'

'Why didn't it burst in?'

'I suppose the doors were very strong. And this house was on higher ground. In fact, I think built *against* higher ground. That's what we drilled into further back. The mud would have rushed over like a waterfall, exerting no pressure. Like you can walk behind Niagara Falls. Then, because it's higher here, by the time it had filled up below in front and begun to back up it had grown cooler. It had probably begun to go solid, to congeal.'

'I wonder why he shut the doors. Perhaps he was away in Rome.'

Catrina imagined the roar, the empty house shaking, as

the great Niagara of mud poured on and on over it and down into the town below and beside it. And then? Would there be gurgling? Or just silence – like the silence now – as the thick, solidifying mud rose slowly, thickly up?

There was a door on each side halfway down the corridor. Inside the left-hand one as they came from the wall of mud-rock came their first surprise.

It was a small room; even so the torch was now so dim Alex could only reveal it in small close-up sections. The walls were decorated with large white panels, each with a delicate picture painted in the centre and separated by broad black stripes. Along the right hand wall was a bronze bath tub.

'But it's *exactly* the same as baths are now!' cried Catrina.

'Except for the tap,' said Alex, holding the torch above it.

Catrina touched the double-headed phallus delicately with her fingertip. 'I've noticed he likes cocks. Did you see those lamps attached to the pillars outside?'

Next to the bath stood a round marble basin decorated with acanthus leaves. It was supported on a stem of some strange marble speckled red and white. There were two low marble shelves and a marble seat against the left-hand wall under a window. This was a five-inch by ten-inch slit which had obviously also been sealed by a wood and bronze panel.

'It must have been dark,' said Catrina. 'Perhaps he had a lot of enemies.'

'For coolness more like,' said Alex. 'Also burglars.'

The other door had larger fragments of wood still adhering to its iron hinges. But the torch was now too dim to penetrate the blackness. They peered in. Once again, Catrina had the disturbing feeling that someone was standing there, waiting.

'Wait a minute,' said Alex. 'I've found my lighter.' There was a click and then a thin three-inch flame of faintly hissing gas partially illuminated the little room.

They could see ahead a high marble bed looming in the darkness, its front feet two massive carved lion's claws, beside it a marble step held by two cupids. As they came closer, Catrina caught a dull flash of colour.

'Alex – there's some stuff there.'

Whatever had once covered the bed had long since rotted away. Except at the very end. Here, stretched across it, the purples, greens and golds just distinguishable but very faded, was what looked like a length of heavy silk.

Catrina reached out and took hold of it and at once – not like stuff or even cobweb, but like froth, like mist – the centre dissolved in her hand and the two ends slithered apart and vanished into dust on the floor. Even that minute movement caused the remaining board beneath it to disintegrate. It had been completely eaten to powder and fluttered away in flakes of the gold paint that had sustained it.

'It's incredibly dry,' said Alex as they peered down. 'I suppose it must have been damper at some period, at the start. Or perhaps not even then. It's obviously been very dry for centuries. Look – the bronze hasn't been touched at all.'

The table beside the bed, its marble top resting on the delicately veined elongated erections of three smiling backward-bending fauns, gleamed darkly under his lighter.

'More lovely cocks,' said Catrina, as Alex moved away. She stretched out her hand. 'They certainly knew how to make them.'

'And not just cocks, Catrina – fucking. Come and look at this.'

He was holding his lighter high beside the wall opposite the bed. A dark-skinned youth was copulating with a pale-skinned maiden – but copulating with such ferocious bounding abandon that the two lithe figures burst at several places through the restraining walls of the painted panal. It was painted with extraordinary skill, a skill both artistic and erotic. The sensual face of the youth – greedy, eager – was also oddly sensitive. The colours of the long brown taut body, of the tight, disordered curls, still glowed in the feeble light. To one side, leaning against a painted pillar at the edge of the wall, about to lunge into the fray, was the grinning figure of a Priapus, his giant phallus almost fully erect. A cupid sat astride this monstrous satin-skinned steed, reining it in with silver reins that pulled wide the ravenous mouth.

'Does it excite you?' said Alex.

'I think it does – yes. He looks so real, the one doing it. I think it must be a portrait. I don't think this was a man's house. It was a thirty-two-year-old woman's house. That was her seventeen-year-old lover.'

The flame of the lighter had begun to shrink. Alex held it higher.

'It's odd how little furniture there is,' said Catrina. 'Just the bed, that stool, the bronze table.'

'There would have been more wooden furniture, I think,' said Alex. 'Also cushions and things. I'll look at my books again. The walls are all painted. And there's that table there – the bigger marble one.'

This stood against the wall under a window as small as that in the bathroom, its wood and bronze panel still locked in place. The table had obviously been a dressing-table. Scattered about were several blue glass bottles, a silver comb, a silver hand mirror – the handle a figure of a naked youth, holding above his head a flat circular plate of silver, once no doubt highly burnished, now discoloured and dull.

'I think your woman was older than thirty-two,' said Alex. 'That must be a wig.' He pointed to a heap of jet black hair sewn into some material.

'A *wig*? It can't be. The Romans can't have had wigs.'

'In that case it's her scalp. Don't touch. It would fall apart.'

Catrina picked up a ring lying next to it. She put it on. 'Oh dear – I'm afraid you're right. I can get this on my thumb. Almost thumb and finger. A huge fat woman who paid her lover.'

'And bald – or recently scalped,' said Alex, taking the ring. It was a thick gold band with a relief of some classical figure carved from a large red cornelian.

Suddenly he said, 'Rings like this were fetching fifteen hundred pounds, two thousand in that sale. I think one went for four thousand pounds. And little glass bottles like that went for nine hundred pounds. I should think the mirror would fetch four thousand pounds.' He picked it up and as he looked at its flat surface remembered, fleetingly, the smooth bronze panels on the cathedral door at Ravello. 'As for the cock table . . .' he said after a pause.

He turned and they walked over to the three fauns, each balanced on a single carved bronze hoof. 'There's a famous one rather like it from Pompeii all the books show. I should think ours would fetch £100,000. Even if we find nothing else, this room, that basin and the tap next door, the lamp brackets, the rings and the bottles – there must be £400,000 here. If we could saw the bed into sections. . . .'

So it was true. He was rich. For a moment, looking at him, Alex seemed to glow. A force went out from him which stirred her. The sexual power of wealth. At the same time, beneath it, as though something long dominant was stirring in the entombed house, entering him, transforming him, flowing through him to her, she had a sudden strong sense of decadence, of corruption – ultimately, of danger.

'Alex . . .' Catrina stopped. What could she say?

'We must get out of here. This lighter's about to pack up.'

As they reached the broken patch of wall immediately before the light well, Alex dropped the lighter. Catrina waited nervously in the deep still darkness while he groped.

It flared in his hand near the ground, but he did not stand up. After a moment he said, 'There's a step here. I don't think this is a collapsed wall; I think it's a blocked door. We'll look tomorrow.'

Five minutes later they'd crossed the light-well by the precariously balanced ladder, scraped through the hole, pulled the ladder back and climbed up the shaft.

[3]

That night Alex got extremely drunk. Catrina had suggested they went to the Fauno.

'We can't leave this place unguarded now. Just suppose anyone broke in and found out.'

They toasted Dr Schultz in the expensive Blanc de Castellblanch. At one o'clock Catrina, fairly drunk herself, virtually carried him to bed.

They were woken at seven o'clock by the familiar *woof*-bang, *woof*-bang of the pneumatic drill again. Alex stood naked and groaning at the window. 'It's like being in the steam room at the Porchester Baths. Your fucking *scirocco* is still blowing.'

'Why don't we move our bed down into that room in Herculaneum?'

'Why?'

'Well, you remember how cool it was? And how quiet?'

'For Christ's sake Catrina, don't be so stupid. What would happen if someone called?'

Catrina had a sudden hungover spasm of anger and desire. '*Me* stupid?' she burst out. 'You're not just stupid, you're half-witted. You're obsessed about people calling. So what? If we don't hear, they're not going to break in. You could extend the bell. How long would it take to get up here? Three minutes? Anyway – *no one calls*. Those men out there if they want some water or something. Iannucci – *once*. Oh, you do *madden* me sometimes.'

She sprang out of bed. As she passed, Alex grabbed her and held her to him. Her large breasts, the rasp of her pubic hair; her teeth, clenched into a furious portcullis, slowly, reluctantly, opened, beyond her control. The gush of her mouth. As he lifted her and then, spread, she arched hungrily under him on the bed, Catrina, her eyes closed, saw for an instant the taut brown form of the Roman boy on the wall, the gaping mouth straining at the side.

As they were drinking their coffee in the kitchen, she said, 'You know how they were all called House of the Something, House of the Skeleton, House of the Huge Beam. Well, I know what we should call our house.'

'What?'

'House of the Cock.'

After breakfast Alex left her on guard and went into Erco-lano. He was slightly alarmed to see that Iannucci's men seemed to have embarked on their own shaft. When he asked what it was they told him Signor Iannucci wanted a swimming pool.

'*Altero? Profondo?*' he gestured depth.

'*Due o tre metri.*'

It was four days since he'd last been out and the Via Ascione seemed completely unfamiliar, almost dreamlike. As he walked up it, sweating in the clammy grip of the *scirocco*, Catrina's idea suddenly seemed more sensible. Also, it would feel safer actually guarding the things on the spot. But hadn't she said she suffered from claustrophobia?

Alex knew his fear of discovery was largely irrational but he could not control it. While he was digging, he'd often felt he was engaged on something ridiculous and also futile. Now, just as when he'd first thought of it, it seemed the obvious

133

thing to do. Once again, the buried town under his feet seemed almost more real than the one he was walking in. Again he felt that the force of his thoughts, the very presence of the idea in his head, would communicate it to someone else. They would know what he'd done, or start to do the same thing themselves.

He bought two large torches, some spare batteries and some candles. On the way back he found a three-foot iron bar and brought that with him.

'I think there's more scaffolding up,' he said to Catrina on his return. 'I suppose at last they're starting to repair it all.' Catrina didn't answer.

Alex dumped everything onto the kitchen table. 'I've been thinking about sleeping in the House of the Cock. I think it's a good idea. But I thought you said you got claustrophobia.'

'I didn't mean I had a proper neurotic thing,' said Catrina. 'I have to be really trapped in a tiny space. I get a bit panicked by rush hour in the Tube. Or if a very crowded lift gets stuck. Down there would be all right. I'd know I could get out. There's plenty of room.'

He made her put a note on the door saying they were away till evening, and they went down into the stable. He collected the pick, the shovel, the iron bar and the torches at the bottom of the shaft for Catrina to hand across to him, then passed the lower half of the ladder across the light-well.

As she descended for the second time into the silence and darkness of the entombed house she felt that it expected them. It had been waiting to be discovered for nearly two thousand years.

Standing in the cool, still air, and looking down over the elegantly twisted bronze rail which guarded the light-well, they could see clear, by torch, to the jumble of rubble at its bottom. The well itself was painted its length; long graceful trees reaching down to what looked like some arrangement of water.

Immediately below them they could see a second bronze rail and behind it glimpse the darkness of a second room.

'We can easily get down by rope,' said Alex, 'if that isn't a door to a stair or I can't unblock it.'

In fact this didn't prove too difficult. The stone architrave above the door had cracked and been forced half-way down,

134

where it had stuck supporting the rubble above it. The debris beneath was loosely packed.

Ten minutes with the pick and the iron bar and Alex had cleared a three-foot hole through which they could see a rubble strewn stairway descending into the blackness. 'Come on,' he said.

Once again, Catrina had a strong sense of someone waiting. 'You could find a living man down there.' With beating heart she bent to follow him.

The room, criss-crossed by their torches, was quite large. The marble floor was thick with dust and covered in lumps of plaster. And everywhere the torch beam lighted there were statues: two naked wrestlers, a sleeping faun, busts and heads, statues in niches, fastened to pillars to carry lamps and candles. Several pillars were badly cracked – brackets at acute angles – as were the painted walls between; some of the busts had been shuddered off plinths or out of niches in some long-past earthquake. But all the bronzes and many marbles were intact. In the middle there was what must have been a small fountain – three satyrs back to back in an alabaster basin, swollen wine-skins over their shoulders from which the water would have spouted.

'It really is a treasure house,' whispered Alex.

Their footsteps echoed as they crossed to the same implac-able wall of dark grey mud-rock stretching between the fluted, painted pillars.

'They had double barriers here,' said Alex. His torch picked out the twin grooves cut into the marble. Perhaps for this reason, though the outer panels had largely collapsed, nearly half the inner ones remained, still braced against the mud as though it might decide to go on the move again.

Strangest of all was the large marble table a few feet inside the mud-rock wall. Here there had clearly just been a meal. Spoons lay on plates, glasses – or rather large beakers – stood for wine; on a large flat silver dish there still lay, broken and disturbed by the eaters, the skeleton of a fish.

They stared at it all, both unconsciously listening. At last Alex said. 'Somehow it makes one feel two thousand years isn't so very long after all.'

'It *is* like the *Marie Celeste*,' said Catrina. 'A Roman *Marie Celeste*.' Their voices reverberated in the silence.

'It must have been the *tablinium*, the dining room,' Alex said. Again they stood in silence, looking at the recently abandoned table. Alex had just reached forward to pick up one of the silver plates when suddenly, clutching violently at his arm, Catrina let out a high, terrifying scream. Alex twisted round.

'Look!' she whispered, pointing at what her torch had picked out. 'Oh my God Alex – *there's a man.*'

Following her finger, he felt the hair rise on his scalp and down his spine. From the other side of the room a young man was watching them coolly through a six-inch gap above a partly collapsed door. He was smiling slightly and the whites of his eyes gleamed in the dark skin.

For a minute Alex stared petrified. Then, still directing his torch at the unflinching, unblinking gaze, he slowly let out his breath.

'It's a statue,' he said. 'Let's go and look.'

The heavy door had collapsed away from its hinges as the wood rotted, but sufficient remained round the massive iron lock to hold it half upright. They stepped inside and saw two skeletons sprawled on the floor. One, the slightest, lay against the wall; the skull of the larger had been crushed beneath the marble block which had obviously fallen from the space through which the statue had looked.

But it was the statue that held their eyes. Catrina thought she had never seen anything so beautiful in her life before.

It was a naked youth poised on his toes with hands held out as if in welcome. The smiling face was at once sensual and delicate, the nostrils slightly flared. The delicate veins on the half-outstretched hands and heel-lifted feet just raised the satin surface of the bronze. You could sense the tension rising through the calves and smooth thighs to the delicate and provocative bulge of the buttocks. The statue seemed almost alive, eager to follow the direction of the piercing blue eyes set in whites of startling brightness. Not quite life size, he was standing in an alcove, two chains from metal clasps round his biceps pinning him to the rough hewn walls. The alcove was about four feet from the ground so his eyes were exactly level with the top of the door.

'I should think it's worth nine million pounds,' said Alex, 'though God knows how we could sell it.'

'But look at his face,' said Catrina. 'Doesn't he remind you of someone?'

'No.'

'I think he looks like that boy in the mural.'

'You're obsessed with that mural. He's far more likely to have been a god. I've totally forgotten Greek, but I think that – Ἐρῶς – means Eros.' He pointed to the inscription on the marble slab, which had been shaken from its place in front of the alcove and now hung dangerously above them.

He stepped back and they stood looking at the skeletons. 'I think they ran in here seeking the protection of the god when the volcano erupted. He was killed by that block. The smaller one was overcome with fumes.'

Catrina knelt. 'Poor things,' she said. 'Strange how skeletons are still so human somehow. Look, this one is wearing two rings. Perhaps she was the woman the house belonged to.'

'Some woman,' said Alex. 'Look at those bones. I think it was a man.'

Beside the smaller skeleton lay a silver plate with an exquisitely sculpted five-inch torso of a naked boy rising from its middle. Alex picked it up. 'Five thousand,' he said, 'Perhaps ten.'

They explored for another hour. Opposite the little temple to Eros, if that was what it was, was a door onto a stairway which led, quite unblocked, to what Alex said must have been the *atrium*. Here they found further confirmation that Alex's theory was at least partly correct.

The windowless wall opposite the light-well was intact except for the door. This had finally given way under the pressure of the mud – but it was mud that must have already solidified until it could barely flow. A thick, eight-foot high, gritty wedge had been extruded through the door some fifteen feet into the atrium. There, even before it could do more than begin to fan out, it had hardened into rock.

The statues here were almost entirely of animals. In all, at a rough first count, they found thirty-two – twelve of which were bronze.

'I should think there must be ten million pounds' worth,' said Alex, as they ate lunch in the kitchen. 'Perhaps more. Eventually we're going to be very very rich *indeed*.'

The immediate problem, however, was the precise opposite – and far more familiar.

'I can't believe it!' cried Alex. 'How is it possible? It's like some terrible vendetta. They pursue you to the ends of the earth. You flee England, change your bank, practically change your name, start afresh – suddenly, there they all are again: electricity bills, overdrafts, grocery bills – the same evil grinning faces. So what is it?'

Their account at the Banco di Napoli was virtually empty. They owed Iannucci two months' rent, one in advance, one in arrears; the *alimentari*, handsome Signor Russo – fifty thousand lira; the *macelleria* – forty thousand lira.

'And don't forget the deposit cheques on that drill,' said Catrina. 'They'll have been presented.'

'Presented and bounced,' said Alex. 'Do you mean we're totally broke?'

'I've £150 in travellers' cheques I saved for emergency.'

'We'll spend it – and not on those bills. The point is, we're going to be *rich*. We'll take enough small things back to pay off all this and keep us going two or three months. Raise, say, ten thousand pounds. Then we'll work out how to sell the big stuff. I think Eddie Segal's the man to see.'

Alex hacked out the entrance into a hole approximately three feet in diameter; he also took off the lower two feet of the lava block at the top of the light-well. He bought another ten-foot ladder in Torre del Greco and secured it across the well by lashing it to the bottom of the bronze railing. With some ten inch spikes from the *ferramenta* and lengths of nylon rope he fixed hand-lines to make the crossing feel safer. He also bought 250 feet of flex; switches; bulbs and light fittings; and ran a wire throughout the buried house.

The *scirocco* finally blew itself out, but they moved down into the room with the mural all the same. It was still one of the hottest Augusts on record and Iannucci's swimming pool continued its deafening progress. Alex bought some planks and sawed them to fit the slots in the marble bed; Catrina brought her make-up, hair conditioners, face-creams and vitamins and arranged them on the marble table. She put scent in one of the little glass bottles.

Their sleeping in the House of the Cock involved Alex in elaborate security. He hammered more wood onto the already blocked stable window. He put additional bolts on all the doors. A second bell was extended and hung on the wall by the light-well, rippling, when tested, the obstinate silence with its trivial and incongruous trill.

'Pity we haven't one of those musical chimes,' said Catrina.

Alex didn't smile. His anxiety seemed to have been augmented by the security of the house itself, with its two minute windows and massive doors. He hardly went outside. No matter how drunk – and he was again drunk most nights – he always remembered to check the locks and padlocks and pull back the old stable doors which now permanently concealed the entrance to the shaft.

But a second obsession had now been added to the fear of burglary.

Catrina had had another fantasy when they'd first descended underground. They were entering the subconscious; they would now discover the buried truth about themselves and about each other; they would get to know each other totally.

But she realised quite soon that this was as absurd as her idea that she would somehow discover the true nature of Alex's love for her; or if, indeed, he loved her at all.

He had, he made plain, a job to do and he did it. With the two books on Pompeii and Herculaneum – the Kraus and one by Grant – but more particularly with the Christie's and Sotheby's sale catalogues and price lists, he set out to value everything. He also took photographs to show dealers. Especially did he photograph the beautiful boy Eros.

Yet, though he prowled through it continually, lifting, peering, it seemed to Catrina he didn't really take the house in at all. Exploring with her torch – the feeble current of Ercolano and the scattered bulbs doing no more than lighten the deep gloom – she discovered that there were themes in the elaborate decorations. In the *atrium*, where the statues were of animals, the colour was predominantly blue. Between the pillars were panels framed by painted struts entwined with seaweed. In the centre of these panels was a smaller panel, each showing some underwater scene. One showed sea-snakes and brightly coloured fish cavorting round a wreck.

The under-sea scenes continued on the curved, deep blue wall of the light-well – with winged sea horses, an octopus, lobsters, a dolphin with the head of a bull.

As she moved her torch beam up, Catrina saw that the blue grew lighter. By the floor above, the *tablinium,* it had become a rustic pool, from which slender, half-formalised tree trunks soared up to vanish out of sight. The panels between the pillars here, in the *tablinium,* some badly cracked, were of pastoral scenes – parks, men hunting, nymphs and dryads.

At the edge of the pool on the light-well there was a naked foot-high man amongst the pale green foliage, his long, half-tumescent cock garlanded with tiny vine leaves.

When Catrina pointed him out, Alex said, 'It's a Priapus. He was the god of the gardens. I've been reading about cocks; I'd forgotten. All the Romans used them in decoration. It was very common. They brought good luck and warded off evil.'

'But don't you think it's an extraordinary painting?'

'Yes.'

'I don't think you'd even noticed it. Just because it can't be cut out and sold.'

'On the contrary, it could be cut out and sold.' He flipped rapidly through one of the catalogues. 'Here you are. This was a mural from Sicily actually – £43,000.'

The colours, though sometimes faded, were often still bright and glossy enough for her to imagine how light and airy and beautiful it must have been when sunlight poured in between the pillars and down the light-well.

Now, however, the darkness was threatening, the great walls of mud-rock menacing and oppressive. The absolute silence and stillness seemed unnatural, almost sinister. Catrina began to imagine she heard noises, creakings. In particular, the statue of the young god began to grow sinister. There was something corrupt about the lascivious smile, the direct but sly expression of the blue eyes. So alive did he seem, the blood still pumping in those minutely raised veins, that it was clear the chains had been put on to stop him escaping.

Catrina avoided the alcove. Before long she was beginning to linger over the shopping again and pay visits to La Pinetta.

Alex's self-imposed job suddenly seemed pointless. 'Why

value it all so carefully?' she said. 'We know it's worth a lot. Why can't we just take some small things, rings and things, and go to London? I'll have to give Signor Russo something soon.'

'If I don't know roughly what it's worth we'll just get ripped off,' said Alex irritably.

But she saw that what he really liked doing was looking at the objects obsessively again and again. He enjoyed this for its own sake, for the money dream. It gave him pleasure just to pick it up and decide, even if it was for the fifth time, that it was probably worth two thousand pounds, or three thousand, or four thousand. She wondered whether perhaps he wasn't frightened that he'd succeeded. He'd come to prefer fantasy.

Though he spent all day down in the house, he was far less alert than her even to its details. 'Have you seen behind the window panels? It's a sort of crystal stained yellow like burnt sugar. It shows you must be right – how slowly and gently the mud was rising when it got up to that level.'

And at the same time, despite her fears, her claustrophobia, her distrust of the smiling youth, every day she continued to notice and delight in something new that was fresh, delicate and fastidious: the birds' heads whose curved marble beaks formed the feet of the dressing table; the little aerial carriages driven by grasshoppers between the feathery green leaves climbing the light-well; the dolphin twining its tail round the girl in one of the bathroom panels.

For this reason she was shocked to find one evening that Alex had sawn the elegant bifurcated bronze phallus off its lead pipe in the bathroom.

It was exactly seven days after they'd first broken in – an anniversary. They'd carried down two chairs, four bottles of Chianti, butter, fresh rolls, parma ham, mayonnaise, crab, lettuce, cheese and fruit. They drank out of the big glasses they'd found on the table, ate off the same plates. They'd put candles on the table and in some of the brackets on the pillars.

Catrina wouldn't have mentioned it, obscurely sensing it concealed explosive, if Alex hadn't started them on the third bottle.

'Why *did* you saw the tap off in the bathroom?' she said, watching him pour the blood-red wine into the tall beaker, the bright liquid clouding as it swirled behind the pale blue, slightly opaque glass.

'Why not? It's small.' His voice was already somewhat slurred. 'I should think it must be worth five hundred pounds.'

'Do you only think of how much everything here might fetch?'

'Isn't that why we came here?'

'No. I came here, I helped you, because I love you.'

Alex felt a sharp, deeply buried stab of fear. He refilled his glass beaker and half-emptied it almost in the same gesture.

'I couldn't have done it without you.'

'Rubbish. Any girl you fancied could have encouraged you. But it's true you couldn't have done it without my money.' It was suddenly all quite clear. She had hoped to find the roots of his feelings for her in the depths of Herculaneum and she had done so.

Alex stared at the table. His heart was beating hard. He wore his schoolboy expression but a schoolboy caught out. He filled the beaker.

'There you are – getting drunk again. When anything goes wrong, you simply drink.' Neither of them spoke.

'I think you've used me,' said Catrina.

'I haven't used you. Of course I love you. You've helped me make the first real achievement of my life. Half of this is yours. Three-quarters if you like.'

'Thanks, I don't want it. What do you mean "of course"? You haven't said you love me once.'

'I'm not good at saying it.'

'You're not good at saying it, because you don't feel it. Whenever I've had to say we're married, why have you always looked as though you were going to faint?'

'That's rather different.'

'Oh, is it? I also think it's horrible sawing the whole place up like that.'

'Why?' He used a calm, reasonable voice to force back a sudden upthrust of drink-fury. 'We're eventually going to sell everything in it.'

'Sell sell sell. Exactly. You didn't dig down here because you love me. You dug down for money and you needed my money to do it.'

Alex didn't say anything. Why did women always want love? Why did they always need to have it all said?

'The fact is that I do now know your true nature. You're just totally mercenary. I don't suppose you've *ever* loved someone. Have you?'

Alex felt he was burning. He was on fire. His hand was trembling as he half-emptied the glass.

'Go on,' said Catrina. 'Why can't you answer me? Why do you always look quite mad when I say we're married?'

Alex suddenly leapt up and flung his beaker of wine violently at the wall of mud-rock immediately behind her head. '*Why can't you shut the fuck up?*' he shouted.

For a moment he stood shaking, staring down at her beautiful face, feeling the rage and drink roaring in his head. Then two tears slipped from her eyes, slid down her cheeks and it all confusedly began to ebb away. He bowed his head.

'Why did you have to goad me like that?'

She watched him weave across the marble floor and disappear into the darkness of the stairs. Why had she goaded him? Wasn't it obvious? When she stood up, she caught the flash of white from the statue's eyes. She stared at them, and then turned and looked at the dark grey mud-rock bleeding where the blue beaker had smashed against it. She sat for a long time, running her finger to and fro in a pool of wine on the smooth marble of the table. Why had she goaded him? Had she been right? He'd looked about fourteen.

And yet, as though what had happened had been an invasion from outside, now nearly over, he woke up when she climbed into bed and took her in his arms. Although he'd drunk most of the three bottles, he was, as always, still able to make love to her and their row dissolved away in that act which does always, however momentarily, do what it says.

[5]

They were woken by a loud crash as something fell from the table and broke. The bed, the whole room, the house were shivering in the darkness as though in a fit.

'Alex, I'm frightened. What's happening?'

'I don't know.'

143

'Is it an earthquake?'

'I think it must be.'

The shivering stopped as abruptly as it had started, but was followed instantly, as though set off by it, by the shrill sound of the door bell echoing in the light-well.

Alex turned on the light which he'd fixed above the bed and frantically pulled on his shorts. 'Christ alive, why does this sort of thing always happen with a hangover?'

'Because you always have a hangover.'

She sat and listened to him clattering across the aluminium ladder. She thought, One day one of us is going to fall. Nothing had changed in the bedroom except motes of dust were drifting down from the ceiling.

Alex was back in five minutes. 'It was Iannucci. He said it wasn't an earthquake but an earth tremor. Is that what *scossa di terremoto* means? He quivered his hands like this.' Catrina nodded. 'He looked pretty shaken. He said there'd been a lot of rumours in Ercolano in the last few weeks that another earthquake was coming.'

Catrina felt a chill of fear. She hesitated, then said, 'Actually Dr Schultz said something about that too.'

'What?'

When he heard what the American archaeologist had told her, Alex hit the end of the bed with his fist.

'Why the hell didn't you tell me this before?'

'I thought you had enough on your mind. You certainly couldn't have dug any faster.'

'But for Christ's sake Catrina – do you think I'd have hung about all this week if I'd known that? It would be too much to have got this far and have the whole thing ruined by an earthquake. I wish to hell you'd told me.'

He stared angrily at the tousled figure in the bed. Catrina said, 'Iannucci can't have come about earthquake rumours. What did he want?'

'The rent.'

'What did you say?'

'I said I was going to London to get more money and would pay him in two weeks or so. I said you'd be staying here to look after the place and asked him to keep an eye on you.'

There was a silence. Catrina braced herself against the high

144

cold marble back of the bed. 'I'm not staying here alone while you go to London, if that's what you mean.'

'Why not? We can't possibly leave this unguarded.'

Why had it all suddenly become so difficult? 'I don't care,' said Catrina, 'I'm afraid I just can't. This place would scare me on my own. It does give me claustrophobia after all – a bit. It's sinister – that statue looking at me all the time. And it might take a month to raise enough money. You don't know these people. I'd be too frightened. No one's going to break in.'

Alex sat heavily down at the end of the bed. 'In that case we'll just have to bury it all again.' He held his head in his hands, shaken by the hangover. 'I feel frightful. I must have some vitamins.'

The Vitamin B Forte bottle dropped back loudly onto the table as he picked it up. 'Why can't you screw on lids?' said Alex. 'Christ, what a mess. Look, it was one of these glass bowls that broke. One like that fetched three hundred and fifty pounds at Christie's last year. It didn't use to be here.'

'I got it from downstairs. Odd it should break now after two thousand years.'

'It's not odd at all, crammed on the edge with all your clobber. We're living in an antique shop, no, a *museum*, Catrina,' said Alex, emptying Vitamin A into his parched mouth.

'Sorry,' said Catrina, deciding not to point out that he'd said, three days ago, that the beaker he'd thrown at her might be worth eight hundred pounds.

During the morning Alex collected the two silver plates with the sculpted torsoes rising from their middles, three glass bowls, a flask, the phallic tap head, two of the five-inch statues with erections and the three golden rings. He carried the Acker Packsack kit, pickaxe, pulley, and sledgehammer down to the bottom of the shaft. He sawed the old stable doors so that they fitted across the shaft resting on the space where he'd cleared the earth away round its top. He covered them with sacks.

The emergency travellers' cheque money was finished, but Catrina said there should be enough in her London account from her allowance to pay for the tickets. The Banco di Napoli somewhat reluctantly took a Eurocheque card.

After an early supper at the Fauno that night, they drove out to the deserted quarry where Catrina had dumped the debris from the months of drilling and digging, and she showed him where she'd emptied the first sacks of earth from the stable floor.

A nearly full moon was high among the stars and the earth stood out black. The shadows of the brambles were dark and sharp against the old quarry face, but sharp as in a dream. Sharp too were the tiny claws. The end of an arched branch caught at Catrina like an importunate kitten. Once, her neck was pierced, drawing blood. Every so often they stopped shovelling the earth back into the van and stood sweating and panting in the silence. But at last with a scarcely perceptible sigh there came the first gentle touch of that long flow of cool air which would stream down from the mountains for the rest of the night, blowing the great heat of the day out to sea.

As they left the moonlit quarry, Catrina had a feeling that a dream was ending. Now would come the last act in their drama. Or perhaps the first act. All before had been a game.

They got back at twelve-thirty. Alex piled the earth back on top of the stable doors till it reached floor level. He parked the van obliquely so that anyone trying to reach the now invisible shaft would have to get behind it. Finally, he took out the distributor head.

'We'll get a taxi to Capodichino outside the station,' said Alex. 'There's usually one there by ten o'clock.'

'That'll take the last of our spare lira,' said Catrina. Already, reality was closing in.

Chapter Nine

[1]

Gas, electricity and telephone had all been cut off in the Stockwell flat. These were the only envelopes Alex opened.

'The rest will have to wait till we've got some money.'

Catrina said she thought she could pay the electricity and telephone from her allowance money. She'd check.

Alex was still at that particular disadvantage in his conversation with Eddie Segal next morning which comes from having to feed in tenpence coins every twenty sentences. The conversation, however, did not last long.

'So you're back,' said Eddie. 'I thought you said a week.'

'Did I? It took longer than I thought.'

'Well, fortunately for you – and for us – there were unavoidable delays and the Nigerian business is still very much on.'

'Nigerian business?' said Alex blankly, coin poised. 'What do you mean?'

'You can scarcely have forgotten your solemn undertaking, your word, to carry out a commission for Dexter's in Nigeria?'

Alex did now vaguely remember a preposterous proposition that he should risk life and limb on some terrifying, ill-paid and dangerous mission in the middle of Africa. 'Yes of course. But something big has come up Eddie. I need to put some things in your antiquity sale.'

'Do you mean,' said Eddie slowly, suddenly remembering Alex at Cambridge, 'my offer on your uppers, your solemn word – you are refusing? After my introduction to Dr Montesano?' His car, borrowed without permission, driven into the Cam. Huge, supposedly joint, bills always left to him. He listened while Alex shoved in another tenpence piece.

'I'm sorry Eddie, but this is really big. You'll make a lot of money. Could I put some things in your sale?'

'Of course not. The catalogues went out months ago.'

147

'Well, what can I do?' said Alex.

'I haven't the faintest idea,' said Eddie, putting down the receiver.

'*Arseholes*,' said Alex angrily, joining Catrina outside the telephone box. 'He hung up. I'd forgotten what a little prig he is. He won't do it. What shall we do now?'

'Well, we must get some money. Let's get one of those plates and the smaller ring valued and then take them to a dealer. Take them to the British Museum or the V and A or somewhere.'

'The British Museum,' said Alex. 'Eddie said that man Henderson was very good. I'll just have to risk that he didn't see me in Ercolano.'

[2]

One of the chores – but an essential one – Keepers and Assistant Keepers had to undergo in most departments of the Museum was looking at an endless stream of objects brought for identification. Usually it involved little more than the dispelling of illusions. Occasionally something extraordinary turned up. But for Thomas, that morning, it was to be fairly devastating.

Mark Warren, one of the Assistant Keepers, knocked on his door and put his head round.

'Can I come in, Thomas? I thing there's something you might like to see.'

He handed over one of the Museum's baize-lined trays. In it lay a ring and a silver plate. At the sight of the plate Thomas felt the unaccustomed Mogadon hangover magically disperse.

It was about eleven inches across with a slightly raised edge and delicately plaited silver rim. From the middle, its base surrounded by a smaller plaited relief, rose the exquisitely sculpted torso of a young man about five inches high. Thomas turned the dish over. It was in immaculate condition.

'It's magnificent isn't it?' he said. 'You know the Boscoreale one, of course.' He turned it over again. 'I wonder if this mightn't be Egyptian work. You find that in the first century sometimes.'

148

'He wanted it valued, as usual,' said Mark. 'But he also wants to sell it to the Museum.'

'Does he indeed?' said Thomas. He looked at the form lying in the tray. Alexander Mayne. An address in South London. The name meant nothing. Under *Brief description of object to be identified* was written: Family possessions. Roman plate? Roman ring?

'I'll have a word with him,' said Thomas.

He took the tray and limped through the antiquities department to the anteroom. By some oversight the door had been left ajar and he was able to step silently through.

The boy had his head down and was reading something in his paper. All that Thomas could see was an untidy mane of gorse-bloom-coloured hair. For one terrible, hallucinatory moment he thought he was looking at his son Philip. He stared for a space of five seconds, his heart thudding, his stomach contracting painfully, and then stumbled forward and half-fell into the chair.

'Are you all right?' Alex looked up, startled, and then rose hurriedly to his feet.

'Yes, yes,' muttered Thomas. 'I'm sorry. It's my leg. A war wound. It sometimes catches me like this.' With an enormous effort he forced himself to look up and face the yellow-haired young man who had now finally, at the least opportune moment, materialised in front of him. 'I understand you wish to sell this plate?'

'If it's worth it. I don't know what it's worth.'

'I imagine my colleague told you the Museum never gives a valuation.' He remembered clearly where he'd seen the young man before. He remembered also the girl he'd seen then. His work had given him a very tenacious and very exact memory for appearances. Typical that of all mornings he should turn up on this one. Fate was unerring in its ability to twist the knife.

'Well yes he did,' said Alex. 'But would you be interested?'

'The ring is not out of the ordinary,' said Thomas. 'But the dish is a very fine piece indeed. The only one I've seen rather like it is in the Louvre, the Boscoreale Collection. Where did you get it?' He had an abnormal desire to keep him talking.

149

'Oh it's been in the family for years. I think my great-grandfather brought it back from Italy.'

Thomas felt at once that he was lying. He looked still more closely at the rather ravaged, handsome face which so reminded him of his son. Of Philip as he might have become. The thick untidy yellow hair made him look younger than he was. 'Your great-great-grandfather?'

'Someone in the family anyway. There's another one. They've always been knocking about.'

His son would have lied as well. 'Look,' said Thomas almost gently, 'don't think I'm trying to impute anything at all. I say this to everyone. We have to be quite certain that anyone from whom we buy has absolute legal ownership of what they are selling. To put it bluntly, the Museum never buys stolen goods or goods smuggled illegally from a foreign country. You may find unscrupulous dealers who do so – but you'll get less than true value, very much less. Now, as I say, I've no doubt things are as you describe. In which case I'm sure there must be documentation – mentions in wills and old letters. I doubt such pieces would go unnoted. You might even find an old Italian bill of sale.'

'And if I did, would the Museum buy?'

'Well, the Museum can hardly ever compete in the open market any more. By the same token I have to tell you you'd probably do better at auction. However, there are advantages if it's a question of death duties. Is there anything of that sort in your family's wish to sell?'

'Well yes – that sort of thing,' said Alex, beginning to feel increasingly guilty under the concentrated gaze. He gathered the plate and the ring up to put back in the Sainsbury's bag.

No sooner had he left than Thomas wanted to call him back. He owed it to Dr Montesano to question him more closely. Had he been to Sicily? What had he been doing in Ercolano that day, those last two times?

In fact, neither these nor other obvious questions and warnings were uppermost in Thomas's mind. All he felt – and he was astonished, not that he felt it, but at the force with which he did so – was a desire to help. A desire, almost, just to get to know him.

However once again, though he got to the door only a few seconds behind him, when he looked out Alexander Mayne

150

had vanished. Thomas hadn't the strength to pursue him. All very well talking about the secret of a long life being learning to forget – but what was he to do when events conspired like this? He felt thankful his trip to Naples and Dr Montesano's conference were only a week or two away.

Since the evening four months before when Cynthia had showed him the strip of stained aluminium foil and they'd discovered her eighteen-year-old son was on heroin, Thomas had been drawn inexorably and inevitably into her fight to save him. How after all could he refuse? He'd seen no danger to himself in helping. Though not a day passed that he didn't think of his son, Thomas had long since, or so he thought, come more or less to terms with his feelings about him.

The night before, for the first time since her son had started treatment, there had been a crisis. He had failed to come home. He had also failed to turn up at the Clinic for his methadone. At 11.30 Cynthia, distraught, had rung Thomas for the third time. Wearily, to calm her more than anything, he'd agreed to go and look for him.

August in London that year was hot and wet. Seventeen years before, on that terrible night when he'd set out on an almost identical expedition after his son Philip, it had been the middle of ice-bound February.

This time Thomas got back at a quarter to one. He phoned at once. 'I've looked in all the obvious spots round Piccadilly and Soho. He's not there. I don't know his habits. He could be anywhere in London. Try and get some sleep. He'll come back.'

'It's unbearable.'

'I know.'

It was unbearable; somehow it was borne. Seventeen years before his own anguish had been unbearable; somehow that too had been borne. Yet tonight, standing in the hall he felt nothing at all. Perhaps that should have been a warning.

Coming into his bedroom, Thomas at once noticed the position of his slippers kicked off when he'd changed his shoes to go out. They lay face down, a foot apart, a little turned in – the slippered feet of an invisible man lying on his face. He sat abruptly on the bed, staring at the two slippers. He felt slightly sick and had begun to shiver.

It, too, had been a Monday – Monday 19 February. He'd

returned slightly drunk from dinner to find his flat had been burgled.

There was no indication as to how the burglar had got in and the signs that he had done so were infinitesimal. The drawer of the table in the hall a quarter open. Things moved on his desk. It was the bedroom cupboard door standing ajar that alerted Thomas. He opened it wide and felt for the inside pocket of his dinner jacket. The wallet was empty.

He knew at once it was Philip. Only Philip and Sheila knew his habit of keeping an emergency hundred pounds in that wallet. And Philip still had a key to the flat.

Suddenly he felt furious. No matter that by chance there was only five pounds left. Dr Ifford had rung him that morning. This was a crucial point in the treatment. He was trying to wean Philip off Methadone. The boy had not turned up that morning. He was particularly vulnerable to overdosing at this moment. On no account was Mr Henderson to give him money, as he had on occasion in the past. He had also spoken to Mrs Henderson.

'I've given him money exactly twice. It's not always easy, not to help your son.'

'You don't help him by giving him money with which he can buy heroin. I don't want him OD-ing now. You must get him to come to me. He can come to my house if the clinic is closed.'

'Very well.'

Philip himself had rung just before lunch. Thomas had refused to give him money. He had, after the familiar altercation, persuaded him, or so he thought, to go and see Dr Ifford. Philip had reluctantly promised. And now this.

Thomas pulled on his coat angrily and went out to the car. It was very cold, thick clouds moving slowly up from the horizon across the clear frosty sky.

He drove to a disco off Leicester Square where he knew Philip sometimes went to collect. He pushed through the din, scanning faces under the flickering lights.

There was no sign of him, but sitting at the bar was a thin young West Indian called, he thought, Mick. Thomas never knew and did not care what these acquaintances of Philip's thought of him when he appeared like this. They often lied to protect Philip. But Mick, who only took cocaine, had lost three friends to heroin. He'd helped in the past.

'Good evening,' said Thomas, not liking to risk "Mick". 'Have you seen my son around?'

'No, man.'

'Any idea where he could be?'

'You tried the Eldorado in Greek Street? And there's a new squat in Islington he sometimes crashes out in when he's got some smack.'

Thomas wrote the address in the back of his address book. 'Thank you.'

'It's nothing, man.'

He drew a blank at the Eldorado. The house in Islington looked scarcely more promising. Tall and gaunt, the ground floor windows had planks nailed across them. It looked completely empty.

The heavy cloud had now covered the moon, and the nearest street lamp was unlit. But as his eyes grew used to the near-darkness, Thomas thought he saw a faint glow in one of the windows on the top floor. He collected the torch from the car and climbed the steps to the door. This was held loosely shut by a piece of wire. Thomas untwisted it and went in.

The hall was dark and cold. It smelt faintly of urine. In the beam from his swiftly swung torch Thomas saw peeling stained walls, a broken bicycle, the staircase. He pushed the door to and set off up into the darkness.

He had been right. A faint band of light showed under the door opposite the top of the stairs. Thomas stepped across, listened a moment and then opened it.

The temperature in the small room was raised a few degrees above freezing by a fire dying in a grate littered with cigarette ends. There was a candle in a saucer. A torn pillowslip hung over half the closed window. To the right of the fireplace near the door was a pile of old blankets and newspapers. On the other side his son was sitting slumped on a mattress, a blanket over his shoulders, leaning his head with its untidy mass of yellow hair against the wall.

They stared at each other. Then Philip said, 'What do you want?'

'I came to find you.'

'Why? I don't want to see you.'

'I was worried about you. Also I wanted to know why you burgled my flat.'

'I didn't.'

'Don't lie, Philip. You broke in and took money from the wallet in my dinner jacket.'

'I came in with the key. I didn't *break*, in as you call it. It was only five lousy fucking pounds.' There was silence.

Suddenly Philip stood up, swaying, shivering violently. Then, his hair wild, desperate, almost vicious in his trap, he was screaming at him, 'Don't call me a liar. Can't you see the state I'm in? Why can't you give me some money? You mean bastard.' He sprang at Thomas across the room and was upon him before he could move aside.

Instinctively – and yet also suddenly giving vent to the pent up despair, pain, frustration and anger of the past eighteen months, letting it burst out – Thomas swung his fist in a hard right cross.

It was a blow that would probably have broken Philip's jaw had it connected. Even though it only caught him on the shoulder he was flung violently back against the wall, to slide down onto the mattress.

Thomas stood looking at him, anger and remorse instantly contending, making him tremble uncontrollably himself. At last he reached out his hand. 'Philip. . . .'

'Go away. I'm quite all right. I'm expecting someone.'

'Come with me. I'll take you home.'

'You won't give me any money?'

'No, Philip. You know you'll only use it to get heroin. Come back with me in the car.'

'Go away. Leave me.' He turned his back and pulled the blanket up round his thin shoulders.

Thomas hesitated and then slowly left the room. Snow was falling in dense heavy flakes as he drove to Regent's Park. He remembered there had been quite a lot of blankets. Several times he had to fight a longing to go back. Yet what could he do? He couldn't force him into the car. Or perhaps that is what he should have done.

The telephone was ringing as he came into the hall. It was a call box.

'Dad, it's me.'

154

'Yes?'

'I'm in the shit. You've got to help me, Dad.'

'I'll come and get you now.'

'Dave hasn't turned up. I've got to have just one shot. I didn't go to the Clinic. I didn't get my methadone. Help me have one shot and I swear I'll do anything you want.'

'You know I can't do that. I'll take you to Dr Ifford now. He'll give you something.'

'Oh fuck off then. *Fuck off.*'

He'd hung up. Once again, Thomas resisted an almost overwhelming desire, a direct automatic physical response, to go to his son. He did not get to sleep properly till nearly five o'clock. When he woke at seven it was to struggle slowly up from fathoms of horribly disturbed depths. He knew at once that something dreadful had happened, or that he had to do something that he dreaded. He lay trying to remember what it was.

Philip. He had to go to him. He dressed without shaving and left at once.

The snow had been falling all night and was still floating gently down all over London. The traffic was in chaos. Thomas's sense of dread increased steadily as he slithered with the other cars. 'Oh God let him be all right,' he murmured, hardly aware he did so. 'Oh God let him be all right.'

The front door of the house was half-open. Thomas stepped through and shouted 'Philip! Philip!' and then started up the stairs two at a time, his feet echoing in the silence.

It was as cold as death. He was dimly aware of open doors and empty rooms strewn with mattresses, broken beds, broken chairs, waste paper, cigarette ends, milk bottles, filth.

Thomas stopped at the top, his heart thudding. The door of Philip's room was shut. Slowly he limped three steps forward and opened it.

He saw first the soles of Philip's feet, a foot apart, slightly turned in. He was lying on his face, his mop of gorse-bloom hair uppermost, one arm flung out. There were two syringes lying on the floor beside the mattress.

Thomas knelt down and very gently, as though frightened to wake him, shook one foot. The body had already gone rigid and he moved the whole leg.

Suddenly – sitting on his bed, still staring at the two slippers – he heard an agonised cry just behind him. It was more a howl, as though some desperate animal had managed to get into the flat.

Thomas jumped up and looked round. There was nothing. It took him a few moments to realise that it was he who had cried out.

Oh God, he thought for the thousandth time, 'if only I'd gone to him. If only I'd done what I wanted to do.'

He kicked the slippers into the cupboard and went hurriedly downstairs. He poured out three-quarters of a tumbler of whisky, added a little water and drank it down while he forced himself to become calm.

He'd been asking for it, to search for Cynthia's son like that. Some memories, it seemed, were too strong, some guilts too bitter, to be resolved. They could only be buried away in cement and steel blocks deep in the rock, in salt mines, below the bed of the sea. To go after her son was like sending a probe deep down into the radio-active waste left from the fierce fire of that terrible pain, that terrible event, and to find it, not finally dead, grey and harmless as he'd thought, but just as virulent now as it was seventeen years before when first sealed away.

In bed, the whisky already working, he took the Mogadon. But before he shut it all away again he allowed himself to remember one of the oddest things about that final memory. It had come out at the inquest that Philip had died on his back. That is how the ambulancemen had found him. He had inhaled his vomit. But not then, not now, not ever, could Thomas bear to remember having looked upon his son's dead face.

[3]

'Well they refused to value them,' said Alex, when he arrived back at Stockwell. 'I saw Henderson. I think he did spot me at Ercolano. He obviously thought I'd stolen them.'

'So what now?'

'I don't know. It'll take months to get them into an auction. Dealers will give us less. A bent dealer, which we need in the long run, will rip us off. We've got to persuade Eddie. He's sharp, but I trust him. He's a trifle bent – sufficiently. And we need someone on a continuing basis. We've got to sell this stuff continuously over years. I'll get these photographs developed. There's a 24–hour place in Stockwell.'

'But that'll cost £20 at the rate you were photographing. We need money *now,* this minute. I've nothing left in my account and about ten pounds in my purse. Can't you just sell one of the rings?'

'I suppose we may have to. But I hate the idea of all that work and then getting half the value. Let me just do some more humiliating coin-box work.'

This revealed that Eddie Segal was away till Thursday. He arranged to phone him then. 'I said I'd a business proposition. That'll intrigue him.'

'Isn't there someone we could borrow from?' said Catrina.

'The trouble is that the people I can borrow from I already owe huge sums to. I could offer to do more location work. The trouble is, even if he has any work, which is unlikely, David never pays in advance and we can't afford the time to arse about really working for him.'

Later in the afternoon, Alex took the smaller gold ring, the one with a relief carved into the garnet, to a dealer in the King's Road. He got four hundred pounds, and at once opened a new account at the Midland Bank in Clapham High Street.

'One virtually identical fetched fifteen hundred in a sale,' he said, when he got back, pointing to a price list.

'I suppose they have to make a profit.'

'*Profit!*' said Alex bitterly. 'It's a total rip-off, as I'd expected. Everything really depends on that prig Eddie. I wish to hell the telephone had been restored. You sent your cheque, didn't you? How long do they bloody well take once you've paid your bill?'

[4]

Eddie, however, had been intrigued. After listening for some minutes when Alex rang him two days later, he said, 'The fact that you have behaved quite monstrously, Alex, naturally

157

doesn't preclude us doing business. Come round in a couple of hours, at twelve.'

When he saw what Alex produced from the Sainsbury's bag he became suddenly attentive. He examined them all in silence. At last, his black eyes moving rapidly back and forth over the photographs, the objects and Alex's face, he said, 'Where did you get these, Alex?'

'I'm afraid I can't say.'

'Quite, quite. Of course. It wasn't in Sicily by any chance?'

'I can't tell you, Eddie.'

'You went to Naples of course,' said Eddie, holding the silver dish close to examine the figure. 'Was Dr Montesano helpful?'

'Very. I went there to research a film. It had nothing to do with this. Will you help me sell these things?'

'Naturally, in principle, Dexter's would be glad to help you dispose of these for you – either at auction or privately. But I should have to discuss it with Willie Calman, our expert. These look perfectly genuine to me, but antiquities are not my field.'

'They're genuine all right.'

'I'm sure. I'm sure. But there are all sorts of aspects I need to discuss.' Eddie lifted a telephone, spoke for a few moments, smiled at Alex. 'Willie can manage four o'clock. Okay by you?'

'All right. And Eddie, I need cash badly, and quite soon.'

'I'm sure we can come to an arrangement.' He smiled and held out his hand, a hand so small and smooth and perfect it was itself like some valuable object bought at auction. 'I'm so glad we've been able to make it up, Alex.'

'Yes.'

Eddie watched Alex start with rangy strides up Duke Street. You had to hand it to these public-school types, the old varsity type, when they went to the bad they did it with style. He lifted the phone. 'Can you come in now, Willie? Something rather interesting's turned up.'

While he waited he picked up the paper the objects had been wrapped in. *Il Mattino*. He couldn't remember how much of Italy that covered, but he thought it most likely that Alex had somehow got involved in the operations apparently going on in Sicily. Stunt men, in Eddie's view, were virtually a branch of the criminal classes – like pugilists in the Regency.

He was impressed. He looked out of the window again, but there was no sign of Alex.

Alex himself, enjoying the reversal of roles, had been aware of the admiration. But there had been something else behind the expression in the rapid intelligent eyes; some message in the delicate pressure of that exquisite hand with its nails buffed to mother-of-pearl.

As he turned into Jermyn Street, he realised with a slight shock what it was. Eddie thought he was a crook, a fellow crook. His expression and pressure had been ones of recognition, of welcome and complicity.

Up to that moment, except for a twinge in the British Museum, Alex hadn't thought of them as doing anything particularly wrong. He'd known the selling might involve some minor dishonesty. But the getting, that surely was just treasure hunting. It was a non-crime, like stealing old banknotes or computer fraud. Now, seeing a policeman coming towards him from the direction of Lower Regent Street, he turned abruptly up the Princess Arcade.

Willie Calman was a thin, spindly man with an enormous bald head and glasses. At first glance, as he rose from beside Eddie Segal's desk that afternoon, Alex took him to be about fifty. Then Eddie said, 'Willie was at Cambridge the same time as us. He read Classics at Corpus.'

The objects Alex had brought were spread on the desk, as were the photographs.

'Willie and I have discussed this, Alex,' said Eddie, 'and we have some good news. Willie tells me two small lots have been withdrawn from the October sale – one of rings, and one of glass. He feels with proper announcement, some ringing around, we could substitute some of your things. What sort of prices, Willie?'

'This ring?' Willie held the heavy gold ring with the engraved cornelian Alex and Catrina had found on the bedroom table. 'I should hope to get two to three thousand. This glass bowl – fifteen hundred. This flask – perhaps four hundred.' His long fingers were like pale, skin-encased tweezers.

'So,' said Eddie, with his sly, fellow-criminal smile. 'Five thousand within six weeks. Not bad.'

'What about the other things?'

'We won't have another sale for about nine months,' said Willie. 'But I can certainly sell these plates privately.' He turned to Eddie. 'Pierre Melon would buy one, perhaps both. Twenty thousand pounds each. Perhaps a little less if he bought both.' He turned back to Alex. 'You know? The Swiss actor.'

Tense with excitement, Alex felt a huge greed growing in him, a monstrous appetite. He wanted to hear the word million. 'I really meant the other things. The photographs.'

'Ah – the photographs.' Willie picked one of these up in his fastidious tweezer fingers. There was rather a long pause. 'Eddie tells me you think they are genuine?'

'I *know* they are genuine. There is not the faintest doubt. All these objects on the table come from the same source.'

'These people can be very cunning. They plant genuine things among very clever forgeries. I should have to see them. But. . . .' Once again Willie paused, turning the photographs over and over. 'But just *suppose* all these are genuine first-century AD and earlier, like the objects themselves, why then this is the most astonishing discovery. It will rival the collection from the Villa of the Papyri or the Boscoreale Collection in the Louvre.'

His excitement, carefully controlled, was evident. Alex swallowed.

'*If* they are really genuine.'

'They are totally genuine. I can't tell you how I know. Not yet. But I have absolute proof.'

'Then, of course, that may also prove difficult.'

'How do you mean?'

'Well, take this statue of a young man, this boy.' Willie turned the photograph he was holding to Alex. 'It is about, what? Two-thirds life size?'

Alex nodded. 'About.'

'It looks as though it could be a masterpiece, though the photographs aren't terribly good. It reminds me a little of the Raicia statues at Reggio in Calabria. If you dig something up like that or pull it from the sea, you simply *can't* sell it to reputable people. Something so tremendous would just *have* to be known about. You follow?'

'And if you do sell to disreputable people?'

'You have to accept much less. Probably as little as one-twelfth of the real market value. This is because there is a long process of selling to various dealers to cover tracks, and at each step there will be a hundred percent mark-up. Let us say you sell a bronze head for twenty-five thousand pounds. Your dealer will sell for fifty thousand. The final dealer will get a hundred thousand. But even that is one-third the real market value. At auction, with a proper provanence, your head would be worth three hundred thousand. That is to say, you have to sell for twenty-five thousand pounds something that is really worth three hundred thousand.'

Alex felt his stomach sink, the marvellous hungry greed, the money lust, dying away. 'But do you mean you can't sell any of the good pieces? You remember that bronze head Eddie? Lots of the stuff here is far better than that in my view. Certainly in far better condition. Do we just let all that go?'

'Not necessarily.' Willie put his finger tips together. 'To create a proper provenance isn't as difficult as you might think. For one thing, eighteenth-century sale catalogues were much less precise than those now. They seldom gave dimensions. You can often find a vague description of something five or ten inches high and attach it to a life-size statue which the description fits just as well. It would take some work, but I'm quite sure I could create provenances for several things in your collection.'

'But what about the things that aren't remotely like anything in old catalogues? Do we just let them go for a song?'

'We *never* let things go for a song,' said Willie, smiling. He too, to Alex's eyes, suddenly looked reassuringly crooked. 'There are people – I know quite a number – who are prepared to own beautiful things they know are not totally above board. A lifetime is a long time. Suppose you yourself bought a first-century bronze head today. You would have it to enjoy for forty years. There are people who don't mind showing it to a few friends, but they don't want it *known* they have it. They prefer that it is *not* known in fact, so that they

161

don't have to pay the insurance. Insurance is so high today that you pay two or three years' premium and you've *bought* a major work of art.

'In fact, Eddie, I think that is how we should dispose of the bulk of the collection,' said Willie, turning from Alex to Eddie and then back again. 'If we assume it is genuine – and I shall have to see it all at some point of course – then the small things, some of the smaller statues, at auction. The larger pieces, taking our time, to private collectors. Texas is an excellent place for disposing of things of this kind. So – we cut a little off the market value. But we don't sell really cheap through crooked dealers in the way I described. And there are big tax advantages. Auctions are public. We have to declare prices. You have to pay tax on them, often a great deal. But I can get Pierre Melon, say, to agree he paid 10 thousand pounds for that plate when in fact he paid 20,000. You declare ten thousand pounds, the other ten thousand we put in a Swiss bank account.'

'So what do you think you won't be able to sell?' asked Alex.

'I see difficulty only with the statue of the boy. Given time we can dispose of all the rest. But I'm talking of the pride of the collection. This could be millions.'

'How many millions?'

'I should have to see it first. Who can say? Four million pounds. Five. . . .'

'What about Bill Davis?' Eddie said suddenly, in the rather long silence the millions had produced.

'I'd forgotten Bill Davis. Worth trying.'

'Who's Bill Davis?' said Alex.

'He was Chairman and President of the Branson Oil Corporation, apart from being a director of about forty other things,' said Eddie. 'He's spent his life collecting, especially since he retired. But his house on Ischia is almost completely bare. He's *terrified* of theft. The cellar of his house is lined with three-inch steel. It is simply the vault of a safe. After dinner he'll say, "What would you like – a Titian? A Raphael?" One will be brought up, admired, discussed, sent back. It's probably better than having them hanging everywhere and being passed with glazed eyes.'

162

'You think he'd buy the boy?' Alex felt the money-lust flaring violently, uncontrollably, again.

'I think he might. I've got things for him. Hardly anyone knows of his collection. He is the true collector – it's the pure pleasure of owning, the vanity, the appetite for it. He would never be so foolish as to buy anything very well known that had been stolen. But something of this sort. . . . Yes, I think he might.'

'I thought that little Michelangelo cartoon you got him was stolen,' said Willie.

'Not exactly,' said Eddie.

They had only one small altercation, over Dexter's commission.

'Ten percent?' said Alex. 'That seems a great deal.'

'It's normal.'

'Yes, but this collection isn't. I went through hell to get it. Also, I understood you made reductions to get big things like this. Five percent.'

'I don't think you'd get Christie's and Sotheby's handling this,' said Eddie silkily. 'But in view of our old friendship – seven and a half percent.'

'All right,' said Alex.

As he was leaving, after much cordial handshaking, Willie suddenly said, 'Oh, Mr Mayne. I hope you haven't touched the statue of the boy.'

'I'm not sure,' said Alex. 'I can't remember. But I certainly intend to. Why?'

'Because it may bring bad luck. I did a very rough translation of the inscription on that rather precarious-looking slab above it.' He held out a sheet of paper.

On it, in a minute hand, Alex read:

Do you wish to hold this Eros boy of mine? If so, may baneful fate carry you off in shameful death.

[5]

Alex opened yet another new account, this time at a second nearby branch of the Midland Bank. One by one the life support systems were restored. He repaid Catrina the money she'd spent to bring this about.

Unfortunately he had an encounter, followed by an unsuccessful chase, with an old-fashioned bailiff in a bowler hat. The fact of his presence then seemed to spread by some process of creditors' telepathy.

Their life in the Stockwell flat, as they waited for the Dexter's sale on 11 October, took on elements of siege. Catrina answered the telephone. The door bell they never answered. They came and went by a back door on the ground floor. This meant climbing a five-foot wall into the yard of a timber merchant's.

Obsessively planning ahead, Alex rang a firm of metal casters called Burley Fields and asked how much a bronze statue would weigh. Life-size, said Burley Fields, would be about 600 lbs. Two-thirds life size, 250–300 lbs. The better the casting, the thinner the bronze and the lighter the statue. Alex decided that the beautiful cursed boy would weigh about 200 lbs or even less – well within his scope using the big pulley.

He'd decided not to tell Catrina about the curse. He guessed it would upset her.

On Sunday, 19 September, with as little movement as possible so as not to wake Alex, Catrina spread the *Observer* across her knees in bed and saw at the bottom of the first page the headline:

Below Vesuvius a town trembles with anticipation
Scientists monitoring the over-forty-years quiescent Vesuvius, report some disturbing developments. Over the last four months an area of approximately 6 kilometres to the west of the volcano has risen over half a metre.

Attributed to molten rock shifting its position 4 or 5 kilometres down, the uplift has been accompanied by earth tremors at the surface. The little town of Ercolano, at the centre of the disturbance, is currently experiencing as many as 40 slight tremors a day.

With growing dismay 'she read that the vulcanologists of Naples University and the Vesuvius Observatory would only say that if there was to be an eruption, they could give forty-

164

eight hours' notice. The authorities required a minimum of five days to evacuate the whole area. Rumours were rife. People in Ercolano and neighbouring Torre del Greco were refusing to sleep in their houses at night. A good many, especially those who had experienced the 1980 earthquake, had already fled.

This was more serious than hangover recovery. Catrina gently shook Alex awake. When he'd read the item, he sprang shaking from the bed.

'I don't trust that bloody mountain an inch. Ring that crusty old professor of yours and ask how bad it is.'

'I can't. I don't know his home number. There must be ten pages of Williamses.'

'I think we should get out there at once,' said Alex. 'Suppose there was another AD79 and we lost the lot.'

After several cups of coffee he rang Eddie at his flat, said there was trouble in Italy, he was going out, he needed five thousand pounds.

'I can't possibly advance that, Alex. That's more than we expect from the sale.'

'It's precisely what you expect from the sale. Besides, you've got both those plates as security – say forty thousand pounds. I'm not in this alone, Eddie. I have colleagues to deal with. If I don't get out there at once with some money there may be nothing.'

After much grumbling, Eddie agreed to two thousand pounds.

Catrina phoned Professor Bill Williams at London University on Monday morning. She spoke, or rather listened, for a considerable time.

'He says it's impossible to tell what's happening. This particular thing hasn't happened near Vesuvius before as far as he knows. But it's quite common near Pozzuoli. It probably does mean Vesuvius is boiling up to erupt, but it could take years. Between 1970 and 1972 Pozzuoli rose three and a half metres and then went quiet for ten years. Apparently in 15–something,' Catrina looked at her notes, 'in 1503 it did this and was then calm for thirty years. So Vesuvius might do nothing for twenty years. I asked him if it would be like AD79. He said definitely not. Vesuvis hadn't erupted for at least a thousand years then. Not nearly enough force will have built up this time, if it comes.'

'Anything else?'

'He did say that if he were buying property in Italy he wouldn't buy it near Vesuvius at the moment.'

'Well, that's just it. We've got property near Vesuvius. We must get it out.'

He stood looking through the open window. There was, he thought, the faintest feeling of autumn in the light wind blowing in on him over the sloping grey roofs below the back of the flat. Suddenly Catrina said into the silence, 'Odd name.'

'What?'

'I've always thought Pozzuoli an odd name. It *sounds* like something swelling. I'm not surprised it happens there.'

Early that afternoon Alex went round to Dexter's to pick up the cheque. Eddie had prepared a document for him to sign in which he undertook to sell exclusively through Dexter's. He skimmed through it. He didn't see how they could possibly stop him or even know if he wished to sell privately in Italy or indeed anywhere else.

Honeymoon conditions still prevailed at the Midland Bank. There was seventy pounds left in the account and he arranged to draw this out in lira the following day. On the strength of the Dexter's cheque they let him have four hundred pounds in cash, the bulk to be sent to Torre del Greco as soon as the cheque was cleared. Catrina too arranged to get some emergency lira.

Seats were fairly easy on flights to Naples, and they flew out the following day, Tuesday 21 September, on the evening flight that arrived at nine-thirty.

[6]

It was plain the moment they landed that summer wasn't over in in Southern Italy. Even the air conditioning blew warm from the cabin roof, and waves of heat acrid with diesel rose up over them as they descended to the tarmac.

The first taxi refused to take them to Ercolano; so did the

166

second. It was too late, too far. When the third refused, Alex said, 'They're scared. It's a very good fare.'

They took one into Naples and caught the last Circumvesuviana of the night from the Piazza Garibaldi, arriving in Ercolano at 11.07.

The moon was high and full that night and they noticed the change the moment they came down from the platform – scaffolding three and four storeys high up the apartment blocks round the deserted space in front of the station.

The Via IV Novembre was empty too, and here again there was scaffolding strung out sparsely down the street. It gave the seemingly abandoned town an oddly rickety air in the moonlight, as though they were looking down behind the back of a cheap film set.

A man came out of the Caffè Fauno at the bottom of the street and started to weave erratically towards them under the tram lines up the middle of the road.

It was not just drink that dictated his progress. As they passed the Ufficio Turistico near the top of the street, they experienced the first of the hundreds of tremors to which they were to be subjected over the next week. The word described it perfectly – a slight quivering, as though an exceptionally large underground train had passed underneath. But it was sufficient to dislodge three tiles which crashed down onto the pavement fifteen yards in front of them. Alex took Catrina's arm and they moved out into the road.

Attillo was shutting up the bar as they came in. He was pleased to see them. 'I thought you'd left with the other rich,' he said to Catrina. 'Dottoressa Schultz goes to America in ten days. They say they close the *scavi*.'

He described the growing fear, the endless rumours: there was to be an earthquake; an eruption; nothing would happen; it was dying away. Not that the tremors, most of them, were that big. They'd felt one then. But tremor after tremor after tremor – cracks appeared, tiles fell, in one of the slum houses a staircase had suddenly collapsed. Nights were worst. The feeling of something menacing beneath you. People were leaving. Many slept with relatives in Naples. Those in the Via Ascione had taken to sleeping in the tomato fields.

They said goodnight and left. The crack at the bottom of the street now stretched right across it, four inches wide.

167

Catrina thought of the huge angry boil below them, swelling and swelling, its base five kilometres down, upon whose thin distended splitting skin they dared to walk.

They knew the moment they came into the kitchen that the house had been broken into. Glass from the window above the sink was scattered on the floor. Drawers had been pulled out and emptied.

Catrina ran into the sitting room. 'Typewriter's gone,' she said.

But Alex was pointing at the door down to the stable. They had left it bolted on both sides. It had been kicked wide open.

'I knew this would happen,' he said grimly, starting forward. 'Pray God they didn't find the shaft.'

Chapter Ten

[1]

The thin-faced middle-aged man opposite him had his eyes closed. Thomas had already been struck by something blank and expressionless about the flat pale lids not caused by sleep. Then he noticed the white stick, retracted into a magician's wand, tucked under his thigh. It was because the skin was smooth and unlined round the eyes. Functionless, they had long ceased to respond.

He had come out a few days before Dr Montesano's symposium. Partly because there were some details of his address he wanted to check in Naples. Partly because Dr Montesano had said there was some anniversary celebration the new Soprintendente at Herculaneum was hoping he'd attend. But principally he'd come early to escape. And already, as he'd hoped, Cynthia, the nightmare of her son, were receding behind him.

The train was gliding down a valley, terraced vines up its steep sides. There was a sudden faint increase in noise through the sealed windows, a slight pressure in the ears, and for three minutes Thomas had himself to look at until they sped out of the tunnel into the late afternoon sun again.

Now the earth had flattened, the terraces turned to fields of vine. How richly covered it was, how fertile – vines, olives, broom, forests of oak and chestnut. A Roman aqueduct for a hundred metres virtually intact. The mound in that field looked promising. Romans had tilled there, before them Samnites, Etruscans. Invaders turned natives, possessing it, why shouldn't they dig up its treasures if they wished?

And possessing it so briefly. It was as though the train was stationary and the past streamed backwards beside him almost too fast to catch. Romans, Gauls, Greeks, Etruscans, Samnites, Sabines, Oscans – each clasping this lovely rich

169

land for a few centuries. And if they wanted to dig it up, why shouldn't they sell or smuggle what they found? There was so much left, so much they would not find.

At seven-thirty, the sun was setting gold and pale crimson. By the time he returned from the dining car it was night and in the window he once again had only himself for company. The long broken hiss of the wheels made it feel as though they were sliding south through the darkness. He remembered the train rhythms of his youth, that insistent rhythm, smuts blown into his eyes. He remembered waking, a little boy on the top couchette, when the train stopped at night in Continental stations – Lyon, Carcassonne – blowing steam, clanking, strange voices. All journeys are journeys into the past.

At Naples, Thomas took the blind man's elbow at the steep steps down to the platform. The man murmured, 'Thank you', in English and Thomas wondered how he'd guessed.

He heard English voices, French, two Germans on the platform. We are the invaders now, he thought.

[2]

The bulb in the stable had broken, but by the light from the living room Alex could see the van was resting on bricks. The wheels had gone.

He ran down the steps, across the floor and squeezed round the bonnet. For a moment, his eyes not accustomed to the darkness, he thought there was a gaping black hole. Then he felt forward carefully with his front foot, step by step, and touched firm earth.

'It's all right,' he called to Catrina still standing at the door. 'They didn't find it.'

The bulb replaced, they found that not only had the wheels gone, so had the tools and the spare wheel. 'They would have taken the whole thing if I hadn't removed the distributor head.'

The earth he'd piled onto the old stable doors to conceal the entrance to the shaft had settled into a shallow depression. 'It's amazing they didn't spot that and dig down,' said Alex, pointing.

'I don't think it's in the least amazing,' said Catrina. 'I suppose it might have given way when they stepped on it and they'd've gone crashing through.'

Upstairs they found all the clothes they'd left had gone, the radio, a small suitcase. Only Alex's one good suit, which had fallen down behind the chest of drawers, had been missed.

Three litres of wine had been left. 'That's the difference between English and Italian burglars,' said Catrina. 'English would have drunk it.'

Alex opened one of the bottles. 'Clearly there are starting to be looters. We'll really have to watch this place.'

Several times during the night Catrina was woken by earth tremors. Even though most of them were fairly mild – it might have been some heavy lorries pounding past – she lay rigid with apprehension before eventually falling asleep again.

But just before dawn there came something much more definite. Catrina heard the structure of the old, shoddily repaired house crack and shift and there came a faint crash from downstairs.

She wanted to wake Alex, whose even, rather stertorous breathing was not reassuring. In the end she lay staring at the ceiling. What was this leading up to, what cataclysm? When? There were several long new cracks in the ceiling. This time she was still awake at the next tremor, quite mild. There had been a gap of half an hour.

When she went into the kitchen to make the coffee there were two large pieces of plaster smashed on the floor.

'I think we should move into the House of the Cock again,' she said, pulling the wooden chair up to the bed.

Alex, blearily half upright, reached onto the tray between them. 'Why?'

'Because it would be safer. It's survived two thousand years of this and it's fine.'

'But things aren't so bad, are they?'

'You were heavily asleep all night. It was terrifying. One shock really shook the house. It'll collapse soon. Also my blue dress is down there and some of my make-up.'

'Well – it's true, it would certainly be the safest place. But I don't want to open the shaft till the last possible moment. Once open, we obviously couldn't leave it a second unguarded. As I said last night, as this gets worse the place'll be swarming with looters. And we've still got a bit of time.'

'How do you know? I think it could go up any minute.'

'The *Observer* said they could give two days' warning before an eruption and there's no sign of them evacuating yet. Also you said Dr Schultz was in touch with the Observatory, and she isn't going for ten days.'

'I know. It's odd. Something must have held her up. The way she spoke to me sounded as if she was off more or less then. Anyway, what are you going to do?'

'I'm going to try and sell the statue of the boy. That's the big one. If we can sell that for half, even a third of its value, we're made for life. We've got to move fast. I'll try and get the names of the biggest dealers in smuggled stuff out of that policeman Dr Montesano said he'd introduce us to. I'll see Eddie's man Davis as soon as I can.'

'But that's mad, Alex,' said Catrina. 'I want to get out now. Why don't we just load up with as much as we can carry and get out?'

'What's the point? Getting in here at all was gambling everything, going for the top. You said so yourself.' How could he explain the hunger as strong as sex that had flared in him when Willie had said five million pounds? It was on him now.

'Yes – but there wasn't about to be a colossal earthquake or whatever then. Surely you can make nearly as much with the other things, and we could be away safe.'

'No,' said Alex obstinately. 'It's got to be the statue. A killing. There's plenty of time for the rest. Suppose I can't sell the boy, or they give two days' warning. A day is ample to load all the bronzes and anything we can carry into the van, and then away.'

'You won't get far without any wheels.'

'That's the second thing I'll do after getting hold of that policeman. Go and deposit our money and see if I can buy some more wheels. Thank goodness it's a Ford.'

But in fact he had hardly finished shaving when there was loud knocking at the kitchen door and Signor Iannucci was standing there.

He had called, it seemed, by chance; also by chance carrying his rent book. But his pleasure at receiving a cheque for 720,000 lira was almost immediately swamped by his outrage at the burglary.

He took it as a personal insult. When Alex got Catrina to ask him if his brother-in-law the *meccanico* would have five wheels that would fit their Ford van, Signor Iannucci swept the idea angrily aside. All the possessions would be found and returned. He had a good idea who had perpetrated this *offesa*. Everything – wheels, typewriter, tool box, clothes – would be returned. Meanwhile, his men – still apparently building while the rest of Ercolano was shaking to pieces – would repair the door and the window at once.

'This will test his powers,' said Alex. 'See you later. I'm going to the Fauno to telephone.'

Catrina made a shopping list and followed him soon afterwards.

Ercolano was still functioning but had the feeling and appearance of a place at war, somehow incongruous under the peaceful blue sky and high hot sun. Several shops had shut, their windows boarded up. Two-thirds of the market was empty, the stalls and barrows still at work all pulled well away from the walls. There was far more scaffolding than had been apparent at night, except in the poorest streets like the Via Ascione. Everyone Catrina spoke to had different, usually terrifying news about what was going to happen. Yet they all seemed astonishingly calm about it to Catrina, who wouldn't have stayed in the place an instant if she could have persuaded Alex to go.

And regularly, twice an hour, the whole little town, the buildings, the scattered hurrying people in it, trembled as though fearful of what might come.

From one point, at the bottom of the Via IV Novembre where it joined the Corso Resina, it was possible to see Vesuvius. For some reason, despite its history, Catrina had always seen the mountain as beneficent: a squat mother-form brooding protectively over her children determined nothing should harm them.

But now it seemed to have moved closer and tilted forward slightly, howitzer-like. It was even possible to imagine, to trace in imagination, the trajectory of the four– or five-ton projectiles that would roar up from its mighty barrel and

173

thunder down on them as that great rock had thundered down and blocked the light-well two thousand years before.

Alex was already back when she returned and was pouring wine for himself and Iannucci's workman.

'I should have taken you,' he said, helping her with the bulging plastic carrier bags. 'I'd forgotten Montesano hardly spoke English. In the end he had to get a secretary to interpret between us on another telephone.'

'Did you arrange anything?'

'He's going to try and fix a meeting with Capitano Barbatelli. I'm to ring the *carabinieri* later today.'

'Ercolano's absolutely buzzing,' said Catrina. 'Carmela, you know, my friend, says Mario has heard there is definitely going to be an eruption – but not for a month. Maria at the *alimentari* said they were preparing a camp at the Parco di Capodimonte in Naples and everywhere will be evacuated at the end of the week. Carlo Abate, where I get the wine, said it wasn't Vesuvius but there'd be another 1980 earthquake. The Church of Santa Caterina is practically on fire with candles. Lots of them have left.'

Late in the afternoon, when Iannucci's men had finished their work, Alex and Catrina went down to the Fauno.

Capitano Barbatelli would be pleased to see them at the *carabinieri* offices in the Piazza Ignazio at four o'clock the next day. Eddie Segal was not so accommodating.

'I don't understand why you have to see Davis now. We can't rush something like this. It has to be led up to.'

'We haven't time. I'm in dead trouble, Eddie. Some of these men I'm dealing with are pretty rough. We may not be able to get our hands on all the stuff. I must know if he's prepared to pay a proper sum before I decide what to do.'

'He certainly won't say anything without seeing it. In fact, he won't even if he does see it. He'll want Willie or someone comparable to vet it. Shall I send Willie out now?'

'No. Just explain the situation to Mr Davis and, if he's interested enough, arrange for me to see him as soon as possible.'

'How can I explain the situation? You tell me nothing. In any case, I don't like it, out of the blue like this,' said Eddie. 'It's too hurried. Too impersonal.'

'Look, Eddie. You've got to trust me. I'm having great difficulty with some of my colleagues. If you won't do it, I'll ring him myself.'

'You can't, he's ex-directory.'

'Then I'll go to Ischia and call on him. I'll find him somehow. Eddie – do you want us to go on working together, or do you want me to go ahead alone?'

'You can't do that. You signed a contract.'

'I'd be interested to see how you'd stop me.'

'Very well, very well,' Eddie's voice was high with irritation. 'I'll try. He's extremely elusive. Where are you?'

'I can get to Ischia quickly enough. I'll ring you tomorrow. And remember – this is urgent.'

'Not tomorrow. Tomorrow is impossible. Friday.'

They were just sitting down to supper when there was the sound of a car and then vigorous honking.

It was a triumphant Iannucci. He'd discovered who'd broken into their house. He had already recovered the wheels of the van. They were in his car. If Signor Mayne would be so kind. . . . He'd get back everything, probably tomorrow.

When they'd rolled the wheels into the stable and Signor Iannucci had refused a glass of wine, Catrina asked him who the burglar was. Iannucci wouldn't say but he could promise them – narrowed eyes, finger along his nose, and then a curious scissor movement with his fingers in the air – he wouldn't do that sort of thing for a very long time.

'What a sinister gesture,' said Catrina. 'What did it mean?'

'Castration,' said Alex.

[3]

Maresciallo Capitano Barbatelli of Napoli I, the *carabinieri* of the Special Operations Group, had a small office overlooking the Piazza Santa Ignazio. Aged about forty, he had short dark hair, a neat grey suit, perfectly manicured hands and a gentle musical voice. Art exhibition posters covered his walls. He smoked continuously, the smoke streaming after his hands as he gestured.

He spoke in long articulate periods, pausing to let Catrina translate. He understood they were making a film on smug-

175

gling antiquities for the BBC. This was no doubt connected with the interest of the Italian Government in the matter at present. He would be happy to help. But to understand the smuggling it was necessary to know first about the stealing of antiquities.

There was a vast amount of robbery in archaeological areas all over Italy. It was not organised, it was not as yet big crime. It was done by people who lived in the area. They would have other jobs. Then once or twice a month, usually at night, they would go to the *scavi*, or a tomb, or some villa they had stumbled on and dig something up. Often these places had been known for generations and passed on from father to son.

There was little danger. They did not consider themselves criminal exactly – nor, it was clear, did Capitano Barbatelli. Nevertheless, every now and then large amounts of money were involved.

The important figure here was the *intermediario*. These were the men with contacts, amateur archaeologists who disposed of the goods. They would inspect them and assign them to a class – 1, 2 or 3. One and two would be sold in Italy, often in the same area they were found.

Class three were the important finds – a bronze torso, say, found accidentally by some underwater fisherman. Couriers from abroad, specialists in antiquities, would come and inspect. Nearly always they were from Swiss dealers. They were trained to spot fakes. Even so, sixty percent of what they bought was fake. There was a huge and very skilful industry in faking antiquities.

But the intermediaries were the ones who made money and the best people for Signor Mayne to talk to. They were clever men who usually organised the smuggling. They were specialists – one dealing in Etruscan objects say, another in Greco-Roman antiquities. You could tell a good intermediary by his collection of books. They very often had other jobs, but were in fact very rich. He knew one who was supposed to be in charge of a cemetery. He hadn't seen a coffin in years! He had contacts all over Italy. All over Europe, indeed.

Capitano Barbatelli's job was catching smugglers. It was clear that it was the ingenuity of the smugglers – and so the ingenuity needed to outwit them – that delighted him.

176

'Tell him,' he said to Catrina, 'some of these intermediaries – astounding what they do. I remember a case of a valuable statue being *rushed* across the border in an ambulance, a doctor on board, sirens wailing, *en route* to a Swiss clinic. Then there was an entire Etruscan tomb, all walls painted. They had it cut into six huge blocks and sent to Switzerland as pre-fabricated building blocks. I actually found it in crates in Geneva like that.'

There was a fund of tales. Alex found his attention wandering.

'But you see,' ended Capitano Barbatelli, 'to go to such lengths shows what a lot of money can be involved. Yet until recently organised crime, the Mafia, the Camorra, had been uninterested. Now – since the Sicilian business – the Camorra in particular are getting very interested. And very angry. This is bad.'

'But I thought they'd been smashed,' said Catrina. 'There was a huge trial some years ago.'

Capitano Barbatelli said yes, it was true there was a trial. But the Camorra had soon revived. Now its tentacles covered Italy again – smuggling, robbery, prostitution, kidnapping, intimidation of shopkeepers.

'In Ercolano, where you are, the shopkeepers will probably pay dues to some local Camorra gang. It isn't bad there. I could take you to some really bad areas. Torre Annunziata down the coast is far worse.'

But before Capitano Barbatelli could expatiate further, Catrina suddenly asked him something. For several minutes they jabbered in front of Alex. 'What was all that about?' he asked when they paused.

'I told him about Iannucci. He said he sounded very like a leader of the local Camorra gang. That was why robbing us was so insulting – poaching on his patch. He said if they don't murder their rivals they kneecap them. And he was interesting about his building work and our rent book. Apparently the Camorra are very into illegal building deals. Our bit of Ercolano is probably going to be sold to the *scavi*. Iannucci is after compensation.'

Barbatelli explained that the recent discoveries of illegal antiquities in Sicily had suddenly alerted the Mafia and the Camorra to the value of this particular criminal activity. And it was extremely valuable – clearly some rich villa had been uncovered. The Camorra were especially incensed that they hadn't been cut in, since they had a tradition of smuggling, respected even by the Mafia.

'Ask him what I should do? How can I get in on all this?'

Capitano Barbatelli had the very person – the cemetery custodian he'd mentioned earlier. His field was Greco-Roman antiquities, which meant he was extremely interested in the Sicilian development. He was a distant cousin of the Bellomunno, the rich undertaker family. He was called Tommaso Bellomunno. He was also high up in the Camorra. But most important, he was a charming man, cultivated, who spoke excellent English.

'What should I say I'm doing?'

'Tell Signor Mayne,' said Capitano Barbatelli, scribbling addresses and phone numbers on a piece of paper, 'perhaps not to mention the BBC. That is perhaps too much publicity. Tell him he is writing a book. Don't believe two-thirds of what he tells you. He will boast. But he will give you a very good idea of the situation.'

As they found their way back to Ercolano through the Naples traffic, Alex said, 'We haven't time to arse about with my pretending to be a writer. We'll ring him up tonight and say we've something that may interest him. A business proposition.'

[4]

Catrina sat outside, her table on the very edge of the pavement for fear of tiles, while Alex went into the Caffè Fauno to telephone.

The line to London was atrocious. 'I'll ring again,' he shouted. He dialled seven times unsuccessfully. When he finally got Eddie again it was even worse. 'What?' shouted Alex. 'What? You'll have to shout.' Eddie had fixed for him to have dinner with Mr Davis. It was impossible to hear how Eddie had introduced him. Alex wasn't even sure if he'd got the address right. It sounded like Forio. 'I'll ring again later,' he shouted. 'I can't hear you.'

178

Signor Tommas Bellomunno wasn't in. Alex shouted to Catrina to come and take over.

'What shall I say?'

'Say we would like to meet him as soon as possible, today if he can manage it. Tell him we have a business proposition we think would interest him.'

Catrina spoke volubly, listened, said goodbye and put the phone down.

'Well?'

'His manservant or secretary or whoever it was suggested we turn up at six-thirty. He thinks he'll be in then. He thinks he'll see us. I couldn't get him to be more definite.'

'How did you put it?'

'Just as you told me to. I also called you an English gentleman.'

As they came out into the sun, the ground suddenly shivered beneath their feet again. It was slight this time, but Catrina was sure the shocks were growing stronger and more feequent. She took his arm. 'Let's get out of here, Alex. It frightens me. Let's go into Naples and buy some shirts for me and have a late lunch there.'

'All right, we'll eat at that place behind the Theatre. *Amici Miei.*'

Signor Bellomunno had an enormous first-floor apartment near the front in the Piazza dei Martiri. It was so grand you weren't allowed to park. Alex found an empty meter in the Via Carlo Poerio and they walked back.

'It's about five thousand to one to find a meter in this part of Naples,' said Catrina.

A concierge waved them towards a wide, shallow marble staircase.

Outside number four Alex said, 'I haven't the faintest idea how these people operate. I suppose the only thing to do is to say what we want and see what happens.'

Catrina nodded. She had a sudden strong impression they were being watched.

After several minutes the door was opened by a diminutive maidservant. Catrina started to explain who they were, but the girl interrupted her. '*Si, si – prego venite da questa parte.*'

The high rooms, cool after the afternoon sun, sparsely scattered with reproduction Louis Quinze furniture, were decorated like most Italian houses to impress and not to live in. There were some marble busts and heads which looked genuine.

Signor Bellomunno was in the third and most human room – made so by shelves of books. Tall, sliqhtly stooping, silver-haired, he had the air of a distinguished retired diplomat in a film. His left foot was in plaster. It was difficult to imagine he held a high position in an organised network of often violent criminals.

'Please come and sit down.' He spoke excellent, musical English. 'Please have a glass of Cinzano.'

When the tiny glasses were filled, he inclined to Alex. 'You are here for long, Mr Mayne?'

'Only two days,' said Alex.

Signor Bellomunno inclined to Catrina. 'And where are you staying?'

'At the Excelsior,' said Catrina.

He addressed them both. 'A very good hotel. You must see – perhaps you have already – some of our treasures: the Museo, Paestum, Pompeii, the excavations at Herculaneum.'

'Isn't that a bit dangerous at the moment?' said Catrina.

'Ah, Mrs Mayne – we Italians of the Campania have lived for thousands of years in the shadow of Vesuvius. We benefit from her riches. We have to tolerate the price she occasionally asks.'

There seemed no reply to this. At last, after a long slightly interrogatory pause, Signor Bellomunno said, 'I believe you had something to discuss with me?'

Alex held up his still untouched glass of Cinzano, a blob of gold, and swallowed it in a mouthful. 'Yes,' he said.

'May I ask what it is?'

'We wish to dispose of an extremely valuable Roman bronze. For reasons you will appreciate we cannot do this in the normal way. I was told you were the best person to help us.'

'Do you mind my asking who gave you my name?'

'I'm afraid I can't tell you. I'm afraid I am not at liberty to tell you a great deal.'

'Well I have some nice pieces. I am more of a collector now than anything,' said the cemetery custodian, waving his hand at objects round the room. 'But it is true I have contacts. I can sometimes place something. What is this precisely?'

'It is a very fine first-century AD, two-thirds life-size bronze statue of a boy in perfect condition. I have some rather poor photographs.'

Signor Bellomunno took the photographs but did not look at them. Instead he looked at Alex. 'Do you know about such things, Mr Mayne?'

'I am not an expert. I worked at Dexter's for some years.'

'Dexter's?'

'An auction house in London.'

'Dexter's?' said Signor Bellomunno, beginning to fan the photographs but still not looking at them. 'My dealings are principally with Switzerland and Austria. Your Sotheby's and your Christie's of course I know well. But Dexter's . . . no. What in your opinion is this statue worth?' He was now, at last, looking at the photographs.

'I think on the open market at auction anything between five and six million dollars. It might be more. I would not, of course, require that. I would want a minimum of one and a half million dollars.' Alex's heart was beating and his mouth dry. He longed to walk across the room and empty the bottle of Cinzano.

There was the minutest perceptible pause in Signor Bellomunno's scrutiny. 'These are large sums, Mr Mayne. Very large.' He took a glass from his pocket and bent closely over one of the photographs.

'Yes,' said Alex. He had a feeling Signor Bellomunno disapproved. He was rushing things. But what else could he do? He was rushed.

There was a long pause as Signor Bellomunno looked at the photographs one by one. At last he raised his head. 'Of course, I cannot tell much from these photographs. I would naturally have to examine this statue very very carefully myself. If I placed it, my client would certainly send someone to look.'

'Of course. But I will be frank, Signor Bellomunno. I want to know if you can find money of that sort, and if you would be prepared to pay me that sort of figure. If you can't, or if you don't want to, then we need talk no further.'

Signor Bellomunno put the glass back in his pocket and,

reaching across, handed back the photographs. 'I too will be frank. If something like this had been found round here, something as good as you say, I should have known about it. You may know something about antiquities, Signor Mayne, but you do not know the Campania. Here there are many many fakes. Good fakes. Even experts are fooled. *I* 'ava been fooled myself!'

'You think this is a fake?'

'How can I see?' said Signor Bellomunno, two tiny spots of colour on each cheek. He spread his hands. 'It may be so. It may not be so. How can I say I can get such a sum, or say I give you such a sum until I see? I cannot promise in advance. But coming from here, me not knowing – yes, it is probable it is a fake.'

'What makes you think it comes from round here?' said Alex. He wanted a cigarette.

'I understand you to say that,' said Signor Bellomunno, looking faintly surprised. 'You are here. You say someone tell you about me. Naturally I assume it is found here.'

'Your reputation stretches further than Naples, Signor Bellomunno,' said Alex. 'I cannot tell you precisely, or more than roughly where it was found. But . . .' He suddenly remembered something he'd read by an actor. Don't pause; but if you have to pause, pause for as long as you can. The room was very quiet. At last Alex said, 'The statue was found in Sicily.'

'*Ho capito,*' whispered Signor Bellomunno softly. It seemed to Alex that his eyes had sharpened, they actually glittered. 'You mean I would have to go to Sicily to see it? I would have to see the site. I think that would be necessary.'

'First,' said Alex, 'I must know. Can you get one and a half million dollars?'

'Well, that is a large sum of money. I 'ava dealt in large sums before. But I cannot commit myself till I 'ava been to Sicily and see it.'

'You will not go to Sicily. Myself and my colleagues will bring it here. You will be collected and driven out to see it. You will not be followed. When you have satisfied yourself – and I can promise you you *will* be satisfied – as to its value and its genuineness, then we will discuss terms.'

182

'I see,' said Signor Bellomunno. There was a pause while he looked at his fingers. 'Very well,' he said.

Alex stood up. Signor Bellomunno pushed himself out of his chair. 'You will have another drink?'

'No,' said Alex. 'We are late. We have to go. I'll ring you as soon as we're ready.'

Signor Bellomunno turned and limped to a bell-pull hanging beside the ornate marble fireplace. 'You will forgive me not seeing you away. Two weeks ago I foolishly break an ankle.'

They shook hands. Signor Bellomunno bent over Catrina's hand, just not touching it with his lips. He watched them go, smiling, one hand raised.

As soon as the little maid had shut the door, he turned and limped hurriedly over to an internal telephone.

'Giovanni,' he said rapidly, '*Io voglio che tu segui quell'omo inglese e la sua ragazza. Se vanno al albergo, scopri quando lascieranno e poi gli seguirai. Se hai tempo, chiama suario per aiutarti. Se prendono il treno per la Sicilia, anche tu lo prenderai. Voglio sapere dove vanno, chi vedono tutti sui movimenti. Subito. Vai.*'

As Alex drove down the choked Via Carlo Poerio, Catrina said, 'I thought you were brilliant. But I don't trust him. He'll try and cheat you.'

'I thought so too. But we haven't much choice. If Davis isn't any better, I'll try and get the statue up into the van. And if that's not possible to do quickly, load as much of the lighter stuff as we can and get out.'

'Oh please Alex, please can't we do that now? You don't know these men. They're utterly ruthless. This isn't a game. They're quite capable of murder. Let's get out now.'

'I know it isn't a game, thank you. Doesn't a million pounds mean anything to you? *A million pounds, Catrina.*'

'I wish we'd never found that bloody statue.'

The dense, hardly moving traffic of Naples rush hour was a suitable setting for their angry silence.

At the start of the Corso Umberto, Catrina said, 'Go left here. I know a way through the side streets to the Piazza Garibaldi.'

As they followed the stream of traffic up onto the *autostrada* and joined the race towards Salerno, Alex said, 'I think we're being followed.'

'Why?'

'Look behind us, a blue Fiat 1100 about three cars back. I noticed it when we took the short cut to Garibaldi. Then it practically caused a crash getting behind us past the station. Hold on.'

Changing down, he flashed his indicator and pulled the van abruptly left into the fast lane. A furious Alfa Romeo blasted its horn and turned on its headlights.

The van, given a following wind and downhill, could just make seventy. Ignoring the Alfa Romeo, Alex kept his foot to the floor. As the Romeo swerved from side to side trying to force its way through, he caught glimpses of the Fiat racing in pursuit.

Abruptly Alex braked and pulled in right between a lorry and a VW Golf. The Alfa roared past, its driver shaking his fist. He could see where the Fiat had once again tucked itself in three cars back.

'There you are. No doubt about it.' His heart was beating.

'But why? Who is it?'

'It can't be Barbatelli. He knew we were going there. He thinks we're *bona fide* BBC. Iannucci doesn't need to and wouldn't. It must be Bellomunno. He didn't trust us. He wants to see where the stuff comes from, or who our contacts are or something like that.'

'Or murder us. What can we do?'

'I'd like to try and throw them off but we haven't a chance in this.'

'Why don't we stay the night at the Pensione Eden?'

'No. I don't want to go anywhere near Herculaneum. Anyway, I don't suppose it's open.'

'Well, Salerno then. We can stay at a hotel.'

Alex looked at the petrol gauge. It was registering two-thirds full. 'Perhaps. But suppose the Fiat was still there in the morning. In any case we can't afford the time. Oh *shit*, now look what's happening. It's that toll place.'

The traffic fanned out into five lanes at the five pay gates, and moved slowly forward. Although at 8.30 the temperature was beginning to ebb, the throbbing engines radiated heat. Alex hung one arm out of the window; the index finger of his other hand tapped rapidly on the steering wheel. The Fiat was two behind them. If he could get a good start after the gate. . . .

Suddenly Catrina said, 'I know. Take the turning off the autostrada at Torre Annuziata, then follow signs to Ottaviano.'

'Why?'

'We can go to my grandparents.'

'That's a fucking *ridiculous* suggestion,' said Alex furiously. 'We can't possibly do that.' The relief, if momentary, was enormous.

'I don't mean stay with them. You don't understand. Don't get so angry. Let me think.'

Even after the gates, the cracks in the road as they came up to Ercolano kept the traffic bunched and slow, making escape impossible. It was noticable that scarcely any cars took the exits to Ercolano or Torre del Greco.

'It's a huge estate about fifteen kilometres from here,' said Catrina, speaking very rapidly. 'There's a wall right round it. Just after Terzigno, a road leaves the main Ottaviano road and runs left alongside the wall. This little road carries on to the village of Pompilli, but about halfway along it there's a small road at right angles following the wall round to the right. And just off this are the back gates. They're locked. Do you see what I mean? If you could get ahead of the Fiat on the Pompilli road and then suddenly turn off, we could get through the gates before they could catch us.'

The traffic was beginning to speed up again. A sign said: Torre Annuziata – 6 km.

'How, if they're locked?'

'There's a lodge. Nina the head gardener's wife opens them. We'd just have time.'

'And then what?'

'We can get round to the front gates through the woods. We can't be seen from the house. Anyway, they won't be there. They'll have fled to Rome.'

'All right,' said Alex. 'It'll give me a chance to practise my skid turns, and I can't think of anything. Light me a cigarette.' One at a time, he wiped the palms of his hands on his trousers.

Cars poured off the *autostrada* at the Torre Annunziata exit, and for some minutes, with mounting relief, Alex thought

185

they'd lost the Fiat. Then, as they reached the top of a rise a little way from the exit, he saw it appear round the corner at the bottom.

Alex's stomach tightened, but he said easily, 'I've never been followed before, but I don't think they're very good at it.'

The road, pitted and broken, lay through urban sprawl, near-slums, mess. But gradually it became more open. There were vines in the dense black earth, a few pine trees. Here and there outcrops of lava. A sign said: Terzigno – 3 km. They must be getting close. The shadows of trees and houses were now thrown right across the road and Alex turned on the car's sidelights. Neither of them spoke. He looked in the rear mirror. The Fiat was still there.

All at once Catrina was pointing. 'There. You see that sign to the left? Turn there.'

Alex drove slowly. He wanted the Fiat to relax and also, anxious not to be seen, to drop back.

'Here,' said Catrina.

The road stretched straight ahead in the dusk, alongside a high stone wall. Behind this rose the graceful forms of the umbrella pines. Alex slowed again, until the Fiat came in sight again, then accelerated up to thirty.

'Tell me when we're two hundred yards from the turning.'

The Fiat was dropping back, as he'd noticed it always did on extended straights. Some way ahead an old man was slowly bicycling towards Pompilli. As they passed him, Alex thought he saw blackberries on a small bush beside the road.

'There,' said Catrina 'The turning's immediately opposite that big pine with the white paint on its trunk. Just there.'

It was at least two hundred yards. Alex pressed the accelerator steadily towards the floor. He wanted to pull away from the Fiat without alerting it.

They were doing at least fifty-five as they came up to the tree. Alex heeled and toed into a skid turn, flicking off the sidelights as his heel hit the brake. The van lurched violently and, as it skidded round, lifted onto two wheels. Then they were down again racing up the narrow road, engine roaring.

'Here,' shouted Catrina. 'Go right here.'

Once again he heeled and toed, sliding the van round. Immediately he had to brake again, grabbing up the handbrake too. Even as they slewed to a stop three feet from the tall double gates, Catrina was out and running to the little bungalow among the trees.

Alex revved the engine, his eyes on the rearview mirror. Moments passed. What were they talking about? Have a drink? Coffee? He suddenly struck the wheel with his fist. *For Christ's sake, Catrina – hurry up.* He wanted to press the horn, but was frightened in case the Fiat should pass and hear.

At that moment the Fiat did appear, flashed across the rear mirror, was gone. Almost at once Alex heard the squeal of tyres and at the same time Catrina came through the door dragging a large fat woman behind her.

'Run,' yelled Alex. 'They've spotted us.'

The fat woman had clearly not run for years, if ever, but she did now manage a rolling waddle. She reached the gates. There were moments of deliberate fiddling. They swung open.

Alex flung the van forward, aware of the Fiat accelerating furiously backwards in his rear mirror. Catrina leapt in, slamming the door. He saw the gates pulled together and the woman turning away just as the Fiat skidded to a stop in exactly the same place he'd been fifteen second before.

'Right here, Alex. Turn right here.'

It was gloomy enough among the pines for the headlights. Alex was trembling. 'Why did you take so long?'

'I didn't take long. I had to explain things to poor Nina. She nearly collapsed when I appeared.'

'What did you say? Will you light me another cigarette?'

'I said he was a jealous lover. She wasn't to let him in. She wasn't to say anything to Grandpa and Grandma when they got back – they *are* in Rome.'

'Did she believe you?'

'I expect so. It desn't matter. She's known me for years. She'll be fine.'

It was dark when they reached Ercolano again. Catrina had taken them back via Poggiomarino and Scafati as a precaution, but they didn't see the Fiat.

Her heart sank as they entered the slum town, now bristling with scaffolding as though in the process of being built.

'I must try and get hold of Eddie,' said Alex, stopping at the bottom of the Via IV Novembre.

But the Caffè Fauno was shut. A card was pinned to the door: '*Chiuso fino al prossimo avviso.*'

'Hell,' said Alex. 'The whole place is panicking. I can't face that phone box. I'll try tomorrow. Have we any food?'

'Bread and eggs. Two litres of wine.'

'Two litres? Good.'

Chapter Eleven

[1]

Twice during the night Catrina, lying sleepless, rigid with terror, was quite certain the house was about to collapse on them. The second time, when the shaking lasted a good three seconds, there was a loud crash from outside.

But even the regular tremors were now definitely harder and more frequent. It was as though a tremendous battle was gradually drawing closer, the ground quivering from the concussion of giant cannon.

She insisted he carried the living-room table outside the kitchen door and they had their coffee looking at Iannucci's now deserted building operations.

'I can't spend another night like that, Alex. You've got to open up that shaft before you go.'

'It didn't seem too bad. I thought I heard one faint noise.'

'Faint noise! That was just the whole of the Via Ascione collapsing. Did nothing else penetrate your drunken slumbers?'

Alex glanced up the Via Ascione which, though as decrepit as usual, appeared to be standing.

'All I'm saying,' said Catrina, 'is that if you want the place guarded while you're away, you'll have to open the shaft. I am not going to sleep another night upstairs in this house. Also, I told you, masses of my make-up is down there and vitamins and my blue dress.'

'All right, all right, don't go on.'

The earth was loosely compacted and it took Alex under an hour to dig a hole two foot by three down to the stable doors. He ranged the five sacks against the wall.

'Aren't you going to fix the lights?' said Catrina, as he went over to the stable doors and undid the padlock.

'I haven't time,' said Alex. 'You just have to throw the flex

189

down and plug it into the extension lead at the bottom. And don't forget to hang the bell down the light-well.'

'But there's masses of time. The Forio ferry doesn't go till one-forty-five.'

'I daren't risk it. I know it's a thousand to one, but that Fiat might spot the van. I'll have to take the Circumvesu-viana. Could you take the van out while I change and pack?'

The Circumvesuviana will be quicker not slower, Catrina wanted to say. But she realised this was the price for making him dig out the entrance to the shaft, and climbed irritably into the van.

As they turned from the Corso Resina up towards the station, Catrina saw that Attillo was taking down the shutters from between the scaffolding that now embraced the Caffè Fauno. 'Panic's over,' she said. 'Hadn't you better ring Eddie?'

'I'll do it at the port. I don't want to waste time here. I want to get a hook, a pulley and some more rope in Naples for the statue.'

At the station, he kissed her abstractedly and said, 'You'd better hurry back. We've left the shaft open. If you go out, put a couple of boards over that hole and cover them with sacks. And could you leave the van here for me tomorrow afternoon? There'll be no taxis and I'll be carrying quite a lot. I'll get back as soon as I can.'

It was when she was repadlocking the iron gates at the end of the Via Ascione that she saw that half the roof had nearly collapsed in the semi-ruined house one away from theirs. She had a sudden fantasy that the stable ceiling would have fallen in, filling the shaft. They would have to go home.

Nothing had happened. Catrina had a shower, washed up the breakfast and supper, made the bed, swept up several chunks of plaster. Finally, reluctant and apprehensive, she forced herself to lower the light flex and bell down the shaft and, holding the torch, stepped onto the ladder.

It felt strange going down into the coolness and darkness of Herculaneum again, half-familiar, half-dreamlike. Once more she had a curious feeling that she was descending into her subconscious.

Nothing had changed. The delicate green of the light well painting, clear in the naked sixty-watt bulbs, the fluted painted pillars and elaborately decorated walls in the *tablinium* had no further cracks. There was a certain amount of dust, that was all.

It occurred to Catrina, staring with new eyes at the naked statue, that this house, like the others, buried in their buried streets all round her, was not just the safest place to be during these tremors and quakes, but the safest place in the world. Locked into their sixty or seventy feet of concrete-like mud, they would survive everything. All human life could vanish in the nuclear holocaust; ten million years of frost and sun and rain finally eradicate its cities and its plains. Eventually the only record that man had ever existed would be preserved in Herculaneum, the last representative that lascivious and lovely boy.

She turned away with a sudden shiver of distaste and fear. He wasn't lovely at all. The blue eyes seemed to be looking above her head, but he could see her. He was sinister.

She ran quickly up the stairs to the bedroom. Here too the only sign of disturbance was a certain amount of dust. Catrina stood looking at the mural and thought of Alex making love to her.

It wasn't just her subconscious. It was Alex's as well. It had now finally overwhelmed him, obsessing him not any more with the need to prove himself – surely that had been achieved – but with straightforward greed for money, corrupted by the sly and obvious enticement of those outstretched bronze arms – 'take me, have me, I'm yours'. She hated it. It made no difference to her feelings for Alex. After a while, it seemed, love was nothing to do with what the person did.

It was while she was reassembling her make-up scattered among the vitamin pills and bits of Roman debris on the marble table that the house was struck by a tremor. It was a mild one, but after it had passed Catrina stood listening intently. Surely she'd heard a noise. She went to the door, her head on one side.

At once she had a strong feeling – part-fantasy, part-sensed – of something happening down there. The house, Herculaneum itself, entombed by the malevolence of forces deep in the earth, could only rise again by the agency of those same

191

forces. Gradually, with the quivering of the mighty womb in which it rested, the ancient city was coming alive.

Swept by sudden panic, Catrina ran past the bathroom, clattered across the ladder and scrambled to the top of the shaft.

The panic did not begin to leave her until she stood panting in the sunlight. Even then she looked behind to see if she was pursued, and she had to force herself back to cover the shaft top roughly and lock all the doors.

One of Carmela's little girls was playing in the gutter of the Via Ascione as Catrina came through the iron gates.

'Is your mother in?'

'No.'

'Tell her I'll come and see her this afternoon.'

She walked down the Corso Resina and found herself automatically heading for the Caffè Fauno. But it was true that Signor Russo's *alimentari* there was one of the few still open. Also she wanted to know why Attillo had come back.

'Have you heard something? Is it all going to stop?'

'Signor Abate came and pulled me out of bed himself – what does he care? He lives in Salerno. I'm scared. As soon as the shit' – he used the word *stronzo* – 'goes back, I'm off again.'

Catrina sat in the sun sipping her *cappucciono*, table at the pavement's edge. She was scared as well. Fear made her hate Herculaneum, long to get out, yet she too was involved. What was in her subconscious? Was it the power she felt as she saw Alex about to become very, very rich? Had she been corrupted too? She thought, Men are our medium.

'Hi, Catrina! Why haven't you gone yet? I told you way back in July this place was going to blow up, didn't I?'

A huge shape blotted out the sun.

Catrina looked up. 'You did, Dr Schultz. But Attillo said you weren't going till next week yourself.'

Dr Schultz lowered herself onto one of the little white chairs, obliterating it.

'Yeah – well I've advanced it to Tuesday. And it'd be today, only I've a little vendetta work to perform on Monday.'

'What's that?'

'The sham archaeologist was going to announce his plans for the *scavi* to the whole world at some damn fool celebration of his. I warned him that if he did that I'd get up and make a speech that'd knock the shit outa him. I aim to be there and see if he dare do it. Come along. Could be fun.'

'We haven't really been invited,' said Catrina. 'At least only very vaguely, some time ago.'

'*I'm* inviting you,' said Dr Schultz.' She stood up again. 'I'm late for Carlo. But mind you be there – Monday, one o'clock at the Antiquarium.'

[2]

Catrina had been right. Alex had an hour and a half to wait for the Forio ferry even after he had bought a small pulley, a hook and a further length of nylon rope.

The ferry rose out of the sea onto skis and skimmed. Water obscured the windows. Alex, becoming more and more apprehensive, wished it had been a paddle steamer.

This absurd speed meant further hours to wander round the hot little town of Forio. He discovered at the quayside that there would be no difficulty in finding Mr Davis. The first taxi he asked knew at once who he wanted – *il Americano millionario*. Half an hour away. No – less. *Meno*. Alex said he'd be back at 7.30.

It occurred to him after his fifth *espresso* – harsh sips of adrenalin that were beginning to make him both shaky and exhausted – that nothing had been said about staying the night. The Pensione Nettuno was big enough to be a hotel. Alex sank with relief onto the usual gimcrack bed and tried in vain to doze.

At 7.30, after two quick brandies, he was back at the quay. The road twisted up above the town and then wound south. '*Santuario del Soccorso*,' said the taxi driver pointing through the fading light; '*Citara*' – and then something that sounded as if they were passing above a nuclear reactor. He felt edgy with nerves. If only Catrina were there.

The Villa of San Michele was isolated at the end of a long private road, immaculately tarmaced compared to their dusty, cratered passage from Forio. The taxi stopped before tall double gates set in high walls. Alex paid and it drove off into the dusk.

193

The wall was ten foot high, plastered smooth and topped by wire. The heavy wrought-iron gates were handleless and had steel plates bolted down their vertical bars. Alex saw a telephone recessed into the stone wall to the left. He lifted it. After a moment a man's voice said, '*Prego?*'

Alex cleared his throat. 'It's Mr Mayne here. I believe I'm expected to supper. To dinner.'

There was a pause, then the Italian said, 'Please to wait at the gates, Signor Mayne. Someone come.'

Alex replaced the receiver. So far so good. At least Eddie had got through to Davis and it was the right day. He stepped out and looked along the wall. He could see now that at intervals along the wire there were notices showing a skull and the zig-zag symbol of lightning. Once again he wished Catrina were with him.

Five minutes later the big gates swung smoothly open. A man in a pale grey suit gestured him through and silently opened the back door of a large pale grey Mercedes.

The grounds were laid out in lawns and dotted with trees and shrubs. Alex twice saw men patrolling with alsatians on the short winding drive to the Villa itself.

This was built of plastered stone to resemble the fortress it clearly was – massively square, creeperless, with narrow windows, the ground-floor ones barred. The Mercedes crunched to a stop on the gravel. At the single heavy wooden door there was further brief communication by telephone.

Waiting at the gates, and again crossing the gravel, the heat of the day hung heavy on the still air. But Alex was surprised by a sudden chill outpouring. Davis's fortress was air-conditioned.

This underground dungeon coolness was reinforced by the bare walls and narrow windows – a shut-inness unrelieved until Alex was shown into a large room at the end of a featureless corridor.

The whole of the long wall facing him was glass. It was filled, from where he stood, by an immense panorama of sea. The Villa of San Michele was built right on the edge of a high cliff. To the left, far below, a toy lighthouse blinked. Alex felt his palms sweat.

'I see you appreciate my view, Alex. Come on down – I'd like you to meet some very good neighbours of mine.'

194

Somehow expecting they would be alone, Alex was disconcerted to see the backs of two small grey heads, just visible above the back of a huge white sofa. But his host already had him by the hand.

Bill Davis was big and bald and loose. He looked like one of those large, nearly tasteless southern vegetables that had been peeled. Keeping Alex's hand in his soft, hot-water bottle grip, he led him down.

'Mr Mayne works for Dexter's, Denzil. This is Mr Denzil Fedden, Alex – I'm sure you've heard of his collection – and this is Alicia Fedden.'

The little man, two sticks leaning beside him, looked about ninety-five. But his glance, under bushy grey brows, was sharp enough. 'Please excuse my not rising, Mr Mayne,' he said in a rather high voice.

Mrs Fedden, her doll-like face criss-crossed with lines, looked scarcely younger. Alex shook each frail, age-spotted hand.

The two men were in dinner jackets, Mrs Fedden in a long blue tube. Well – at least he hadn't come clanking in with his hooks and pulleys.

'Let's fix you a drink first, Alex.' Davis steered him round the low, plate-glass table and then, after the grey-suited servant behind the bar had poured, soda'd and iced a whisky, took him over to the vast window.

It hardly seemed safe. Alex could see vertically down to where the waves were breaking about a mile below. Once again he felt his hands sweating.

'That's the lighthouse on the Punta dell' Imperatore to the left,' said Davis. 'Away over there you can just see Forio. Yes, I don't think even Denzil here would deny me the finest view on the island.'

'I wouldn't dream of it. I wouldn't dare deny you the finest everything.'

'Well, I can't match your porcelain and you won't let me buy it. Sit down Alex, sit down.'

'You work for a fine auction house,' piped Mrs Fedden at Alex. 'Didn't Colin Stubbs join you recently from Christie's?'

'I don't really know,' said Alex. 'I don't actually work full-time. I'm an adviser.'

'On what?'

'Well, sort of general. That is – several areas. Not porcelain, I'm afraid.'

'Any particular period?'

'Middle,' said Alex, feeling increasingly annoyed with Eddie Segal. 'That is – roughly medieval.'

'What?' said Mr Fedden, cupping his hand to his ear.

'Middle. Medieval,' said Alex.

He was saved by the announcement of dinner. It took some time to get Mr Fedden to his feet.

The food was airline first-class: a large, pre-cut, bright orange segment from a completely tasteless melon, followed by bland slices of grey veal in a flavourless gravy, with small heaps of highly coloured, equally flavourless vegetables.

Alex was appalled to see only one bottle of white Bordeaux. He'd noticed before how drinkers of very expensive wine – who might be expected to enjoy the stuff – behaved as if it were poison.

'How long have you worked in the art world, Mr Mayne?' said Mrs Fedden from his left.

'About ten years,' said Alex. 'But I do far more work with films now.'

'Film?'

'Yes. Collections of early films are becoming very valuable. I'm getting a sale together at the moment.'

'What sort of thing?'

'Well, you know,' said Alex. 'Chabrol, Buzan. Galimard. The early directors. Though Buzan was basically a cameraman, of course.'

'How fascinating.' Mrs Fedden raised a wineglass dwarfed even by her shrunken hand, and took the mouthful of a humming bird. 'I've certainly heard of Chabrol.'

Fortunately, however, he did not have to play much part. Bill Davis flowed over them in an endless series of conversational waves. Or something even more formless than waves – an oceanic swell of words, hypnotically boring.

At last the airline fodder, separated by interminable pauses, came to an end. They followed the shuffling Mr Fedden back into the next-door room.

When they were all sitting down, Davis went and stood with his back to the big window. He was smiling. After a considerable pause he said, 'So, what's it to be tonight, Denzil?'

'I understood you to say the Bouts had arrived, Bill,' said Mr Fedden. 'This would also fall in with Mr Mayne's period, as I understand it.'

'Is that so, Alex?'

'Yes,' said Alex.

'Right you are – Derek Bouts it shall be.'

He raised his head and nodded at one of the servants, then came and sat heavily down on the sofa between Mr Fedden and his wife so that they tilted towards him. 'I think you'll enjoy this, Alex,' he said, smiling across at him.

It was done with some theatricality. An easel was set up in front of them. The lights were dimmed and two spotlights trained on the easel. After a considerable pause, a large painting draped in a velvet cloth was placed on the easel. Davis waited a moment, then raised his hand. The cloth was deftly removed.

Alex saw a shiny painting of an infant Christ in a manger, flanked by Mary and an angel, against a medieval landscape. There was silence. Everyone seemed stunned.

'Incredible!' breathed Mrs Fedden at last.

Mr Fedden began to rattle his sticks.

They moved over to the painting. Alex, his jaws already aching from lack of alcohol and the continuous effort to appear alert, forced his features into an expression of almost maniacal interest. He bent close, noting from a small gold plaque on the frame that Davis's Derek was in fact Dieric. 'Very, very fine,' he murmured. 'Very fine.'

'Mr Mayne will correct me,' almost squeaked Mr Fedden, 'but I believe a lot of Bouts is on linen?'

'Yes,' said Alex.

For ten minutes they looked. Alex could think of nothing whatsoever to say except to suggest – which he didn't – Rentokil Woodwork Fluid. He hoped his silence would be taken for wonder. Davis did indeed bask. He might have painted the thing.

At last the cloth was replaced, the painting removed, the lights turned up. Mr and Mrs Fedden had to go. Alex must visit next time he was in Ischia. Davis accompanied them out. Alex waited.

'Finest private collection of antique porcelain in the world,' said Davis as he came back through the door. 'I've made him an offer. He's not budging. We'll see.' He moved to the bar. 'Mario, give Mr Mayne a drink,' he said, giving that grossly underworked figure something to do at last. 'What'll it be, Alex?'

'Brandy,' said Alex.

'That'll be all, Mario,' said Davis. He came and sat down in the big white chair beside the plate glass table. There was a silence. Alex felt himself sweating despite the air-conditioning.

'Eddie Segal tells me you have a statue he thinks might interest me, though he hasn't seen it. So what is this statue?'

'It's a two-thirds life-size Roman bronze of the first-century AD. It's exceptionally fine. Really exceptional. And it's in perfect condition – even the eyes.'

'*Perfect* condition? So it wasn't found in water? I understand from Segal you are reluctant to reveal your source – but it must have been a remarkable place?'

'It was. I can't say where. What I can say,' said Alex and then, once again about to play his ace, he paused. He took a sip of his brandy. At last he said, 'What I can say is it was somewhere in Sicily.'

'Sicily? Do you mean actually *found* there?'

'Yes.'

'That's a big pity, a real big pity.'

'A pity? Why?'

'Yes Alex. For several reasons. The heat's on that stuff down there. I'm not having anything to do with something as hot as that. For another – well, I have a good number of contacts in the Special Branch at Rome. I understand they no longer think the find is there. It's somewhere in southern Italy – probably in Calabria. It's being channelled through Sicily. That's what I understand. The third reason? Well, I hope you'll excuse this, Alex – but you don't strike me as a professional. It just don't figure to me, you being involved down there.'

Staring at his glass, Alex felt his heart sink. He'd blown it. He'd seriously underestimated Mr Davis.

'Look, Alex, would you take a word of advice from me? If we're to do business tonight you've got to be honest with me. Oddly enough, in ordinary business transactions you can often cut a few corners. But where the business *is* cutting corners, if you follow me, you can't. Do you follow me?'

'Yes. I lied. I'm sorry. But I said that to an Italian and it worked.'

Davis's eyes sharpened again. 'Excuse me, you've tried to sell this already? Who to?'

'A chap called Bellomunno.'

'Bellomunno, Bellomunno. It rings a bell. Did he see it? Does he know where you are?'

'No. Neither. He wanted to see it. But Sicily stopped him wondering where it came from. I hoped it would do the same with you.'

'You don't want to get mixed up with those Italian go-betweens and suchlike,' said Davis, frowning.

'Listen,' said Alex, 'if whether you buy it or not in the end depends on knowing where it came from, I'll almost certainly tell you. For the moment, I promise you it was nowhere near Sicily or Calabria. And I found it myself. No one else is involved.'

There was another pause. Davis shifted upright in his chair. 'Whether I buy it or not depends on whether it is authentic, on its quality, whether I like it, and on the price. This is what I propose. You get the statue here. I'll have Eddie Segal and that chap he has with him – what's his name?'

'Willie Calman?'

'Yeah. I'll have Calman and Segal fly out. I'll have a chap I use in New York fly out. If they all agree it's as good as you say, if I like it as well, here's what I'll do. I'll give you one million dollars or one third what they think the market value would be, whichever is the lesser.'

'One million dollars?'

'Yeah. Unless they say it's worth one and a half – when I give you five hundred thousand.'

'OK. I agree,' said Alex. His heart was beating hard.

Mr Davis wouldn't hear of him leaving for the Nettuno. 'I'll have Mario ring them. You stay here tonight. I have to leave early tomorrow but the car will take you down.'

'When shall I bring the statue?'

'I get back Thursday.'

'I was hoping to bring it earlier than that.'

'Sure. If you've been talking to Italian dealers and suchlike

199

round Naples or wherever, then the sooner it's in my vaults the better. You bring it here as soon as you like. I'll tell Mario to expect you. Then we'll all meet up here again Thursday evening.'

Alex's bedroom was as bare of picture or ornament as the rest of the house. Padding barefoot to the bathroom across the thick carpet, he thought of the Titians and Rembrandts and goodness knows what else somewhere in the rock beneath him. He was glad of Mr Davis's immaculate brown silk pyjamas in the curious underground coldness of the air conditioning.

His final conscious thought was to look up the exchange rates the moment he got to Naples.

[3]

Catrina spent the afternoon and evening with Carmela. The whole family had moved into a single room. Her friend, normally equable and humorous, was edgy, slapping her children, her sallow face drawn and tired.

'The Comune spend millions of lira propping up the rest of Ercolano. There's nothing here. They want these houses to fall down. Only the Via Ascione sleep in the fields.'

'At least the weather's still good enough for that.'

'Yes, and that's another thing – it has no right to be like this. By this time of year there should have been some thunderstorms, some rain. What's it saving itself for, I'd like to know? Something bad.'

Catrina could offer no comfort since she shared Carmela's fears. Carmela's other great worry was money. As Ercolano ran down it became increasingly hard for Mario to get enough of the cardboard boxes he collected for a living. He'd tried going closer to Naples but the territories were all carved up.

'I may be able to give you some money soon,' said Catrina.

'What – you? The wife of *uno scrittore inglese*? Everyone knows *uno scrittore* makes nothing.' Nevertheless, Catrina noticed a gleam in her eye.

As it grew dark, Catrina grew more and more apprehensive about sleeping alone in their house. It was not so much fear of an earthquake. She knew she'd be safe enough in the House of the Cock. It was far more her own private fear, completely irrational, that after two thousand years Herculaneum was stirring again, rising from the dead. In the end she asked Carmela if she could sleep in the fields with them.

She collected some wine and cheese as well as a sleeping bag. Mario lit a fire and Carmela cooked spaghetti.

Catrina slept better than she'd done since returning from England. Nevertheless she was conscious all night of the regular trembling of the earth. It was as if they were living on the flank of some vast prone beast, stirring and quivering in its sleep, that might at any moment wake with a roar and destroy them.

Alex returned late on Sunday evening. Catrina, who was sitting waiting outside the house, ran to the van. He got out and at the sight of her face took her in his arms. 'Is everything all right? What's happened?'

'Nothing, nothing. I'm just scared. There's a really huge new crack in the bedroom ceiling, and another right down the stable wall. This place is shaking itself to bits.'

'I know. We're getting out. We're going tomorrow.'

'Why – was it no good?'

'On the contrary, it was fine. At least, I think so. I'll tell you. Read this. I must have a drink.'

The front page of *Il Corriere della Campania* had, next to a smudged photograph of Vesuvius, a single word in huge letters: '*QUANDO?*' – WHEN?

'The 10–kilometre-square region of recent seismic activity, comprising principally Ercolano and Torre del Greco, is now suffering up to sixty shocks a day of intensity between 3 and 4 on the Mercalli Scale.'

Already thoroughly alarmed, Catrina skimmed on. A furious row had broken out between scientists in the Observatory and the University. The first said the area should be evacuated immediately; the second that the danger was passing and would soon be over.

'I can't read this terrifying stuff,' she said as Alex came out of the kitchen. 'What is the Mercalli scale?'

'I don't know. Like the Richter scale, I suppose. But obviously we ought to get out. A man on the Circumvesuviana – which incidentally may also stop running soon, there were notices up – said they were going to evacuate at the end of the week.'

'And can we sell the statue?'

'I think so. I'll tell you.' He described what had happened on Ischia. When he'd finished, Catrina said, 'It all sounds a bit sinister. Guards with alsatians.'

'I trust him far more than Bellomunno. In fact, I think if he does buy it, I will tell him and Eddie about it all. I'll bring them here. We can't do it on our own.'

'It would certainly be a huge relief. Is a million dollars enough?'

'Yes. It's a hell of a lot of money. The pound is more or less at parity with the dollar at the moment.'

While Catrina cooked supper, Alex took the hook and pulley he'd bought in Naples down into the House of the Cock. She could hear muffled hammering from the top of the shaft.

He took her down to the *tablinium* after they'd eaten and pointed to the hook secured in the ceiling between the statue and the marble slab with the inscription. The pulley was attached to the hook and from this a nylon rope, its other end dangling, was secured round the statue under the arms.

'I hacked away the plaster and found that beam. It's extra-ordinary. It's just as hard, harder even, than when it was put in. I had to use the bar to screw the hook in and it takes my weight easily. Those people in London said a two-thirds life-size bronze would weigh about two hundred and fifty pounds. I reckon this one will be two hundred. Both of us will be able to lift him off his feet quite easily. We'll leave him chained to the wall tonight for safety. In the morning I'll get some-thing on wheels, we'll lift him up, let him swing out of the alcove, lower him down, and wheel him to the light-well. The big pulley in the stable is far more powerful. We'll haul him to the surface, swing him into the van – and that's it. Away.'

Catrina looked at the bronze boy staring out as he had when, terrified, she'd first seen his eyes; as he had for two thousand years. She pointed to the marble block with the inscription hanging apparently precariously in front of the hook.

'Can't you shift that? It looks so dangerous to work under.'

'I've tried. It isn't dangerous. You can't budge it. It's

202

wedged right in. Whatever earthquake left it like that also jammed it solid.'

When they were in bed, Catrina described her encounter with Dr Schultz.

'I see,' said Alex. 'If it comes to a fight, I doubt Dr Gandolfino will last the first round.'

'Please, Alex, if there's time, couldn't we just look in for a moment tomorrow at his party? I absolutely *long* to see what will happen.'

'There won't be time.'

'But if there is?'

'If. All right. Come here. I want you. This is our last night.'

'Our last night down here, you mean,' said Catrina sliding under the bedclothes.

'Yes. And I can promise you one thing.'

'What?' said Catrina, engulfed in wine fumes.

'The earth will move.'

[4]

They woke much later than Alex had intended. He dropped two Alka-Seltzer into the Roman beaker on the faun table beside the bed and shoved Catrina with his foot.

'We must get up. It's nearly ten.'

They gulped coffee, then Alex fixed the big pulley to the beam in the stable and let the long nylon rope down through the shaft. With one end tied to the rail outside the bathroom, the other easily reached the rail on the *tablinium* below.

'Right. I'm off to get something to cart it in.'

'But you'll be *hours*. We'll never have time to go to Dr Gandolfino. I'll be frightened here alone. What shall I do?'

'I shan't be hours. I'll try and borrow something – a pram, anything. I'll see if I can get a porter's trolley from the station.'

'There aren't any,' said Catrina, irritable with fear. 'You're thinking of Paddington.'

'Here,' said Alex, wrenching open the back of the van and pulling out the folding tool chest. 'Get the hacksaw from this and saw the two chains holding the statue to the wall. Then you can pack. Not everything – essentials. If I'm still not

203

back, which I will be, bring anything you can carry from down there – heads, glasses, knives, *anything*, the mirror – and pile it in the corner there and cover it with sacks. We'll take as much as we can.'

Catrina watched with sinking heart as he backed the van out, opened and relocked the gates, and then roared off up the deserted Via Ascione. She opened the toolbox. It was always impossible to find anything in a toolbox, but she was soon certain there was no hacksaw. She went slowly up to the old bedroom, fetched the suitcase, and with difficulty got it down the shaft.

She had opened it on the bed and was about to load in the vitamin pills, when there was a sudden violent tremor – at least 50 on the Mercalli scale. Without a pause, still clutching the Efamol, she was carried on the wave of panic over the lightwell, up the ladder and out panting into the sun.

Again, it was not fear of the house collapsing. She felt secure underground. The tremors had a different quality. On the surface there was a feeling of being shaken. Below, gripped by the mud-rock, it was steadier, more integral. It was as though the evil force rising form the depths had now finally taken possession. Herculaneum had become the shaker. It was another manifestation of the buried city coming alive.

Catrina looked at her watch. Eleven o'clock. He'd be at least an hour. Everything in Torre del Greco would be shut too. He'd have to go to Torre Annunziata. And the whole operation of getting the statue up, loading the van, getting away, would take till evening at the least. They'd need food and drink. Thank God her purse was in the kitchen. She'd take half an hour off to shop.

Chapter Twelve

[1]

Thomas sat outside the small café at the bottom of the Via IV Novembre and waited for his *cappuccino*. He'd experienced his first tremor ten minutes before on his way down from the station and been shaken in more ways than one.

As far as he could gather from what he'd read, no one quite knew what was happening or what might happen. An article in *Il Mattino* that morning said that the repeated tremors had, as often at Pozzuoli, now dissipated the forces built up below and stability would soon return. Nevertheless it seemed foolhardy, to say the least, just to step into the eye of the storm like this for no really pressing reason. He had no particular obligation to the new Soprintendente of Herculaneum. Dr Gandolfino had shown no more than the normal, almost obligatory curtsey to a visiting academic.

I wouldn't have felt like this twenty years ago, he thought.

The young man brought him his coffee.

'*È pericoloso?*' Thomas asked, spreading his hand to the scaffolding and up the street.

'*Cho lo sa? Io non ci starei qui se dipendesse da me.*'

Thomas agreed. He wouldn't stay here either. Looking down the street, he saw a pretty girl crossing the road, in front of the *scavi*. His eyes followed her for a moment and then, distracted by the open gates, he looked at his watch. He was due at one o'clock. It would be ironic, he thought suddenly, if the final result of two and a half centuries of excavation – the first spectacular discovery of which Dr Gandolfino's gathering was to celebrate – were for all visible remains of Herculaneum to be shaken to the ground.

He turned restlessly, searching up the Via IV Novembre, afflicted with that nagging sense of psychic loss which comes when interrupted watching a pretty girl walk past. But she had vanished.

All at once he saw her again. She was coming out of the *alimentari* opposite. Her dark head of thick black curly hair was bent but he recognised her at once.

Swiftly, he turned his head away. Then turned back. Absurd precaution. She'd hardly glanced at him in Herculaneum. In the museum, if indeed she'd been there that time, she hadn't seen him at all.

He watched her striding up the street and turn out of sight into a square.

He finished his coffee. The young man was occupied inside the cafe. Thomas left fifteen hundred lira to cover the thousand-lira ticket under his saucer, and set off up the Via IV Novembre. He had more than an hour to kill.

The scaffolding was so thick on the pavement it was necessary to walk on the road. As did the few people about anyway, probably to avoid falling tiles. It was strange seeing her here like that. Few if any tourists would be coming to Ercolano at the moment. Did that mean that young man – what was his name? Mayne – was young Mayne here too?

There were only two stalls in the market, one vegetable, one fruit. He watched from the far end as she bought from both of them. She obviously knew the owners, chatting at length. Odd she should be here at all, even odder if she lived here or was staying here – when clearly two-thirds of the population had fled.

As she turned out of sight at the far end, Thomas set off past the Scuola Media Statale, his limp barely discernible. This time he would not be left behind.

He followed her wavering route for nearly ten minutes, during which time the whole of Ercolano once more shuddered beneath his feet. She too was obviously killing time, either with nothing to do but chat to the people she met, or else reluctant to get to wherever it was she was going.

Thomas was still more surprised when she turned into the Via Ascione. This must have been one of the poorest parts of the town. Several of the houses, unsupported by scaffolding, had already suffered considerable damage. Thomas stood and watched as she walked down the middle of the little street. She turned into the house at the end on the right. He waited a few minutes and was about to set off after her when she emerged and went to the gates at the end.

Thomas reached them himself just in time to see her disappear into the last house on the left, the only one in the whole street which showed signs of rough repair.

Catrina dumped her plastic bags on the kitchen table and felt in the pocket of her skirt for her purse. It wasn't there. She emptied first one bag, then the other.

She must have left the purse at one of the stalls in the market. Thankfully, and with an instant's guilt that she must partly have done it with this in mind, she escaped from the kitchen again and turned up past Iannucci's abandoned workings. This time she noticed an elderly man, obviously English, standing outside Carmela's house and wondered for a fleeting moment what he was doing there.

She'd left both gates and the door of the house open. Thomas walked through the gates, down past the padlocked stable doors and into the house.

There was nothing particularly revealing in the kitchen, nor in the little bedroom above it. Indeed the absence of mattresses, and bedclothes on the two iron beds showed they didn't even sleep there. The room next to the kitchen had a typewriter but seemed quite unlived in. A door led off this, and the moment he had opened it Thomas stopped in astonishment.

He was at the top of some steps leading down into what had obviously once been a stable. In semi-darkness this end, the far end was lit by a single bulb hanging from the beam. From the beam there hung also two strands of flex and a rope round a large pulley. The rope and the flex disappeared into a hole in the earth floor. It was this that held Thomas's eyes. His instinct had been right.

He hurried across the stable and bent over the two-foot by two-foot opening to the hole. It was quite deep, twenty-five feet or so, but he could just see light coming through an opening in the side at the bottom. Thomas turned and lowered himself carefully onto the ladder.

Three minutes later he was standing, panting slightly, beside the railing round the light-well. He looked about him in amazement. It was unbelievable, impossible. Yet it was true. He put his hand onto the elegantly twisted bronze rail and shook it. Firm as a rock. He leant over. Light came dimly from a floor below, and still more dimly from another below that.

Thomas paused, listening. He must hurry. But he was astounded, already fascinated by what he saw. Ancient reading rushed back. The stylised reality of the painting on that wall opposite, those delicate but formalised leaves, that was the third period, he seemed to remember – say AD 25.

He peered across at it with intense curiosity, then pulled himself up. Yes, he must hurry. Yet it was amazing. It was untouched. He turned back and went into the room on the right. The bathroom: the bold black and white panels (a later period, surely), the basin on its porphyry stem, the bronze bath – a typical design. He dropped onto his knees. At the back, under the bath near the wall, he found a six-inch long scraper, curved like a small flat pelota racquet – a strigil. Not completely untouched, it seemed; he saw from the gleam of fresh bronze that someone had recently sawn the tap head off the lead pipe.

And in the bedroom, superficially at least, it was very considerably touched. The millennia had telescoped. On a cluttered table against the wall, a large box of Tampax rested on a first-century burnished silver hand mirror, eye shadow and mascara were jumbled with Roman flasks. There was an Alka-Seltzer carton on the floor under the fine ithyphallic table. He looked at the great marble bed facing the wall painting, at the frozen storm of its blankets and sheets. He was glad they were together. He would have been glad for Philip to have had a good-looking girl like that.

There was still glass in the little window above the dressing table – or rather not glass, but the tough, extremely expensive *lapis specularis*, crystallised gypsum. How dark it must have been. Thomas imagined the tapers and candles flaring and smoking in their phallic holders. He imagined a young man sitting on the marble seat in the bathroom, scraping off the dirt-laden oil with the strigil.

He realised that his old idea about Herculaneum, his fantasy of the sculpture locked in the rock, was unsubtle. It was an entire world hidden there, a teeming life; the image was that of some great novel of lost time still shrouded and waiting words.

Now totally absorbed by what he was seeing, he left the bedroom. He had to stoop low, almost crawl, at the opening to the short stair next to the bathroom, but at the bottom he was once more struck still and staring in amazement.

Dim as the light was from two small bulbs, the walls and pillars were brilliant with colour; the room was crowded with statues. The owner had obviously been very rich. Also a Philhellene. All the portrait busts – save one, which looked like Nero – were, he thought, of Greek kings and heroes.

Thomas wracked his brains to remember his early studies. It had been over thirty years before, at the start of his interest in antique marble that, among numerous places, he'd read quite deeply about Pompeii and Herculaneum. But his memory had always been his strength as a scholar. Surely there had been some mild controversy about Herculaneum. Space had been scarce in the little town. There had been an evolution from the more usual horizontal plan in Roman towns towards the vertical. This house would certainly support such an argument. He was standing in the *tablinium*. The *atrium* would be below, presumably through the door on the far side. He must go and look. There would have been a further storey, perhaps open to the air, above the bathroom and bedroom. The cubicle behind that well-preserved door hanging on its lock would have contained the *lares,* shrine to the household gods. He would find some effigy or model temple there.

At that moment, however, it was the floor which interested Thomas. It was an intricate but at the same time bold marquetry of rare marbles – serpentine, variegated, pava-razzo, porphyry, antique green.

But in that place where he would gladly have spent six months of his life he was only to be allowed ten minutes alone. He had just knelt and spat on his handkerchief to clear the dust off what looked like an extraordinary yellow marble, probably African, when he heard the rattle of the aluminium ladder.

It was the girl, or else the young man. He got reluctantly to his feet. It was distasteful, but he would have to confront them. He limped towards the stairs, his rope-soled shoes soundless on the dust-covered floor.

When Catrina turned and saw the tall grey-haired man

emerging from the half-cleared door, the terror flung her back against the bronze railing. She might have fallen over had Thomas not stepped out and grabbed her.

'I'm sorry. I should have given you some warning.'

She pulled her slender wrist furiously from his grasp. She was trembling.

'Who are you? What do you want? How did you get in?'

'I followed you. I got in when you ran out and left the door open.'

'Get out. You had no right to do that.'

'Perhaps not. But then, if you'll excuse my saying so, you have no right to be here either. I followed you because I saw you here five months ago. I saw your friend Mr Mayne in the Museum, when he brought a plate and a ring to show me. My name is Thomas Henderson.'

He paused. Catrina looked at him. What did he expect? Handshakes?

Thomas said, 'There was something about Mr Mayne's story which didn't ring quite true. It seems I was correct.'

'What do you mean, we have no right here? We rent this house. These things belong to no one else.'

'You know perfectly well they belong to the Italians, to the Italian state. That's why Mr Mayne lied about where they came from.'

'What are you going to do?'

'I shall report this to the authorities in Naples.'

Catrina stared at him. She felt suddenly sick. 'You can't,' she whispered.

'Well, I don't want to get you both in trouble. Why don't you report it yourself?'

But Catrina continued to stare at him, tears in her eyes, two, three, four tears rolling down her cheeks. 'You can't,' she whispered again. 'It would kill him. Oh, poor Alex.'

Thomas looked for a moment at this beautiful representative of the new invaders. 'Listen,' he said gently, 'have you sold much of this?'

Catrina shook her head. 'Only a ring. We've put a few things in a sale in October – two more rings, some pieces of glass.'

'Withdraw them. The point is, what you've both done, what you've discovered, is quite extraordinary. It's unique.

210

There's nothing like it anywhere else in Italy, anywhere in the world. There are substantial rewards for finding and reporting things like this. I am by no means unknown to the Museum in Naples. I would certainly help and make sure, if I could, that you are not punished and that you are suitably rewarded.'

Catrina looked at him and for the first time took in the deep lines of his face, the expression half-melancholy, half-remote, but also kind. 'You don't understand. Alex has gambled everything on this. His whole life. *Himself.*'

Before Thomas could answer, they heard, muffled, the momentary sound of the van's engine in the stable above, then silence, the doors banging, silence again.

'That's Alex,' said Catrina.

Thomas nodded. They both waited. Suddenly the two ropes hanging down the shaft and the light-well began to move rapidly as one of them was pulled to the surface.

'Catrina,' shouted Alex. 'Catrina – I need help. I've brought a wheelbarrow.'

Catrina cupped her hands. 'Alex – there's someone here.'

'What?'

'There's someone *down* here,' shouted Catrina.

The ropes stopped moving. There was a short silence. Then Thomas heard the aluminium rattle again, this time of the extending ladder in the shaft.

Alex looked ready to fight as he stepped over the railing. Thomas, unconsciously registering the pinched nostrils and drained face, found himself tensing.

'How the bloody hell did you get in here, Mr Henderson?'

Thomas explained, and at once Alex turned furiously on Catrina. 'I told you never to leave those doors open.'

'I know. I'm sorry. I was frightened. These tremors have got me down.'

'What do you intend to do?' said Alex, taking Thomas in. He was big, but he was old. Alex doubted he was as fit as he was after months of digging.

'It's not so much what I intend to do but what you intend to do,' said Thomas. 'I've told your friend – I'm afraid I don't know your surname – I've told Catrina that I will do all I can to mediate between you and the authorities if there is any trouble. And I would like to emphasise that what you

211

have achieved is very remarkable. But obviously you realise that. I think it quite possible you would get a substantial reward. I would certainly help bring this about. Whether you do or not, the Italian Government pay a proportion of the value of recovered antiquities.'

'Don't be ridiculous,' said Alex. 'Proportion of the value – they pay about one-hundredth. In any case, this will all probably turn out to be Iannucci's. I haven't the faintest intention of going to the authorities as you call them. I found this, I dug it out, and I shall do what I like with it.'

'Then I have no alternative but to go myself.'

'I shan't let you.'

They faced each other, the older man apparently quite calm, the younger shaking, white-faced, distraught with fury and frustration.

Alex, looking about him wildly, suddenly saw the iron bar he'd left lying by the rail the night before and bent swiftly down to seize it.

Even as he raised it above his head, Thomas stepped under his arm and drove his right fist expertly into his solar plexus. At the same time he swung a left hook, catching the young man high on the right temple.

The two blows hurled Alex sideways and back against the wall, down which, doubling up, he slid to the floor.

'Alex!' cried Catrina and, thrusting between them, she knelt beside him.

Panting, less with effort than from released tension, Thomas stepped back. 'We won't solve this by violence,' he said. 'I don't want to hurt you, but I shall defend myself.' He moved to the railing. 'I'll give you two and a half hours to think this over. At three o'clock I shall come back. If you are still determined to try and exploit this on your own I shall report it myself.'

Neither of the young people took any notice of him. Alex, badly winded, was still gasping, bent over. Catrina massaged his stomach. Thomas swung himself onto the ladder and began the somewhat perilous return.

It was seventeen years since he'd struck out like that. Walking up the Via Ascione in the sun to keep his appointment in Herculaneum he noted, wryly, the coincidence of who it was he'd struck. He should of course have turned them in at once. But he would have given Philip a chance.

It was not, however, only that uncanny and unsettling resemblance which had led him to be so lenient. That perhaps excused it, a gesture to long-suffered, long-buried remorse. But there was another reason just as if not more important. Thomas couldn't resist letting himself have one more look at that perfectly preserved first-century Roman house. Before Dr Gandolfino and his minions descended to analyse, photograph, catalogue – and eventually cart away and shut up some or all of the inmates in the huge locked cages of the Naples Museum zoo.

[2]

It was ten minutes before Alex was fully recovered. He leant against the wall.

'He's as strong as hell. It was like being kicked by a horse.'

Catrina rubbed his stomach. 'What are we going to do?'

'What do you think? You heard what that thug said. We've got two and a half hours. Say two. We'll try and get the statue out. If it's too difficult we'll load the van with as much as we can and get out. Did you manage to saw through the chains?'

'I couldn't, Alex. There's no hacksaw.'

'Christ *alive*, Catrina,' Alex shouted, at once furious again. 'What's got into you? You used to be a help. Of course there's a hacksaw. Or you could have borrowed one from Carmela's husband.'

At the top of the shaft he emptied the tool chest all over the stable floor. There was no hacksaw.

'I'll have to go and get one. Go down there and start bringing up anything you can carry. Cover things with those sacks.'

'Let me get the hacksaw, Alex. I know all these people. I'll get one in a minute. And you'd be far quicker bringing things up. You'll take hours again, going into Torre Annunziata.'

'I shan't go into Torre Annunziata. I'll borrow one here.'

'*Please*,' said Catrina desperately, feeling she was about to cry. 'I *hate* going into that terrifying place alone.'

213

'Oh don't be so childish,' said Alex coldly. 'Listen, you've already nearly destroyed the only thing I've ever achieved, my one chance of getting rich. I said there was danger from burglars. You denied it. We were burgled. I said we must always lock up. You said no one ever came. You don't lock up and someone comes and we've fucking nearly blown it. Will you please, just this once, at the end of it all, do as I say? Go and rescue some stuff from down there.'

Catrina watched him open the stable door and back the van out. She felt humiliated, miserable and defiant. As he drove off she shouted. 'I shan't.'

Despite the urgency, he stopped the van outside the iron gates and came slowly back to carefully and deliberately relock them.

'I shan't go down into that beastly place, Alex,' Catrina shouted again, now blinded with tears. 'I'll go to Dr Gandolfino's party. I'm warning you.'

But Alex didn't even look up. He turned, got back into the van and roared off up the Via Ascione.

She walked slowly back to the kitchen and then up to the shower cubicle to get their washing things and some clothes. She'd pack all she could above ground first – though it was as frightening here in a different way as in the House of the Cock.

She'd come down to the kitchen with the suitcase when to her surprise she heard the van again. He was back already. She pushed the door into the living room nearly shut and stood against the walls, listening.

She heard him shout, 'Catrina!' And then a moment later, muffled, probably with his head poked through the hole at the bottom of the shaft – 'Catrina.'

Alex had managed to borrow from Signor Russo at the *alimentari*. There were now exactly two hours ten minutes before Henderson had said he'd return.

'Catrina,' he shouted again, standing beside the light-well. There was no sound at all in the buried house. Alex ran to the bedroom to see if she was sobbing on the bed. Empty. Her bright red shoes lying kicked off on the floor.

She was not in the *tablinium* either. 'Oh *fuck*,' said Alex aloud. He stood irresolute, and then turned abruptly and hurried into the small room with the statue. Eyes fixed, smiling, the beautiful boy stared sightless through the gap above the broken door.

Alex had taken four strokes of the hacksaw when he threw it down and jumped from beside the statue.

Something was wrong. Had she left him? He had a moment of panic. He couldn't finish it without Catrina. Or had she really gone to Dr Gandolfino's? Surely she hadn't been serious?

Or had she? Now a wave of fury swept him. He suddenly realised that that was precisely what she'd done. She'd probably watched him pass in the van. He ran swearing towards the stair.

Catrina heard the van start up just as she'd decided to emerge and join him. She ran out of the kitchen shouting, 'Alex! Alex!' But he must, for once, have omitted to re-padlock the gates on his return. The van was already halfway up the Via Ascione, the gates swinging wide.

She guessed at once where he'd gone. How long would he be? Five minutes to the *scavi* and down to the Antiquarium, three minutes to find she wasn't there, five minutes back. At the outside. He'd hurry.

After ten minutes she went to the shaft and slowly began to climb down it. Although she felt slightly guilty and a bit apprehensive about Alex's anger, she was more frightened of the buried house. But he could only be a few minutes now.

It was as she was crossing the light-well that another tremor struck. Catrina clung terrified to the two guide ropes as the ladder shook. She heard it rattling against the uprights of the railing. And she heard another sharp metallic noise in the depths of the house. It sounded as though the statue was jumping, shaking its chains, trying to escape.

But as she was coming out of the stairway into the *tablinium* she heard the noise again. It came from below in the *atrium*, a distinct metallic clink like two swords striking. Catrina stopped, her heart thudding. Once again she remembered Dr Schultz, 'You could find a living man down there.'

'Hello,' she shouted. 'Is anyone there? Mr Henderson? *C'è qualcuno là?*'

Suddenly, right opposite her, in the blackness beyond the door leading to the *atrium* she saw the whites of two eyes

215

gleaming in the light cast from the bulb outside. Now she could make out a sharp aquiline nose, the outline of a face.

Catrina was too frightened to move, too frightened even to cry out. Her hand at her mouth, she stared petrified in the doorway.

When he stepped out of the blackness and advanced wordlessly towards her, she thought for one hallucinatory and terrifying moment that he was dressed in the garb of a Roman soldier. But as he grabbed hold of her, his face streaked with dirt, she saw it was only jeans and a shirt.

The touch of his hand broke the grip of panic. She struck out with her free hand and kicked at his shins. 'Alex!' she screamed. 'Alex!'

He was far too strong. But struggling to break free, trying to bite his thumb, she thought she heard the rattle of the ladder. 'Alex – help?' she screamed again. 'Quick!'

There was another man. He had a jacket raised. Just before it was flung over her head, enveloping her, stifling her, she caught a glimpse of his face and was almost sure she recognised it. It was the man Dr Gandolfino had introduced as his Chief Engineer and who had led them so expertly through the old eighteenth-century tunnels – Signor Carlo Vincenzi.

[3]

Alex arrived at the lecture room in the Antiquarium six minutes after leaving Catrina. Dr Gandolfino was just finishing his address.

This had been much truncated. As the Soprintendente and his wife had arrived at the entrance to the *scavi* a young *carabinieri* had stepped up beside the car, saluted and handed him an envelope.

It contained a short, confidential message from the chief of police. The authorities had decided to evacuate the Communes of S. Georgio a Cremone, Portici, Ercolano and Torre del Greco, also all areas seven kilometres east, at dawn the next day, Tuesday 28 September. There would inevitably be some panic. Key personnel, among whom was included the Soprintendente of the *scavi di Ercolano*, were advised to leave at once.

Dr Gandolfino's immediate instinct was to turn the car that instant and drive full speed to Naples or even Rome.

His wife Sophia was made of stronger stuff. A striking black-haired woman twenty-five years younger than her husband, she told him not to be a fool. Cut his speech short. She would get away and collect some things from their apartment. He was to follow as quickly as he could. They'd meet up at the hotel in Naples they'd stayed in on their arrival from Milan.

Dr Gandolfino restructured his speech to its keynote and climax. The glory of Herculaneum was its courage. Its courage against the worst that earthquake, Vesuvius or time could do. A glory, he could now for the first time publicly reveal and inaugurate, about to be crowned by a new era of excavation – the glorious resurrection of the Villa di Papyri.

Bowing now to the applause, Dr Gandolfino was pleased he hadn't fled. Some local figures were absent – he couldn't see the Mayor of Torre del Greco, nor Capitano Pinto of the *carabinieri*. No doubt they too were 'key figures'. But most of the Naples people had come. Dr Montesano was there. He was pleased to see Professor Carlo Gilberto of the University.

Out of the corner of his eye he saw Sophia slip off her chair behind him on the low dais and make for a door at the back of the room. Soon he would make some excuse and hurry away.

Dr Schultz, advised by her friend in the Observatory, had advanced her departure by five days and was leaving that evening. Although she could hardly be refused entry, she had not in fact been formally invited to the celebration. However, when Signor Vincenzi had told her that as a mark of protest he and his workforce of three would not be turning up she had felt her position was vindicated. She had abandoned her plans of public confrontation, as outlined to Catrina, and had decided to come in a spirit of reconciliation. She might even drop her de-funding plans.

Dr Gandolfino's speech had reduced her to quivering breathless fury. Boasting loudly and at length about his mad Villa di Papyri plans, it was a deliberate public humiliation. There could be no reconciliation now. Her feelings were so strong she feared she might have a seizure.

She had to strike one more feeble blow for feminism. She

217

wished it did not have to be so feeble. She wished she had something other than her handbag, albeit weighted with a now empty flask, with which to strike it. Without ceremony, Dr Schultz elbowed her way to the front.

The first that Dr Gandolfino – now desperate to escape, edging surreptitiously towards the door – knew of her arrival was a blast of neat spirit as from an over-heated, over-brandied Christmas pudding thrust onto his nose.

'Just a minute,' hissed Dr Schultz in English. 'I want a word with you.'

'Nota now,' pleaded Dr Gandolfino, backing away. 'I hava urgent appointments. *Urgente.*'

Dr Schultz felt her control going. She reached out and grabbed Dr Gandolfino's ear. 'You're not getting away this time, you lousy skunk,' she said.

Dr Gandolfino was suddenly shaken by a violent pulse of panic. Instead of retreating, he lashed out.

In an instant, battle had developed. Bystanders rushed to separate them. Someone fell, bringing down several others into something that now resembled a rugger scrum.

It was this extraordinary scene which held Alex, standing on a chair at the back of the room, for a few vital minutes. All at once, he impatiently drew his eyes away and once again searched the heads below him. Where was she? What had she done? He could see no sign of her tight black curls.

'Who are you looking for?' It was the Museum man, Mr Henderson.

'Catrina, the girl I was with. Have you seen her?'

'She hasn't been here. I should certainly have noticed her. Has something happened?'

'I don't know. She's vanished. I'm worried. I feel something's wrong.'

'Perhaps she's gone into the town.'

'No, no she wouldn't do that – not now. Anyway, she's just been into the town. No – something serious must have happened.'

Alex pushed through the crowd to the door. He was aware that Thomas was following him. He didn't want this; at the same time he had an odd sense of inevitability.

At the van he turned. 'Why are you coming too? You said we had until three o'clock.'

'I meant it. I'll go back if you like.'

Alex didn't answer.

'If something has happened, I might be able to help,' said Thomas.

'Yes,' said Alex. He couldn't understand why he suddenly felt so apprehensive. He found it comforting to have the big man beside him.

At the bottom of the Via Ascione, he stopped and ran into Carmela's house. There was no one there.

He drove the van into the stable, re-padlocked the doors, and preceded Thomas down the shaft.

He looked once more in the bedroom and the bathroom and then hurried down into the *tablinium* below. He now saw one of Catrina's blue espadrille's beside the satyr fountain.

'She can't have gone out,' he said to Thomas. 'Unless she went with one shoe on and one off. She only had two pairs of shoes here. We were burgled. The red are upstairs. I didn't see that the blue one was here before.'

'Tell me exactly what happened?'

'We had a row. I was going to get a hacksaw. I told her to go and collect as much stuff out of here as she could. She was frightened and refused. Incidentally, you must have guessed what we'd do?'

'I knew you might.'

'Why did you give us the time?'

'I wanted to give you a chance to do the right thing. I didn't particularly want to turn you in. If you hadn't, you wouldn't have got far. I took the number of the van. You would leave it as late as possible. The Italian police are perfectly efficient.'

'I see,' said Alex. 'A trap. Also extremely patronising.'

'Have you searched the place thoroughly?' said Thomas. 'In the *atrium* – that is, I presume, down there? Above ground? One of these tremors might have dislodged something and struck her. Have you. . . .' Suddenly, in mid-sentence, Thomas started forward, shouting urgently, '*Look out behind you, Mayne.*'

Alex jerked his head half round and was just able to raise his arm sufficiently to partially deflect the pickaxe handle so that it glanced violently off the top of his head.

Temporarily stunned, though not unconscious, he could

219

offer little resistance to the two men who rushed him back up the stairs and then manhandled him up the shaft.

It took them ten minutes to finally subdue Thomas. Two he was a match for; another two were too much. Even so, they had to club him down as well. Arms pinned, he saw the blow coming and managed to heave himself sideways so that he took the brunt of it on his shoulders.

Chapter Thirteen

[1]

They put Thomas in one of the small ground floor store/stable rooms typical of the slums. His hands and feet were tied and he lay on the earth floor where he'd collapsed when they'd half-carried, half-flung him in.

His head and shoulders ached and throbbed where he'd been struck by the pickaxe handle. He raised his bound hands and gingerly felt the side of his head. The hair was spiky and hard with dried blood. The knuckles of both hands were bruised and painful. He'd landed a few good blows. He remembered one of the faces as he'd knocked it back. It had seemed oddly familiar.

After a while he managed to force himself to sit upright and lean against the wall. Sunlight streamed in thin rods and beams through cracks and holes in the big wooden door; also through a small grimy window high in the facing wall. The whole of one end was piled high with an assortment of boxes, rolls of chicken wire, a pram, two rusty iron bedsprings, the frame of a bicycle.

He supposed he was still in Ercolano, or at least not far away, because the tremors were continuing. Thomas was interested how quickly he'd grown used to them.

He looked at his watch – 2.45. It had been about 1.45 when he and Alex Mayne had left Gandolfino's reception.

He rolled painfully over onto his side and then frontwards onto his elbows and knees. Pressing down with his tied wrists he pushed himself onto his feet. He wanted to look through one of the cracks in the door and see where he was.

Three or four ungainly hops jarred his head so painfully that he turned and shuffled back. What did it matter where he was?

At five past three there was another tremor; and another

at three-twenty-five. Every twenty minutes. Seventy-two in twenty-four hours.

Slowly the rods of sun moved round, the angles widening as the sun went down. Then one by one they were cut off. Finally the little window went grey. Thomas dozed.

He was woken by the sound of the big wooden door being unlocked. It was quite dark in the store. The door opened and a moment later a single bulb came on in a socket above it.

There were two men standing looking at him. They came over without speaking. One knelt to untie his feet. The other produced a long oily rag and began to bind his eyes.

'*Attenzione! Attenzione!*' said Thomas sharply, his wound smarting. 'Tie it higher – *più alto.*'

'*Mi scusi,*' said the man.

When they'd pulled him to his feet, Thomas said, '*Dove mi porta?*'

'*Vedrà,*' said the man who'd untied his feet.

They guided him out and helped him into the back of a van. The last to get in was the driver and Thomas heard the right hand door slam. He supposed they were in young Mayne's van.

He was driven for about half an hour, but it was a circuitous route, presumably to make him think they were going further than they were.

They stopped. Thomas was helped out and led by the arm through a room and up some stairs. A door was opened, his blindfold was removed and he was pushed through.

It was a bare whitewashed room with a single window covered by a sack. Thomas noticed hooks in the ceiling; there were also some metal rings at chest height in the wall to the left of the window. Perhaps it had once been used for storing grain or meat.

Catrina and Alex were sitting at a small table. Both had their hands tied behind their backs.

Catrina got to her feet and came to him, her face drawn. 'What have they done to you, Mr Henderson?'

'Do I look so dreadful?'

'Your face is bruised. You've bled a lot.' She went behind him. 'Your head's been cut quite deeply, by a nail or something like that.'

'I'm better than I felt earlier. I'm not as young as I was.' He limped to one of the chairs and sank onto it. 'Are you all right, Mayne?'

'Yes,' said Alex. 'Just a bloody great bruise.'

They were all silent. All at once, so familiar now yet still strange, the house shivered and was then still.

'We can't be all that far away,' said Thomas.

'They blindfolded Alex and me. But from what I heard one of them say I think we're somewhere behind Ercolano.'

Again there was a silence. 'What do you think they'll do to us?' said Catrina.

'I don't know,' said Thomas. 'I had a feeling I'd seen one of them before.'

'The one with the scar and grey hair?' said Catrina. 'That was Signor Vincenzi. He's the chief engineer. We met him with Dr Gandolfino.'

'I see,' said Thomas slowly. 'I must have met him with Dorothy Schultz at some point. Chief engineer. Did he follow you down as well?'

'He's been opening up the eighteen-century tunnels, and I think digging some of his own. It's one of Dr Schultz's pet schemes. Tell him, Alex.'

But before Alex, slumped in morose silence, could speak, the door opened and an oddly formal procession came in. Signor Vincenzi led, followed by a second man carrying a tray on which were three plates and glasses, a bowl of spaghetti and a bottle of wine. A third man carried a shotgun.

They all showed signs of the recent fight. Signor Vincenzi had a pronounced black eye. He looked both worried and truculent. He muttered to Catrina while untying her wrists. 'He says that he has told Giuseppe to use that gun if we try anything.'

The relief at being free was considerable. Thomas rubbed his wrists and stretched his arms, then reached out and filled the three tumblers. The red wine was rough and fizzy.

'Ask Signor Vincenzi what he intends to do with us,' he said to Catrina, having decided not to try his rudimentary Italian.

Catrina asked. The reply was terse. 'It depends on his boss.'

'His *boss*?' said Alex, for the first time showing slight animation, 'He can't mean Dr Schultz, can he?'

This did not require translation. Vincenzi was clearly shocked. Dottoressa Schultz knew nothing about all this. How could they suppose such a thing? The gravest injustice had been done to her by the *Società Archeologico di Ercolano*.

'Ask him,' said Thomas, intrigued by the vehemence of this short outburst, 'if he isn't ashamed to betray his work like this. Does he intend to hand in any of the things he has found?'

Once again, Vincenzi was stung. '*Senti chi parla. Cosa facavate là sotto? Imballando il tutto per portare al Museo Nationale?*'

'He says,' said Catrina, 'that we can't talk. What were we doing down there – packing it all up to take to the Museo Nationale?'

But Signor Vincenzi was clearly also very anxious to explain and excuse himself. He could barely pause to let Catrina translate.

He and his fellow workers had begun in secret about a year before, more to test Dr Schultz's ideas than anything else. He said that they'd planned, if successful, to reveal the results in a few months – '*Per rivendicare la dottoressa*'. To vindicate the doctor.

Two things happened. Early on they came upon a number of very fine objects – a bronze head, two marble portrait busts. The second, well, they – he gestured at the three of them – would not understand what was happening in Naples. He himself was employed, he was all right. But he had three brothers, all unemployed. He had two sons who could scrounge a living, and frequently not even that. Did they know what it was like to have no money? No work? His workmen were the same – all with poor relatives in desperate need. Anyway – to whom did this stuff belong?

One of his brothers had a wife who came from Sicily. Her family, especially her brother, were mixed up in that sort of thing – smuggling, tomb-robbing, all harmless stuff on the side. This man got very good prices for the bronze head and the portrait busts. He paid them a very fair percentage. He promised to sell anything they found. He promised to protect them if there was any trouble. He would take all the risks –

224

including transporting their finds to Sicily. But in return, everything they found they had to give to him.

Then Dr Gandolfino arrived. It became quite clear that nothing which had anything to do with Dottoressa Schultz would be listened to. Anyway, they'd now gone too far to turn back.

Signor Vincenzi now embarked on a speech in which Alex's name featured several times. Catrina didn't bother to translate, merely saying, '*Si, si,*' several times and finishing her spaghetti.

'What's he saying, Catrina?' said Alex at last, exasperated. 'It seems entirely about me.'

'It is,' said Catrina. 'He's saying nothing they found is anything like what you've done. He says it's truly remarkable. He says it proves Dr Schultz was quite right. What he is really doing is saying we are in the same boat as him.'

'Hardly an accurate description of the situation,' said Alex.

There was a short silence. Catrina suddenly said, '*Cosa faresti se un Siciliano ti dicesse di ucciderci?*'

Signor Vincenzi stood up abruptly. '*Non succederebbe mai.*'

He turned away from the table and told one of the men to take away the plates.

Each of them in turn was then taken by Giuseppe, shotgun held across his chest, and allowed to use a basin and cracked, seatless toilet.

Thomas was last. In the square of mirror he looked like some tramp murderer – or his victim. He wiped away the worst of the dirt and dried blood. Turning his head, he could see the long scalp wound.

When he got back, Alex and Catrina, their wrists retied, were sitting on two mattresses along the wall opposite the window.

Thomas, however, was taken to a third mattress alongside the window.

'He thinks you're the dangerous one,' said Catrina.

Vincenzi tied Thomas' wrists with the nylon rope and then threaded it through one of the metal rings. He left sufficient for him to lie down. Without a word he walked to the door, turned off the light and shut the door. They heard the key turn in the lock.

The house shook again. Thomas heard the metal rings tap against the plaster in the darkness.

Alex said, 'What did you say that upset him, Catrina?'

'I asked him if he'd kill us if the man in Sicily told him to. He said it wouldn't arise.'

'I don't think it will arise,' said Alex. 'He's obviously out of his depth. I just hope some catastrophe makes it impossible for him to take anything out of our house.'

Thomas thought it would certainly arise. The way in which Vincenzi and his men had attacked him and Mayne had been both violent and ruthless. Why should they be allowed to live? They put in jeopardy enormous sums of money – millions of pounds. He did not look forward to the next day one bit.

He said nothing. They were all still shocked. Alex Mayne must have been shattered at the total collapse of all his hopes. He could almost feel sorry for him.

'I think it's amazing they went on digging when the whole place is shaking itself to pieces,' said Catrina.

'That was the reason,' said Thomas. 'Like you, they wanted to find and get out as much as they could while it was still possible.'

He realised the silence that followed was slightly hostile. He'd separated himself from them, put them together with Vincenzi. The silence extended. He felt very tired. He shifted slightly, pulling the blanket higher with his tied hands.

Suddenly Catrina said into the darkness, 'Did the Romans have wigs, Mr Henderson?'

'Yes,' said Thomas. 'They were rare, but a few of the richer ones did. Chinese hair. Why?'

'I just wondered,' said Catrina.

[2]

Thomas was woken at seven-fifteen by the sound of a loud-speaker. He lay a moment, then threw off the blanket and pulled himself up by the rope running through the metal ring.

He ached all over. It wasn't until the day after a boxing match that you learnt how much punishment you'd taken. He'd taken a good deal.

His rope just reached to the window. Thomas pulled down

226

the sacking and tried to open it but the base had been nailed to the frame. He pressed his forehead to the glass.

They were high up behind what must have been either Ercolano or Torre del Greco. He could see in the distance the blue expanse of the sea, as calm as though it were a fallen segment of the empty sky.

The house they were in, the only one with a balcony, was the only old one in a line of four or five newly built, the rest of which he could just see to the right.

Across to the left, over a road, were scattered houses among fruit trees and vegetable plots. In the road was a police car with a speaker on the roof. A *carabinieri* was standing beside it talking to a small highly excited and gesticulating group.

'What's going on?' Catrina was sitting up, puffy with youth and sleep.

Thomas looked out again. The *carabinieri* was getting back into the car. 'I'm not sure. Come here. You may be able to hear what they're saying.'

The police moved slowly off down the road towards the town.

'*Le autorità ordinano di lasciare libera questa zona immediatamente.*' The harsh sound of the speaker was oddly menacing and disturbing. *Chi non trova alloggio presso i parenti potrà recarsi al campo di emergenza, vicino al Cimitero del Pianto. Non è il caso di lasciarsi prendere dal panico.*'

The car stopped just in sight about a hundred yards down the road. Another little group gathered round the young *carabinieri* officer.

'Could you catch what they said?'

'Something about evacuating immediately,' said Catrina. 'They said go to the Pianto cemetery if you'd nowhere else to go. No need to panic.'

'No need to panic indeed,' said Alex. 'What shall we do? We must get out.'

'We'll have to wait,' said Thomas.

'But they can't just leave us here. Suppose an earthquake brought the house down?'

'I imagine they'd be delighted.'

They stood and watched the houses empty. Most people must have left before. From their line there came only one car with a couple in it and filled with hastily thrown in

227

bundles. An old man with a handcart was methodically loading it from the house next to them.

Suddenly Alex said, 'I can't stand this,' He walked over to the door and kicked out violently backwards with his heel. 'Hello!' he shouted. 'Signor Vincenzi? Are you there?' He stopped. They all listened. There was no sound. Alex kicked the door again. 'Signor Vincenzi,' he shouted, '*Let us out.*'

'They've gone,' said Catrina.

Alex beat on the door with his fists. 'Signor Vincenzi! Signor Vincenzi!' he shouted, then turned. 'I'm not going to stay trapped like this waiting to be blown up. What can we do?' He looked about him, his yellow hair wild, at bay, desperate.

Thomas turned away, wincing. 'I think you could kick in the panels of the door,' he said. 'They don't look very strong.'

But Alex had already picked up one of the chairs in his bound hands. 'Look out,' he said.

He brought it to the window and despite the feeble grip and awkward angle eventually managed to smash open one side of the casement. He climbed out onto the balcony and stood resting his hands on the balustrade.

The only person in sight was the old man. He had finished loading his cart and was about to set off.

'Hey Signore,' called Alex. '*Attenzione!* Help! *Per favore* – come and let us out.'

The old man looked up, then bent to his task. The cart began to move.

'You shout to him, Catrina,' said Alex.

Catrina clambered out onto the balcony and shouted to the man as he moved slowly out into the road.

'*Per favore signore – siamo chiusi qui dentro, venite a liberarci. Ci vorrà un minuto solo. Per favore aiutateci.*'

The old man took no notice. He paused once in the middle of the road while a tremor shook them, then continued imperturbably until out of sight.

'I don't fancy trying to get down off here with my hands tied,' said Alex, bending over the balustrade.

Thomas looked at his watch. There was now a ten-minute interval between tremors. 'Kick in that door,' he said to Alex again. 'You've already split it where you kicked before.'

Alex bent and climbed in through the window. He returned

to the door and began to hack backwards at it with his heel. Almost at once the wood began to splinter.

In five minutes he'd kicked out sufficient space for him to force his way through. There was a click of the key and the door opened. 'Come on,' he said to Catrina. 'Let's go down.'

They were gone some time. When Alex returned he was alone, carrying a kitchen knife. 'We're going back into Herculaneum to try and get out that statue.'

'Which statue?'

'Didn't you see the statue of the boy?'

'I didn't have time to see anything properly.'

'Well, it's the most valuable of the lot. I'm going back to get it out.'

'I think that's very foolish. Obviously something is about to happen here. We should get out at once.'

'I don't see why. The scientists said they could give two days' warning. That gives us at least a day. Will you help us?'

'No,' said Thomas.

'Then I can't let you go.'

Alex had his eyes down, fixed on the knife.

'You'd leave me tied up here, with the strong possibility that I'd be killed?'

'I can't risk it,' said Alex. 'If I let you go you'd simply go straight to the nearest *carabinieri*. If we have a day or so to get away we've a very good chance.'

'Do you suppose anyone would listen to anything like that now? They certainly wouldn't send a lot of police back into the danger zone just to pick you up.'

'I can't risk it,' said Alex obstinately.

'So you'll leave me here like this?'

'It's your choice, not mine. Will you come and help us or not?' His expression was hunted.

'I've already given you my answer.' After a pause, Thomas added, 'Does Catrina know that this is what you're planning to do? Does she agree?'

'Oh shut up.' Alex turned angrily away and went out slamming the door. Thomas thought he heard their raised voices downstairs, then there was silence.

Thomas leant back and felt the house shudder as another shock struck it. The iron rings tapped against the wall. This time he heard, deep in the earth, a sound like a muffled explosion.

He wondered if he was near death – and if so if he was frightened. He had long realised he was not really capable of love; not, that is, as women seemed capable of it. He had never loved as he had been loved. Only his son had raised in him such a powerful, almost frantic feeling. When Philip died he'd thought, that's it – nothing else can really hurt me. And with no compelling reason to live – no reason outside himself – he had, he thought, ceased to care very much about death.

He was relieved to find that it was so. He felt no fear; he felt resigned, perhaps even a little curious. He moved the length of his tether and stared out of the window. The great bay sparkled two miles or so away in the September sun. Out of the blue was an exact description. On just such a day as this, a day of blue sky, blue sea, had disaster struck nearly two thousand years before. But they too must have had warning – shocks, tremors.

He looked at his watch – eight-thirty. He remembered that August of his research – thirty-four years ago now – how he'd stood on the balcony of his hotel room on the front in Naples. It would be in the dead heat of morning – ten o'clock – but he would look intently to the horizon waiting to discern in the distance the thin black line that would eventually resolve itself into the day-long cooling breeze.

Suddenly Thomas's eye, vacant in memory, sharpened. Surely that was a line of wind-raised waves racing across the bay now. But, surging towards shore with incredible swiftness, this was something of far greater turbulence than those soft summer streams.

The line of tossing waves vanished from view. They must have struck with great force because clouds of dust rose from the houses near the shore. It was as this cloud swept inland that Thomas realised what was happening.

Just in time he flung himself down against the wall, crouched with his head between his knees, bound arms and hands bent up to protect his bowed head. As he did so, there came a surging subterranean roar as though a furious herd of bulls were charging through the earth below.

The whole house was violently shaken. It shook for about twelve seconds. There was the din of collapsing masonry and plaster rained from the ceiling. Then the roar faded into the distance. There was silence, broken once by the crash of a tile falling, once by a slide of rubble. Dust filled the room.

Thomas got to his feet and brushed himself clumsily. He hadn't been hit, though heavy blocks of plaster littered the floor. The room was intact, except for the wall to his right which had been wrenched back at an angle so that at the top he could see out past the roof to the sky.

One of the houses across the road was in ruins. It looked as if the front wall of the house at the end on the right had fallen out. The balcony outside the window had vanished.

Thomas turned back and examined the room more closely. He was fortunate it had not collapsed. Great cracks split it from floor to ceiling. One of these, he now saw, went straight through the point at which his ring was pinned into the wall. He raised his hands, gripped the rope and pulled. The ring came out as if set in butter.

He stared for an instant in disbelief, then with a surge of excitement coiled in the rope and set off, carefully keeping close to the wall till he reached the door.

It was still unlocked. The staircase had pulled away from the wall for the length of three steps but the fourth one held his weight and stepping gingerly, once more pressed to the wall, he reached the bottom safely.

There was a knife on the kitchen table, the same knife Alex Mayne had been holding. Thomas put it blade up and gripped it between his knees. It took six minutes to sever the last thread and he pulled his hands apart. He was free.

The cracked toilet with its nail hung with torn newspaper was waterless. Nor did the tap run. He ran his hand through his hair, then set off from the house towards the town.

He went at a steady limping trot, keeping to the middle of the road. He rubbed his wrists and bent and straightened his arms as he ran. Not for the first time in the last two days he blessed the years of squash that had kept him fit.

As he ran down the tarmac road the houses gradually became more numerous and the extent of the damage increased. Hardly any had escaped unscathed; one or two were in ruins. The tremors were now coming at irregular five– to ten-minute intervals. Twice Thomas stopped as the ground shook. There was no sign of any people, though several times he heard dogs barking from empty houses, presumably left behind to deter looters.

The tarmac gave way to large flagstones and the road turned a corner into the first street. Here, suddenly, he came upon a scene of frenzied activity. A van and a small Fiat were parked on the right-hand side of the descending road outside a house whose roof had partly collapsed in onto the first floor. At the wheel of the van sat a youth of about twenty; in the Fiat a short, bald man of about sixty. Both engines were running. The man had his door open and was shouting back towards the house.

As Thomas came towards them, an elderly woman tottered from the house. Although three-quarters hidden by the pile of dresses and boxes she was carrying he could see she was enormously fat. She staggered across the pavement, half-shoved, half-let fall her burden into the back of the van and turned to hurry back into the house.

At this the man leapt out of his car, ran some way towards the house and stopped, shaking both hands above his head.

'*Tu sei una pazza lunatica,*' he shrieked. '*Vuoi ammazzarci tutti? Lascia le tue cose, lasciale. Vieni. Lunatica! Lunatica!*'

Without pausing in his stride, almost without thinking, Thomas swerved as he passed the van, jumped into the Fiat, slammed the door, set off the brake and shoved in the gear. As the little car shot forward, he saw the man start after him, then stop and stand gesticulating.

He knew the sensible thing to do would be to drive as fast as he could to Naples. Instead, he drove on down, guessing Ercolano to be more or less straight ahead. He was haunted, as if from the past, by the image of the young man, the young man with his desperate hunted face and his yellow hair.

The first signpost came at a garage – Ercolano, Torre del Greco left. Soon after that an appalling road, taken at speed, went steeply down to the right, signposted '*Centro Città, Scavi*'. It passed under the *autostrada*. Five minutes later Thomas joined the Via IV Novembre.

The damage here was much the same as higher up the

slopes of Vesuvius. Many buildings had partially collapsed, none had entirely escaped. The tram lines were down and spread down the road like an immense cat's cradle. The little slum town was deserted, waiting silent in the sun.

Just past the Caffè Fauno Thomas had to slow and almost stop. There was now a foot-wide crevice stretching right across the road and continuing in a large crack up the wall of the *alimentari*. He turned right up the Corso Resina. The tramlines here were still intact, but sagging badly. Their street, as far as he could remember, was second or third on the left past the buried Teatro.

The Via Ascione had been almost totally devastated. But again, the shock wave, as freakish as blast in its effects, had kept the street itself quite clear. The old slum houses, weakened by weeks of earth tremor, had simply fallen in on themselves.

At the bottom he found the iron gates unpadlocked. The house itself was still standing, although most of the plaster had been shaken off the walls and the house next to it had yet further collapsed. Two bicycles had been flung down outside the stable.

The heavy beam holding the pulley and the light and bell wires seemed only just in its socket. Thomas gave a quick glance above his head then descended as quietly as he could into the shaft.

He stood listening when he'd crossed the light-well. He could hear Alex's voice from below. 'Mayne,' he shouted. 'Come up here, both of you. It's me – Henderson.'

There was silence, then he heard running footsteps on the short stairway. It was Catrina who appeared, looking dishevelled and frightened. 'Thank God you're all right. I was terrified something terrible might have happened to you.'

'You've got to get out of here. Another shock like the last one and the building will come down. You'll be trapped.'

'I can't get Alex to come. He's mad. You've got to help me get him out. I can't leave him.'

She turned and disappeared. He followed her, bending into the stairway.

Alex was standing staring up at one of the most beautiful statues Thomas had ever seen. As the buried city shook again so that he steadied himself against the broken door, the statue

233

held him for a moment transfixed. Even then his scholar's mind automatically noted, analysed. The eyes were unusual. Almost certainly *lapis lazuli* set in ivory.

'Thank God you're here,' said Alex, oddly echoing Catrina. He seemed to have forgotten the events of an hour before. He'd forgotten everything except the statue at which he was again staring with fierce intensity.

'You can't stay here,' said Thomas. 'We've got to get out at once. There's either going to be an eruption or another earthquake or both.'

Alex appeared not to hear. 'I hadn't noticed he was fixed to that marble plinth, which still hasn't been set into the rock. Of course, with that as well he weighs far more than three hundred pounds. It's too much for one person. There isn't time to get the big pulley. But if you and I pulled, we could do it. Catrina can then pull the statue clear and we can lower it into the barrow.'

'But we haven't got the van,' said Catrina. 'It's impossible. How can you possibly get away? Please leave it, Alex, and let's get out of here.'

'Mr Henderson came by car, didn't you?'

Thomas nodded automatically, without answering.

'You see?' Alex turned to Thomas. 'Will you help us?'

Thomas didn't answer. He was staring with fixed eyes at the distraught and hectic face, the wild, gorse-bloom hair.

'For God's sake,' cried Alex, reaching out his hands, his voice breaking, 'please help me. Can't you see I'm in the shit? You've got to help me. Please.'

There was a long silence, while Thomas stood without speaking. And suddenly Catrina had the feeling that he too had descended, had been forced down like them into some unconscious region of himself.

Almost as if alone, looking at Alex but not addressing him, Thomas said, 'Yes, all right. I'll help you.' At once he was aware not just of an extraordinary release but of something that was much deeper. He was swept by a sense of atonement.

He walked over and joined Alex by the rope hanging from the pulley. Catrina went and stood in front of the statue. For a moment none of them moved. Then Catrina, almost as though hypnotised, stretched out her hand and gripped one

234

of the delicately veined ankles. It was the first time she'd touched it. The dark bronze was as smooth as skin.

'Right,' said Alex. '*Now!*'

He and Thomas braced themselves and took the strain. As they did so, as if they had released some mechanism, there came from far below the city that same sinister rumbling muffled roar. The ground began to shake in a series of convulsions so violent that Thomas was thrown backwards to the ground, striking the side of his head painfully against the wall. The roaring was accompanied by deep detonations like bombs going off under water.

It lasted about fifteen seconds. The rumbling faded, but this time instead of stillness and silence, the ground continued to shake. Thomas lay, his head throbbing. It was not so much shaking as shuddering. He heard Alex stir near him and then heard him cry out, 'Oh my God.'

Thomas sat up. Alex was pressed back against the wall, his eyes fixed wide in horror.

In front of them, spreadeagled on her face in front of the statue, her arms back, palms up, lay Catrina. The marble block with the inscription, jammed for centuries, had finally been dislodged. It lay across her head like a pillow she'd pulled to block out the noise.

Thomas moved so fast he was not aware of rising. He was bending over, both hands gripping the marble. But one glance showed it to be too late. Death had obviously been instantaneous. He could just see the dark curls parted by a massive split from which the force of the blow had extruded a wedge of brain matter. The rest of the crushed skull and face was mercifully hidden by the marble block.

Before he could straighten, he was thrust aside by Alex, who seized the three-foot marble block at either end and bent his knees to try and lift it.

'I shouldn't,' said Thomas gently. 'Best leave it.'

Alex looked up at him. 'You mean she's dead?'

'Yes, I'm afraid so.'

Alex looked at him as though trying to understand a foreign language. Then he turned away and struck his open hands violently against his face. 'Oh, Christ,' he said, 'What have I done? What have I done?'

Thomas stood awkwardly, feeling the blood from his re-opened wound running down inside his shirt. He put out his hand, then withdrew it and walked out into the *tablinium*.

Here nothing seemed to have changed. Except, as he stood looking about him, he could feel the ground thrumming under his feet. It was as though whatever it was below, now frantic to get out, had started to vibrate the bars of its cage.

Thomas stood irresolute. He could hear Alex being sick. Poor bloody boy. Yet if he himself hadn't. . . . Instantly, he shut his mind. He refused to think about it, about that sweet girl lying there. Had he laid one ghost only to raise another?

The marble shivered under his feet. They had to get out. But Alex needed a little longer – give him a moment longer.

He was still standing there three minutes later, when there came a rending crash from above them and the lights went out.

At once he heard Alex, his voice high, cry out, 'What's that? What the hell's happened now?'

'I don't know,' said Thomas, arms out as he moved forward. 'I'm going up to see if I can find out.' He prayed that what he feared hadn't happened.

He felt Alex brush roughly past him in the dark. 'No – you stay with her. I'll get the torches from the bedroom.'

Keeping his arm out, Thomas felt his way along the wall and into the stairs. Mounting slowly in the dark he could hear the ladder across the light-well rattling as the ground vibrated.

All at once there was a beam of light through the round opening at the top of the stairs. He bent through and found Alex standing at the light-well directing his torch across. As Thomas had feared, the entrance was blocked.

Alex appeared unable to take it in. When Thomas took the other torch from his left hand, he turned and looked at him blankly.

'I'll get across and see if I can shift it,' said Thomas.

A look of fear suddenly contorted Alex's face, and without speaking he turned and disappeared down the stairs again.

Thomas tightened the cords binding the ladder to the rail, then gingerly crossed it. Here his worst fears were realised. The shaft was completely blocked with wood from the stable roof, including the main beam. There was hardly any rubble, indeed he could shine his torch through and see up the shaft in several places. But heave and wrench as he did, the mass of wood was unshiftable. They were trapped.

He re-crossed the ladder and went slowly along to the bedroom. As he remembered, there was a jug of water besides the beaker on the table by the bed. If they were to be rescued, how long would they have to wait? Vesuvius could erupt, in which case nothing was predictable. But it now seemed more likely that this was another earthquake spasm as in 1980. If that were so, he thought, the worst was probably over. They'd had two severe shocks. There would be after-shocks, but not for days, even weeks. People would soon return. They must listen; then shout.

He limped back down the marble corridor. No one would come and look for them. Not only did they suppose the place evacuated, they had no idea the buried house existed. By the time they got around to clearing up the rubble he and Alex would be long dead. At least it gave some point to that girl's death. She would be spared the worst.

As for him, once again he felt no fear. He would have time to study the place now. If he had to die, what better place to spend his last few days than here?

Alex was standing in the dark when he came back to the statue room. Thomas kept his torch pointing at his feet, then turned it off to conserve the battery. There was no knowing how long they'd need them.

'I can't believe she's dead,' Alex said. 'It's not possible to take in. Her hands are still quite warm and soft.'

There was a pause. 'I'm extremely sorry,' Thomas said.

'Do you blame me for it?'

There was a short pause. 'No.'

'I think I shall – when I can think about it.' After another pause he said, 'I don't want to leave her here now. Let's get her to the surface, wash her, make her comfortable.'

'We can't,' said Thomas.

'Why not?'

'The ceiling has collapsed and blocked the shaft. It's unshiftable. We're trapped.'

'We'll have to take the tunnel then.'

'What tunnel?'

'The one Vincenzi and that lot took Catrina out by.'

'I didn't know about that.'

'No – I suppose she told me before you got there. But I imagined you'd guessed. He told us about digging out the eighteenth-century tunnels. That's how they found the place. They pulled her out the same way.

'I see. Somehow I imagined they'd come in as I had. It doesn't matter.'

Thomas noticed with detachment how his philosophic acceptance of death vanished the moment there was hope. His heart was beating rapidly. 'Let's go and find it. We ought to get out of all this and up to the surface as fast as we can.'

'You mean we must leave her here?'

'Yes,' said Thomas gently. 'Leave her. For the moment. We can come down later for that.'

'I suppose so,' said Alex.

But he didn't move. They stood silently together in the blackness, in the trembling house. At last Thomas said, 'We must go.'

Alex didn't answer. For a whole minute they stood, and then suddenly he turned on his torch and cast it slowly over Catrina's body at his feet and on up to the statue above her. For the last time the bronze boy's *lapis lazuli* and ivory eyes flashed and were gone. Alex stepped past Thomas and he followed him across the *tablinium* floor.

Signor Vincenzi and his men had had time to hack only a narrow two-foot high passageway through the tongue of mud-rock which had finally forced its way into the *atrium*. Once Thomas and Alex had crawled fifteen feet or so down this they found themselves in one of the old eighteenth-century tunnels which had followed the Roman street.

Here Alex turned left and set off into the darkness. But this too had been re-dug out little more than three foot high and Thomas had to bend double. Quite soon they were stopping to rest.

After fifty yards the tunnel divided. 'I don't know which way to go,' said Alex. 'Catrina didn't describe the way or anything.' Suddenly he added, 'God, I wish these tunnels weren't so bloody *low*.'

His voice was shaking. Thomas flashed his torch briefly and saw that Alex's face – the face of his long-dead son – was dead white. There were flecks of foam at his lips. The shock was coming to him.

'Let me go in front for a bit,' Thomas said.

Alex let him squeeze past without answering. Bent double, scraping their backs, already sweating profusely in the heat, they hurried on. Another thirty paces and the tunnel divided again. Now it was so low they were crawling, backs pressed to the roof.

'I can feel it pressing down. It's not safe,' said Alex, the rising note of panic now marked in his voice.

'Shut up,' said Thomas sharply. 'Don't be such a bloody fool. Of course it's safe. These tunnels have survived much worse than this since 1738. We're safer here than on the surface.'

Without pausing to think, he took the right-hand tunnel and crawled forward. After about fifteen feet the tunnel came to a dead end.

They knelt in silence. Thomas was acutely conscious of the weight of seventy foot of rock above them, seeming about to shudder down and crush them. He desperately tried to visualise the turns and direction they had taken relative to the *atrium* and the buried house itself. It was impossible.

'We're either going to get out at the old Theatre or at the *scavi* themselves,' he said. 'Or at some new entrance which Vincenzi made. We can't know where that would be. But the Theatre and the *scavi* would be downhill and I have the feeling we've been going slightly uphill.'

They crawled back the last fifteen feet, then Thomas squeezed past Alex again and they retraced their way to the first divide. After about twenty doubled-up paces down the right-hand tunnel it suddenly grew high enough for Thomas to stand upright. The relief was extraordinary and instantaneous. He quickened his pace to a run, although he was now limping badly and could feel his old war wound with every step.

Too late, intent on piercing the blackness ahead, he suddenly saw at his feet a two-foot wide crevice. He just had time to shout, 'Look out, Mayne!' and step wide across it when he heard Alex cry out behind him and there was a sharp noise like a pistol shot.

It was not particularly deep – not more than eighteen inches. But at the bottom it narrowed to seven inches or less. He could see Alex's foot had been rammed up by the force of his descent at a savagely acute angle. He cried out twice as Thomas freed him. Slipping his hand up inside the trouser, Thomas could feel the ligament bulge half-way up the calf.

'I'm sorry,' said Alex, sitting leaning against the side of the tunnel. 'I think I'm going to faint.'

'Put your head between your knees.' He supported him, helping him bend forward. Alex was drenched in sweat, breathing quick and shallow and shivering violently. As he held the young man, moved by his vulnerability, waiting for the spasm to pass, Thomas heard below them, deep in the vibrating rock, another of the sudden muffled explosions, the underwater detonations, which had accompanied the last shock.

Alex's breathing eased. He pushed himself upright. 'What have I done?'

'Your Achilles tendon's snapped. How do you feel?' He knew Alex's leg would soon be very painful indeed.

'Not too good. Look,' said Alex. 'I'm going to hold you up. There's no sense in us both going just because of me. You get on and get out.'

Thomas didn't even bother to answer this. 'The tunnel's too narrow for two abreast. We'll get you up and then you put your arms round my neck. Keep them low to avoid the wound at the side of my head.'

Though Alex was fairly heavy, Thomas would not ordinarily have found it too difficult. But he hadn't much strength left.

Fifteen paces further on the tunnel divided again. Breathing heavily, Thomas paused to rest; then took the right-hand turn. He had an uneasy feeling they were completing three sides of a square.

Another twenty paces and suddenly the roof dropped four foot. Thomas stopped and let Alex down.

'We'll have to crawl again. Do you think you can manage it?'

'Yes.'

They crawled for about twenty yards. Several times he heard Alex gasp with pain. Then the tunnel roof became still lower. Thomas stretched out flat. And now, for the first time, be began to think they were finished. He was old, far, far too old. He pulled himself forward – a snake, a rat. Behind him he heard Alex gasp again.

Forty yards, fifty – how far had they gone? He had a sudden strong suspicion that this height of tunnel – no longer a tunnel, just a hole – was quite new. It was slowly being crushed flat. The wave of panic was almost uncontrollable. Muffled, he heard Alex cry out.

And then all at once, the walls widened, the roof rose. Thomas was able to kneel, to stand. He directed his torch ahead. Seven feet in front of them was a wall of solid rock. The tunnel was blocked.

He leant panting against the wall and then sank into a sitting position. The old wound in his leg was throbbing painfully. Nothing to what Alex must be going through. They would have to retrace their steps. To go where? To crawl, to squirm more and more exhausted through this maze until they dropped? But in fact he already knew he could go no further, back or forward, whether it were possible or not.

Alex, still lying on his front, was playing his torch onto the rock face. 'Wait a minute,' he said suddenly. 'Catrina did say one thing. Apparently they stopped at one point. She was able to stand up again. She couldn't see anything – they'd blindfolded her – but she had the impression that Vincenzi or one of them was opening a door. That block may not be as solid as it looks.'

Thomas stood up and moved wearily to the tunnel's end. It felt solid enough. He ran his hands over it. Rock hard. But suddenly, by the light of Alex's torch, he noticed something rather curious. The surface was divided into segments roughly a foot square by barely discernible but continuous hairline cracks. He took out his own torch and looked closely. There was no doubt about it – a grid of artificially square blocks not noticable at a quick glance but obvious on examination.

Thomas put his hands on one side and shoved. The rock face was firm but he thought he felt it move a little, not in time to the relentless vibration of the whole rock-bound city, but as a result of his efforts.

He moved to the left, placed his shoulder to the rock and heaved. Slowly he felt it start to give and then, all at once, pivoted in the middle, the entire constructed tunnel-face spun forward and round and he found himself standing in darkness on the far side. He had only to repeat the process to spin it back again.

As he pulled Alex through, hopping on one foot, the dangling foot caught and he cried out. The tunnel beyond was nearly head high but again too narrow for them to walk abreast. Thomas heaved Alex carefully onto his back again.

He was near the end of his strength now. He had to stop every ten or fifteen paces, pouring with sweat, his heart pounding, to lower Alex onto one foot and get his breath back. Each time it was harder to go on.

Twenty times or more they stopped, then the torch showed the tunnel spreading into a wide junction off which numerous other tunnels branched. As it widened, Thomas put Alex down and then stood leaning forward, hands on knees, trembling with exhaustion.

At last he forced himself upright. 'Put your arm round my shoulder. I'll support you while you hop forward.'

'Can you manage it?'

'Yes.'

Moments later they were through a high square opening and standing on the stage of the buried theatre.

The relief at being out of the confined tunnels was enormous. They stood swinging their torches and, though it was years since he'd been there, Thomas suddenly recognized in the roof high above them the small round black hole of the eighteenth-century peasants' well. The subterranean explosions were now coming regularly every few minutes and reverberated in the hollow darkness.

Each step they took jarred Alex's ripped tendon. He too was now near the end of his strength, and by the time they reached the bottom of the ninety steps to the surface, Thomas was virtually carrying him again.

It took them twenty-eight minutes to haul themselves, step by step, to the top. At the bottom of the long last flight, slippery with water, Thomas saw something gleaming from the top. For a terrible moment he thought it was fire, then he realised it must be daylight.

As they slowly neared the top, the light grew stronger. He turned off his torch. At last they staggered into the small, summerhouse-like entrance room and both collapsed on the floor.

242

Stumbling, crawling, through the endless tunnel streets of the buried city, it seemed impossible there could be light anywhere. The world had been plunged into never-ending darkness. But here was sunlight streaming in through broken windows. Sunlight and space.

Almost at the end of his endurance, Thomas did not dare rest. The vibrating was growing steadily in intensity, the subterranean explosions now almost continuous. He lifted aside some eight-foot marble columns which had fallen sideways in front of the wooden door, then kicked this open and walked slowly back to Alex.

It was clear even in the Via Mare that Ercolano had not escaped the second of the major earthquake shocks. The two houses immediately down from the Teatro were strewn in rubble across the little street.

But the full extent of the damage began to be revealed when they had dragged their way up the steps to the Corso Resina. Great cracks spread across the trembling road itself. Opposite, the church of Santa Caterina was two-thirds ruins. Roofs had collapsed, fronts fallen in, not a building, not a house had escaped. There was so much dust about that the very air seemed to vibrate.

They advanced to the middle of the road over fallen tramlines and strewn rubble. Thomas was bracing himself to turn and start in the direction of Portici and Naples when Alex suddenly cried, 'Look!'

Thomas raised his head. Unbelievably, zig-zagging wildly to avoid the debris scattered in its path, an army jeep was racing towards them. As it came close, he had a sudden feeling that the driver was too frightened to stop, but at the last moment it skidded up beside them.

A tense-faced officer beside the young driver jerked his thumb over his shoulder. '*Di dietro. Presto.*'

Thomas helped Alex over the tailboard and hauled himself after him. The jeep jerked forward. As it did so there came from the direction of Vesuvius a deafening, earth-rending detonation, then a deep, sustained roar. At the same moment as the volcano exploded into life the terrible vibrating and shuddering came to an end. The monster, so long pent up, shaking the earth in its frustration and fury, had at last burst free.

Chapter Fourteen

The fourth major eruption of Vesuvius since the present series began in 1872 was by no means the most violent, but it was unique in one way which set it apart from the others in the cycle. Not since the eruptions of 1631 and 1765 had there been such tremendous outpourings of lava.

It flowed in a relentless stream due west down the flanks of the volcano. By the morning of the second day it had cut a destructive swathe as far as Pugiliano. It was thus posing an immediate threat to Ercolano.

Lessons learnt in recent years from attempts to control the lava flows from Etna now bore fruit. Barriers had been prepared, a route blasted. The lava was successfully redirected down the Via Cuperella and thence down the Via Ascione.

In the evening of the second day – watched, as it had been for almost its entire progress, by the world's TV – a tongue of lava entered the stable at the bottom of the Via Ascione and poured down the shaft. The temperature at the centre of the flow was still nearly eleven hundred degrees Centigrade. It consumed in an instant the few wooden beams at the bottom of the shaft, cascaded down the light-well and flooded out to fill the *atrium*.

By this time it had solidified sufficiently to stop all further flow through the narrow entrance at the bottom of the shaft.

Meanwhile, the main body of lava continued to flow out of the Via Ascione and spread harmlessly over the cultivated land below until the eruption spent itself on the fifth day. By this time there was some fifteen feet of cooling lava the length of the ruined slum street, filling the stable of No. 46 and covering the half-built new house next to it.

Thomas continued to see Alex. It was at his suggestion –

though, to his surprise, it did not require a great deal of persuasion – that Alex withdrew the various objects due to be sold at Dexter's on Thursday 11 October. They, together with the two silver plates with the five-inch statue torsoes, were sent to Dr Montesano at the Naples Museo Nazionale.

With one exception, no compensation was paid to anyone in the Via Ascione for the additional destruction of their houses due to the redirection of the lava. It was said their houses had been due for demolition in any case.

The exception was Signor Francesco Iannucci. He was paid a sum equal to that of two newly converted tourist villas, one with swimming pool. The rent receipts he was able to produce proved invaluable here.